OSLG

‖‖‖‖‖‖‖‖‖‖‖‖‖‖‖‖‖‖‖‖‖‖
W9-CFX-848

This Large Print Book carries the
Seal of Approval of N.A.V.H.

MAY 2007

LORD OF THE BEASTS

LORD OF THE BEASTS

SUSAN KRINARD

THORNDIKE PRESS

An imprint of Thomson Gale, a part of The Thomson Corporation

Detroit • New York • San Francisco • New Haven, Conn. • Waterville, Maine • London

THOMSON

GALE

LIBRARY OF CONGRESS CATALOGING-IN-PUBLICATION DATA

Krinard, Susan.
    Lord of the beasts / by Susan Krinard.
      p. cm. — (Thorndike Press large print romance)
    ISBN-13: 978-0-7862-9465-7 (alk. paper)
    ISBN-10: 0-7862-9465-5 (alk. paper)
    1. Veterinarians — Fiction. 2. Large type books. I. Title.
PS3611.R5445L67 2007
813'.6—dc22   2006102632

Published in 2007 by arrangement with Harlequin Books S.A.

Printed in the United States of America on permanent paper
10 9 8 7 6 5 4 3 2 1

To the Animals.
"I think I could turn and live
with animals, they are so placid
and self-contain'd,
I stand and look at them
long and long."

— Walt Whitman

ACKNOWLEDGMENT

Thanks to Kathy Flake, who hosted my first trip to the beautiful Cotswolds. She is a true friend to the animals.

CHAPTER ONE

London, 1847

The woman was beautiful as no earthly creature could be, flawless in form and carriage, her hair cascading over her shoulders like Fane gold spun by a master weaver. The world of men had names for her kind: Fairy and Daoine Sidhe and Fair Folk among them — but no such description could begin to capture her radiant perfection. Her ivory face shone with a stern radiance that no mortal could gaze upon without recognizing that he was nothing but a low, wretched brute in the presence of divinity.

Donal wasn't afraid, though Da had left him alone with the Queen of Tir-na-Nog. The man known by humans as Hartley Shaw — the Forest Lord, stag-horned master of the northern forests — had been cast out of the Blessed Land, driven away by his own mother because he would not give up his love for the mortal Eden Fleming. But now Queen Titania gazed down at her grandson and spoke, smothering the little spark of defiance Donal nursed in his six-year-old heart.

"Your father has made his choice," she said, her voice sweeping over Donal like a blast of cold north wind. "But you are young, and your blood may yet serve your people."

Donal had heard those same words a hundred times before, and always he gave the same answer. "I want to go home, with Da."

"Home." Titania flicked her slender fingers, and silver leaves shook loose from the stately tree beneath which she stood. "The vile sty mortals have made of the good, green earth. That is what you return to, child."

Though Donal knew there were many bad things in the world, he knew it was not as terrible as his grandmother said. Animals still ran free in the forest beyond the Gate. Ma and Da had seen to that. No matter what happened anywhere else in the land called England, Hartsmere would always be safe.

"But not for you," Titania said. "Never for you, grandson. You will find no peace at your mother's hearth. You will always be torn between two worlds, and your father's choice will haunt you for as long as you live among mortals." Her lovely face darkened as if a cloud had passed over the ever-shining sun of Tir-na-Nog. "Hear me, and remember. If ever you should love as my son loves . . . if ever you fall into the snare of a mortal female's wiles . . . you will lose the gift that lifts you above the People of Iron. The voices of the beasts will vanish, and you will be alone. You will have nothing . . . nothing. . . .

Donal Fleming woke with a start. The voice in his mind faded, and in its place rose the clamor and din of morning at the Covent Garden market.

Only a dream, he thought. Not a memory, real as it seemed . . . at least not his own. But Tod had been there on that terrible day twenty-five years ago, and the hob had told Donal the story so many times that Titania's threat had become unquestionable fact.

Donal flung aside the coverlet and swung his legs over the side of the bed. He massaged his temples, seeking in vain to quiet the incessant noise that was inescapable in the vast metropolis called London. With a groan he set his bare feet on the faded carpet and staggered to the washbasin to splash his face with the tepid water that remained from the night before. The few drops that passed his lips tasted of the smoke and coal dust and grime that hung in the London air. He scrubbed his skin with the towel so thoughtfully provided by the hotel staff, but no amount of washing would remove the city's taint.

He draped the towel over the back of his neck and went to the window overlooking the square below. The competing cries of vendors — sellers of vegetables and fruit, meat pies and bread and sausages, flowers of every va-

11

riety — mingled with the clatter of cartwheels and hoofbeats, penetrating the thin glass as if it were tissue. Swarming humanity ebbed and flowed between the stalls and shops, kitchen maids bumping elbows with waifs buying violets to sell on street corners and bleary-eyed dandies gulping coffee after a night of theater and tavern.

It was an alien world to Donal. He closed his eyes and thought of the moors with their deep silences and broad, clean skies. At this hour, the farmers would have long since been up milking cows, feeding chickens and mending walls, going about the same business they did every spring morning. And he would be out visiting Eliza's new litter or helping Mr. Codling and his fellow farmers through the lambing season. He might not utter a word all day, for the taciturn husbandmen of the Dales had little use for idle chatter, and the beasts spoke without need of human language.

With a sigh of resignation, Donal selected an oft-mended shirt and his second-best coat from among the few garments he'd brought from Yorkshire. He was aware that his clothes were sadly out of date, if only because his mother had brought it to his attention on more than one occasion. Lady Eden laughingly despaired of her eldest son, and of his ever finding a wife who could overlook his stubborn refusal to accept his proper

12

station in life.

The station of the bastard child who had been given everything the son of an earl could desire, and cast it all aside. All but his love for his parents and brothers, his memories of Hartsmere and the distant family connections that brought him so far from home.

Donal replaced the towel around his neck with a slightly frayed cravat and worked it into a simple knot at his throat. He glanced in the mirror just long enough to run dampened fingers through the unruly waves of his hair. Surely the august Fellows of the Zoological Society of London had better things to do than critique the appearance of a country veterinarian.

He considered and discarded the notion of a visit to the hotel dining room before setting out for Regent's Park. He doubted his stomach would tolerate even his usual light breakfast, and he had no desire to see greedy, overfed tourists stuffing their mouths with slabs of beef and rashers of bacon. Instead, Donal unwrapped a hard roll left over from yesterday's journey and broke it into small bits, wishing he had a friend to share it with.

As if in answer to his thoughts, someone scratched at his sitting room door. The sound came from very near the floor. Donal hurried to the door and opened it, meeting the bright brown eyes of his unexpected visitor.

"Well, now," he said, squatting to offer his

hand. "Have you come to share my bread?"

The parti-colored spaniel cocked his head and gravely regarded Donal's crumb-dusted fingers. He was no street cur to go begging for his meals; his red and white coat gleamed with the luster of frequent grooming and good health, and he wore his handsome, studded collar as if it were the crown of the Cavalier King who had given his breed its name.

Donal set the roll on the ground and listened. For all his well-bred dignity, the spaniel's thoughts were clear and honest in the way of his kind, and he gazed at Donal with absolute trust. The dog's natural intelligence had warned him that something was amiss when his human would not rise from his bed to take him for his morning walk. When his friend only groaned at the patting of a paw and an encouraging lick, he had set aside good manners and barked until another human had come to investigate the uproar. Then he had dashed between the startled woman's feet and run as fast as his legs would carry him, straight to the one place in all London where he knew he would be understood.

"I see," Donal said, resting his hand gently on the spaniel's broad forehead. "Of course I'll do what I can." He stuffed the roll in his pocket, rose and followed the dog into the hallway and around two corners to a door indistinguishable from his own. He knocked, but there was no answer. The spaniel whined anxiously.

Donal turned the knob, and the door gave at his push. Immediately his nostrils were assaulted by the smell of sickness. The sitting room was far more luxurious than his own modest suite, with thick Oriental carpets and furnishings that a wealthy nabob might find acceptable.

Donal strode to the bedchamber, took one glance at the rumpled bed's motionless occupant and gave a sigh of relief. For all the signs of recent illness, the spaniel's master was neither near death nor in urgent need of a physician's care.

He dampened a towel at the washstand and sat beside the stout, middle-aged object of the canine's adoration. The man had the look of prosperity about him, but he had clearly behaved with intemperance and paid the consequences. He mumbled an irritable query under his breath and subsided back into sleep.

"It's nothing to worry about, Sir Reginald," Donal said to the dog as he bathed the florid, mottled face and listened to the steady pulse beating in the man's bejowled throat. "He's only drunk more than is good for him."

The spaniel jumped onto the bed and intently studied his master's face, silky ears lifted.

"What he needs now is rest," Donal said, rinsing the towel and laying it across the man's forehead. "He'll wake when he's ready."

Sir Reginald hesitantly wagged his tail. Donal tucked the bed's coverlet under his master's chin and clucked his tongue in invitation. After a last glance at his human, Sir Reginald followed Donal from the room.

No one paid any heed to a respectable guest and his dog as they strolled casually from the hotel lobby. Sir Reginald liked the hubbub of the market no better than Donal, so they beat a hasty retreat to the dining room, where Donal ordered steak and water for the dog and plain eggs and toast for himself. A pair of severe business men at a nearby table cast disapproving glares at the spaniel, who crouched patiently between Donal's boots.

The waiter returned a few minutes later with a harried-looking young man whose high collar points had scratched red welts into his cheeks. The young man scurried about Donal's table, craning his neck to see under it, and came to a nervous halt just out of arms' reach.

"I beg your pardon, sir," he said, jerking his head very high, "but I have had complaints . . . it is my understanding that you have brought an animal into the dining room."

Sir Reginald cringed, his naturally ebullient nature suppressed by the uneasy hostility in the young man's approach. Donal quieted him with a quick pat and got to his feet.

"I have brought a friend to dine with me," he said quietly, meeting the young man's eyes. "I'm sure you can see that he is not inconveniencing anyone."

The fellow looked pointedly toward the businessmen. "Are you a guest at this establishment, sir?"

"I am."

"Then surely you will agree that it is our duty to see that respectable standards of decency and cleanliness are upheld. If you will kindly provide the direction of your room, I will send a porter to return the beast —"

A low-pitched growl sounded from under the table, and the young man shuffled a few steps back. Donal smiled. "Sir Reginald prefers not to be disturbed," he said, "but I will personally attest to his good behavior."

"You refuse to remove the animal?"

In answer, Donal resumed his seat and pretended interest in a neatly mended tear on his coat sleeve. The young man sputtered. "You leave me no choice then, sir." He signaled to a waiter, who scurried off toward the kitchen doors.

By now the scene of dispute had attracted the attention of the other diners, who shook their heads as they continued to gorge themselves from overflowing plates. A waiter with a thatch of bright red hair sidled up to Donal and leaned close under the pretense of delivering a copy of the morning paper.

"I likes dogs, sir," he whispered, smoothing the paper as he laid it on Donal's table. "Thought you should know that they've sent for the constable." He passed a wrapped bundle into Donal's hand. "This'll do for the little mite. You'd best make yerself scarce, sir."

Donal concealed his surprise and accepted the package with a nod. Sir Reginald emerged from beneath the table and politely wagged his tail at the waiter, then set off at a purposeful trot for the door to the street.

Donal casually rose and followed the spaniel, ignoring the critical gazes of the men who awaited the drama's denouement. He reached the door and opened it, admitting a rush of noise, dust and pungent odors from the market. He closed his eyes and cast his thoughts outward like a net. Here and there, like drifting bits of flotsam in an ocean of humankind, the questing sparks of intelligent animal minds searched for the means to survive another day.

Donal called out an invitation, and they answered. Sir Reginald fidgeted on his haunches and pricked his ears toward the silent tide gathering from every quarter of Covent Garden. The wave was lapping at the very shores of Old Hummums Hotel when the officious young waiter reemerged from the rear entrance with a tail-coated constable.

By then it was too late. Donal scooped Sir Reginald into his arms and stepped out of the doorway just as the first hungry mongrel skittered into the dining room. The head waiter stopped in his tracks, open-mouthed, and one of the businessmen rose to his feet. But the flood could not be stemmed. As the dog on point skirmished toward the nearest table, his company surged in after him, a wash of furry projectiles, large and small, in every imaginable color of dusty white, brown, red, black and yellow. Yapping with the joy of sinners facing the promise of salvation, the dogs leaped upon the feast — the largest hounds planting enormous paws on table tops as they wolfed steaks and loafs of bread with equal fervor, the smallest dashing beneath to collect the fallen scraps. Not one was left wanting.

There were no ladies present in this honorable bachelor establishment to swoon at the terrifying sight of filthy beasts pilfering meals intended for their betters. Most of the men had the sense to get out of the way. One fat gentleman struggled over a roast chicken leg with an equally stubborn mastiff, whose jaws proved more effective than plump fingers accustomed to counting money and lifting nothing heavier than a silver spoon.

In a matter of minutes it was over. The

constable was vastly outnumbered, and had better sense than to try to control a score of overexcited canines whose only goal was to fill their empty bellies. No human being was injured in the melee. And when the dogs had cleared every plate and licked up every crumb from the floor, they took Donal's advice and raced back out the door to scatter and lose themselves again among the two-legged folk who could not be bothered to take an interest in their welfare.

Sir Reginald squirmed with delight and licked Donal's chin. Donal slipped out the door on the heels of the last stragglers. Someone shouted behind him. He closed the door and strode briskly into the milling crowds of the marketplace, losing himself as thoroughly as the four-legged thieves.

He knew he could find a way back to his rooms without attracting undue attention, and certainly no rational man could suggest that he'd had anything to do with an unprecedented invasion of street curs. Nevertheless, the waiter's advice to "make himself scarce" seemed very sound at the moment, and once Donal had restored Sir Reginald to his human, he would lose no more time in visiting his mother's acquaintance in Regent's Park.

The hallway leading to his rooms was deserted. He went on to Sir Reginald's lodgings and knocked on the door, hardly expecting a response. But the door opened to the sober face of a tall man in well-cut but modest garments who raised an inquiring brow and kept the door half shut against any intrusion.

"I beg your pardon," Donal said. "I am seeking the gentleman who has engaged these rooms. I've been looking after his dog and wish to return him."

The tall man glanced at Sir Reginald, comfortably ensconced in Donal's arms, and shook his head. "I fear that will be impossible, sir," he said. "Mr. Churchill has but recently passed beyond this mortal coil."

"He's dead?" Donal asked, stunned. "I saw him only an hour past, and he . . ."

"It was very sudden, I believe." He bowed his head for a moment of respectful silence. "I am Doctor Tomkinson. The maid summoned me when she found Mr. Churchill fallen on the floor." He frowned into Donal's face. "You say you saw him alive?"

"He was indisposed, to be sure, but with a strong pulse and no indication of severe illness."

"His death was due to complications of dropsy, a weakness in the heart. Are you a physician yourself, sir?"

"I am Dr. Fleming, a practitioner of animal medicine."

"I see. Then you were a friend of the deceased?"

"We were never acquainted. His dog came

to me in some distress, sensing his master's illness." Donal held the little dog more tightly, knowing the animal had not yet recognized his loss.

"A clever beast," Tomkinson said without inflection. "Unfortunately, there is no one to care for it here. I understand that Mr. Churchill was a bachelor with no relations who might take the animal. You must have the means to see it humanely destroyed. . . ."

With a wail as wrenching as any child's cry, Sir Reginald launched himself from Donal's arms and dashed between Tomkinson's legs into the room. Donal didn't hesitate to follow the spaniel to the sheet-draped form on the bed.

Sir Reginald crept onto his master's motionless chest, rested his head on his paws and whined piteously.

"This is hardly appropriate . . ." Tomkinson began. Donal turned, silenced the man with a look and knelt beside the bed.

"He is gone," he said gently. "I failed you, my friend."

The spaniel made no response. Donal knew Sir Reginald would remain here with the body until he pined away from thirst and starvation, but neither Tomkinson nor the hotel staff would permit such a display of self-sacrifice. They would turn him over to the dog-catchers or put him out on the street to fend for himself.

Donal gathered the limp dog in his arms and tucked Sir Reginald beneath his coat. "Tomorrow we'll leave London," he said. "I have one obligation to fulfill, but if you wait for me, I'll take you to a place that I believe will be to your liking."

Sir Reginald sighed and closed his eyes. He would not be comforted now, but he was a dog; in time he would accept and find joy again. That was the way of the animals . . . to live fully in the moment instead of wasting the gift of life in regret, resentment and fear of the future.

It was not so unlike life in Tir-na-Nog.

Donal walked past Tomkinson to the door and paused when the physician cleared his throat.

"You don't really believe that beast understands you?" Tomkinson asked.

"He understands far more than you can imagine. And he very much fears that if you continue to overindulge in hard drink, you will meet the same fate as Mr. Churchill."

Tomkinson might have managed some affronted response, but Donal didn't wait to hear it. He returned to his room, made a nest of blankets and pillows on the floor in a corner tucked behind the bed, and left the steak and a tin of fresh water for Sir Reginald. Once he was satisfied that the spaniel would at least be comfortable in his grief, Donal gave the dog a final pat and collected his bag.

He was almost out the door when a rush of warmth and unrestrained love washed over him like summer sunlight. It was enough to carry him through the grim, unhappy streets of London, and nearly enough to make him glad that he was half-human.

CHAPTER TWO

"It is quite beyond anything I had imagined," Theodora said, brown eyes sparkling in her plain and honest face.

Cordelia Hardcastle squeezed her cousin's arm and smiled, though she could not entirely share Theodora's fascination with the many diversions available to the privileged visitors of the Zoological Gardens in Regent's Park. She, Theodora and their friend Bennett Wintour, Viscount Inglesham — who had so amiably escorted the ladies on this sojourn to London — had already viewed the museum with its collection of stuffed birds, exotic skins and every conceivable sort of animal horn and tusk; admired the pleasingly arranged gardens and buildings; delighted in the antics of the beavers in their ponds and marveled at the Australian kangaroos, African zebras and South American llamas.

But perhaps Cordelia had not marveled quite so much as Theodora and the other men and women who strolled about the grounds on this bright spring morning. For she, like a few of the Zoological Society Fellows who had established this impressive display in the very heart of the world's greatest city, had actually seen many of these beasts in their natural habitats. And the sight of such creatures displayed for the general amusement of the Fellows' guests filled her with a certain discomfort.

"You can't expect Cordelia to be impressed, Theodora," Inglesham said, flashing his easy smile. "She has been twice around the world with Sir Geoffrey and has a menagerie of her own. I fear she may be finding this excursion rather tedious."

Theodora searched Cordelia's face. "Is it all frightfully dull for you, my dear? Shall we return to the house?"

"Certainly not." Cordelia cast Inglesham a reproving glance and tucked her cousin's arm through her own. "It was I who suggested this visit, after all."

"And have you found the answers you sought?" Inglesham asked.

Cordelia suppressed a sigh and steered Theodora toward a bench under the spreading shade of an elm. "Lord Pettigrew was most generous with his time and advice," she said. "But even he cannot suggest a reason for my animals' malaise."

"I do not see why they are unhappy," Theodora offered shyly. "Edgecott is a most beautiful estate, and they have pens of ample size. No one could care for them more conscientiously than you, Cordelia."

"One might even say that you devote far more attention to those beasts than you do your friends," Inglesham said with a teasing grin. "A husband might object to such neglect."

"Then it is fortunate that I have never remarried," Cordelia said, folding her parasol with a snap. It was an old game between them, this sparring over his lazy but persistent courtship and her polite but firm rejections. They had been friends since childhood, and in spite of the game there had always been an unspoken understanding that one day the refusals might become acceptance. They got on tolerably well together, the viscount would never think of forbidding his prospective wife to make use of her fortune as she saw fit, and her father thoroughly approved of the match.

But Cordelia wasn't ready to assume the duties of wedlock, however light they might be. She had loved her first husband with a young woman's passion in the few brief months of their marriage. Such passion was no longer a part of her plans for the future, and she would have to accept the conjugal responsibilities of marriage even if Inglesham demanded little else of her.

She would know when the time was right. Until then, she had more than enough interests and responsibilities to keep her heart and mind thoroughly occupied.

"We have not yet seen the elephants," she said briskly. "Unless you would prefer to rest a little longer, Theo?"

"I am quite ready," Theodora said, adjusting her bonnet. "If it is not too inconvenient, perhaps we might also see the chimpanzee? I have heard . . . Oh!"

Theodora's faint gasp called Cordelia's attention to the broad avenue that ran through the center of the gardens. Top-hatted gentlemen and ladies in bell-shaped skirts suddenly scattered away from a high wrought-iron gate, abandoning parcels and parasols, and the breeze carried faint cries of alarm and shouts of warning.

The cause of the disturbance was not far to seek. Through the open gate charged a great gray behemoth, an ivory-tusked colossus flapping large ears like wings and moving with amazing rapidity as it bore down on the crowd.

Theodora clapped her hands to her mouth. "What is it?" she whispered.

"That, my dear, is your elephant," Inglesham said, shading his eyes for a better look. "Gone rogue, from the look of it. And coming this direction."

"Of the African species," Cordelia added, her mind crystal clear in spite of the danger. "They are said to be far more aggressive than the Indian."

Even as she spoke, the elephant paused, swung toward a nearby bench and upended it with a flip of its powerful trunk. A woman shrieked in terror.

"Perhaps it's best if we move out of its way," Inglesham said. He took Theodora's elbow in one hand and Cordelia's in the other. "If you'll permit me, ladies . . ."

Cordelia planted her feet. "The animal has obviously been mistreated," she said, "or it would not behave in this fashion. No matter its origin, any creature, when handled with firmness and compassion, must ultimately respond to —"

"Your theories are all very well, Delia, but now is not the time —"

Cordelia gently worked her arm free of Inglesham's grip, set down her parasol and started up the avenue.

"Delia!" Inglesham shouted. Theodora echoed his cry. Cordelia continued forward, her eyes fixed on the elephant. The beast was still moving at a fast pace, but she was not afraid. Enraged the animal might be, but even it was not beyond the reach of sympathy, kindliness and reason.

The pleas of her companions faded to a rush of incomprehensible sound. Cordelia was vaguely aware of white, staring faces to either side of the lane, but they held no reality for her. The elephant barreled toward her, broke stride as it noticed the obstacle in its path and began to slow.

Cordelia smiled. *That's it,* my friend, she thought. *You need have no fear of me.*

The elephant shook its head from side to side and blew gusts of air from its trunk. The small, intelligent eyes seemed to blink in understanding. The space between beast and woman shrank from yards to mere feet, and Cordelia drew in a deep breath.

She had scarcely let it out again when a blurred shape passed in front of her and set itself almost under the pachyderm's broad feet. Cordelia came to a startled halt, and the elephant did likewise. The shape resolved into a man, hatless and slightly above average height. He placed one hand on the elephant's trunk and stood absolutely still.

Cordelia's heart descended from her mouth and settled into a quick, angry drumming. "I beg your pardon," she said, "but I believe it is generally considered dangerous to step in front of a charging elephant."

Still maintaining his light hold on the pachyderm, the man half turned. She caught a glimpse of raised brows and vivid green eyes in the instant before he spoke.

"And yet you apparently believed you could stop her, madame," he said, his words crisp and patrician in spite of his slightly shabby coat and scuffed boots. "Did you perhaps believe that the thickness of your petticoats would protect you?"

Cordelia found that her mouth hung open in a most vulgar fashion. She closed it with a snap and looked the fellow up and down with a cool, imperious gaze.

"Were you under the impression, sir, that *you* were protecting me?"

A mischievous glint flared in his emerald eyes. "I have no doubt that you could bring an entire army to a halt, madame, but this lady —" he scratched its leathery skin "— requires rather more delicate handling."

Turning his back on Cordelia, the ill-mannered rogue leaned against the elephant's leg and whispered to the animal. The beast curled its trunk around his neck in something very like an embrace and gave a low, pitiful squeak.

Cordelia took firm hold of her patience and carefully moved closer. "You seem to be familiar with this animal," she said.

"We have never met before today."

"Yet she trusts you."

He didn't answer but continued to stroke the pachyderm's trunk as delicately as he might caress a newborn baby's skin. Cordelia took another step. "Is she hurt?" she asked.

Once more the man glanced over his shoulder, as if he found her question remarkable. "You seem more concerned for Sheba than any men she might have injured."

"She would not have acted so without

reason." Cordelia frowned. "If you have never seen her before, how do you know her name?"

"She told me."

"Indeed. And what else has she confided to you, pray tell?"

He turned fully and stood tucked beneath Sheba's head, careless of her sheer weight and impressive tusks. "She has been mistreated in the past," he said with perfect seriousness. "She was taken from her home as a child, and the men who bought her believed that only force and cruelty could compel her to obey."

A look of black and bitter rage crossed his face, so intense that Cordelia almost retreated before the menace so thinly held in check. But then he smiled, and it was as if the sun had burst gloriously through the clouds.

"Sheba knows you mean well," he said. "She would not have hurt you, and thanks you for your kindness."

For a moment Cordelia was mute with consternation, torn between judging the fellow mad as a hatter or simply addled by some harmless delusion. Certainly he appeared sane in every other respect. His clothing, while worn and several years out of fashion, was clean and neat. His voice was cultured, his language educated and his manner — though it more than verged on the impertinent — was that of a man raised in a respectable household.

As for his face . . . Cordelia's gaze drifted over the shock of russet-brown hair, its waves barely contained and in need of cutting, followed the intelligent line of his brow, paused at those startling eyes and continued over a strong, aristocratic nose to mobile, masculine lips and a firm, slightly dimpled chin.

His was a face most would call handsome, even if he lacked the artful curls and long side-whiskers favored by the most stylish gentlemen. At first blush, she would have thought him the son of some hearty country squire, well accustomed to brisk rural air, a horse between his knees and the feel of good English earth sifting through his fingers.

She emerged from her study to find him regarding her with the same bold stare, noting her well-cut but sensible gown, her plain bonnet and simply-dressed hair. What he thought of her features it was impossible to discern.

"Can it be, sir," she asked, "that in spite of your intimate acquaintance with elephants, you have never observed a female of the species Homo sapiens?"

That imp of mischief snapped again in his eyes. "I have had occasion to examine a few in their natural habitats, but seldom have I had the privilege of beholding such an extraordinary specimen."

"Extraordinary because I do not swoon at the first sight of danger?"

His face grew serious again. "Extraordinarily foolish," he said. "If I had not —" He broke off, his gaze focusing on something behind Cordelia. A moment later she heard the tread of boots and Inglesham's familiar stride.

"Cordelia! Are you all right?" He stopped beside her and took her arm in a protective grip. "The brute didn't touch you? I came as quickly as I could, but when I saw you had the beast under control, I thought it best . . ." He paused as if noticing the stranger for the first time, and Cordelia sensed his confusion.

"I fear I cannot take credit for calming Sheba," she said a little stiffly. "This gentleman reached her before me."

"Indeed." Inglesham gave the other man a swift examination and assigned him to a station somewhat beneath his own. "In that case, my good fellow, I owe you a debt of gratitude. Are you an employee of the Zoological Society? I will see that your courage is properly rewarded. If you'll remove the animal to a place where it can do no further harm . . ." He favored Cordelia with a look of somewhat overtaxed tolerance. "Miss Shipp is quite beside herself. She feared for your life."

Cordelia suffered a pang of guilt and glanced down the avenue. "I'll go to her as soon as I've had another word with —"

She stopped with chagrin as she realized

34

she had never learned her would-be savior's name. When she turned to remedy the oversight, she found that man and elephant had already moved away, about to be intercepted by a small herd of uniformed keepers who carried various prods and manacles designed to subdue and restrain.

Whatever they might have intended, the auburn-haired gentleman clearly had the upper hand. The keepers kept their distance, and Sheba continued on her majestic way unhindered.

Cordelia considered it beneath her dignity to run after a man who so clearly had no desire to further their acquaintance, so she accompanied Inglesham back to the bench and spent several minutes reassuring Theodora that she had never been in any real danger. But even after they returned to the townhouse and enjoyed a soothing cup of tea, Cordelia could not pry thoughts of the stranger from her mind.

It was true that he had not done anything she hadn't been prepared to do herself. But the casual ease with which he approached and touched the elephant, the manner in which it responded to him . . . all suggested a man with considerable experience in the area of animal care and behavior.

Unlike Inglesham, however, she was not convinced that he was merely a Zoological Society employee. It had occurred to her that he might even be one of the Fellows, a scientist in his own right. Her father was a cogent example of a titled gentleman who often dressed and sometimes behaved with no more sophistication than a common farmer.

So the green-eyed stranger remained a mystery. In a brief moment of fanciful abandon, Cordelia christened him Lord Enkidu after the legendary companion of Gilgamesh, who had been raised by animals and could speak their language. Several times during their last few days in London, Cordelia considered writing to Lord Pettigrew and asking him if he knew Enkidu's name and direction. Each time she remembered his hauteur, and how he had simply walked away without as much as a goodbye.

In the end she allowed Inglesham to distract her with a few more London entertainments and resolved to dispense with all further speculation about Lord Enkidu. But when she retired to her bed in the pleasant comfort of her father's townhouse on Charles Street, she was troubled by the strangely stimulating notion that she and Lord Enkidu were destined to meet again.

The dreary streets of London seemed to echo Donal's mood as he made his way back to the hotel. The fine spring morning had lapsed into an evening thick with choking fog, a miasma that left Donal wondering how any creature could long survive with such foul stuff constantly seeping into its lungs.

But he had learned that the mere act of fighting for life was far more cruel in the city than in the countryside, where struggle was a natural and accepted fact of existence. Here he had seen ragged children selling wilted flowers for a few pennies, and hollow-eyed women selling their bodies for only a pittance more. Men beat their children and their wives and each other, their breath and clothes stinking of liquor. Starving dogs and starving humans scuffled over refuse even the hungriest wild scavenger would disdain to touch.

Donal could not hear the silent cries of the men, women and children in their daily suffering, but he heard the animals. He strode along broad avenues where the carriages of fine ladies and gentleman dashed from one amusement to the next, attempting to shield his mind from the wretched travails of overworked cart horses who might be fortunate enough to live a year or two before they broke down and were sent off to the knackers. The contented thoughts of pampered lap dogs, safe in their protectors' arms, slipped past his defenses, but he could not warn them that a dismal life on the street was only a stroke of misfortune away.

Once again his thoughts turned to last night's dream of Tir-na-Nog. In the Land of the Young there was no stench, no starvation, no drunken violence. What men called hatred did not exist. Anger, like joy and thanksgiving and affection, was the work of a moment, quickly forgotten.

At times such as these he could almost forget why he had chosen to throw in his lot with mankind.

He stopped at a street corner to take his bearings, blinking as a lamplighter lit a gas lamp overhead. Behind lay Regent's Park and Tottenham Court Road, and between him and his hotel at Covent Garden stood the filthy warren of tumbledown houses and bitter poverty known as Seven Dials. He had been warned by the staff at Hummums to avoid the rookeries at all costs, but he had little concern for his life or scant property. The wilderness of his own heart was a far more frightening place.

When he had traveled up to London at the request of Lord Thomas Pettigrew, an old acquaintance of his mother's and Fellow of the Zoological Society, Donal hadn't expected to face anything more arduous than the work of healing he was accustomed to doing in his Yorkshire practice. Certainly he had never before been asked to examine an exotic beast from beyond England's shores; he had been content to limit his sphere to the common animals he had known all his life. But Lady Eden Fleming had too much pride in her children to hide their lights under a bushel, and so Lord Pettigrew had been convinced that her gifted son must give his expert opinion on several difficult cases that had defied solution by the usual string of local experts.

That was how Donal had come to see the tiger. She had been refusing food since her delivery at Regent's Park, and her keepers feared she might starve herself to death. So Donal had sent all the other men away and listened to a mind unlike any he had touched before.

It was not that he had never entered the thoughts of creatures that survived by taking the lives of others. He had run with foxes on the moors, hunted with badgers among limestone grykes and ridden the wings of soaring falcons. But those familiar souls were simple and mild compared to that of a beast who had stalked swift deer in the teeming forests of India, undisputed mistress of all she surveyed.

Donal had shared the tiger's memories and her deep, inconsolable grief for what she had lost forever. That joining had left its mark on him, but he might have come away unchanged if not for the others: the giraffes and zebras with their dreams of running on the vast African plain; the chimpanzees whose seemingly humorous antics had meaning no ordinary human could understand; and

Sheba, who remembered what it was to bask in the mud with her kin and glory in a world of which she was an irreplaceable part.

The sights and smells and sensations of those "uncivilized" lands had reduced England to a narrow cage of ordered fields and hedgerows, shaped by man for mankind's sole purpose, and the animals' wild souls had awakened a yearning within Donal that hearkened back to his father's ancient and unearthly heritage . . . feral blood that recoiled at the thought of returning to the sheltered, safe existence that Dr. Donal Fleming had believed would content him for the rest of his life.

He shivered and continued on his way toward the hotel, stepping into Crown Street with little awareness of the changing scene around him. In his imagination he crept through a dense and dripping jungle where only a few men had ever walked, breathing air untainted by civilization's belching chimneys and grinding machines. His fingers sought purchase on the sheer side of a mountain peak while pristine snow lashed his face. His legs carried him at a flying run over a plain where the only obstacles were scattered trees, and the horizon swept on forever.

And sometimes, in the visions of freedom that possessed him, a nameless figure walked at his side. A woman with bold gray eyes, severe brown hair and a foolhardy fearlessness she wore as if it were a medieval suit of armor. A female of the type he thought he despised: meddlesome, supremely well-bred and absolutely convinced of her own infallibility.

But he couldn't drive her from his thoughts, so he accepted her presence and set off across a sun-scorched desert, searching for the life that lay hidden just beyond his reach. . . .

The scream shattered his pleasant illusion. He jerked upright, letting his eyes adjust to the darkness of the narrow, lampless street. The half moon crept behind him like a timid beggar, offering only the faintest illumination, but it was just enough to show Donal how far he had gone astray.

The rookeries of Seven Dials rose around him, unglazed windows and empty doors glaring like hollow eye-sockets and toothless mouths. The air was still and heavy, poised as if awaiting a single misstep from an unwelcome visitor.

Donal had no memory of how he had come to be in the very heart of the slum. Ordinarily he would have simply turned and walked away. But the cry of one in deathly fear still quivered in the silence, and he could not pretend he hadn't heard. He listened, breathing shallowly against the stink of raw sewage and rotten food. There was no second scream.

The sagging walls of cramped tenements seemed to press in on him with the sheer weight of the misery they contained, and he almost chose flight over intervention. But he continued to linger, casting for the thoughts of the stray dogs that knew each corner of every maze of alleys and crumbling shacks.

Almost at once he found the source of the trouble. He unbuttoned his coat and followed the agitated stream of images that flowed through his mind like water over jagged stones, abandoning the illusory safety of the street for a dank, noisome passage between two dilapidated buildings. Slurred laughter floated out from an open doorway, and a man's voice uttered a stream of curses in a hopeless monotone. Donal felt the dogs' excitement increase and broke into a run.

The passage ended in a high stone wall. The sound of coarse, mocking voices reached Donal's ears. He turned to the right, where the wall and two houses formed a blind alley, a perfect trap for the unwary. And this trap had caught a victim.

A child crouched amid a year's worth of discarded refuse, her back pressed to the splintered wood of a featureless house. The dress she wore was no more than an assemblage of rags held together with a length of rope, and the color of her long, matted hair was impossible to determine. It concealed all of her thin, dirty face except for a pair of frightened blue eyes.

A trio of nondescript dogs stalked the space

directly in front of the girl, facing an equal number of men whose manner was anything but friendly. It was their voices Donal had heard, and they were far too intent on their prey to notice Donal's arrival.

" 'ere, now," a fair-haired giant said, wiggling his blunt fingers in a gesture of false entreaty. "Don't be so shy, love. We only wants to show you a good toim. Ain't that roight, boys?"

" 'at's roight," said the giant's companion, a skinny youth whose jutting teeth were black with decay. "Yer first toim should be wiv true gents like us. We won't disappoint you."

"Maybe you'll even be able t' walk when we're done," the third man said, wiping the mucus from his nose with the back of his sleeve. All three broke into raucous laughter, and the girl shrank deeper into the rubbish while the dogs bared their teeth and pressed their tails between skinny flanks.

"You come wiv us now," the first man said, "and maybe we'll let yer doggies go. 'R else —" He nodded to Rotten Teeth, who drew a knife and slashed toward one of the dogs. The animal darted back, shivering in terror but unwilling to abandon the girl.

Donal set down his bag and stepped forward. The dogs pricked their ears, and the girl's eyes found him through the barrier of her tormenters' legs. Her cracked lips parted. Fair-Hair's shoulders hunched, and he began to turn.

With a flurry of silent calls, Donal shrugged out of his coat and tossed it on a slightly less filthy patch of ground.

"I regret to interrupt your sport, gentlemen," he said softly, "but I fear I must ask you to let the child go."

CHAPTER THREE

The three blackguards spun about, wicked knives flashing in their hands. Fair-Hair lunged, and Donal leaped easily out of his reach.

"Now, now," he said. "Is this the welcome you give strangers to your fine district? I am sadly disappointed."

Fair-Hair, Rotten-Teeth and Snot-Sleeve exchanged glances of disbelief. " 'oo in 'ell are you?" Snot-Sleeve demanded.

"I'm sure you're not interested in my name," Donal said, "and I am certainly not interested in yours. Let the child go, and I won't report your disreputable behavior to the police."

Rotten-Teeth snorted. "Will you look at 'im," he said. "Some foin toff who finks 'e can come 'ere and insult us."

"Oi remembers the last toim someone did that," Fair-Hair said. "Not much left o' 'im to report to anybody."

" 'at's roight," Rotten-Teeth said. "You

lookin' to 'ave yer pretty face cut up to-noight, nancy boy?"

"That wasn't my intention," Donal said, listening for the scratch and scrabble of tiny feet, "but you are certainly welcome to try . . . if you have enough strength left after your daily regimen of raping children."

Snot-Sleeve aimed a wad of spittle at Donal's chest, which Donal deftly avoided. He glanced past the men to the circling dogs. They heard his request and made themselves very small, waiting for the signal to move. The girl remained utterly still.

" 'e must be crazy," Fair-Hair muttered, peering into the darkness at Donal's back. " 'E can't 'ave come 'ere alone."

"There ain't no one else," Rotten-Teeth insisted. "Let me 'ave 'im first."

"Oi got a be'er idea," Snot-Sleeve said. " 'ooever takes 'im down gets first crack at the girl."

"Oi don't loik this," Fair-Hair grunted. "Somefin' ain't roight. . . ."

Without waiting to hear his friend's further thoughts on the matter, Rotten-Teeth crouched in a fighter's stance and advanced on Donal. The stench of his breath was so foul that Donal almost missed the subtle move that telegraphed his intentions. Rotten-Teeth's hand sliced down at Donal's arm, and Donal stepped to the side, grasped his attacker's shoulder and twisted sharply.

Rotten-Teeth yelped and fell to one knee.

Fair-Hair and Snot-Sleeve rushed to their companion's defense, but they had taken only a few steps when the rats spilled from their hiding places. Rotten-Teeth gave a high-pitched whine as half a dozen dark-furred rodents swarmed over his feet. Another fifty rats and a few hundred mice raced in an ever-tightening circle about the other men's boots, breaking rank only to nip at the humans' ankles.

Fair-Hair swore and stabbed ineffectually at a bold male who sat on his haunches and mocked the human with a twitch of his whiskers. At the same moment the dogs sprang into action. They darted at the men, seizing sweat-stiffened woollen trousers in their jaws. The hiss of ripping fabric joined the squeaking of the rodents and the villains' cries of fear and disgust.

The battle was over almost before it began. After failing to reduce the number of rodents by stamping his oversized feet, Fair-Hair chose the better part of valor and stumbled past Donal in a wave of terrified stench. His bare buttocks gleamed through the large hole in his trouser seat. Snot-Sleeve was hot on his heels. Rotten-Teeth came last, frantically dragging his twisted ankle behind him as if he expected to become the rats' next meal.

A restless silence filled the little space between the walls. Donal gave his thanks to the rodents and sent them scurrying back to their nests. He retrieved his coat and casually shook it out, watching the girl from the corner of his eye. She had scarcely moved since his arrival, and her gaze held the same stark fear with which she had regarded her tormentors.

No, not fear. She had been frightened before, but now those blue eyes held far more complex emotions: suspicion, anger and a glimmer of hope swiftly extinguished. She held out her arms. The dogs wriggled close, licking her face as if she were a pup in need of a good cleaning.

They told Donal all he needed to know. He started cautiously for the girl, holding his hands away from his sides.

"Are you hurt?" he asked.

She lowered her head between her shoulders and peered at him from beneath her dark brows. "Wot do you want?" she demanded.

Her directness didn't startle him. A child left alone so young would have been educated in a hard school. She had probably been hurt so often that she regarded pain as a simple fact of life, like hunger and the casual cruelty of strangers.

"I mean you no harm," he said, settling into a crouch. The dogs grinned at him in apology but remained steadfastly by their charge's side. "I heard you cry out —"

"Oi never. You 'eard wrong."

Donal studied her face more carefully, noting the blue bruise that marked her right eye. "Did those men touch you?" he asked.

She hugged the dogs closer. The spotted, wire-haired male whined anxiously, striving to make her understand. She cocked her head and frowned. "You ain't no rozzer, is you?"

"I am not a policeman."

"Did you bring the rats?"

Donal considered the safe answer and immediately discarded it. "Yes," he said. "They wouldn't have hurt you."

"Oi know." She pushed a hank of hair out of her eyes. "Why didn't you let 'em eat them nickey bludgers?"

Her hatred was so powerful that he felt the fringes of it as if she were more animal than human. "Rodents are naturally secretive creatures," he said seriously, "and I already asked them to do something very much against their natures. Would you ask your dogs to eat a man?"

She giggled with an edge of hysteria and wrapped her arms around her thin chest. "They ain't *my* curs," she said. "But some-toims they 'elps me, and Oi 'elps them."

"They're very brave, and so are you."

She shrugged, and the gesture seemed to break something loose inside her. "Wot're you going to do now?" she whispered.

Her bleak question reminded Donal that he hadn't considered anything beyond rescuing the child from her attackers. The smallest of the dogs, a shaggy terrier mix, crept up to Donal and nudged his hand. The animal's request was unmistakable.

"What is your name?" Donal asked, stroking the terrier's rough fur.

"That ain't none o' yer business."

"Mine is Donal," he said. "Donal Fleming. How old are you?"

"Twelve years," she said sharply, narrowing her eyes. "Wot's it to yer?"

Donal's hand stilled on the terrier's back, and the dog growled in response to his sudden surge of anger. "Where do you live?" he asked, keeping his voice as level as he could. "Do you have anyone to look after you?"

She concealed a wet sniff behind her hand. "Oi don't needs nowbody."

"What if the men return?"

Blinking rapidly, the girl scraped her ragged sleeve across her eyes. "Oi won't let 'em catch me."

But her efforts at bravado were hardly convincing, and the dogs knew how truly afraid she was. Donal got to his feet.

"You'd better come with me," he said.

Her eyes widened, gleaming with moisture in the dim moonlight. "Where?"

"To my hotel. I'll see that you have decent clothing and a good meal. And then . . ."

And then. What was he to do with a child? His thoughts flew inexplicably to the woman from the Zoological Gardens and skipped away, winging to his farm in Yorkshire. He hadn't the resources to take the girl in, but there were a number of solid families in the Dales who owed him payment for his care of their animals. Surely one of them could be convinced to give her a decent home.

Relieved that he had found a solution, Donal smiled. "How would you like to come north with me, to the countryside?"

The dogs burst into a dance of joy, their tails beating the air. The girl pushed to her feet and brushed scraps of refuse from her colorless dress. "Away from Lunnon?" she asked in disbelief.

"Far away. Where no one can hurt you again."

She stared at the ground, chewing her lower lip as she watched the dogs gambol around her rag-bound feet. At last she looked up, brows drawn in a menacing frown. "You won't try nuffin'?"

His smile faded. "I have no interest in abusing children," he said. "Your dogs know that you can trust me."

"Oi told you, they ain't my —" She broke off with an explosive sigh. "Can Oi takes 'em wiv me?"

Donal briefly considered the obstacles involved. "Perhaps we can sneak them in. I already have a dog there. His name is Sir Reginald."

The girl snorted. " 'At's a flash name for a cur."

"But he isn't puffed-up in the least. You'll like him."

"Well . . ." She kicked an empty tin and sent it spinning across the alley. "Awroight. Me name's Ivy."

Donal bowed. "Pleased to make your acquaintance, Miss Ivy."

She made a rude sound, but her eyes were very bright. "Come on, then," she said to the dogs. "Oi'm ready for a spot o' supper, even if you ain't."

They arrived at Hummums after midnight. The market was quiet, awaiting the arrival of the next day's wagons, though a few coffee stalls accommodated fast gentlemen and women of the street trolling for their night's business. There were no "rozzers" present to complicate Donal's scheme.

He left Ivy and the dogs in a quiet niche around the corner from the hotel and retrieved his greatcoat and a blanket from his rooms. He threw the coat over Ivy and gave her the smallest dog to hold while he wrapped the other two in the blanket and bid them keep absolutely still. Ivy proved adept at moving quietly, and they passed through the lobby without attracting more than an indifferent glance from the night clerk.

Sir Reginald greeted them at the door to

Donal's rooms. He stiffened when he smelled the strange dogs and retreated to a safe place under the sitting-room sofa. Ivy set down the terrier, gazing about the room in silent appraisal as Donal released the other dogs from the blanket. He crouched near the sofa and coaxed Sir Reginald into his arms.

"Sir Reginald," he said, "this is our guest, Ivy. Ivy, Sir Reginald."

The spaniel wagged his tail but continued to regard the canine interlopers with suspicion. The three street dogs were on their best behavior, as if they recognized that they had been granted a privilege they must not abuse.

Ivy sat down on the carpet beside them and sniffed loudly. "It's flash enough," she conceded. "You said we could 'ave some food?"

Donal set Sir Reginald on the sofa and brought out the basket of bread and fruit he had bought before he left for the Zoological Gardens. "I'll purchase more when the market opens in the morning," he said, "and I'll find you a dress." He surveyed her slight form, reflecting on how little he knew of women's garments. Surely anything would be an improvement on her current wardrobe. "I think it best that you remain here when I go out."

Ivy snatched the bread from the basket and broke it in half, dividing one part among the dogs and sinking strong, surprisingly white teeth into the other. "You ashamed o' me?"

she asked with studied indifference.

"Not in the least. But you will have to take a bath —"

Ivy shot to her feet, crumbs showering from her patched bodice. "I ain't takin' off me clothes!"

"I'll have them send up a hip bath and hot water while you hide behind the bed," he said patiently. "Then I'll leave you alone. Only the dogs will see you."

She thumped back down and reached for an apple. "I scarcely remember what it feels like to be clean."

Donal glanced at her sharply, aware of a sudden change in her voice. Gone was the thick rookery accent; she had pronounced every word with the perfect diction of the educated class.

"Who were your parents, Ivy?" he asked.

She noticed his intent look and hunched protectively around the basket. "Oi don't remember nuffin'."

"Nothing at all?"

"You sayin' Oi'm a liar?"

Donal sighed and sat on the nearest chair. "You've had a difficult day. I suggest you try to get some sleep."

She glanced toward the door that separated the two rooms. "Only if you stay in there."

"Wouldn't you rather have the bed?"

"Ain't used to 'em." She grabbed the blanket and wrapped it around her shoulders.

The dogs snuggled close. "Go on."

Donal picked up Sir Reginald and started for the bedchamber. "You will still be here in the morning?"

" 'Course Oi will. You promised me a new dress."

There was nothing else to be done but obey the girl's command. Donal entered the bed-chamber and closed the door, sending a last request to Ivy's canine friends. If the girl attempted to leave, the dogs would warn him. In any case, he had no intention of sleeping until he and Ivy were safely on the train to York.

He stretched out on the bed fully-clothed, Sir Reginald tucked in the crook of his arm, and let the intoxicating scents and shrouded mysteries of the jungle close in around him. He stalked with the tigress, his ears twitching as he caught the movement of deer in the bush. She paused to meet his gaze, inviting him to join in the hunt, and her golden eyes turned the somber gray of a winter-bound lake.

"Can it be, sir," she purred, "that in spite of your intimate acquaintance with tigers, you have never observed a female of the species Homo sapiens?"

Donal snapped awake to the sound of scratching on the door. Daylight streamed through the window. In an instant he was on his feet, his head ringing with the dogs' sorrowful apologies. He flung open the door.

Ivy was gone. She had left the blanket neatly folded on the sofa beside the empty basket.

Sir Reginald trotted up behind him and pawed at the leg of his trousers. The mongrels tucked their tails and whined. They were as disconcerted as Donal, for somehow the girl had got past them in spite of their vigilance. Not one of them remembered the moment of her departure.

Ivy was clearly no ordinary child. Donal had severely underestimated her, and miscalculated her trust in him. He had made entirely too many errors in judgment since coming to London. This world left him as addled as a sheep with scrapie, and he would begin to question his sanity unless he were quit of it soon. Quit of men and all their troublesome works.

But he had made a commitment to Ivy. Even if she had chosen not to trust him after all, he wasn't prepared to surrender her to the streets.

"We will find her," he assured the dogs firmly. "One of you will come with me."

The little terrier gave a piercing bark and leaped straight up in the air. Donal set out a bowl of water for the dogs and made a hasty change of drawers and shirt, leaving his jaw unshaven and covering the tangle of his hair with his black top hat.

A few minutes later he squared his shoulders and plunged into the forbidding wilderness of Covent Garden.

Midmorning in London's biggest market was a riot of color, sound and utter confusion. Theodora took in the sights with the same wide-eyed fascination that she had viewed the Zoological Gardens, the Tower of London and Buckingham Palace, while Cordelia thought of home and Inglesham kept himself busy shielding his charges from jostling or any other annoyance. Here costermongers and fishwives rubbed elbows with ladies in extravagant layers of petticoats and gentlemen in velvet-collared frock coats and tight woollen trousers, all of them shopping for bargains in a place where nearly anything could be had for the right price.

Theodora caught sight of a flower stall overflowing with bouquets of every variety of flower and stared at it wistfully until Inglesham recognized her longing and steered her through the crowd. Cordelia lagged behind, her senses strangely on the alert, and so she was perfectly positioned to observe the next sequence of events.

She saw Theodora cradling a spray of primroses, absorbed in their scent as the flower-seller haggled with Inglesham over the price. Inglesham half turned toward Cordelia, an indulgent smile on his handsome face.

And just as he turned, a figure in the remnants of a faded dress darted from between a pair of chattering kitchen maids, slipped behind the viscount and dipped her hand inside his coat.

The thief had no sooner relieved Inglesham of his purse than he spun about and caught her wrist, nearly jerking her off her feet. Theodora dropped the flowers, her mouth opening in shock. Cordelia glimpsed the pickpocket's face — a piquant visage that might once have been pretty — and pushed her way to the viscount's side.

"You little mongrel," Inglesham was saying, shaking the girl from side to side. "Thought I'd be easy prey, did you? Once I have you up before a magistrate —" He noticed Cordelia's approach and set the girl back on her feet. "Mrs. Hardcastle," he said formally, "perhaps you should escort Miss Shipp to a place of safety while I deal with this cutpurse. I shall summon a constable —"

"Wait," Cordelia said. She studied the girl's face more carefully. She appeared to be no more than eleven or twelve years of age, and her eyes — when they flashed defiantly up at Cordelia — were a surprisingly fetching bright blue. But her hair hung in matted hanks about her shoulders, its color indistinguishable, and her feet were bound in rags instead of shoes.

"What is your name, child?" Cordelia asked

gently.

"Her name is of no consequence," Inglesham said. "She is a thief and must be punished."

"But you have recovered your purse, Lord Inglesham," she said, matching his cool tone. "The child is obviously poor and desperate, or she would not be driven to such extremes. Where is the harm in letting her go?"

"The *harm* lies in permitting her to continue her thieving ways. Surely you, of all people, do not approve of flouting the law."

"Surely the law can occasionally err on the side of mercy."

"I agree," Theodora said. "I should hate to think —"

Inglesham shook his head. "Forgive me, ladies, but you know nothing of these things. I —"

"May I be of assistance?"

Cordelia turned to face the speaker and started in surprise. There, dressed in the same rather shabby coat and bristling with a day's growth of beard, stood Lord Enkidu. His green eyes moved quickly from Cordelia's face to Inglesham and then to the girl, assessing the situation in an instant.

"We require no assistance," Inglesham said gruffly, "unless you would be so good as to fetch a constable."

The girl stared at Lord Enkidu and suddenly dropped her gaze. "Oi'm sorry," she muttered.

Lord Enkidu doffed his hat and offered a slight bow. "Forgive me for my presumption," he said to Cordelia, "but it occurs to me that we have not been introduced. I am Donal Fleming."

Inglesham stiffened at Fleming's impertinence, but Cordelia spoke before the viscount could issue a scathing set-down. "I am Cordelia Hardcastle," she said. "My companions are Viscount Inglesham and my cousin, Miss Shipp."

Mr. Fleming bowed again and met Inglesham's eyes. "I would be happy to take the child in custody, sir, if you wish to escort the ladies to a more congenial location."

Inglesham's immaculately shaven chin shot up. Cordelia again intervened. "As you see, Mr. Fleming, Lord Inglesham is of the opinion that the girl should be given over to the police. Would that also be your intention?"

Fleming held her gaze, and Cordelia lost herself in it just long enough to make the silence uncomfortable.

"I should not like to contradict the viscount," he said softly, "but it seems that this child has suffered more than enough to atone for any small transgressions she may have committed."

"Fortunately for the welfare and property of honest English citizens," Inglesham said, "the matter is not in your hands." He glanced around and fixed his eyes on some point beyond the opposite stall. "If you ladies will go on to St. Paul's Church, I shall meet you there when this business is concluded."

Fleming followed Inglesham's stare. His eyes narrowed. Without another word to Cordelia he withdrew, neatly losing himself in the crowd. Cordelia was about to argue with Inglesham when a small, scruffy terrier trotted up to the viscount, lifted his hind leg, and relieved himself on Inglesham's spotless black ankle boot.

Inglesham jumped, kicking out at the dog with a curse. The terrier evaded his foot. The little thief wrenched her arm free of the viscount's hold. He snatched at her sleeve, and as she struggled a silver pendant at the end of a frayed cord swung out from beneath her torn collar. She shoved it back under her bodice, writhing wildly, and her sleeve gave way in Inglesham's hand. She was off like a fox before the hounds.

"Oh!" Theodora exclaimed. "Are your boots quite ruined, Lord Inglesham?" But her eyes met Cordelia's in a flash of almost mischievous satisfaction.

Inglesham took himself in hand, dropped the filthy scrap of cloth and straightened his hat. "I beg your pardon, ladies," he said. "I have obviously failed in my duty to protect you from such unpleasantness. Perhaps it would be best if I return you to the house."

"Of course," Cordelia said. "I believe Theodora has had her fill of the market . . . haven't you, cousin?"

Theodora paid the flower seller for the blossoms she had dropped. "Indeed. It has been a most trying day."

"Then let us put this incident behind us," Cordelia suggested. "We shall be on our way home tomorrow, and the country air will soon put us to rights."

Inglesham smiled, offering an arm to each of the women. "A very sensible suggestion, my dear Mrs. Hardcastle," he said. "What would we do without you?"

His words were light, dismissing their recent quarrel. It seemed impossible for Bennet to hold a grudge; he could be quick to anger, and just as quick to forgive. His sincerity was beyond question.

And yet, as Inglesham hailed a hackney cab to take them back to Russell Street, Cordelia found herself watching for Mr. Donal Fleming, wondering why he had come and gone with such mysterious haste. She thought of the little dog who had appeared so fortuitously after Fleming vanished into the crowd. A very peculiar coincidence indeed. And what an exceedingly trying and vexatious gentleman, with those unwavering green eyes that seemed to judge and challenge her at one and the same time. . . .

As the cab rattled away, Cordelia could have sworn that she saw Fleming with the girl, deep in conversation while the little terrier trotted happily at their heels.

She resolved then and there that Donal Fleming would not remain a mystery much longer.

The girl was alive.

Béfind paced across the silver floor of her crystal palace, her slippered feet beating a muted tattoo that shattered the morning's perfect stillness. It had been many long years since she had felt such blinding rage. Life in Tir-na-Nog provided little cause for the primitive emotions that so consumed the lives of mortalkind; Fane might quarrel over a pretty trinket, or play spiteful tricks upon each other for the sake of an hour's amusement, but such minor conflicts were as quickly forgotten as one's latest love affair.

No, Béfind had not felt so since she had left the human world forty mortal years ago. She had never had any desire to return. The passions that ruled mankind — love and hate, joy and sorrow — were like some foul disease, defiling everything they touched.

Even a great lady of the Fane who had lived three thousand years.

With a whispered curse, Béfind went to stand between the fluted columns that framed a flawless view of the emerald lawn. The sun shone like a vast jewel in a cloudless sky, reigning over unblemished meadow and forest, lake and stream. Deer and horses of every hue grazed among the flowers. A sweet, warm wind ruffled the grass with playful fingers.

A female halfling, great with child, wandered among trees heavy with fruit and blossoms. She strolled beside a dark-haired Fane, laughing at his jests as if she enjoyed her pitiful condition. A mortal visitor to Tir-na-Nog might never realize that the girl was little more than a broodmare . . . an exotic, captive creature pampered and petted for one reason only: to save the Fane race from extinction.

Humankind had but one advantage over the Fane: their blood was strong and hearty while that of the Fair Folk grew thin and weak. Few pure Fane matings produced children, but the spawn of Fane and human were extremely fertile. For as long as Béfind could remember, it had been the duty of each and every Fane to seek a mate among the humans and return to Tir-na-Nog with a halfling child whose own offspring would buy the Fane another few centuries of existence.

Béfind had done her duty. She had forced her body to endure months of ugly thickening, sacrificing her beauty to the thing growing in her belly. Idath had been beside her on the day she delivered the half-human brat. High Lord Idath, who had been her lover for a hundred years and more, had informed her with seeming regret that her babe had died upon its birth.

How the gossips had enjoyed telling her, all these years later, that Idath had lied.

Béfind hissed between her teeth and watched Fane men and women ride ivory steeds in a hunt for the stags of the golden forest. The hunters' arrows would bring no suffering to the beasts when they died, only a swift and gentle sleep. Pain was banished from Tir-na-Nog. Regret had no place here. But there was still room for vengeance.

Béfind lifted her hands and called, summoning the hobs and sprites and lesser Fane who served her in her splendid isolation.

"No matter how long it takes," she told them, "you will find her. Find the girl and report to me."

The hobs and sprites knew better than to utter cries of dismay at the task she had set them. They scattered and vanished, flying swiftly for one of the last remaining Gates that connected Tir-na-Nog and earth.

Béfind turned away from the window with a smile and idly changed the color of her gown from glossy amber to flaming scarlet. Tonight she would summon young Connla to her bed and see how well he pleased her. Tomorrow she would choose another. Let Idath enjoy his victory now; he would soon see who played the cleverest game.

Sooner or later, the girl would be hers.

CHAPTER FOUR

The rolling hills and peaceful fields of Yorkshire should have filled Donal's heart with
welcome relief after his sojourn in London.
Perched on the seat of old Benjamin's farm
wagon, he could see the outbuildings of Stenwater Farm as the road curved into the dale.
Flocks of sheep grazed on the fells, and the
beck tumbled cheerfully between limestone
outcroppings thick with wildflowers.

One would never believe, looking at such a
peaceful scene, that a mad place like London
could exist, or that a belching, roaring
locomotive had carried Donal and his new
charges all the way from the world's greatest
metropolis to the equally ancient but far less
pretentious city of York.

And yet, for all the sense of unreality that
had accompanied Donal on the journey
home, he could not deny that his life had
already undergone a profound alteration.

He had almost been able to forget how
much had changed while he and a cleanly-

washed, cleanly-dressed Ivy shared the small, private world of the railway car. During the long hours rattling through the countryside of the Midlands, he and the girl had come to a kind of understanding, and Ivy had expressed regret for the mistrust that had led her to flee the hotel and resume her previous occupation as a purse snatcher.

Donal wasn't sure if the fact that she was caught in her thievery contributed to her remorse, but she seemed sincere enough in her desire for a new start. Her three mongrels — christened Billy, Jack and Daisy — had infected her with their enthusiasm, and Sir Reginald honored her by falling asleep in her lap. She spent every moment of daylight with her nose pressed to the window, devouring the sight of fresh grass and hedgerows and spring-green trees as if she were on her way to heaven itself.

Donal's thoughts had taken other directions. Again and again he drifted into dreams of the wilderness, lost in the memories of beasts born in lands that called to him more urgently with every passing day. And only one human being invaded those dreams: the gray-eyed Athena named Cordelia Hardcastle.

It was a strangely appropriate designation for her. She was no delicate beauty; her gaze was direct, her speech without coy flattery or empty pleasantries. "Hard" was too strong a word for her determined manner, and yet she was not unlike the castle in her name: sturdy, uncompromising and completely impregnable.

A man of her type and class . . . like Viscount Inglesham, perhaps . . . might be tempted to breech her defenses and scale her walls. Even Donal had not been immune to her obvious intelligence and compassion for those weaker and less privileged than herself. And if he were honest, he would be compelled to admit that something deep inside him had responded to the undeniable, lush femininity she held in check beneath those layers of corsets and petticoats — no more or less instinctively than the way a stallion responds to a mare.

But, encroach on his dreams though she might, Miss Hardcastle belonged to a world in which he had no part.

Donal tried to push such speculation aside as the wagon rolled up the last rise to Stenwater Farm. He had plenty of business to attend to when they reached the farm; there were animals to be visited, accounts to peruse and neighbors to consult regarding Ivy's future. The girl sat with the dogs in the bed of the wagon, her blue eyes wide with excitement, still ignorant of his plans for her. He didn't look forward to explaining how she would be much better off with a good farming family, who had children close to her age and could provide a growing child with a conscientious upbringing.

And I may soon be gone, he thought, gazing up at the cloud-dappled sky. Taking leave of his animals would be difficult enough without the additional burden of a child. There were a few humans he might trust with the dogs, cats, sheep, cattle, horses and pigs — men who would not consign his friends to the cook-pot — and Benjamin would gladly remain at Stenwater as caretaker for as long as he was needed.

And what of Tod? The little hob had been his closest companion for a quarter of a century, a constant playfellow and wise advisor throughout Donal's awkward childhood and youth. But Tod was bound to England as surely as if he wore shackles of iron on his swift brown feet. He was a part of the woods and fields and streams of this island, and there was no telling if he could survive being separated from it. Even though Tod would always find a welcome at Hartsmere with his former master, the parting would be painful for man and hob alike.

The wagon rolled to a halt. Ivy was out before Benjamin could set the break. Daisy, Jack and Billy scrambled out of the wagon, quivering with joy at the myriad scents and sounds, while Sir Reginald patiently waited for someone to help him down.

Donal scooped the spaniel up in his arms and gently set him on the ground just as a half-dozen farm dogs barreled around the corner of the byre. Sir Reginald dived under the wagon, but the street curs held their ground, legs and tails stiff. Soon enough they had determined the vital matters of status and rank, and the entire pack dashed off together.

Ivy twisted a handful of her skirts between her hands and bit her lip. "It's so big," she said. "I ain't never seen so much . . ."

"Space?" Donal offered, briefly resting his hand on Ivy's shoulder. "You'll become used to it in time. The air is clean here. You'll have fresh-baked bread, eggs from our chickens, potatoes and carrots right out of the good earth. You can run as far as you like without fear."

She sniffled, pressing her knuckles to her nose. "But wot will Oi do?"

If it were up to him, she would be free to do whatever she liked . . . help Benjamin with the chores, wander the moors, spend days reading the books in his library. But of course she probably couldn't read at all, and would have to be taught by whichever family agreed to take her in.

"There is something you can do now," he said. "Sir Reginald is a bit frightened by so much change. If you could care for him until he has settled in . . ."

Ivy blinked, emerging from some inner world of her own, and nodded. "O' course.

I'll look after 'im." She bent down and coaxed the spaniel from under the wagon. "You stick wiv me, Reggie, and you'll be just foin."

Donal nodded to Benjamin, who led the horse and wagon off to the stables. Still murmuring to Sir Reginald, Ivy followed Donal up to the house, passing the border of flowers Benjamin had planted along the path. He opened the door to the cozy kitchen and let Ivy look around.

"We live simply at Stenwater," he said. "Benjamin and I share the cooking duties, and we have a cleaning woman and laundress come in once a week. Benjamin cares for the larger animals . . . we have several horses and a pony you might ride, if that suits you."

" 'Ow many animals 'ave you?" Ivy asked, her gaze moving hungrily about the room with its hanging pots and massive box stove.

"Oh, a score of dogs, and as many cats . . . most live in the byre and stables . . . several milch cows, a small flock of sheep and a dozen cattle up on the fells . . . six horses and the pony . . . ten pigs, at last tally. Perhaps forty chickens." He cocked his head, surveying the farm in his mind. "Sometimes we have a fox or a badger visiting us, if they need tending. I've never tried to count the mice."

Ivy giggled, a burst of nervous sound that seemed to relieve some internal pressure. "D'you eat 'em . . . the sheep 'n' cows 'n'

71

pigs, Oi mean?"

"Since I consider them my friends, it would hardly be fair, would it?"

"Then 'ow d'you keep from starving?"

"You would be surprised how much nutrition one can derive from the fruits of the earth," he said. "Our chickens are willing to provide us with eggs in plenty, and our cows are happy to supply all the milk we can drink."

Ivy considered this for several moments. "Oi guess Oi'd rather not eat yer friends, either."

Donal laughed, took her face between his hands and kissed her forehead. She jumped back, regarding him with something akin to shock.

Donal sobered instantly. "I'm sorry, Ivy. I shouldn't have —"

"It's awroight," she said, glancing away. "You just surprised me, is all."

Of course he had surprised her. She'd likely received far more blows than kisses in her short lifetime. And he was not in the habit of doling out caresses to any creature whose skin was not covered in fur or feathers.

Nevertheless, though Ivy would not be with him long, he must remember that she was human. Whatever affection he might hold for her or any other person, the communion he enjoyed with the animals could never be shared with a member of her species.

After he had shown Ivy the kitchen and parlor, he led her through the hall to the bedchambers. The room he kept for guests had a window that looked out on the informal garden, and it was furnished with a brass four-poster adorned with a hand-quilted coverlet.

"This will be your room," Donal said. "If there is anything it lacks, you must tell me."

Ivy crept through the doorway and slowly set Sir Reginald down on the braided rug. "This . . . is fer me?"

"Yes. I'm sure you will want things . . . suitable for a young girl. What we can't purchase in the local village we will surely find in York."

Ivy scarcely seemed to hear him. She approached the bed warily, ran her hands over the coverlet, and cautiously sat down. Sir Reginald jumped up beside her and immediately made a comfortable nest out of one of the pillows. He sighed in complete contentment.

"Mine," Ivy breathed. She rubbed her fist across her eyes, shot from the bed and hurled herself at Donal. Her thin arms closed around him with desperate strength.

"Thank you," she whispered into his waistcoat. "I don't know . . . how I can ever repay you."

Once again her rookery accent had vanished, but Donal was too startled to give much thought to the transformation. He patted her back awkwardly.

"You owe me nothing," he said. "But I do think you have had enough stimulation for one day. If you and Sir Reginald would care to rest, I'll fetch your luggage and see what I can find in the kitchen."

She pulled back and studied his face. "You won't leave me?"

"If I leave the farm, it will only be for a short time, and Benjamin will be here."

"I want you to show me the animals. Your friends."

"After you've rested."

Her lower lip jutted with incipient rebellion, but she thought better of it. With a final sniff she returned to the bed and drew back the coverlet. She crawled under the sheets, holding very still as if she feared her mere presence might sully such luxury. Sir Reginald tucked his body against her, one long, fringed ear draped across her chest.

"Sleep," Donal said, backing out the door. "I'll wake you in time for dinner."

But her eyes were already closed, and she didn't stir again. Donal shut the door and walked silently back down the hall. He met Benjamin in the kitchen, checked the contents of the larder, and asked the old man to prepare a simple but hearty meal. Then he left the house and began his rounds.

The old gelding and the pony in the stable greeted him with whinnies of welcome, telling him of the new litter of kittens born in the loose box. The proud mother cat put in an appearance and allowed Donal to examine the babies. He cradled each tiny, blind body in his hand and felt the new seeds of consciousness beginning to awake.

His next stop was the byre, where the elder cows chewed their cud and gossiped in their bovine way about their youngest sister and her knobby-kneed calf. A quintet of canines followed Donal to the home pasture and maintained a polite distance as he called upon the other horses and cattle, checking hooves and eyes and ears and assessing the gloss of sunwarmed coats. He climbed alone up the fell, standing quietly while the sheep gathered about him and nuzzled his coat and trousers.

Nothing had changed in his absence. All was as it should be, the animals absorbed in the continual "present" of their lives, altering little from one hour, one day, one year to the next. They trusted in the natural order of the universe. And like Nature herself, moor and fell and beck would persevere for a thousand generations, their metamorphoses measured not in decades, but eons.

No, Donal's world had not changed. Only *he* was different. With every step that he walked across the rolling pastures or scaled the low stone walls, he felt it grow — the strange, undeniable sense that the unnamed thing his life had always lacked lay beyond this spare, immutable landscape, somewhere in the sweeping veldt of Africa, the high desert of Mongolia or the jungles of Brazil.

And what of Tir-na-Nog? he asked himself. *What if that is what you truly seek? Endless beauty and freedom from responsibility in a land humanity can never taint with its madness . . .*

A land that had banished his father for daring to be "human." A country Donal had rejected in favor of the challenges of a mortal existence, the chance to do good where it was most needed. To return to the Land of the Young was to surrender his humanity.

And would that be so terrible a price?

Donal descended the fell as twilight settled over the dale and the farm buildings. The scent of cooking drifted up to him on the breeze. Soon the comfortable routine he and Benjamin shared, sitting at the kitchen table in their customary silence, would be broken. Ivy would be there. And tomorrow he must go to the local farmers and learn which family was best suited to caring for a bright but troubled child. . . .

The fox darted under his feet, nearly tripping him into a tumble down the fell. He righted himself quickly, his mild oath turning to laughter as the fox began to chase its own bushy tail, leaping and gamboling like a red-furred court jester.

"Tod!" Donal said, easing himself onto the

grass. "Are you trying to do me in?"

The fox came to a sudden stop, cocked its clever pointed head, and jumped straight up into the air. It landed on two small feet and grinned at Donal from a face neither child nor man, nut-brown eyes dancing with merriment.

"My lord is home!" Tod said, dancing nimbly just above the ground, his tattered clothing fluttering about him. Even at full stretch, he reached no higher than Donal's waist. Like all his kind, lesser Fane of wood and wildland, he was shaped to hide in the forgotten places men tended to ignore. And no human saw him unless he wished it.

Donal returned Tod's grin to hide his sadness. "You would think I'd been gone a year," he teased. "You couldn't have missed me so very much, busy as you were at Hartsmere."

Tod flung himself onto his back and gazed up at the twilit sky. "Tod always misses my lord," he said, spreading his arms wide. "The mortal world is dreary and dull without him."

Donal passed his hand through his hair and sighed. "What news of my parents?"

"They are well, but yearn for my lord's company." His mobile mouth twisted in a scowl. "The Black Widow was there."

The "Black Widow" was Tod's nickname for the woman with whom Donal had shared an intense and harrowing affair. She was indeed a widow . . . or had been, when Donal broke off the relationship.

"My brothers?" Donal asked, eager to change the subject.

"Both prosper. They, too, would call you back." He hopped up, balancing on one bare foot. "Shall we return, my lord?"

Donal gazed down at the grass between his feet. "Not now, Tod. Perhaps not for some time."

Tod leaned forward to peer into Donal's face. "What troubles my lord?" he asked. "Did the Iron City do you ill?"

Donal shook his head. He acknowledged to himself that he was unprepared to admit the truth: that his trip to London, and his time with the animals in the Zoological Gardens, had finally convinced him that he had no place in a world ruled by humankind.

"I saw much cruelty in the city," he said. "I did not return alone."

"Tod met the new dogs," Tod said eagerly. "They praise my lord with every breath."

"Not only dogs, Tod. There is a girl . . . a child from the worst part of London. She's come to stay in Yorkshire."

Tod went very still. "A female?"

"A young girl. She's seen much sorrow in her life, and I wish to give her a brighter future."

Tod was silent for a long while, frowning up at the emerging stars. "She stays here?" he said at last.

"Only until I can find a suitable home for her." He gave Tod a coaxing smile. "You'll like her, Tod. She has spirit."

The hob hunched his shoulders, his face hidden beneath his thick shock of auburn hair. "As my lord says."

Donal got to his feet and held out his hand. "Walk with me," he said. "Tell me all my mother's gossip from Hartsmere."

Tod perched on the windowsill and watched the girl sleep. She did not look so terrible now, her small form smothered in blankets and her face relaxed against the pillow. But appearance could so easily deceive. No one knew that better than Tod himself.

Since Donal's childhood he had been the boy's closest friend and companion. Together they had wandered the ancient woods of Hartsmere, running with the red deer and conversing with the badgers in their setts. The Fane gifts Donal had inherited from his father had made him an expert healer . . . and kept him forever apart from those of his mother's human blood.

But Tod had made certain he was never alone. Wherever Donal went, he followed . . . except when his master ventured into one of the cities of Iron, which few Fane could tolerate. Only once before had anything or anyone come between them, when the Black Widow caught Donal in her web.

Now there was another.

Tod closed his eyes, almost longing for the tears no true Fane could shed. For the first time in the many years he and Donal had lived at Stenwater Farm, Tod had been banished from the house during the evening meal. "Ivy wouldn't know what to make of you," Donal had said. "Perhaps you'll meet her later, when she's accustomed to her new life."

But Tod had taken no comfort in his master's promise. He had listened to their laughter as they sat at the table, sharing bread and cheese in the warmth of the kitchen. Ivy had gazed at Donal with such a look of gratitude and admiration in her eyes that made Tod's skin prickle and his hair stand on end. Donal had smiled at her as if she had earned the right to his affection. And Tod had known then that if he were not very, very careful, she would take his place in this small, sheltered world he had learned to call "home."

Tod glared at the girl, wondering what arcane powers she might possess. He was certain she did not know what she was, and neither did Donal. Perhaps it was his mortal blood that made him blind. Perhaps it was instinct that had drawn him to rescue her, though the gods knew how she had come to be living in the streets of the Iron City.

Whatever the nature of her past, the danger now was very real. Tod was no High Fane to place a curse upon her. All he could do was watch, and wait. And if she did not go to live with some local human family, he would find a way to drive her from Donal's life.

The letter arrived at Edgecott the evening after Cordelia's return. Half-dressed for dinner, she dismissed Biddle and sat down at her dressing table. With deliberate care she slit the envelope and removed the neatly folded paper.

When she had finished reading, Cordelia remained at the table and gazed unseeing in the mirror, oblivious to the passage of time until Biddle discreetly tapped on the door to remind her of the impending meal. She let the maid button her into her dress and work her hair into some semblance of order, but even Biddle noticed that her mind was elsewhere.

She and Theodora ate alone, as usual, while Sir Geoffrey dined in his rooms. After Theodora had retired, Cordelia changed into an old dress she reserved for work outdoors and walked across the drive, past the kennels and stables and over the hill to the menagerie.

The animals were often at their most active at dawn and dusk — restless, perhaps, with memories of hunting and being hunted. Othello, the black leopard, paced from one end of his large cage to the other, his meal of fresh mutton untouched. The two Barbary macaques pressed their faces to the bars and barked at Cordelia before scrambling up into the leafless trees that had been erected for their exercise and amusement. The Asian sun bear, Arjuna, lifted his head and snuffled as he awakened from his day's sleep, but showed no inclination to rise. The North American wolves lay on their boulders and twitched their ears, golden eyes far too dull for such magnificent creatures.

Cordelia sat on the bench facing the pens and rested her chin in her hands. She had done everything Lord Pettigrew recommended when she had set up the menagerie upon her final return to England. The cages were generous and consisted of both interior and exterior shelters, and Cordelia had added tree trunks, branches and boulders collected from the surrounding countryside to lend interest to the enclosures. Each animal had a proper diet carefully prepared by a specially trained groundskeeper. The cages were kept scrupulously clean. The fearful conditions under which the beasts had once lived were a thing of the past.

I want only what is best for you, she thought as the twilight deepened in the woods at the crest of the hill. *Why can you not understand?*

The animals could not answer. She knew she was mad to hope otherwise. And yet there was a man who talked to such creatures as if they were people, a man who could quiet a rampaging elephant and believed that it spoke to him. . . .

Cordelia rose and walked slowly back to the house. She was absolutely convinced of her own sanity, and perhaps that was part of the problem. She seldom found occasion to ask for help in any of her affairs. Perhaps, for the sake of those dependent upon her, she would have to set aside her pride and seek the assistance of one afflicted with just the very madness she required.

CHAPTER FIVE

Stenwater Farm, a mile on poorly graded roads beyond the village of Langthorpe, was almost exactly what Cordelia had expected. It had something of the slightly rough and yet unpredictably charming qualities of its owner, and the moment the carriage pulled up in the yard, a round dozen dogs of mixed parentage charged around the farmhouse corner.

Before the horses had a chance to shy or bolt at the unexpected assault, the dogs stopped and sat in a ragged line like schoolboys who had just remembered their manners. The coachman descended from his perch and let down the step, and as Cordelia climbed out she saw the horses twist their necks about to stare at the farmhouse door.

Theodora stepped out after her, pausing to take in the scene. "Are you quite sure that Dr. Fleming will welcome such an unexpected visit?" she asked.

"I do not know if he will welcome it," Cordelia said, "considering his failure to respond to my letters. However, he is a doctor of veterinary medicine, and as such I assume he is available for consultation." She followed Theodora's gaze. "I assure you, the dogs are not vicious."

"They certainly do not appear to be. I wonder if Dr. Fleming sends such a welcoming committee to greet every guest?"

"I rather doubt he has many guests." Taking Theodora's arm, Cordelia started up the flower-lined path. The dogs melted out of her way as she approached, a few wagging their tails while the others looked on solemnly and fell in behind her.

"I feel as if I am being examined like a ewe at market," Theodora whispered.

"Doubtless Dr. Fleming intends such an effect," Cordelia said. She strode up the flagstone steps to the porch, smoothed her skirts, and knocked on the door.

It went unanswered for several minutes, though Cordelia was quite sure that she heard noises within the house. Finally the door swung open and an old man, slightly stooped but still of vigorous appearance, peered at the women with raised brows.

"Good morning," Cordelia said crisply. "I am Mrs. Hardcastle, and this is Miss Shipp. We have come to see Dr. Fleming on a matter of some urgency."

The old man blinked and let his gaze drift

from Cordelia's feet to the top of her bonnet. "T' doctor is oot o' t' 'oose at t' moment," he said.

Cordelia quickly translated the man's thick dialect and nodded. "Can you tell me when he will return?"

" 'E's with t' coos in t' byre yonder."

"I see." Cordelia suppressed a sigh and smiled patiently. "Perhaps you would be so kind as to tell him that he has visitors who wish to consult with him in his professional capacity?"

The old man grunted. "Weel, noo. 'Appen Ah can fetch 'im. If thoo'll bide 'ere . . ." He closed the door, leaving Cordelia staring at peeling blue paint.

"What did he say?" Theodora asked. "I didn't understand a word."

"He said he would fetch the doctor." She shook her head. "Like master, like man. One can hardly expect courtesy from Dr. Fleming's servants."

"Perhaps it is simply the way of the people here."

"Perhaps." Grateful that she had worn sturdy boots, Cordelia lifted her skirts and set off across the somewhat muddy expanse of trampled earth between the farmhouse and the outbuildings scattered in a rough semicircle sheltered by rocky hills. A hay meadow stretched out to the east where the little valley was widest, and there were several fenced pastures between the byre and what appeared to be a stable. Drystone walls marched up the hills, undulating with the curves of the landscape.

She saw no other farmhands or laborers on her way to the byre, but of animals there were plenty. Chickens and geese wandered at will, snapping up grain and other tasty morsels spread out for them, and a pair of pigs had made a wallow where the mud was several feet deep. Horses in the pasture trotted up to the fence and poked inquisitive heads over the railing. A cat and five kittens paraded toward the meadow, tails twitching. Cows lowed and sheep bleated. Cordelia doubted that she would be surprised to find an elephant among the farm's residents.

The servant's gravelly voice floated from the byre, followed by the familiar, educated accent Cordelia had heard twice before. Lord Pettigrew had been somewhat vague when he had written of Dr. Fleming's background; Cordelia suspected that he knew more than he was willing to tell, but he would surely not have dealings with a man whose past was less than respectable.

The social position of Dr. Fleming's family was irrelevant to Cordelia's purpose so long as he could provide the services she required. She turned to make certain that Theodora was behind her and picked her way to the byre's doors.

". . . did you tell her I was in, Benjamin?" Fleming was saying. "I've already received three letters from the woman, each one more demanding than the last. I haven't time to cater to some fine lady's pampered pets. The very fact that she has come all this way proves that she won't be dissuaded unless she can be convinced —"

"Convinced of what, Dr. Fleming?" Cordelia said, stepping over the threshold. "That some gentlemen are so averse to human company that they will do anything to avoid it?"

Fleming shot to his feet from his place beside a spindly, spotted calf, and the flare of his green eyes stole the breath from Cordelia's throat. He opened his mouth to speak, stared at Cordelia's face, and seemed to forget what he was about to say.

"Ah told 'er ta bide at t' 'oose," Benjamin said mournfully, sending Cordelia a reproachful look.

His words seemed to shake Fleming from his paralysis. "I have no doubt," he said. "Mrs. Hardcastle," he said with a stiff bow, glancing past Cordelia to Theodora. "Miss Shipp. I trust you have not been waiting long."

Cordelia matched his dry tone. "No longer than expected," she said. "Have we interrupted you in your work?"

He looked down at the calf pressed against

his leg and idly scratched it between the eyes. "Nothing that cannot wait." He turned to Benjamin. "Put the poultice on his leg as I showed you, and I'll see to him later."

"Aye, Doctor." Benjamin gave Cordelia a final, appraising look and knelt beside the calf. Fleming brushed off the sleeves of his coat — which, like his waistcoat, trousers and boots, was liberally splashed with mud — and started toward the door. Cordelia noted that he wore no cravat, and his shirt was open at the neck, revealing a dusting of reddish brown hair.

His face was as she remembered it, handsome and bronzed by a life spent outdoors. His brown hair was windblown and still in need of cutting. But he could barely restrain a scowl, and Cordelia felt that his slight attempts at courtesy were more for Theodora's sake than her own.

"I apologize for my appearance," he said, sounding not at all apologetic, "but I didn't expect guests. I fear I lack adequate facilities to entertain ladies."

"We are not here to be entertained," Cordelia said.

He stopped, gestured the women ahead of him, and followed them out of the byre. "Have you come far this morning, Mrs. Hardcastle?"

"From York," she said. "And previously by train from Gloucestershire."

"A long journey."

"Since I did not receive a reply to my letters," Cordelia said, sidestepping a puddle, "I feared they had gone astray. One can never be sure of delivery in the countryside."

Fleming cleared his throat and offered his arm to Theodora when she hesitated at a muddy patch. "I have been . . . much distracted since my return from London," he said. "I am not a practiced correspondent."

"Then you have read the letters."

He released Theodora at the foot of the flagstone steps and faced Cordelia, his hands clasped behind his back. "Yes." He glanced away. "Have you breakfasted this morning?"

"We have. Dr. Fleming . . ."

"Would you care to come in for tea?"

"I would not wish to put you to any trouble, Doctor."

His eyes acknowledged her feint, and his lips curved up at the corners. "No. You would only have me abandon my practice and attend to your private menagerie in Gloucestershire."

Theodora stifled what might have been a gasp. Cordelia returned Fleming's smile. "Perhaps we shall accept your offer of tea, Doctor, if it will allow us to have a civilized conversation."

Fleming bowed again, far too deeply, and opened the door to the house. "Please regard my humble kitchen as your own," he said.

Humble the kitchen and house might be — certainly they bore no signs of luxury or a woman's refining touch — but at least they were orderly and clean. Donal seated his guests at the long kitchen table and set about preparing the tea himself. As water heated on the massive stove, he disappeared and returned with a tray holding a pot of honey, a pitcher of cream and a plate of scones.

"We were fortunate to receive a fresh basket of scones from Mrs. Laverick this morning," he said, deftly placing the pots and plates on the table. A moment later he set out a fine china teapot and dainty cups and saucers.

"How lovely," Theodora said, unable to conceal her surprise.

"An inheritance from my mother," Fleming said shortly. He completed the preparations in silence and strained the grounds into the teapot with the same grace he had shown in stopping a charging pachyderm. "Will you pour, Mrs. Hardcastle?"

She accepted his invitation and served the tea, which Fleming took absolutely plain. Once they had all spent a suitable time savoring the tea and scones, Fleming set down his cup and fixed his direct stare on Cordelia.

"It is not my intention to be rude, Mrs. Hardcastle, Miss Shipp," he said, "but it is impossible for me to accede to your request."

In spite of her previous meetings with him, Cordelia discovered that she could still be taken aback by his bluntness. She placed her cup on its saucer and folded her hands in her lap.

"Surely, since we have come so far, you will allow me to elaborate on the subject before you dismiss it," she said.

He sighed. "Perhaps I misunderstood. Did you not suggest that I travel to your father's estate in Gloucestershire to examine the animals in your private menagerie?"

"I did." She held his gaze. "When we met at the Zoological Gardens, I was most impressed by your dealings with the elephant. I made inquiries based upon the assumption that you had some connection with the Zoological Society. Lord Pettigrew is an old acquaintance of my father, Sir Geoffrey Amesbury. He told me of your profession, and that you had come to London at his request. He said that you were able to improve the health of a tigress and several other exotic animals within only a few days."

Fleming rose from the table and paced halfway across the room. "I went to London only because my family are also acquainted with Lord Pettigrew, and he presented his case as a matter of life or death for the animals concerned."

Cordelia also rose. "Perhaps I was not clear enough in my letters. My case is also urgent."

He came to stand at the opposite end of the room, pressed near the wall like a cornered animal prepared to fight for its life. "You wrote that your pets are suffering from a general malaise. This is hardly surprising in creatures forced to endure unnatural captivity."

She held onto her temper. "You can hardly judge what you have not seen, Doctor."

"I have seen cages," he said, his voice growing distant and strange. "One is little different from another."

"I do not agree. I, too, have seen cages, all over the world, and beasts nearly starved or beaten to death." She swallowed her anger. "My animals receive care equal to that of the Zoological Gardens. Expense is no object where their well-being is concerned . . . and that includes generous compensation for an expert practitioner such as yourself."

He emerged from the grip of memory and made a sound not unlike the snort of an irritated horse. "Sir Geoffrey Amesbury," he said. "A knight?"

"My father is a baronet."

"And your husband, Mrs. Hardcastle? Does he take an equal interest in your hobbies?"

She stared at him, abruptly realizing that she had never clarified her marital status. "My husband, Dr. Fleming, is deceased. I am a widow."

Fleming gaped at her and then had the grace to look embarrassed at his faux pas. "I am sorry," he said, tugging at his cravat. "I had not realized . . . When we first met in London, I had thought you unmarried. But your letters . . ."

"Were not perhaps as clear as they might have been," Cordelia finished. "My father is often indisposed, and has left the administration of the estate in my hands. So you see, I possess all due authority to request your assistance at whatever price we both deem reasonable."

Dr. Fleming was silent for several moments, regarding her as if she had confounded all his expectations. He collected the tea tray and carried it to a scarred sideboard. "You must be very comfortably situated, Mrs. Hardcastle," he said at last. "My circumstances must seem extremely limited by comparison."

"If I have judged you in any capacity," Cordelia said, "it has not been by your family — of whom I know nothing — your profession, or your residence."

"But you have judged that I must be in need of money." He clasped his hands behind his back and gazed out the large kitchen window. "Do you believe that is my chief motive for the work I do, Mrs. Hardcastle? Are you attempting to bribe me with promises of fees I could never earn in such a backward place as this?"

Cordelia strode to join him, her skirts hissing like a goaded serpent. "It seems I remain most ignorant in matters of your character,

Doctor. Pray enlighten me. Why does a man of your obvious skill, whose abilities are lauded by a personage such as Lord Pettigrew, choose to hide himself in the wilds of Yorkshire? Why does he so discourteously reject a respectable offer of employment to heal the very creatures whom he so obviously prefers to humankind?"

He turned on her, the color of his eyes shifting like leaves dancing in and out of shadow. "Tell me, Mrs. Hardcastle," he said, "why can you not bear to be refused? Have you never met a man who declines to tremble in awe at the force of your indomitable will?"

His words hung in a sudden, shocked silence. Cordelia took a step back, her fists clenched at her sides, and tried to remember the last time any man had spoken to her with such contempt.

No, not contempt. She gathered calm about her like an Indian shawl and considered him with cool deliberation. She had been correct in her assessment of him: he *was* hiding, here among his animals, and anyone who might drive him into the open must be considered a threat. A threat to be chased away by any means necessary.

"You must have been hurt very badly," she said, softly enough so that only he would hear. "I pity you, Doctor. I pity you more than I can say."

Fleming blanched. For once he seemed unable to think of a suitably cutting response. Cordelia's heart clenched with a pang of regret. Had she not spoken too rashly, out of pride and anger? Had she not sworn to herself a thousand times since returning to England that she would never again allow passions of any kind to rule her life?

She had opened her mouth to offer some sort of apology when a furious scratching began at the door. A moment later the door burst inward, and the dogs from the yard rushed toward Cordelia like a pack of wolves.

She braced herself, half expecting the pain of fangs tearing at her flesh. But the dogs, all nine or ten of them, simply ran around her and pressed against their master, licking his hands and whining as they milled about him. It was if they had sensed his distress and responded to it in the only way they could.

Their devoted attentions freed Fleming from his preoccupation. He met Cordelia's eyes for only an instant and then walked past her to the door.

"Forgive me for this disturbance, ladies," he said. "The animals of Stenwater Farm are accustomed to an unusual degree of liberty." Something in his voice, and in the half-twist of his lips, suggested that he counted himself among the fortunate beasts. "May I offer you anything else before you return to York?"

The dismissal was gentle, and absolute. Theodora rose, her fingers pinching the folds of her skirt. Cordelia smiled at her reassuringly and led her toward the door. The time for apologies was past.

Dr. Fleming showed them the courtesy of escorting them to the road and summoning the coachman. The dogs watched from the porch, ears pricked and bodies quivering. The cat and her kittens leaped up on the drystone wall bordering the road and regarded Cordelia with haughty disapproval. Even the pigs heaved out of their wallow, complaining like old men grudgingly roused from a sound sleep.

Fleming's expression was mild and disinterested as he handed the women into the carriage and wished them a pleasant journey. It was as if he and Cordelia had never exchanged a single barbed comment or harsh word. Cordelia brooded for all of a half-mile before she signaled the coachman to stop.

"This will not do," she said. "This will not do at all."

Theodora touched Cordelia's arm. "Perhaps it is for the best," she said quietly. "Surely you can find another veterinarian for the menagerie, one who is more congenial."

Cordelia frowned. "Did you find him so unpleasant?"

"Not unpleasant. Unusual, perhaps." Two vivid spots of color rose in her cheeks. "He does not seem to need anyone."

"You notice more than you admit, my dear."

"I noticed that you did not dislike him as much as you pretended."

"Oh?"

"Forgive me, but it is true that you are not used to being refused. If that is the only reason you would . . . I mean . . ." She sank into the seat, avoiding Cordelia's gaze.

Cordelia tapped her lower lip and stared out the window. Green, rolling hills marched away from the road, dotted here and there by clusters of sheep. She opened the carriage door and hopped to the ground without waiting for the coachman to let down the step.

"I think I'll take a turn about that meadow," she told Theodora. "The wildflowers are quite lovely. I shall only be a few minutes."

Theodora offered no protest, and so Cordelia started at a brisk pace for the wall at the side of the road. She found a stile and entered the meadow, her skirts brushing the petals of cow parsley, yellow celandine and buttercup, blue forget-me-not and speedwell. Bees filled the air with their droning. Cordelia climbed to the top of the hill, letting her mind wander between the remote beauty of the Dales and the vexatious puzzle that was Dr. Donal Fleming.

She saw the figure in the white dress while it was still some distance away. At first Cordelia couldn't judge either age or appearance, but as the girl came nearer it became apparent that she was no shepherdess or farmwife going about her daily chores. The young woman's black hair fell loose about her shoulders. She wore no gloves or bonnet. Her gown was simple but well-cut, adorned with lace at bodice and sleeves, and the ruched skirts were too full for those of a working woman. She was walking directly toward Stenwater Farm, and a small brown-and-white spaniel trotted at her heels.

Curiosity aroused, Cordelia descended the hill to intercept the stranger. The young woman saw her and stopped, her slender form frozen as if she were considering flight. The spaniel pressed against her skirts.

"Good morning," Cordelia said.

The girl, whose soft and pretty features proclaimed her to be no more than seventeen or eighteen years of age, performed a brief curtsey. "Good morning, ma'am," she said. Her voice was cultured and held no trace of the local dialect that had been so distinct in Fleming's servant.

"I hope I have not disturbed your walk," Cordelia said. "I am a visitor to this county, but I have seen no one since I left Stenwater Farm."

The girl's bright blue eyes flew to Cordelia's face. "Stenwater Farm?"

"Yes. Do you know it?"

"Yes. That is, I . . ." She stammered in confusion, lifted her chin, and thrust out her lip in defiance. "I am a friend of

Dr. Fleming."

"Are you indeed? I have just spoken with the doctor about his traveling to Gloucester-shire to treat the animals in my menagerie." She noted the dismay that briefly crossed the girl's face. "What a charming little dog. What is his name?"

"Sir Reginald." She looked to the west. "I beg your pardon, but I must —"

"How remiss of me," Cordelia interrupted, offering her hand. "I am Mrs. Hardcastle."

The girl's grip was a bit too firm for strict courtesy. "I am pleased to make your acquaintance, Mrs. Hardcastle," she said without sincerity. "I hope you will enjoy the remainder of your visit, but I must be on my way." She had taken several steps before Cordelia caught up with her.

"Are you going to Stenwater Farm?" she asked. "I would be more than happy to conduct you there in my carriage."

The girl cast Cordelia a frowning glance. "I often walk across the fells," she said. "It is no trouble to me."

"But you will ruin your lovely dress."

Once more the girl seemed flustered, almost as if she had been caught in a lie. Without another word she rushed off, the hem of her skirts already stained green from the grass.

For reasons even she did not understand, Cordelia hurried back to the carriage and instructed the coachman to return the way they had come. Once the coach was within a few hundred yards of the lane to Stenwater Farm, Cordelia called another halt and climbed one of the hills that circled the farm to the east, moving as stealthily as her confining garments would allow.

She crested the hill just as the girl and her dog were approaching the byre from the rear. The young woman looked this way and that, obviously afraid of being seen, and entered the byre.

Cordelia weighed propriety against instinct, and for once she gave instinct its head. She half slid down the hill, watching for Fleming or his servant, and reached the bottom undetected. She found the back door to the byre and entered cautiously.

There was no immediate sign of the girl, but a flash of white in the darkness caught Cordelia's eye. She found the grass-stained gown draped over the edge of the hayloft. When she was satisfied that the young woman had left the byre, Cordelia crept through the front door and looked across the yard.

It appeared that every one of Fleming's animals had deserted the area, even the somnolent pigs. The silence was so complete that Cordelia could hear the sound of voices from the house . . . those of Dr. Fleming and a young girl. She lifted her skirts and dashed to the side of the house, keeping her body low.

". . . must return to the Porritts, Ivy," Fleming said, his words carrying distinctly out the half open window. "They will be worried."

"Oi won't go back," the girl said. "Oi don't loik them farmers. Oi wants to stay 'ere, wiv you."

Cordelia leaned against the wall to catch her breath and wondered how she had sunk so low as to sneak about like a common housebreaker and eavesdrop on a private conversation. And yet she sensed that there was something peculiar going on . . . particularly since the girl's voice, apart from the thick London accent, was almost identical to that of the young woman she had met in the meadow.

"You don't want me anymore," the girl accused. "You brought me all the way up 'ere, and then cast me off loik an ol' pair o' shoes." She sniffled. "You're cruel, Donal. Cruel 'n' mean."

"No, Ivy. It isn't that I don't want you here. But you are better off with children your own age, and I don't know how much longer I will be at Stenwater Farm. You have Sir Reginald —"

"Oi *won't* go back!" She began to cry with great, gulping sobs. "Oi'll jump roight off Newgill Scar, just see if Oi don't!"

The thump of running feet was followed by the creak of hinges, and Ivy burst out the front door. Her gaze immediately fell on

102

Cordelia.

"You!" she cried, and backed away so quickly that she almost stumbled on the flagstones. Cordelia absorbed the girl's appearance in a heartbeat: the colorless dress, the bare feet, black hair swept up under a man's frayed straw hat. But the shapeless frock could not quite conceal the womanly curves of her figure, and the dirt-smudged face was instantly familiar.

Ivy was not only the young lady with the white dress, but she was also the ragamuffin who had attempted to steal Inglesham's purse in Convent Garden.

CHAPTER SIX

Ivy glanced at the door and then toward the byre, catching her lip between straight white teeth. The little spaniel planted itself in front of her and growled softly.

"Ivy," Cordelia said, extending her hand. "You have nothing to fear from me."

Fleming chose that moment to step outside. He looked from Ivy to Cordelia, his brows drawn low over his eyes, and folded his arms across his chest.

"Mrs. Hardcastle," he said. "May I ask what you are doing here?"

Cordelia had always believed that the best defense was a swift offense. "I might ask, Dr. Fleming," she said, "what a certain young thief is doing in your house when she was last seen snatching purses in Covent Garden."

Fleming stared at Cordelia, searching her eyes, and let his arms drop to his sides. "The answer is simple enough," he said. "I found this child in Seven Dials, being assaulted by grown men, and did not consider it fitting to abandon her to such a life of squalor. I offered her a home in Yorkshire —" he shot a narrow glance at Ivy, as if he expected her to protest "— and that is why you find her here. The matter of your viscount's purse was an unfortunate misunderstanding."

"I see. A most admirable act on your part, Doctor, one that not many would emulate. It seems that not only the animals benefit from your compassion." Cordelia caught Ivy's gaze. "Do you agree with this description of events, Ivy?"

The girl hunched her shoulders but refused to speak. Cordelia nodded, unsurprised. "You helped her to escape in Covent Garden," she said to Fleming.

"I had no intention of seeing a child go to gaol for such an insignificant offense."

A child. There was no irony in Fleming's voice, no sign of awareness that his protégée was anything more she seemed to be — as, indeed, she had appeared to Cordelia in London.

Cordelia briefly wondered if Dr. Fleming was capable of an outright lie regarding such a matter. If he were — and given the young woman's beauty and older appearance when she was properly cleaned and dressed — it was not such a leap to imagine that he might steal her from the streets of London and set her up as his . . .

Good God, what was she thinking? Fleming might be unpolished and discourteous, but he was no debauche. Clearly he had never seen Ivy in the white dress or any garment like it, and Ivy intended to keep it that way.

"Do I understand," Cordelia said, "that Ivy has been living with a neighboring family?"

Fleming sighed and rubbed the crease between his eyes. "Yes. The Porritts are good people, well-regarded in this part of the Dales. What is your interest in Ivy, Mrs. Hardcastle?"

"I could not help but overhear that she seems unhappy where you have sent her. It must seem a very drastic change from the rookeries of London to the life of Yorkshire farmers."

"Ivy has everything she needs . . . good food, a warm bed, fresh air and the company of young people. What else could she require?"

What else indeed. Cordelia made a quick and admittedly impulsive decision. "Will you allow me to speak with Ivy privately, Doctor?"

He bristled rather like the little spaniel who so fiercely guarded his mistress. "You will not expose her to the law —"

"Certainly not. As you may recall, I was against turning her over to the constable in London." She met Ivy's gaze. "My feelings on that score have not changed."

Fleming's shoulders sagged in defeat. "Ivy,

you have nothing to fear. Speak to Mrs. Hardcastle, be honest with her, and then we'll decide what is to be done."

Ivy shot an uneasy glance toward the byre and reluctantly followed Cordelia into the house. Cordelia closed the door behind them. "Would you like some tea, Ivy, or scones?" she asked. "There were still a few left when my cousin and I departed the farm earlier this morning."

Ivy slumped in a chair, arms shielding her breasts. "I ain't 'ungry."

"Then perhaps you won't mind if I prepare some for myself." The tea things were still lying out from that morning's service, so Cordelia began heating water, moving about the kitchen as if it were her own. Ivy's sullen defiance reminded her far too much of another unhappy girl, only a little younger than this one, and she was grateful to have something to occupy her hands.

"I hope you will allow me to ask a few questions," she said with forced lightness. "I'm a little bewildered at what I have seen and heard today."

Ivy shuffled her feet under the table. "You followed me 'ere, di'n't you?"

"Yes, Ivy, I did."

"Why?"

"Because I . . . I wished to learn more of Dr. Fleming, and since you claimed to be his friend —"

"You di'n't recognize me from Lunnon when Oi had on the dress," Ivy said suddenly, "but you knew roight away 'oo Oi was when you saw me 'ere."

"And you recognized me at once when we met in the meadow," Cordelia said, "but you did an excellent job of concealing it."

Ivy gnawed on her lower lip. "You di'n't tell Donal about the dress."

Cordelia paused in her preparations. "It seems obvious that Dr. Fleming did not give it to you. Where did you acquire it?"

Ivy shuffled her feet under the table. "I . . . borrowed it."

"From the Porritts?"

"Sometoims Oi loiks to dress up."

"Have the Porritts seen you 'dressed up'?"

"Not them."

"Nor, I venture, has Dr. Fleming." She took the kettle off the stove. "I presume that you have pretended to be a child since London?"

Ivy nodded shortly.

"You must have a very good reason for hiding your true age from your benefactor. But I suspect that you have been playing the child since long before you met Dr. Fleming."

Ivy looked away. " 'Ow d'you know so much?"

"I have seen Seven Dials, and places much worse. To survive under such conditions requires great courage and resourcefulness."

For the first time Ivy met her gaze. "Why

should you keep moi secrets, when Oi troi to steal from yer gen'l'man friend?"

Cordelia smiled. "It is certainly true that someone fitting your description attempted to steal Lord Inglesham's purse. But it seems that I have met two Ivys today — one who is quite grown up, speaks gracefully and is obviously of good family, and another who flaunts the vernacular of the rookeries and pretends to be an unlettered child. I have been quite unable to decide which one is real."

Ivy squirmed and stared at the table. "Why d'you care?"

"Is it so astonishing that others besides Dr. Fleming might take an interest in a promising young woman . . . particularly when she has been denied the advantages she so clearly deserves?"

"You don't even know me. 'Ow d'you know wot Oi deserves?"

"From the time I was a young girl, I traveled all over the world with my father. I had to learn quickly how to understand many different kinds of people. It has always been my desire to help those in need, whether they be men, women or animals."

"You loiks animals?"

"Very much. At my father's country house in Gloucestershire, we have horses, dogs and wild creatures few Europeans have ever seen. That is why I came to visit Dr. Fleming, because of his fine reputation as a veterinarian." She sat down across from Ivy and smiled. "May I speak frankly, as between two women?"

Ivy nodded warily, but her blue eyes took on a sparkle of interest.

"I cannot pretend," Cordelia began, "to guess what kind of situation compelled you to live by such desperate means in a place like Seven Dials, but I can surmise why you chose to disguise yourself as a child. You had hoped to avoid the sort of salacious attentions you were suffering when Dr. Fleming rescued you." She paused. "He did rescue you, did he not?"

"Yes." Ivy rubbed at a bitten fingernail and almost smiled. " 'E ran them blodgers roight off, 'e did."

"And when he brought you to Yorkshire, he had no idea that you were older than you had made yourself appear." She stopped to fetch hot water and the teapot, then laid out the cups and saucers in the center of the table. "When I saw you in Covent Garden, you deceived even me. Did you bind your breasts, Ivy?"

Ivy flushed. "Oi 'ad to. When Oi first got to the rookeries, most blokes left me alone."

"How old were you then?"

"Twelve."

Cordelia poured a cup of tea, added a dollop of honey and gently pushed the saucer toward Ivy. "I know that drinking a good cup of tea in a civilized setting is not unknown to you, Ivy. The young woman I met in the meadow wore that gown like one who remembers fine things and better days."

Ivy pulled the steaming cup toward her and clenched her fingers around it. "Oi . . ."

"Can you tell me where you lived before you went to Seven Dials?"

"Wiv me muvver. She died." Ivy lifted the cup to her face, closed her eyes, and breathed in the scent as if it were the ambrosia of the gods. "I don't remember much from before," she said in accentless English. "I just know that I lived in a house with a garden, and I had books and pretty dresses."

Cordelia released a slow breath. She hadn't been sure if she would be able to gain the girl's trust, and she had desperately wanted to. Perhaps it was because Ivy reminded her so much of Lydia. Certainly she needed no better reason than common decency to help the girl, and her persistence had pierced at least one layer of Ivy's formidable defenses.

"You can read and write?" she asked.

Ivy snorted indelicately. "Of course."

"What of your father?"

Ivy jumped up from the chair and began to pace the room, her motions abrupt as if she were resisting the urge to run away. "I don't remember him at all," she said. She reached inside the neckline of her shapeless bodice and drew out a silver pendant hung on a worn leather cord. "He left me this."

"It's lovely," Cordelia said. The silver emblem seemed to be a complex Celtic knot set with a vivid blue stone, but before she could examine it further Ivy pushed it beneath her dress again.

"I think he must be dead," Ivy said. She stopped to stare out the window, her fists clenching and unclenching at her sides.

"And you had no other kin to take care of you," Cordelia said.

"None that I ever met."

Cordelia rose and went to stand behind the young woman. "Whatever happened to your father and mother, they must have loved you very much. They gave you an education, and the spirit to go on living when it must have seemed . . . almost too much to bear."

Ivy shook her head sharply. "I didn't need anyone."

"And yet you came with Dr. Fleming when he offered you a home."

Ivy's voice softened. "He was the first one who was ever kind to me. And the dogs loved him . . ." She pressed her hands flat against the window pane. "But 'e di'n't give me no 'ome," she said, lapsing back to rough rookery speech. " 'E sent me off to live wiv them farmers. . . ."

"Surely he did so only because he wanted what was best for you," Cordelia said. She reached out but let her hands fall before she could touch Ivy's rigid shoulders. "He saw only one part of you, Ivy. He couldn't guess that you might be destined for something better than life on an isolated farm."

"I won't go back," Ivy said, low and intense. "They took me in because they owe Donal a debt, but they don't like me. They think I'm a low, filthy thing."

"Did not Dr. Fleming provide you with a . . . suitable history so that the Porritts would be willing to accept you?"

"You mean did he lie to them?" Ivy asked. "Of course he did. He made sure I was clean and had new clothes, and he told them a story that made Mrs. Porritt weep into her teacup. He paid them to treat me like one of their daughters."

"But you refused to play your part."

"Why should I have done? I hated it there."

"You did not reveal your true age."

"I didn't want them to think that Donal misled them. And I didn't want *him* to know."

"Why not, Ivy?"

The girl scraped her fingers down the windowpane, drawing a frightful squeak from the glass. "I was afraid he would turn me away," she whispered.

"You know that he must be told."

"Yes." Abruptly she spun on Cordelia, a wicked smile curving her lips. "I can't go back to those silly farmers, anyway. I stole that dress from Porritt's eldest daughter."

Cordelia swallowed her instinctive reproach. Thievery was quite likely the very least of what Ivy had been compelled to do in order to survive. Whatever misfortune had led to her fall from respectable life and her apparent loss of memory, her father had almost certainly been of the merchant class, perhaps even a banker or lawyer. Yet Ivy faced a long and difficult climb to regain the state of mind and appropriate behavior that distinguished a well-bred woman. Even the smallest criticism might destroy the fragile truce she and Cordelia had made between them.

"It does not seem a good idea for you to return," Cordelia agreed. "But perhaps there are alternatives."

"I want to stay here, with Donal."

Once again Cordelia suppressed her arguments. It would be unfortunate if Ivy had developed a *tendre* for Dr. Fleming, though not entirely unexpected. He had been kind to her, and he was not without attractions for a girl who had been living among the dregs of humanity for five or six years.

At least Cordelia didn't have to contend with an inappropriate attachment in the other direction. Dr. Fleming showed no signs of regarding Ivy as anything but a child. But before the girl could be made to accept her own best interests, Dr. Fleming must be brought to recognize the complexity and delicacy of the situation.

"I know we do not yet know each other well," Cordelia said, "but if you will trust me, Ivy, I believe I may be able to convince Dr. Fleming that it would be best for you to find a more agreeable home."

Ivy turned and regarded Cordelia through narrowed eyes. "At Stenwater Farm?"

"That I cannot promise. But you may be sure that I will hold your concerns very much in mind."

Ivy weighed Cordelia's offer as if it were a question of life or death. Indeed, it must be against her inclinations to trust any stranger, however well meaning. And yet Cordelia couldn't help but believe that she could offer the girl something she must yearn for with all her heart: comfort, stability, and the constructive discipline that would restore her to her rightful place in society.

"Very well," Ivy said. Without another word she spun and ran for the door, light-footed as a fawn. Her spaniel raced after her.

Cordelia gathered her composure as she collected the tea things and carried them into the kitchen. Something quite remarkable had occurred in the hour since she had followed Ivy to Stenwater Farm. Of course there were perfectly rational reasons behind her decision to involved herself in Ivy's life; she firmly believed it was the duty of any decent person to assist those less fortunate. But there was also an element of irrationality in the situation that disturbed Cordelia, and all she could do was push such thoughts aside as she went to find Dr. Fleming.

When Mrs. Hardcastle emerged from the house, Donal could see that something significant had transpired between her and Ivy.

He had seen a hint of that change in the girl as she'd rushed out the door, flying past Donal with hardly a glance. But Mrs. Hardcastle's face seemed to hold a kind of light he could not remember noticing before, a peculiar and exotic beauty that that had nothing to do with her rather ordinary features. And her eyes . . . those eyes he had seen in his dreams . . . revealed a hint of vulnerability that had a startling effect on Donal's heart.

He rose from his seat on the flagstone steps and held her gaze as she descended to meet him. He did not understand the unprecedented sense of familiarity that assaulted his nerves and turned his mouth too dry for speech. He knew Mrs. Hardcastle no better now than he had an hour ago, and yet she might have been an old and dear acquaintance, a friend in whom he could confide his deepest yearnings. He could share with her his visions of distant wilderness, his need to run in those faraway places, and she would understand. She would even shed those confining, torturous garments and run at his side.

But she came to a sudden stop, almost as if she sensed his thoughts, and her eyes hardened to tempered steel.

"Dr. Fleming," she said, "I wish to discuss a proposal regarding Ivy's future."

Donal shook off his daze and offered his hand to assist her down the remaining steps. "May I ask, Mrs. Hardcastle, what you and Ivy discussed?"

She took his hand with obvious reluctance, her gloved fingers small and firm in his, and broke away as quickly as courtesy allowed. "We discussed her unhappiness with the current arrangements, and I offered to help her find a more suitable situation."

"I see." Donal paced a little distance away, concealing his anger. "You will forgive me if I speak frankly, madame. I am surprised that you consider the judgment of a twelve-year-old girl of greater reliability than my own."

"If she were indeed twelve years of age and a simple child of the streets," Mrs. Hardcastle said, "I might consider your judgment sufficient. But you have been deceived, Doctor. Ivy is at the very brink of womanhood, and it is not too late to mold her into the lady she was doubtless born to become."

"I beg your pardon?"

"It is not overly surprising that you were taken in. It is human nature to see what we wish and expect to see. Ivy is an excellent actress, and she had an extraordinary motive to play her role well. Even I did not penetrate her disguise until I met her again, here at Stenwater Farm."

As Donal listened with growing chagrin, she recounted her meeting with the young woman in the meadow, Ivy's transformation and the girl's admission of her masquerade. She asked Donal to accompany her to the byre, where she revealed the soiled white gown that Ivy had stolen from the Porritts' eldest daughter.

"Ivy maintained her disguise at the Porritts'," Mrs. Hardcastle said, "but she could not resist the chance to be her true self for a short while, even if no one would see her."

"Her true self," Donal repeated slowly. "If she does not remember her life before the rookeries, how does she know what that is?"

"I am fully convinced that she is of good family, and received at least some education. It may be possible to learn more through my father's connections in London."

Donal sifted the fine material of the gown between his fingers and shook his head. "Why was she afraid to tell me the truth about her age?" he asked. A wash of sickness curled in his belly. "Did she think I would abuse her?"

Mrs. Hardcastle walked up behind him. He felt her breath on his shoulder, and for a moment he thought she might touch him. His muscles tightened in anticipation.

"You should not blame yourself, Dr. Fleming," she said briskly, her skirts brushing his boots as she moved past him. "Only a fool would believe such a thing of you." She turned to meet Donal's gaze. "Ivy does not know her own mind, but it is clear that she will not remain with the Porritts."

Donal went to the door of the byre and looked out at the fells, thinking of the preparations he had already begun to make, the arrangements for the farm and animals he was putting in motion. There was no question of taking Ivy with him on his travels. If she refused to remain with anyone but him . . .

He had never thought to have the simple things that most humans took for granted: courtship, marriage, a wife and children. He had too little interest in the ways of human society, and human society had no place for a man of his eccentricities. But he had made a choice in taking Ivy from London. He had made himself responsible for a human life.

Mrs. Hardcastle implied that Ivy ought to become a lady like herself, that the girl would be happiest wearing beribboned dresses and flirting at balls and fetes like the ones Donal's mother loved to give at Hartsmere. Donal had met many such young women before he had left his parents' estate, and he knew the sort of life they desired: a youth of frivolous pleasures followed by a staid and expedient marriage to a man of excellent prospects.

There was hardly an ounce of true spirit, honesty or sincerity amongst any dozen of them.

But Donal had seen something in Ivy that Mrs. Hardcastle had not. He had watched her running on the fells, her feet bare in the grass, her arms spread wide and her face rapt with the beauty of nature. He couldn't imagine her laced into a corset and weighed down by horsehair petticoats. Whatever Ivy's true age or parentage, she had a love of freedom that would not be suppressed.

"I would . . . appreciate your advice in this matter, Mrs. Hardcastle," he said, keeping the despair from his voice. "It seems that I made a mistake in sending Ivy away. I know little of the needs of young ladies, but I believe she can be happy here. If there is anything in particular you feel she requires, I will make the necessary provisions to —"

"She cannot remain with you at Stenwater Farm," Mrs. Hardcastle interrupted. "Surely you understand that an unattached and unchaperoned young woman cannot share residence with a bachelor unless she is prepared to sacrifice her reputation."

Donal flinched. "I am aware that your society is unforgiving of the smallest breach of its nonsensical rules," he said, "but surely Ivy has already put herself beyond the pale . . ."

"Not at all." Mrs. Hardcastle maneuvered

herself so that Donal could not avoid her eyes. "The only people who might recognize her from London are you, myself, my cousin and Viscount Inglesham. When she is decently clothed and in an appropriate environment . . ." She took a deep breath. "Dr. Fleming, what Ivy requires above all else is loving care that includes firm discipline and thorough instruction in the skills and comportment that will secure her future. I believe that I can provide that care."

Donal heard her words with dawning comprehension and bitter realization. "You?" he said. "You wish to take Ivy into your home?"

"Yes." She clasped her hands at her waist almost like a supplicant, but Donal wasn't fooled. "I have the resources to give her what she needs at Edgecott. She will have more than adequate chaperonage there, as well as congenial surroundings and pleasant country society."

Donal strode out of the byre, scarcely waiting to see if Mrs. Hardcastle followed. "Has Ivy agreed to this . . . proposal?" he asked.

"I have not told her," she said behind him. "I knew I must speak with you first."

He turned on her, nearly treading on the toes of her sensible half-boots. "So my opinion is still of some value, madame?"

"Naturally, since it was you who saved her."

"But I am not fit to keep her."

Her nostrils flared with annoyance. "Dr.

121

Fleming, I think you would find your free bachelor's life, as well as Ivy's reputation, much compromised if she were to stay."

"But your life will not in the least be affected."

"I can provide you with any number of references, Doctor, if you require them. I do not believe you will find any cause to object. I have had considerable experience in seeing to the welfare of the people of our village. I am accustomed to having dependents —"

"Perhaps you consider Ivy another addition to your menagerie."

She flushed, and her eyes struck his like hammers on an anvil. "You may regard animals as people, but I most assuredly do not subscribe to the reverse view."

"Humans would be far better off if they recognized their kinship to animals," he retorted. "What if Ivy does not agree to your scheme?"

"I am confident that Ivy and I have established a certain rapport," she said stiffly. "If you place no obstacles in her path . . . if you encourage her to recognize the benefits she will enjoy at Edgecott, I am sure she will be reasonable."

Reasonable. Donal clenched his jaw. "And what benefits do *you* gain by this, madame? What payment do you expect for your selfless generosity?" Before she could reply, he rushed on. "Is this all a convenient ploy to acquire my services for your private zoological gardens?"

"What?"

"Your interest in Ivy is most timely," he said, refusing to relent before the shock in her eyes. "You must know that she finds it difficult to trust anyone, and she'll never go with you unless I accompany her."

Mrs. Hardcastle's small fist clenched, and Donal entertained the absurd image of the woman raising that fist to strike him in the jaw. She was certainly angry enough to attempt it; her usual air of cool self-possession had deserted her, and a tigress crouched behind her outraged stare.

"How poorly you must think of your fellow men and women if you ascribe such motives to me," she said. "I require nothing of you but your permission to help a young person in need."

For all his previous certainty of her ulterior motives, Donal was the first to look away. His breath came quickly, but not out of anger; his senses had turned traitor, making him painfully aware of the woman's body beneath the stout cage of Mrs. Hardcastle's corset. He could almost taste her scent, a subtle blending of soap, lavender and warm skin. And the blaze of her temper only ignited the long-banked fire he had worked so hard to extinguish.

She brought out the worst in him, the very

strength and stubbornness of her character provoking his passions as no other human had done in many years. He should not find her in the least attractive, yet he did. And it was all because of the tigress in her eyes.

God knew that he should do anything but allow himself to be drawn more deeply into Mrs. Hardcastle's sphere of comfortable, self-satisfied English society. But she had spoken no less than the truth where Ivy was concerned. And if he were honest with himself, he would admit that the lady had offered him a reasonable alternative to surrendering his dreams.

All he need do was spend a few weeks in Gloucestershire to see Ivy well established in her new home. And then, once he had completed the arrangements for Stenwater Farm — and made Tod understand why he must leave England — he would book his passage from Liverpool and be on his way.

He eased the tension from his shoulders and essayed a smile. "What is your name?" he asked.

Mrs. Hardcastle had clearly expected another round of sparring, and his mild question took her aback. "I . . . beg your pardon?" she stammered.

"Your given name. Your Christian name."

She perched on the edge of indignation, but she must have recognized that such a minor breach of etiquette was a small enough price to pay for peace between them.

"Cordelia," she said.

"Cordelia," he repeated. "King Lear's loyal daughter."

"You know your Shakespeare, Dr. Fleming."

"Donal," he said. "My name is Donal."

"Irish, I believe?"

"I spent my early childhood in Ireland."

The wariness in her eyes gave way to curiosity. "Is Fleming also Irish?"

"English," he said. "My parents live in Westmorland."

"I have heard the Lakes are very beautiful."

"Yes." He glanced over her head toward the road, searching for a change of subject. "Where is your cousin? She might wish to join us for luncheon, if simple fare meets with your approval."

Cordelia touched her lips. "Oh, dear. I did not intend to leave Theodora alone in the carriage so long. I shall go at once and fetch her . . ."

"That will not be necessary." Donal closed his eyes, picked out the carriage horses' minds from among the other equines in the vicinity, and sent them a brief message. "I believe they are already on their way."

"But how could you know that?"

"Any good doctor — even an animal doctor — must rely on instinct as well as science," he said. He whistled, and his dogs

125

came to him, prancing with delight at the newfound goodwill they sensed between him and his visitor. Cordelia gamely patted a few bobbing heads, but Donal discouraged them from licking her hands or leaping up on her full skirts, and they raced off again to find Ivy.

"I expect Benjamin to arrive any moment with fresh bread and cheese," Donal said. "When Ivy returns, allow me to speak to her alone."

"Then you no longer have any objections to my proposal?" Cordelia asked.

"Not if Ivy is willing to try."

Cordelia quickly looked away, and once more Donal caught a glimpse of the vulnerability he had seen after she had spoken with Ivy. "Thank you, Dr. Fleming," she said, her voice not entirely steady. "You shall not regret it."

"It will only be for a few weeks, Tod," Donal said, crouching beside him in the loft of the byre. "Mrs. Hardcastle — the lady I met in London — wishes to give Ivy a permanent home. I know you've never had the opportunity to know her, but this may be her best opportunity for happiness."

Tod kicked his feet over the edge of the loft, hiding a scowl behind the fall of his hair. "Why must my lord go with her?"

"I've taken responsibility for Ivy. I must

make sure this is the right course for her future." He patted Tod's shoulder. "You're welcome to accompany me, of course. You've never been to the south of England; there are more humans there than here in the north, but Gloucestershire is filled with hills and woods where you can run in freedom."

"The Fane left those lands long ago."

"That may be true. But I wouldn't be surprised to find that a little Fane magic still lingers, even so."

Tod sighed, knowing he could not win this battle. He had thought himself rid of the girl, and still she'd returned; now there was a good chance that she would be out of Donal's life forever. Tolerating her presence for a few more weeks was a small enough price to pay.

"When we come back," he said, tossing hair out of his eyes, "it will be as it was before. My lord and Tod, together."

Donal looked away, and his voice was strange when he spoke. "Only in Tir-na-Nog does everything stay the same," he said. "In this world, change is inevitable."

"Tod never changes," Tod said, touching Donal's hand. "Tod will always be here."

Donal smiled, but Tod felt his grief. It was these females who brought him such pain. But soon they would be gone.

"Tod will go with my lord," he said firmly. "And it will not be long before my lord has peace again."

Donal only bowed his head and gave no answer.

"She is found, my lady!"
"She is found!"
"Found!"

The incessant chatter of the sprites clanged like raucous bells in Béfind's ears, but she did not chastise her servants. She smiled indulgently as they darted about her head, crying out their victory until even they grew weary and settled to the glistening floor at her feet.

It was one of her hobs who gave the report. He related how they had searched high and low, seeking over the mortals' island until they had sensed Fleming's presence in a place far from the humans' cities. There they had watched and listened, learning much that could amaze even one who had lived three thousand years.

Donal Fleming. It would have been a stroke of astonishing coincidence had the players in this drama been human. Fleming, son of the exiled Forest Lord, had found the girl living in squalor in the mortal's great Iron City and taken her to live with him on his little farm in the north. It was clear to Béfind's servants that Fleming had made himself her guardian and accepted his new responsibility with a mortal's tedious gravity. It was equally clear that he didn't know what she was.

Béfind called for a cup of mead and idly tapped her fingers on the arm of her chair. Everyone in Tir-na-Nog knew Hern's story: how he, one of the last of the High Fane to linger on earth, had fallen in love with a human woman and surrendered his Fane powers in exchange for a mortal life as Cornelius Fleming, Earl of Bradwell. Donal was the bastard offspring of his first, illicit union with his beloved, Eden Fleming, six years before he had returned to the mortal realm to woo and win her as his wife.

It was well-known that Donal, whom Queen Titania had sought to claim for Tir-na-Nog, had chosen a dull existence of isolation on earth rather than enjoy a life of ease and eternal pleasure in the Land of the Young. But he kept one companion to remind him of his Fane heritage . . . a hob called Tod, who had once been his father's servant.

Béfind accepted the glass of mead from the hands of a sprite and sipped the honeyed beverage thoughtfully. It should have been a simple matter to reclaim the girl Ivy, but there were a few small complications. Perhaps she could dispose of one of them here and now.

Idath kept her waiting, as she had known he would. He strolled into her palace with a lazy air of indifference, his eyes hooded as he took in her entourage of hobs and sprites, each and every one still drenched in the smell of the mortal realm.

"Béfind," he said, inclining his head. "To what do I owe the honor of this summons?"

She smiled and offered him a golden chalice of mead, which he refused. "Why must we quarrel, my friend?" she purred. "It has been too long since we have lain in each other's arms. Is it so strange that I would ask you to attend me?"

Idath returned her smile with equal warmth. "What do you want, Béfind?"

"I have found the girl."

"Oh?" He yawned behind his hand. "What girl is that?"

She bared her teeth. "I know the truth, Idath. You took my property. You told me the babe was dead and delivered it to your mortal paramour to raise as her own."

"Ah, yes. I begin to remember."

"How could you have forgotten? You believed you could wound and confound me with your lies."

"As you believed you could prove your indifference to me by casting me aside and remaining with your mortal lover for a full year."

Béfind laughed. "Ah. You finally admit your motive — simple jealousy. How petty. How very *human*."

Idath's expression didn't change. "You have always found it amusing to mock the blood of my halfling mother," he said, "and yet I learned much from her that you will never understand."

"Such as love?" she sneered.

"Once, perhaps. There was a time when I cared enough to punish you for making sport of my devotion and cleaving to your mortal for no reason but to show how little you felt for me, even after a hundred years." He gazed out at the lawn. "It was all a game to you, Béfind. I only decided to play by your rules."

"By handing my child over to one who would corrupt her as your mother did you."

"If I had believed any real harm would come to the girl, I would have left her with you. But you did not deserve the acclaim you would receive by bringing a healthy child to Tir-na-Nog."

Béfind burned with fury. "Perhaps you did not know that the child was found living alone in the worst part of the Iron City, hunting her food in the gutters like a *beast*."

Idath leaned against the nearest column and smoothed the scarlet silk of his tunic. "I am grieved to hear it."

"Unfortunate indeed that your lover is dead."

He couldn't quite hide the flash of sorrow in his eyes. "Mortals die. It is their nature."

"But the girl lives. None other than the son of Hern has discovered her."

"Hern's son?" Idath cocked his head. "What does he want with her?"

"His mother's blood taints him with what mortals call 'compassion,' " she said. "He pitied her. And now he intends that she shall have a life among humans."

"She has already lived among humans."

"And suffered because of your spite," Béfind said. "That is over. I will bring her back to Tir-na-Nog."

"I wonder how you will manage that, *a mhuirnín?*"

She stepped away from her chair and came to stand before him. "You cannot stop me."

"It is not I who will stop you." He glanced about at Béfind's servants. "Did they not tell you of the amulet?"

Béfind bristled. "Idath, if you do not —"

He raised a languid hand. "I gave it to her when she was yet with Estelle," he said. "As long as she wears it, none who is Fane may touch the girl or carry her through a Gate to Tir-na-Nog."

"What?"

"I knew you would find her eventually, *a chuisle.*"

Béfind was momentarily speechless. "You . . . you would go so far —"

His eyes grew cold. "Perhaps I judged her better off away from you."

Béfind turned away and composed herself. She faced him again with a smile. "An amusing trick, Idath. But surely the game has gone

132

on long enough." She stroked his sleeve. "Remove the enchantment, and I shall give you whatever you desire."

He looked her up and down. "You possess nothing I desire."

She tore his sleeve with her nails and let him go. "You will not win this battle, Idath. I shall go to the mortal realm myself. I shall tell her who she is, and then —"

"Tell her who she is?" Idath chuckled softly. "Alas, the charm on the amulet does more than forbid any Fane to touch her. None may reveal her true nature. You may speak the words, but she will not hear them."

"You hate me so much?"

"Hatred is a mortal curse, *leannán*."

"So is jealousy, mighty lord."

"And blind ambition. You want the child only because your pride has been wounded and she is proof of your fecundity, a valuable object to be paraded before the Queen and High Fane like a pretty bauble. Perhaps you will not find the prize worth the effort."

"It shall be more than worth it to lay your pride in the dust."

He bowed. "As you wish, Béfind. The battle continues." He swept from the room, scattering the lesser Fane from his path. Béfind shrieked in rage and snatched a delicate crystal sculpture from its stand, shattering it against an ivory column.

"So he thinks he shall win?" she hissed as

the hobs and sprites cowered at her feet. "He dreams that he can best Béfind?"

She threw herself down into her chair and coiled her hair between her fists. So she could not tell the girl what she was. That was not quite the defeat Idath believed. There would be ways to approach the child and groom her for her rightful future, all without challenging the amulet's enchantment. Béfind would not leave such an important task to inferiors. She would go through the Gate herself. She would learn how best to handle Donal Fleming, if he should prove to be an obstacle to her ambitions. And she would have what was rightfully hers, once and for all.

Chapter Seven

There was no part of England, Donal reflected, more thoroughly English than the Cotswolds.

The view from the carriage window was one of gently rolling hills dotted with clouds of grazing sheep, low stone walls turned golden in the clear sunlight, homely farmsteads and quaint cottages with thick thatched roofs. Westmorland and Yorkshire still had their shares of wilderness in crags and sills, heaths and moors, becks and forces and lakes — hidden sanctuaries where patches of ancient woodland and unsullied mountains crouched just beyond the fringes of civilization — but Donal doubted he would find such places here.

He leaned back in the seat and pinched the bridge of his nose. The minds of the animals he had heard along the winding road to Edgecott had been largely contented ones that knew neither worry nor anticipation of the future. Even Sir Geoffrey Amesbury's matched bays were well fed and glossy of coat, never asked to push beyond their endurance or forced to suffer the brutality of the bearing-rein. In the amber sunshine of a bright spring morning, it was almost possible to forget the cruelty and indifference that seemed so much a part of human character.

Donal did not forget. But he allowed himself to be distracted by the look on Ivy's face as she craned her neck to absorb every detail of the neat little village that gave the Amesbury estate its name. Round-faced children and prosperous cottagers waved from the verge of the cobbled lane that passed through the center of the village, and Ivy waved back.

Once she had made the decision to visit Edgecott, her hard shell of defiance and suspicion had dropped away like the halves of a ripe walnut. Soon after she and Donal had boarded the train in York, she had cast off her fears with the impulsiveness of youth and wholeheartedly embraced the excitement of the journey.

Her enthusiasm eased Donal's mind. Seventeen years old she might be, but her childhood had been robbed of so many simple pleasures that she devoured each new experience with innocent delight. Sir Reginald, who had chosen her as his new lifelong companion, perched on her lap and laughed with a lolling tongue, sharing her joy.

Neither girl nor dog had been in the least

constrained in Donal's presence. He had no interest in enforcing arbitrary rules of conduct, and ignored the occasional pointed stares and whispers aimed at "that wild young woman" by starchy matrons and stiff-rumped gentlemen who resembled exotic fowl escaped from their pens. Ivy had not yet been introduced to corsets; her blossoming figure was now quite apparent to Donal's previously ignorant eye. Yet he had no desire to cut short her last days of freedom before Mrs. Hardcastle applied the shackles of rigid morals and genteel hypocrisy.

He prayed that Ivy's courage and adaptability would enable her to accept the world Cordelia intended to make for her.

The carriage rattled out of the village and past fields and pastures bordered by light gray dry-stone walls. Soon it reached the high iron gates that guarded Edgecott's stately park.

The gates stood open in welcome, but Donal regarded them with a shiver of foreboding. They were merely symbols of power and prosperity, harmless in themselves, but to Donal's mind they resembled nothing so much as a cage. A part of him believed that once he passed through them, he would be caught in the snares of civilization forever.

"Look at the trees!" Ivy said. "I never saw such tall ones in Yorkshire!"

The woods of Edgecott's park were indeed impressive. They reminded Donal of the ancient forest of Hartsmere, where his father had roamed for millennia as guardian and protector of every living thing within it. Yet most of these trees had been grown, not by nature, but by Amesbury ancestors who had planted the wood to enhance their prestige and shield their property from the eyes of lesser mortals.

Donal was so lost in thought that he didn't see the great house until Ivy drew his attention with an exclamation of approval. She had good reason for her admiration. The main house at Edgecott was built of the fine native stone, and while it had obviously been altered over several centuries, with a classical wing and ornamentations added well after its original, Elizabethan construction, it was a handsome building as such things went.

Standing in a neat row at the foot of the stairs were several male and female servants, including footmen, maids, an older woman who must have been the housekeeper and a tall man of impeccable dignity whose demeanor declared him master of the household staff. As the carriage rounded the gravel drive, one of the footmen broke ranks and hurried up the stairs.

The coachman eased the horses to a stop before the stairs, and the footman leaped down to lower the steps. Ivy hopped out, ignoring the footman's proffered hand, and stood gazing up at the massive limestone facade.

Donal descended more slowly, not in the least eager to deal with a bevy of servants whose only purpose was to wait hand and foot on their employers. He avoided them by going directly to the horses, thanking them for their work and examining their legs and hooves while the coachman watched curiously.

Ivy inched up beside him, Sir Reginald in her arms. "They're all staring at me," she whispered, glancing back at the servants. "Where is Cordelia?"

Like Donal, Ivy had taken to referring to Mrs. Hardcastle by her given name, and Donal had not discouraged her. "I'm certain she will wish to welcome you herself," he said, giving the horses a final pat.

Ivy gripped his sleeve. "Maybe it wasn't such a good idea to come here after all," she said. "I don't belong in a place like this."

"How do you know, when you've scarcely seen any of it?" he said. But she gave him a narrow look that suggested she knew he was every bit as nervous as she.

"You really are going to stay?" she demanded.

"As long as you need me."

Her shoulders relaxed, but her gaze remained fixed on his face. "You like Cordelia, don't you?"

"Of course I do, Ivy. She has been nothing

but kind to you, and the animals —"

"No. I mean you *like* her."

He reminded himself again that she was no child, and that her very survival in London had depended on the keenness of her observations. He pretended a sudden interest in the knot of his cravat.

"I admire her, certainly," he said. "She is a formidable woman."

Ivy snorted. "You're no good at lyin', guv. I seen 'ow you watched at 'er at the farm, roight enough."

"And how did I watch her, pray tell?"

"The way ol' Rooster Tom looks at the 'ens after 'e's 'ad 'is fill o' crowin'."

"Ivy!" Heat rushed to his face, and he steered her away from the avid ears of the footman who lingered nearby. "It would be best if you abandon rookery speech at Edgecott, since Mrs. Hardcastle hopes to give you the advantages of a lady."

Ivy thrust her nose in the air and performed a deep curtsey. "As you wish, Your Majesty."

He sighed. "Also, consider *what* you say. I have no objections to your frankness, but you'll find that it may be advisable to think before you speak."

Ivy's playful demeanor melted into seriousness. "It sounds like a lot of work."

"It is work to be grown up, Ivy, no matter where you are. Whatever you may face here, it will be nothing compared to London."

Ivy pressed her face into Sir Reginald's warm coat. "Do you think I could be a lady, Donal?"

"I think you can be whatever you choose."

"Then if I work hard and wear pretty dresses, will you look at me the way you look at Cordelia?"

Donal heard Ivy's words with amazement and consternation. His cravat seemed to tighten like a noose. As he struggled to find an answer, a footman emerged from the house and held the door open for the one who followed.

Cordelia Hardcastle swept down the stairs in a rustle of deep blue skirts, a smile animating her resolute features. She walked past the servants and extended her hands to Ivy. There was no mistaking the warmth of her greeting.

"Ivy," she said, "Dr. Fleming. Welcome to Edgecott."

Ivy took Cordelia's hands. "It is a beautiful house," she said with uncharacteristic shyness.

"Thank you, my dear." Cordelia glanced up at Donal. "I hope that your journey was a pleasant one?"

Donal inclined his head. "We found it most enjoyable."

Her gaze lingered on his face. "I am so glad that both of you have been able to join us."

The rote courtesies expected on such occasions flew out of Donal's mind. Somehow he had forgotten a few small details of Cordelia's features in the two weeks since she had left Stenwater Farm: the clean arch of her brows, the tiny dimple in her left cheek, the fullness of her lips that hinted of sensuality kept under strict control.

Those lips parted, and Cordelia's breath sighed out as gently as the breeze stirring the leaves overhead. How easy it would be, how scandalously improper, if he were to lean down and catch her mouth with his own. . . .

"Donal?" Ivy said.

He shook his head and looked away. Cordelia casually put another several feet of distance between them. "I'm certain you must be famished," she said to Ivy. "Cook has prepared a grand luncheon fit for the Queen herself. It will be served at one. You will wish to rest, and change into fresh clothing. Your boxes are already being taken up to your rooms."

"I hadn't much to bring," Ivy said. "Only the dresses you and Donal bought for me."

"Of course, my dear. But we shall soon remedy any deficiencies in your wardrobe, I assure you." She turned to Donal. "Our butler, Croome, will escort you to your chamber, Dr. Fleming. Mrs. Priday, our housekeeper, takes a personal interest in seeing to the comfort of our guests."

Mrs. Priday, who was blessed with the round, pleasant face and stout figure that seemed the very hallmarks of an English country housekeeper, took Ivy under her ample wing. After a brief backward glance, Ivy went with her. Croome stood waiting while Cordelia hesitated.

"I trust that Miss Shipp is well?" Donal said to fill the silence.

"She has a slight ague, Dr. Fleming, which is why she was unable to greet you. I shall tell her that you inquired after her."

"Yes." Donal glanced across the park. "You have a fine wood here, Mrs. Hardcastle."

"Thank you. The Amesburys have always appreciated nature." She paused. "Perhaps you would like to come in?"

Donal looked from the gaunt-faced Croome to the wide, heavy door. A rush of panic caught at his throat. "I should be happy to look at your animals now, if it is convenient," he said.

"Dr. Fleming, I certainly do not expect you to work after such a tiring journey. That can wait for another day."

"Nevertheless, I . . . Do you perhaps have an empty groundskeeper's cottage, or a room above the stables? I believe I would be more effective in working with your animals if I lived closer to them."

She stared at him with raised brows, doubtless wondering whether or not to take offense at his apparent rejection of her hospitality. From her perspective, she must be doing a simple country veterinarian considerable honor by inviting him to stay in her titled father's country manor.

"There is another reason it might be best if I lodged outside the house," he said quickly. "You and Ivy will naturally spend more time together without the distraction of my presence. It is, after all, to our purpose if we encourage her to prefer your company over mine."

"And she will not do so if you are in the vicinity?" Cordelia asked, too sweetly.

He knew he had blundered, but the constant effort of making himself agreeable was wearing on his patience. "Mrs. Hardcastle," he said, "it hardly matters how we attain our mutual goal as long as we achieve it."

Her eyes snapped with annoyance. "I quite agree, Doctor." She spoke to Croome, who signaled to one of the footmen and went inside the house. The footman set out across the park in the direction of the stables.

"I have sent for our head groundskeeper," Cordelia said, "who will know if there is a cottage available. It may require a few hours to arrange. In the meantime, perhaps you will condescend to make use of your room to refresh yourself. You do wish to set Ivy a good example." She started for the door and paused, glancing over her shoulder. "You will, of course, join us for meals. I would not like Ivy to think that I have banished you from the house entirely."

With that, she marched into the house, and the last remaining footman closed the door behind her.

Donal stood staring at the door, feeling very much the fool. For one mad, impossible moment he had been ready to admit to Cordelia the real reason he couldn't bring himself to stay in the house. In that moment he had desperately wanted her to understand.

But if she had ever felt the need to run untrammeled in the wilderness, to cast off all bonds and renounce the walls and bars and conformity of man's civilization, she had long since judged such needs irrelevant to her life. And that would make her no different than a hundred thousand other English men and women who either denied the animal within themselves, or set it free to rend and devour their own kind. For most humans, there was no middle path.

With a sigh, Donal picked up his bag, turned on his heel and strode onto the neatly groomed lawn of the park. He tore his cravat loose and stuffed it in his pocket, finally able to breathe again. Soon he was walking beneath the high, arched canopies of oak, ash, elm and lime. He opened his mind and let it wander, brushing over the small, bright flashes of avian thoughts sparkling among the branches, sensing the horses in the stables and the sheep that kept the grass so well trimmed. Close to the earth he heard mice and voles and rabbits, all busy with the endless work of searching for food or raising the next generation.

But beyond those familiar souls, so like the ones he had known in Yorkshire, were others . . . far less penetrable minds, whose waking dreams were filled with harsher light and deeper shadow than any to be found in England.

Donal followed where the outland voices led him. He climbed a low hill, and on the other side he found the menagerie.

He had not known exactly what to expect, and had dreaded finding tiny, bare cages that would drive any sensible beast to madness in a matter of weeks or even days. But Cordelia's facilities were spacious, well-furnished and separated so that no animal was too close to another.

Donal descended the hill, holding his mind receptive. The animals heard him well before he reached the first of the cages, but there was a stillness in them that told him something was wrong. He deliberately slowed his pace and imagined himself as only another denizen of the park and wood, no threat to any creature, captive or free.

He needn't have bothered. He felt no fear as he approached, and only the barest flicker of curiosity. The floor of the nearest cage, sand and gravel and rock, was so dappled with shadow from thick tree branches that he wouldn't have seen the black leopard if not for his Fane senses.

The animal lay stretched out in the shade near a small doorway that led to the covered portion of its cage. Donal crouched close to the bars.

The roar of gunfire bursts in his ears. He presses them flat to his head, for the sound fills him with terror. But soon all he knows is pain. The bullet has lodged in his flank, and blood spatters on the earth, marking his path for all to see.

He falls back, his legs trembling with effort after so long a flight. They are drawing closer. His ribs heave as he struggles to suck in air. Heavy footfalls shake the ground behind him. He smells the acrid scent of his enemies. Their harsh, alien voices are like the roar of the sky in the season of falling water.

He can go no farther. He closes his eyes, shutting out what he cannot bear to see. The relentless footfalls come to a stop, and the net falls over him as the voices bellow their victory. . . .

Donal gasped and tumbled free, his heart hammering with panic. He slapped at his left leg, certain he would feel the hot rush of blood and the ragged edges of a bullet wound.

But his flesh was whole, no tear in his trousers to mark a bullet's passage. He bent his head between his knees and let the wash of dizziness pass. He had felt such fear in animals before, often when they were in pain and he was preparing to heal them. But never had any bonding struck him as vividly as this.

He straightened and looked into the cage. The panther must have felt his mental intrusion, yet the animal barely lifted his head. His golden eyes blinked once to acknowledge Donal's presence. Then he laid his chin back on his paws, his elegant tail motionless against his flank.

Donal clutched the bars of the cage and got to his feet. His legs were still trembling as he moved on to the next cage. A pair of tailless monkeys — macaques, he guessed — clung to the uppermost branches of the small tree that had been provided for them. As soon as Donal offered his greeting, they leaped gracefully down and ambled toward him. Though they showed a more active interest than the leopard, their intelligent eyes were dulled with sadness.

Bracing himself for another painful memory, Donal opened his mind again.

He clutches his mate's hand and tries to pull her away, but she will not leave the little one, who has already fallen to the raiders. The family scatters, their voices high-pitched with fear and anger. But it is too late to save the youngest; they cry and tremble in their captors' nets. A few lie still among the rocks, never to stir again. . . .

This time the apes themselves broke the contact. They were back up in the branches before Donal fully regained his senses. He wrapped his arms around his chest and heard the cries of his brethren fade away, replaced by the gentle chatter of birds in the wood.

"I am sorry," Donal said, pressing his forehead against the bars. But he knew it was an empty sentiment. These creatures suffered not only from their unnatural imprisonment, but also from the shock of their captures at the hands of callous hunters. He might learn to refine his healing abilities to erase such terrible recollections from the animals' minds, but he would have to work closely with them, live beside them just as he had warned Cordelia.

With weary resignation he moved on. The next cage held no sign of its inmate, but Donal heard the sluggish thoughts of the animal secluded in its den and formed an image of the cage's occupant: a bear, born on another continent, whose memories drifted in lush, warm, green forests. It had chosen to live in its ursine imagination rather than accept the intolerable reality that surrounded it.

Unable to reach the bear, Donal passed to the largest cage. Three wolves paced among the large stone scattered across the enclosure. Two were female, and one, the male, kept watch from a higher vantage. He might have been magnificent save for the dull, patchy quality of his once-thick gray coat, and he stared at Donal for only a moment before dropping his gaze in submission.

Sing for the lost children. Sing for the mother, dead with life still growing within her body. Sing for the mountains and the rivers and the empty dens, ravaged and plundered by the two-legged killers. . . .

Donal bent his head to the leader wolf in a gesture of respect and left them to their endless mourning. Half-blind with grief, he staggered up the hill back toward the house. He was nearly to the door of the manor when he collided with another man heading in the same direction. The man drew back, cursed under his breath and straightened his coat, all the while subjecting Donal to a thorough examination.

Donal came back to himself and met the man's eyes, recognizing him at once. The handsome, fine-boned face was topped by a thick and fashionably curled head of blond hair, and the blue eyes were of the precise color to make ladies swoon with admiration. His tailcoat was designed to broaden his shoulders and nip in his waist, his trousers were snug enough to show a lean length of thigh muscle, and his black shoes had been buffed to a scintillating polish.

Lord Inglesham tapped his gold-headed cane on the drive. "Do I know you, fellow?"

he asked with an air of condescending good humor. "Are you the new groundskeeper Mrs. Hardcastle spoke of employing for her menagerie?"

CHAPTER EIGHT

Donal considered his reply. He was quite certain that the viscount did remember him, in spite of the briefness of their previous meetings and the weeks that had passed. He touched the brim of his hat.

"You are correct, Lord Inglesham, in a manner of speaking," he said. "I am Dr. Fleming. You and I have twice met before, in London, though of course I should not expect such a grand personage as yourself to recall."

The viscount narrowed his eyes and gave a sudden laugh. "Of course. You were the fellow at the Zoological Gardens. An animal doctor, if I understand correctly."

"I am."

"Mrs. Hardcastle did inform me that she had taken on another of her charitable cases. She is much too generous with her time and fortune, but what can one say?" He smiled, an utterly false expression laced with deliberate calculation. "Has she also employed you to clean the stables, Fleming, or have you had an unfortunate mishap?"

Donal took his meaning well enough. He remembered the cravat hopelessly crumpled in his pocket, and the dust of travel filming his trousers and coat.

"I would be happy to assist in the stables if Mrs. Hardcastle requires it," he said. "But if you will forgive me, Lord Inglesham, I must go inside and change for luncheon."

Inglesham's smooth countenance briefly lost its superior cast. "Mrs. Hardcastle is excessively broad-minded when it comes to her servants. I'm sure that you appreciate the honor."

"I have been made quite sensible of it."

"Very good." Inglesham swung his cane and continued toward the house, scratching Donal from the short, rarified list of matters that merited his attention. Donal shook his head and followed, allowing the footman at the door to fawn over the viscount and bow Inglesham into the house before asking a passing maid where his own room might be found.

The maid hurried off to find the proper guide, and Donal was left to examine the entrance hall with its handsome tiled floor, marble columns and ornate chairs set along the walls. A very grand cage it was . . . so grand that one might almost forget how thoroughly it entrapped its occupants. Donal was relieved when Croome arrived to lead him up the grand staircase to the landing, through a picture gallery overstuffed with Amesbury ancestors, and into the guest wing.

The room assigned to Donal was much as he had expected . . . far more imposing and luxurious than anything he would require in his most self-indulgent moments. The bed was large enough for four, and the single room, with its adjoining dressing closet, would have swallowed the spacious kitchen at Stenwater Farm. His few trunks were already laid out and opened, and his coats, trousers, shirts and waistcoats had been carefully transferred to the huge oak armoire.

Donal set his bag on the bed, moved quickly to the window and threw it open, sucking in the fresh air with gratitude. Then he cast off his coat, unbuttoned his waistcoat and paced the room from one elegantly papered wall to the other, debating what to say to Cordelia when next they met. Frank speech would not be possible at the luncheon table, but soon he must confront her with what he had learned of the poor creatures she held in captivity.

If she was something more than an average well-born Englishwoman, as he had begun to suspect, he might make her understand. If she was not, then nothing he might say would pierce the veil of her comfortable illusions.

After he had thought it through a hundred

times, Donal shed the rest of his clothing, cleaned up at the wash stand, teased his hair into tolerable order and donned fresh clothing. He struggled with his cravat and let it lie askew around his collar. As Inglesham had so helpfully pointed out, he was only an employee, and not expected to attain the heights of fashion considered de rigueur among his betters.

He descended the stairs and found another footman to show him to the breakfast room, where the informal luncheon was being served. When he arrived, however, he found that all the diners had finished their meals and gone about their business, leaving plates of cold meats, bread, cheese and a selection of fruit for the laggard. Donal picked through the remains, avoiding the meat, and made a hearty meal while a footman hovered nearby.

When he was finished, he asked after Cordelia and was told that she was occupied with Miss Ivy in her chambers. Donal's first impulse was to flee the house and seek Cordelia at another time, but as he was finding his way to the door he ran across Theodora Shipp.

"Dr. Fleming!" the lady said, performing a hasty half curtsey. "How pleasant it is to see you again. I do apologize for not coming out to greet you when you first arrived."

Donal bowed. "I was sorry to hear that you were ill, Miss Shipp. I hope you are improved."

"Indeed." She flushed and lowered her eyes. "It was only a touch of the ague, and it is already on the wane."

"I am delighted to hear it." He hesitated. "Miss Shipp, may I speak to you in confidence?"

The flush spread from her cheeks to the rest of her face. "I . . . are you sure you would not rather speak to my cousin?"

"It is Mrs. Hardcastle I wish to discuss."

"Oh. I see. Oh . . ." She fumbled with a handkerchief, dropped it and quivered like a rabbit about to bolt for its hole. Donal quickly retrieved the handkerchief and passed it back to her.

"I did not intend to cause discomfort, Miss Shipp," he said, aware once more how ill-suited he was to human company. "If you will excuse me . . ."

"No. No, I am quite all right." She attempted a smile. "I shall be happy to speak with you, Doctor. Perhaps in the garden? It is such a pleasant day. Only let me fetch my bonnet."

She darted upstairs and returned with a straw bonnet that completely obscured the sides of her face. Donal offered his arm, and Miss Shipp gently steered him around the house to the rose garden in back.

Whoever had designed the garden must have held pretensions of grand formality;

well-placed classical statues graced the gravel paths, and wrought-iron benches had been carefully positioned between the neat parterres. Every shrub and hedge was precisely clipped by an expert gardener.

"Would you prefer to sit, or continue to walk?" Donal asked.

"Walk, if you please," she said. "Exercise after an illness is good for one, I have heard." She tilted her head as if she were peering around the brim of the bonnet. "What — what did you wish to ask, Doctor?"

"Please call me Donal," he said. "I realize it is an impertinence, but I am unused to formality among my cows and chickens."

A sound much like a laugh emerged from the bonnet. "I, too, do not care for rigid adherence to convention," she admitted. "I shall call you Donal, if you will call me Theodora."

"Theodora," he said. "I have been to visit your cousin's menagerie."

"Indeed. I know that Cordelia . . . Mrs. Hardcastle . . . was most anxious for you to see the animals."

"Yes. She is right to be concerned about their welfare."

Theodora came to a sudden halt and turned her head enough for Donal to catch a glimpse of her face. "Oh! Are they quite ill?"

"Their lives are not in danger." He met her gaze. "How did Cordelia obtain this menagerie? Did she have the animals captured for her?"

"Oh, no. Not at all, Doctor . . . Donal. Is that what you thought?"

He could not very well explain how the animals' terrible memories had overtaken his mind and left him with impressions of cruelty, pain, and fear. "I did not know what to think," he said honestly. "I did not want to believe it."

She pressed his arm. "You need not. Cordelia . . . she rescued the animals, every one, from their previous owners."

His heart gave a leap. "Rescued?"

"Yes. Perhaps she has not spoken . . . that is, she has not told you of her adventures in a number of exotic countries?"

Donal recalled Cordelia's brief reference to seeing cages "all around the world." "She may have mentioned it in passing," he said, "but she did not —"

"She has been nearly everywhere with Sir Geoffrey," Theodora said eagerly. "India, Africa, the South Seas, the Americas. I can scarcely imagine . . ." She broke off in consternation. "I do beg your pardon. I did not intend to interrupt. But you see, Cordelia is one of the kindest and most generous people I have met. Everywhere she has traveled, she has helped both people and animals in need. The creatures she brought to England were in dire condition before she saved them. She saw each one nursed back to health and has spared no expense in caring for them. If not for her, these animals would surely be dead."

Donal closed his eyes, struck by the keenness of his relief. "Your cousin's actions are most admirable."

Theodora nodded, her face once again concealed in the shadows of her bonnet. "I do admire her greatly. Though she has spent little of the past seventeen years in England, she has already done wonders for the parish since her return, helping the needy and generally improving the quality of life for the people of the village. She cannot abide cruelty of any kind."

"I well remember her attempt to help Sheba, the elephant at the Zoological Gardens."

Theodora put her hand over her heart. "She frightened us dreadfully, approaching such a large beast with no protection. If you had not come . . . but that is so like Cordelia. I am quite certain she has risked her life a hundred times in similar circumstances."

Donal could well believe that once Cordelia set her mind on any action, she would follow through regardless of the hazard to herself . . . and in spite of the opinions of the society she seemed to value so highly. It was only one of the many contradictions in her character that he found so puzzling. And so disturbingly intriguing.

"Lord Inglesham commented on her generosity," he said. "He did not seem to entirely approve of it."

Theodora was silent so long that Donal bent forward to look at her face. She had assumed a blank expression, too perfect to indicate anything but distaste. "Happily," she said, "Lord Inglesham has no say in what my cousin does with her life or her fortune."

"You do not like the viscount?" he asked.

"It is not for me to judge one of such high estate," she said primly.

He almost laughed. "Were his boots quite ruined?"

"I beg your pardon?"

"The boots anointed by the impertinent dog in Covent Garden."

A strangled sound emerged from the bonnet. "You saw?"

"I did."

Theodora raised her hands to her mouth. "He must have been furious," she said, "though of course he wouldn't let Cordelia see. She would not approve of his making a to-do over such a frivolous matter."

"And he cares for her approval?"

"He cares very much." The bonnet turned left and right, and Theodora leaned closer. "He wishes to marry her."

Donal's muscles tightened, and he drew in a sharp breath. "Why?"

160

She withdrew abruptly. "Forgive me," she said. "I spoke out of turn." She gathered her skirts as if to flee, and he touched her arm, certain — for reasons he could not fully understand — that he must learn all he could about Cordelia's relationship with Inglesham.

"I asked to speak to you in confidence," he said, "and you may be sure that I will not share our discussion with anyone else."

She sank down on the nearest bench. "What more can I tell you?"

"Why does Inglesham want to marry Cordelia?"

"Do you think it impossible that a man of good family should wish to marry a widow past the first blush of youth?"

He blinked in surprise. "Such a thought had never occurred to me."

"Then what has my cousin's friendship with the viscount have to do with your care of her animals?"

Her steady question held more than a hint of challenge, though she still looked ready to flee at the slightest provocation. Donal himself felt an unaccountable desire to turn tail and run.

"I frequently do not comprehend human motives," he admitted. "If Ivy is to remain here, I must know that there is nothing that will compromise her happiness."

Theodora searched his eyes and gradually relaxed. "Of course. Your concern is laudable." She sighed. "It might be best if I begin with Cordelia's first marriage. She was still very young when she met Captain James Hardcastle while he was serving in India. Because of her extraordinary upbringing and years away from England, she had little chance to meet eligible men or enjoy a conventional courtship. When she was introduced to Captain Hardcastle, she had only just lost her younger sister, Lydia, to a tragic accident."

"I don't remember her mentioning a sister."

"She seldom speaks of Lydia." Theodora rose and began walking along the path, her hands pressed to her skirts. "Cordelia and James were married after a brief engagement, and Cordelia settled with the Captain in India. They had hardly been together more than three months when he was killed in a skirmish with bandits."

"I am sorry," Donal murmured.

"I had not met Cordelia then, but I know that she left India soon afterward and rejoined Sir Geoffrey in his travels. She has shown no inclination to remarry since her return six months ago . . . but she and Inglesham have known each other since they were children. His estate is only a few miles from Edgecott. The viscount has always been a frequent visitor, and Sir Geoffrey approves of him."

Donal glared at the ground under his feet. "Does she love him?"

"I do not know."

"Does he love her?"

Theodora fumbled with the ribbons of her bonnet. "A peer of the realm may marry for love, if he is fortunate," she said. "A viscount would not be ashamed to marry an Amesbury, even if she is only the daughter of a baronet. But there are often other considerations behind such alliances." She turned to face Donal, her very ordinary brown eyes vivid with some strong emotion. "My cousin is a wealthy woman in her own right, with an inheritance from an aunt that is hers to dispose of as she pleases. Sir Geoffrey is not poor in the least, but he has an unfortunate tendency to gamble and has suffered certain reversals in recent years . . ."

"He wants her money," Donal said flatly, kicking at the gravel with the toe of his boot. "Will she not lose control over her fortune if he marries her?"

"Yes. But Cordelia has no reason to distrust him. She is . . ." Once more Theodora trailed off, and her lips pressed together as if she were sealing away any further comments.

Cordelia is blind, Donal completed for her. But he knew too little of the viscount to condemn him out of hand because of Theodora's suspicions or his own dislike. Nor had he any reason to interfere in Cordelia's personal affairs. Good God, he hardly knew the woman. . . .

And that made no difference at all to his irrational feelings.

"Thank you, Theodora," he said. "You have helped to understand the situation a little better."

She looked away. "I hope that I have not discouraged you from allowing Ivy to stay. I should never forgive myself if I —"

"Dr. Fleming!" Cordelia's voice interrupted Theodora, who appeared relieved at the intrusion. Cordelia rounded a corner on the path, her smile bright enough to encompass both her cousin and Donal.

"Theodora," she said. "Croome said I might find you and Dr. Fleming in the garden." She turned to Donal. "I hope you have not felt too neglected, Doctor. I have been doing my best to make Ivy comfortable in the house. She is resting now, but you will see her at dinner. And we have already planned a trip into Gloucester for fittings next week, if you should care to accompany us."

It was as if she and Donal had parted on the best of terms several hours ago. Cordelia's annoyance with him had apparently been forgotten, and after hearing Theodora's tale about the animals and the loss of her husband, Donal could not feel anything but sympathy. He returned her smile with all the warmth he could muster.

"I am delighted to hear that Ivy is settling

in so well," he said. "If you require my assistance on your visit to town I will be happy to join you, but I should not wish to become a burden upon ladies in pursuit of sartorial pleasures."

Cordelia arched a brow. "How eloquent a way of saying that you would find our excursion dreadfully dull, Doctor. But I quite understand." She indicated that he and Theodora should return to the house. "I have come to tell you that our head groundskeeper has located a suitable cottage where you may lodge while you stay at Edgecott. If you will come inside, we shall have tea and I will tell you more."

Donal slowed his pace. "I am certain it will be —"

"Come, come," she said, her gray eyes teasing. "I know that you have already been to your chambers and the breakfast room, so the house can hold no more terrors for a man who has faced down a charging *loxodonta africana.*"

His skin grew hot. "I . . . of course I will join you for tea, Mrs. Hardcastle. Thank you."

She gave him a smile of triumph and preceded him and Theodora into the house, leading them to a small and pleasant room that received the afternoon sunlight. A tea service was already waiting. Donal sat uneasily in his delicate chair, his gaze fixed on the strip of blue sky visible through the window.

Theodora excused herself after a single cup and retired to her room.

"My cousin seems much improved," Cordelia commented, offering Donal a second cup of tea. "Did she show you the garden?"

He cradled the tiny teacup in his hands and nodded. "It is a very well-kept garden."

" 'Well-kept.' How carefully you say it, though I can see that something does not meet with your approval."

The chair creaked as he shifted his weight. "It is not my intention to insult —"

"I know it isn't. But you do prefer your Yorkshire 'garden' of heather and wildflowers, do you not?"

"I appreciate Nature in her original state," he said, "unfenced and untamed."

"Then you must often be disappointed with what you find around you."

"Yes."

"Even on the moors?"

"Even on the moors there are fences, and animals made to serve men."

Cordelia took a sip of her tea and set down her cup. "Surely you must admit that not all things can exist in their unaltered state, not on the earth we inhabit."

"Certainly not in England."

"Nor in any part of the civilized world."

He let his gaze wander over the contours and planes of her face, wondering anew what had shaped such a paradoxical creature as

Cordelia Hardcastle. "Theodora tells me that you have been all over the globe."

"My father was . . . is . . . a naturalist. He took me and my sister with him in his travels after my mother died."

"Then you must have seen many places where man does not yet hold sway."

"Yes. But I was speaking of the civilized world. It is only natural that men should wish to domesticate the wilderness in order to live in greater safety and comfort. Human beings have done so since the beginning of time."

"Is it for safety and comfort that men place animals in zoological gardens, hunt foxes to their deaths and set dogs and cocks to fight against each other?"

"Animal fighting is an abomination, and does not belong in a discussion of rational human behavior. Hunting is a primitive custom which I hope will eventually lose favor. As for zoological gardens . . . do they not allow men to better understand and thus preserve unfamiliar and exotic species?"

"I only know what the animals feel."

"I concede that no one should be able to guess their emotions better than one of your profession. But in the case where animals are held in captivity, common sense tells us that making the creatures comfortable and helping them adapt to their new situation is by far the most compassionate and prudent approach."

"Prudent," he repeated. "Is that your guiding principle, Cordelia? Prudence?"

Her lips tightened almost imperceptibly at his use of her given name. "You perhaps imply that I showed a lack of such prudence in my decision to offer a child of unknown antecedents a home at Edgecott?"

"It did seem a rather impulsive decision."

"In rare cases, Doctor, it is necessary to leaven one's customary circumspection with a certain daring that may seem, but is not, contradictory."

Donal smiled. "*I* have no quarrel with occasional impulsiveness. In fact, I quite approve of it."

Silence fell between them. Cordelia reached for her cup, missed her aim and knocked it against its saucer.

A light tapping came at the open door, causing Cordelia to jump in her seat. She immediately rose and met the footman as he entered and bowed.

"I am sorry to disturb you, Mrs. Hardcastle," he said, "but Sir Geoffrey has asked that you attend him in his suite."

Cordelia brushed her hands over her skirts and nodded. "Very well, John." She turned back to Donal, avoiding his eyes. "My father wishes to see me. I know we have not yet discussed your cottage, but I will see you again in the drawing room before dinner, at six o'clock."

With those words of dismissal, she hurried out of the room. Donal heard her shoes on the stairs, and then the sound of a door closing.

He could not have said what made him follow her. He slipped into the entrance hall, listened for servants, and casually climbed the stairs as if he intended to go to his own room. At the landing, however, he turned left into the wing reserved for family members, passing through yet another gallery of Amesbury portraits. No sooner had he reached its end than he heard the raised, petulant voice of an angry man.

". . . bringing cursed waifs and tradesmen into the house, the least you can do is have consideration for your own flesh and blood."

"Yes, Papa," Cordelia's voice answered, strangely muted. "But Dr. Fleming is not a tradesman —"

"Whatever he is, I will not have you forget your duty . . ." He paused. "Yes, there on my left temple. Not so firmly, if you please."

Donal moved closer to the door, poised to beat a hasty retreat if anyone should chance by.

"There now, Papa," Cordelia said. "You must take your quinine."

"The stuff is foul."

"You have endured much worse."

Sir Geoffrey made a gagging sound and coughed loudly. "You delight in tormenting me. If I had control over your fortune —"

"Please, Papa. Calm yourself."

"Calm be damned. I wish to see this . . . this animal doctor you have brought to Edgecott. Perhaps he will provide some amusement after all."

"Of course you shall meet him, Papa, when you are better."

"Better? I shall never be 'better.' " He coughed again. "Is Inglesham still here?"

"No, Papa."

"Why don't you marry the fellow, Cordelia, and have done with it? You know that your mother would have approved. More than approved. And I wish it as well."

"I know, Papa." After a moment Donal heard her footsteps moving across the room. The door swung open before he could conceal himself. "Now you must rest. When I —" She saw Donal, and the high color in her face deepened. She backed away, hastily shut the door, and spoke in a low voice to her father. When she came out of the room, her face was composed again.

"Dr. Fleming," she said. "Have you lost your way?"

Donal tugged at his cravat. "I apologize for intruding. I —"

"Doubtless you overheard," she said. "My father suffers from recurrent attacks of malaria he acquired in the tropics. It can be quite disabling, and he has been somewhat worse of late. He was not always so querulous."

Donal retreated a step. "I understand. If you will —"

"I beg you to be forgiving when you meet him." She picked up her skirts and walked passed Donal, leaving him to trail behind her.

He escaped into the warmth of the afternoon, his thoughts a muddle of contrary images. He readily envisioned Cordelia's face in its customary expression of firm and uncompromising determination, as it had been when he first met her, and yet just now it had revealed both chagrin and vulnerability. When she dealt with Donal, Ivy or the servants, her manner was anything but meek, yet with Sir Geoffrey she had been deferential, even ingratiating.

Mistreated animals often reacted to abuse in one of two vastly different ways: they either broke and became trembling, neurotic shadows, or they turned viciously against those who hurt them. But humans could be disturbingly complex. Donal had always enjoyed an excellent relationship with his parents, but he could remember an earlier time when those who had the care of him had ignored and mistreated him. Ivy had suffered in filth and poverty, yet she had emerged from her ordeal with unexpected strength. Cordelia had lost a husband and a sister. Was that all she had lost?

As Donal made his way back to the menagerie, he had the disquieting feeling that the bars of an unseen and very human cage were closing more and more tightly about him.

CHAPTER NINE

Cordelia, Theodora and Ivy emerged from the milliner's salon, carrying their latest treasures carefully wrapped in tissue and ribbon. John the footman, laden with bundles and boxes filled with bonnets, stockings, gloves, shawls, stays, and underclothing, collected at various shops throughout the very busy morning, stood ready to carry them back to the carriage waiting down the street. Cordelia thanked him and sent him on his way.

"I'm hungry," Ivy announced, her gaze darting up and down the lane in search of a likely inn or street vendor. "May we eat now?"

Theodora covered her mouth with her hand and met Cordelia's gaze, amused by the girl's antics. Cordelia shook her head and smiled ruefully. It was not that she didn't appreciate Ivy's high spirits; indeed, during the week since Ivy's arrival it had been as if sunshine incarnate had entered Edgecott's gloomy halls, and Cordelia had often arisen from her

173

bed with a long-forgotten excitement fluttering in her chest.

Ivy was like a South American hummingbird, Cordelia thought — never still for an instant, moody one moment and vivacious the next, always poised to dash hither and thither as the urge struck her. Every day had been filled with new surprises as Ivy reveled in her new life of abundance, and even the small things Cordelia most took for granted acquired a fresh and joyful luster. The house was redolent with the scent of wildflowers Ivy collected by the river; meals became stimulating affairs dominated by Ivy's incessantly curious questions; the library with its vast collection of books was transformed into a land of endless adventure. Cordelia even caught old Croome hiding a grin when Ivy swept through the hallways.

In some ways Ivy was still the child she had for years pretended to be. Cordelia had expected her to be excited about the shopping trip, and the girl had certainly found much of interest in Gloucester. But Ivy had soon grown bored with the ordeal of holding still while the milliner's assistants poked, prodded and measured her for the array of gowns she must have in her new life. Her mood had become increasingly restive, and Cordelia was reminded that soon she must begin to teach the wild girl how to be a lady.

She grasped Ivy's sleeve, preventing her

from racing up the street like a greyhound after a lure. "Do you remember what we discussed?" she asked. "If you remain calm and cooperative, we will have a pleasant luncheon at the inn."

Ivy pulled a face. "I thought I would have new dresses today," she said, "but all we did was wait while them morts stuck pins in my knickers. That ain't no fun at —"

"Language, my dear," Cordelia reminded her. "I know you can do better than that."

"Oi can if Oi wants to," Ivy said airily. "*Donal* never orders me about the way you do."

"Dr. Fleming still thinks of you as a child, Ivy, but I have much higher expectations."

The girl snorted. " 'E knows I ain't no kid."

"Your behavior at this moment might convince him otherwise."

A flicker of distress crossed Ivy's face. "You said you'd make me into a lady!"

"So I did. And when we receive your dresses, you will find the thought of ladylike behavior much easier to bear."

With one of her lightning-swift changes of mood, Ivy whirled round and round with her arms outflung. "I shall be beautiful," she sang, spinning in a dizzy circle. Suddenly she stopped, facing Cordelia. "I shall be beautiful, shall I not?"

Cordelia smiled and cupped Ivy's cheek. "You are already the loveliest girl of my acquaintance."

Ivy kissed her hand. "And when I am dressed up properly, *then* Donal will notice me."

Cordelia felt a chill of inexplicable alarm. "Donal is your friend. He speaks to you often. . . ."

"But he doesn't *look* at me. Not the way he looks at you."

Cordelia swallowed her astonishment. "I beg your pardon?"

"I've seen you two every day at dinner. He watches you all the time . . . and sometimes you look at him, as if . . ." She frowned. "Sometimes I wonder if that's really why you brought me to Edgecott . . . so you could have Donal."

Suddenly weak at the knees, Cordelia took a fresh grip on Ivy's arm and walked her around the corner into an alley where they would not be overheard.

"Ivy," Cordelia said, catching the girl's downcast eyes, "is that what you truly believe?"

Ivy fidgeted, shuffling her feet. "I don't know."

"Do you think I don't want you?"

"I . . ." Tears gathered in her eyes. "I'm afraid."

Cordelia enfolded the girl in her arms. "You must not ever, ever think that I do not want you just for yourself, my dear . . . for the very wonderful person you are."

"But why?"

"Why?" She stroked Ivy's hair away from her face. "I, too, have been lonely, my dear."

"You? But you always have so much to do, at Edgecott, in the village, even in London —"

"Yes," Cordelia admitted. "I am often very busy with my work. But Edgecott has been too quiet, too staid in many ways. I had not realized just how stifling it had become until you arrived. Or how happy your presence makes me."

"You . . . you really mean it?"

"I never lie, my dear . . . it is one of my guiding principles." She set Ivy back and gripped her shoulders. "I knew when we first met that your true home would be at Edge-cott, with me and Theodora. You must never doubt it."

Ivy hugged her fiercely. "And you won't let Donal go away?"

That again. Cordelia stifled a sigh. "Dr. Fleming and I agreed that he should accompany you to Gloucestershire so that the change of scene would not seem so difficult for you. It is true that I asked him to treat my animals, but that was only a secondary reason for his coming."

"If I can prove I'm a real lady, will he stay?"

"I cannot speak for him . . ."

"You don't care if he leaves Edgecott."

A hard lump lodged at the base of Cordelia's throat. "I am quite certain that Dr. Fleming has his own plans for his future. But I very much regret if I have given you any cause to believe that I have . . . inappropriate feelings for Dr. Fleming, or that such feelings in any way motivated my request that you make your home here."

Ivy sniffed. "You really like me?"

"I like you very much, my dear. And I hope you will come to like me."

Ivy rubbed at her face with her arm, and Cordelia produced a handkerchief. She felt unreasonably emotional herself. Perhaps it was because Ivy had so grievously misconstrued her reasons for bringing the girl to Edgecott. And Cordelia had very much set her heart on helping this young lady reach her potential as a woman and a member of society.

But if she looked beyond the obvious explanations for her discomposure, she was equally disturbed that Ivy had claimed to recognize some attachment between Cordelia and Dr. Fleming that simply did not exist. Indeed, the very thought of it was preposterous, an intemperate fancy of a romantic young girl's imagination.

Shaking off her lingering unease, Cordelia smiled and reached in her reticule for the small box she had carefully wrapped that morning. "I have something for you, my dear.

I had thought to give it to you tonight, but —"

"A present? For me?" Ivy asked, grinning.

Cordelia presented the box on her open palm. With eager fingers Ivy undid the ribbons and wrapping, lifting the cover with a gasp of delight.

"A chain!" she said. "A silver chain. How pretty it is."

"For your pendant," Cordelia said. "I think it is past time to retire that ancient leather cord, don't you?"

Ivy quickly untied the thong about her neck, slipped the pendant free and, with Cordelia's help, attached it to the silver chain. She was nearly hopping with excitement as Cordelia fixed the clasp.

"How do I look?" she asked, twirling about on her toes.

"Like a very elegant young lady," Cordelia said. She laughed softly, taking joy in Ivy's pleasure. "Would it suit you to have our luncheon now?"

"Oh, yes. Thank you, Cordelia."

For the remainder of the afternoon, Ivy determinedly applied herself to behaving exactly as Cordelia would wish. Cordelia was immensely gratified by the small but telling victory. She lived by the doctrine that any problem could be solved with steadfastness, compassion and common sense. Once again her philosophy had been proven correct.

But that didn't mean she could relax her vigilance. Ivy's education was just beginning. And Cordelia knew that she must take special care from now on never to give Ivy — or Donal — any reason to doubt her complete disinterest in the doctor as anything but a temporary employee and Ivy's one-time guardian.

Donal had been up before dawn as was his custom, and so he had dressed and arrived at the house well in advance of breakfast. A sleepy footman directed him to the kitchen, where Mrs. Jelbert was just baking the day's bread and brewing coffee for Sir Geoffrey. Donal accepted a mug of the beverage and set off on his usual brisk walk around the park and past the menagerie, returning at last to his own humble cottage.

His first glimpse of his lodgings at Edgecott had been on the day after his and Ivy's arrival, when Perkins, the head groundskeeper, had led him to a cluster of cottages just over a low hill from the menagerie. A pair of scullery maids with an array of buckets, mops and other cleaning implements were leaving as Perkins and Donal approached. Two other maids and a footman in the uniforms of the house stood ready with linens, rolled carpets, a washstand, and sundry other amenities.

Donal had understood that it would do little good to protest that he had no need of such luxuries. Cordelia would not have listened. So he had accepted the gift with good grace and set about making himself worthy of his keep.

Every day for the past week he had spent each morning with the animals in the menagerie, treating their minor ailments and doing what he could to abate their discontent and the general malaise of captivity. The work was frustrating, for he knew there was a limit to what he might achieve under the circumstances, yet he formed a bond with the animals that he believed was of some small benefit to both them and him.

In the late afternoons, after luncheon at the house — when he all too often found himself inexplicably gazing at Cordelia like a veritable mooncalf — he rambled among the wolds or visited the local villages and farms where he observed numerous examples of Cordelia's admirable work among the yeomen and cottagers of the parish.

It was clear that she was deeply respected by the parishioners, regardless of station or profession; the curate praised her Christian charity, farmwives spoke enthusiastically of the school Mrs. Hardcastle supported, and shopkeepers in the village practically fell over themselves to extol the value of her patronage. A prosperous squire, whose carriage horse Donal examined on the road several miles outside Edgecott, was happy to confide that Edgecott itself would be in a sorry state indeed if not for Mrs. Hardcastle's management; the reclusive Sir Geoffrey was hopeless at such matters and left the administration of his estate and fortune in her capable hands.

After hearing such laudatory accounts Donal generally looked forward to his evening meetings with Cordelia, though he despaired of his foolish attachment to her company. This evening was no different. He climbed the hill overlooking the carriage drive, watching for the ladies' return from Gloucester. He remembered how they had looked when they departed that morning: Ivy appearing very grown-up in her long, full skirts and with her dark tresses drawn up close to her head, Cordelia sitting erect in her seat, her face a little flushed by the wind, every hair in perfect order. Even from a distance she exuded a unique and particular force of will.

God alone knew how long they would be at their shopping; if they were anything like Lady Eden, they might even choose to remain in town overnight. Donal shook his head with an indulgent smile and descended the hill. He had meant to visit the stables and kennels for the past several days, and there seemed no better opportunity than the present. He set off at a brisk stride for the stable block behind the house and gardens.

Halfway there he was stopped by an importunate bark from the direction of the manor.

He waited for Sir Reginald to catch up, and the spaniel fell into a companionable trot beside him.

"Do you find the house to your liking, Sir Reginald?" he asked.

The dog cocked his head up at Donal and wagged his tail.

"Doubtless it is no more than you were used to with your former human companion."

The dog's sadness reached Donal briefly, and then Sir Reginald sent a much more joyful message.

"I am glad that you are happy with Ivy," Donal said. "There will be many times in future that she will look to you for comfort. The world can be a harsh place for young people, especially of her sex."

Sir Reginald gave fervent agreement, for he was well familiar with the tales of the three street curs who had come with Ivy to Yorkshire. He whined.

"No. You need never fear that Ivy will return to that life. But it is up to you to remind her how much she stands to gain if she strives for happiness here, where she has so many advantages."

The spaniel paused, sat on his haunches, and regarded Donal severely. Donal squatted beside him.

"Yes. It is true that I hope to leave England within the next few months. But it is not that I wish to be rid of Ivy, or leave you and the other animals. Someday I will return, but . . ."

The spaniel shot him a reproachful look.

"No, I would never give up our conversations, Reggie . . . not even for all the gold in England. Come along, now."

Sighing deeply, the dog accepted Donal's reassurance and dashed ahead toward the stables. Donal reached them a few minutes later.

The stables were large and, like everything else at Edgecott, kept spotlessly clean. Stable boys were at work mucking out stalls or polishing tack, and grooms exercised a pair of handsome bay thoroughbreds. A dozen more horses, including a fat pony and several ladies' hacks, occupied the roomy stalls.

Donal breathed in the air of contentment with a smile. He returned the grooms' greetings and walked along the stalls, acknowledging each occupant. Twelve large, elegant heads pushed over the partitions, nostrils flaring and ears pricked forward. The shaggy pony snorted and danced to show how clever he was. The other horses laughed at him, but gently. There was no hostility or rivalry here, only a calm good fellowship.

Donal soon perceived the source of the general serenity. Though equine memories were far from precise, and consisted more of disjointed images and feelings rather than sequential facts, he was able to discover that one person more than any other framed the horses' tranquil thoughts: Cordelia Hard-castle.

The pony remembered how he had been taken away from a man who had beaten him when he could not pull a loaded cart that would have foundered a draught horse. One of the hacks, a quiet mare who was simply no longer beautiful, had been bound for the knackers when Cordelia rescued her. Almost every horse had a similar story to tell, and even those that had been purchased under more ordinary circumstances had fond feelings for Cordelia and the sugar lumps she brought nearly every day.

The stable cats, who kept carefully out of Sir Reginald's way, found the warm stalls a paradise of plentiful food and stroking hands. Donal toured the kennels behind the stables and judged them to be in a similar happy state. The dogs there had plentiful space to run, and a goodly number of them had also been saved from dog fighters, injury or starvation.

It was impossible to come away from a visit with the domestic animals of Edgecott and think of Cordelia as anything but a saint. For a while Donal drifted along in a golden glow of admiration, but eventually his thoughts turned again to the residents of the menagerie.

As much as Cordelia loved her four-footed dependents, she saw no real difference between the horses, dogs and cats and their wilder brethren. Somehow he must explain that the suffering of the menagerie inmates had little to do with physical sickness and was in every way the result of their captivity, benevolent though it might be.

Making her understand, however, would be neither an easy nor pleasant task. His first attempt at broaching the subject had not met with any great success. As he wandered about the kennels and pondered how he might try again, he heard a high-pitched squeal of rage from the stables, accompanied by the frenzied emotions of a horse in distress. He raced from the kennels into the stableyard to find a groom struggling with a rearing stallion, its lethal hooves cutting the air like scythes.

He was suddenly hurled back in time to his first days as a child at Hartsmere, when he had seen the man known as Hartley Shaw gentle a similar horse with a simple touch and a few soft words. Shaw had been far more than the wandering laborer he'd pretended to be; he was Donal's own Fane father in disguise, come to reclaim the half-mortal son he had lost.

It had not been until he was a young man that Donal learned the full story of his father's courtship of his mother: how Hern, wild lord of the forest, had taken the shape of a well-bred Englishman and eloped with Lady Eden, getting her with child before their wedding day; how she had fled when she'd learned of his inhuman nature and given birth in secrecy and seclusion; how Hern sought to reclaim his child by taking yet another human form and plotting to carry Donal back to the Fane homeland of Tir-na-Nog.

Instead, he had fallen in love with Lady Eden, given up his virtual immortality and became a true parent to a lonely six-year-old boy. From him Donal had learned how to shape and control his inherited ability to understand and influence animals of all shapes and sizes. Now he had cause to put those abilities to good use again.

He sent calming thoughts to the angry horse and walked slowly toward him, ignoring the cursing groom.

"Stay back," the man warned in a thick Irish accent. "He's a bad one, he is."

Donal continued to advance, extending his hand so that the stallion could catch his scent. "What is troubling him?" he asked the groom.

"What's troublin' him?" The man laughed, setting off a fresh bout of lashing hooves. "What isn't? He's a savage beast fit only for the glue factory." He ducked nimbly out of the stallion's way and raised the quirt in his hand as if he would strike, then caught Donal's eye and thought better of it. "You're the animal doctor, ain't you?"

"I am. And you had best step away and let me deal with him."

"And get meself in trouble for lettin' you get stomped to death?" The groom jerked down on the stallion's headstall, temporarily bringing him under control. "Ain't nothin' you can do to save this son of the devil."

Donal shut out the groom's words and gave himself over to the horse's violent thoughts. Fear was the predominant emotion . . . fear of men who had mistreated him, and rage at everything that bore a human scent. The animal might have been handsome in a healthy state, but his ribs projected from his heaving sides, and numerous newly-healed cuts and abrasions made a lacework of scars on his long, runner's legs.

"Easy," Donal murmured. "Easy there." He projected images of the peaceful stalls and the horses inside, well-groomed and fed and safe.

The stallion went very still, his ears swivelled toward Donal. Then he lunged, tearing the lead from the groom's hands, and nuzzled Donal's pocket like a placid gelding looking for treats.

"Impossible," the groom said, like a curse. "That devil can't be tamed . . ."

"That's right," Donal said to the stallion. "Don't listen to him. He doesn't know."

The stallion bobbed his head and stretched his lips to feather over Donal's face. Donal saw bits and pieces of the animal's tormented past; once again Cordelia figured powerfully in the stallion's memories. But before that there had been a place with many other horses, and constant excitement . . . the rush of preparation, the walk out to the starting line, the jostling of the other horses as they tensed their muscles for action . . . and then the signal to run, to stretch legs and devour the track with every stride, all the way to the finish and victory.

But there had not been enough victories for the stallion. He'd been started too young, driven too hard, passed from owner to owner until an injury had forced him to the sidelines; no one had considered him worth the careful nursing required for his recovery. So he had gone to a man who knew nothing of race horses but fancied himself a great sportsman, who believed that beating his new acquisition would force the creature to stop its shamming and become the great champion that would make his fortune. . . .

Then Cordelia had come. She had seen that he was cared for and exercised just enough to bring strength back to his wasted body. But he could not forget the other men, and whenever one of the grooms approached, he fought as if for his very life.

"That time is over," Donal said, stroking the deep brown neck. "You will run again, my friend. Wait and see."

"What're you tellin' him, Doc?" the groom said, his mouth twisted in scowling amusement. "He may stand still for you now, but in another minute he'll be fightin' again. It's his way. Either lazy and refusin' to move, or kickin' at anything within reach."

Donal met the groom's blue eyes. "What is your name?"

The man tugged his forelock in a sarcastic gesture of respect. "Gallagher, Doctor. Head groom at Edgecott."

"You call the horse a devil, but his real name is Boreas, for the north wind."

"Is it, now. That's fascinatin'."

"What Boreas requires is an excess of gentleness, not discipline." He pressed his nose to the stallion's muzzle. "Your patience will be well rewarded."

Gallagher made a rude noise. "The Missus keeps bringing these nags to us, and we have to fix 'em. Pretty soon there won't be no room left to —"

"You do wish to keep your position, don't you?" Donal said softly.

Gallagher stiffened. "Now what d'you mean by that, Doctor? You after gettin' me discharged for doin' me job?"

"I have no influence with the lady of the house," Donal said, "but you *will* take better care of this animal, will you not?"

"I don't take kindly to threats."

"Then perhaps this will encourage you."

He bent Boreas's ear and whispered into it. The stallion quivered. He lifted his head and gazed across the park, seeing not a rolling meadow but a curving track and a crowd cheering him on.

Donal stepped away. Boreas stood still a moment longer, and then he leaped into a dead gallop, tail and mane streaming out behind him. The other grooms paused in their work to stare in disbelief. No one who saw Boreas run could doubt that he was born to race, and that nothing in the world could hold him back.

Gallagher swore an Irish oath and threw his cap on the ground. "Damn me. He can run!"

Donal smiled. Sir Reginald, who had been observing the drama from the safety of the stable doors, rejoined him. They watched as Boreas galloped a wide circle around the park and returned, slowing his pace to a canter, a trot and finally a walk. His coat was darkened with sweat, but his neck arched with pride and joy shone in his eyes. He butted his head against Donal's chest and swung his head to regard Gallagher with lips peeled back from his teeth in unmistakable mockery.

"Now you see what Boreas is capable of," Donal said. "I suggest you treat him with the respect he deserves."

Gallagher was obviously lost in thought, and took Boreas's lead without argument. The other grooms went back to work, muttering among themselves. Donal scooped Sir Reginald up in his arms.

"It's been a long day, hasn't it?" he asked the spaniel. "Even if the ladies aren't back from town, I'd best freshen up before I present myself at the house. Mrs. Jelbert would surely turn up her nose and refuse to feed us at all."

Sir Reginald gave a bark of agreement, and together they made their way back to the cottage. Donal had no sooner stepped over the threshold when Sir Reginald went rigid in his arms and began to growl deep in his throat.

"What is it, my lad?" Donal asked. "Scented a rabbit? I don't feel any —" He stopped, listened, and broke into a grin. "That's one fox you won't want to chase, Reggie. He's likely to lead you into an embarrassing trap."

The spaniel whined and wriggled to get free. Donal laughed.

"You'd best come out, Tod, and set this poor dog's mind at rest."

The fox glided into the doorway and sat on its haunches, yawning widely. Sir Reginald's ears rolled so far forward that their elegant red fringe nearly hung over his eyes. He whimpered in confusion. The fox turned round and round like a dervish, and when he came to a stop he was a fox no longer.

"Good day to my lord," Tod said, bobbing a bow, "and to my lord's friend."

Donal chuckled. "Of course. You and Reggie were never properly introduced in Yorkshire. Tod, meet Sir Reginald. Sir Reginald . . ." He set Sir Reginald down, and the spaniel cautiously advanced on the hob. In a breath they were fast friends. Tod plopped down on the floor and accepted Reggie's enthusiastic kisses.

Donal sat on the edge of the bed, watching Tod with a knot of sadness in his chest. "It took you a long time to come down," he said. "I thought you'd changed your mind."

"Oh, no, my lord," Tod said, scratching behind Reggie's ears. He glanced about the cottage. "This is where my lord sleeps?"

"Yes. Have you seen the big house?"

Tod shuddered. "My lord is wise to stay away."

"That was my opinion as well. As long as you're at Edgecott, you'll stay close to me. Avoid the house and the humans inside it."

"Mortals cannot see Tod."

He was right, and yet Donal couldn't shake the feeling that Tod should be extraordinarily careful while they remained at Edgecott.

And after that . . .

Donal shook his head. Tod was entirely too sensitive to his moods, and there was no point in upsetting the hob prematurely.

He rose from the bed, stretching his arms above his head. "Come with me, my friend. There are a few things I'd like to show you."

CHAPTER TEN

Donal was not himself. Tod had known every one of the lad's moods since Donal had come to Hartsmere as a child, shy and withdrawn and not yet ready to trust. In some ways he was very like his father, wary of humans and more vulnerable than he would admit, for all that he had chosen to live on the earth of Men.

He took Tod to see the animals in their cages, and Tod saw at once that their state distressed him. But he knew it was not this alone that troubled Donal. His judgment was confirmed when he and Tod and Sir Reginald crossed the wooded park and climbed the low wold overlooking the great house.

A carriage rattled up the drive, its open canopy revealing three human females in all their silly, billowing skirts and ruffles. Their faces were concealed by bonnets that encased their heads like ancient helmets, but Tod saw at once how Donal stiffened, heard how his heart began to beat too fast as he watched the passengers alight from the vehicle.

Tod plopped into the grass and hugged Sir Reginald to his side. This was not good. This was not good at all. Tod had delayed his trip south because he was afraid of what he might find; now, it seemed, matters were far worse than he'd imagined.

Donal started down the hill toward the house. Sir Reginald gave a yip of excitement, scrambled out of Tod's arms and dashed past Donal, aiming for the girl in the yellow dress. Tod made himself invisible and flew after him, keeping his distance from the humans clustered by the door.

He did not hear the first part of the conversation as Donal greeted the females, or the brief and meaningless exchange that followed. But he noticed when the two older females went into the house, leaving Donal alone with the youngest.

"How was your shopping trip, Ivy?" Donal asked her.

The girl jerked at the ribbons of her bonnet, tugged it off and dangled the ugly thing just above the ground. "Oh . . . it was all very well, I suppose. I wish *you* had come."

"I would have been entirely useless, I assure you."

"You would have been *dreadfully* bored," she declared, bending to take Sir Reginald in her arms. "You and Reggie were lucky this time. You won't always escape so easily."

Donal smiled faintly. "Escape from what?"

"From me, of course." She laughed and performed a little skipping dance, setting her bell-like skirts to swaying as if a hundred winged sprites pulled it to and fro at her behest.

Tod hovered closer, risking Donal's anger. The girl had changed from the rough, wild creature he had seen at Stenwater Farm. It was more than just the finely-cut clothing, the glowing skin or the dark hair shimmering with health. The way she looked at Donal told Tod that she had become even more of a danger than she had been in the North.

You shall not have him, Tod thought, glaring at the top of her dark head. *I shall make you* —

The girl glanced up with a faint frown, and Tod looked into her eyes. Blue eyes, brilliant as the skies in Tir-na-Nog.

Tod so forgot himself that he nearly became visible again. He shivered as if with some repulsive human illness. His heart beat as fast as a bumblebee's wings.

It must be hate, he thought. Hatred such as he had never felt, as alien to him as mortal love. Hatred of this girl and what she might do to his master. How she might take Donal away. . . .

". . . buy many dresses?" Donal was saying, his words slowly taking shape in Tod's befuddled mind.

"Of course," Ivy said, feigning nonchalance while her gaze eagerly searched Donal's. "At *least* a dozen. Most must still be made, but we brought two back with us. I will show them to you this evening, if you like."

"I look forward to it," Donal said with a courtly bow.

Ivy beamed. "You shall see that I am already becoming a lady."

"I've no doubt of it. Mrs. Hardcastle is clearly an excellent teacher."

"Yes." Ivy set Sir Reginald down and linked her arm through Donal's. "Of course I should never change myself at all unless I knew you wanted me to."

Donal paused, gazing down into her eyes. "It isn't only what I wish, Ivy. We agreed that this was the best course for your future."

Ivy sighed and turned her face away. "I know," she said. "I will make you proud of me, Donal."

Tod did a somersault of frustration. It was clear that Donal still did not know what he faced. This girl had wiles more potent than that of the average female, and Donal possessed all too few defenses against females of any sort. Yet to tell him the full truth would surely not aid Tod's cause . . . not when it was to his advantage for Ivy to remain with the woman Hardcastle.

Donal cast a suspicious glance in Tod's direction and led Ivy toward the house.

"You'll make Cordelia proud as well," he said. "I know she greatly enjoys your company."

Ivy kicked at the ground with the toe of her shoe. "I don't know if I will ever please her."

Donal stopped. "What are you saying, Ivy?"

"Nothing. It's just . . ." She hunched her shoulders. "Cordelia wants to make everything perfect. What if I can never be good enough?"

"Nonsense." Donal cupped her chin in his hand. "Would you like me to speak to Mrs. Hardcastle? Is there something you would have me tell her?"

"No, Donal."

He studied her face a moment longer and then led her to the door. "Remember that you may come to me at any time if something troubles you," he said, "just as I'm certain you may speak freely to Mrs. Hardcastle. We —" He broke off as Ivy whirled about and wrapped her arms around him, pressing her cheek to his coat. His skin turned red, and he tugged one-handed at the tight cloth around his neck.

"Ivy . . ." he began.

She stretched on her toes, kissed his cheek and fled into the house. Sir Reginald slipped in the door at her heels. Donal stared after her, jerked again at his neckcloth and turned to stride up the hill.

"I know you're here, Tod," he said, strain

thinning his voice.

Tod made himself visible and hung in the air just out of Donal's reach. "The girl," he said, his own voice unsteady. "She gives my lord much trouble."

Donal gave Tod a quizzical glance. "What makes you say that, Tod?"

"She is female."

Donal laughed softly. "That she is, and she knows it."

Tod flew alongside his master, gathering his courage. "My lord brought the girl here to give her to the woman Hardcastle."

"To make a good home for Ivy at Edgecott, yes."

"And has that not been done?"

Donal stopped at the crest of the hill and met Tod's gaze. "I have had the feeling since Ivy's arrival at Stenwater that you don't like her, Tod. You usually pay little enough attention to humans or their affairs. What has she done to earn your disfavor?"

Tod squirmed, turning so that Donal could no longer see his eyes. "She makes my lord unhappy."

"Whatever put such an idea into your head?"

"My lord finds no pleasure in this place. Let us go home."

Donal raked his hand through his hair. "Sometimes I don't understand you, Tod. You've just arrived, and my work is far from finished. The animals . . ." He stripped the noose of cloth from around his neck and balled it in his fist. "I can't leave just yet, even if I wished to do so. I have responsibilities."

He continued down the hill, but Tod lagged behind. Donal noticed Tod's absence and stopped. "What is it, my friend? Why Ivy? Why now?"

Tod dropped to the earth, his magic no longer strong enough to hold him aloft. "She will change my lord, like the other one did."

"Like the other . . ." Comprehension lit Donal's face. "Like Mrs. Stainthorpe, you mean?" He closed his eyes. "That will never happen again, Tod. You may trust my word."

He strode on ahead. Tod didn't follow. It was almost too late; Donal had fallen under Ivy's spell. If something were not done very soon, Donal might never leave this place at all.

With an effort Tod lifted himself up again and flew toward the thick patch of woodland that stood in the center of Edgecott's park. A grandfather oak reigned over the lesser trees; it reminded Tod of the ancient oak in the forest of Hartsmere, where Donal's father had once held court among the birds and beasts.

He settled down at the base of the trunk, letting his weariness engulf him. It was not the way of Fane to worry; he had been too long apart from his own kind. If he slept for a time, surely an answer would come to him.

He had just begun to doze when a dozen falling leaves fluttered against his face, waking him with a start. Laughter erupted all around him. He sprang up, spinning about on his toes.

"Tod is not deceived," he cried. "Show yourselves!"

The laughter stopped, and out of the air emerged a winged sprite, hardly bigger than a human's hand. Five of her sisters materialized in her wake, hovering on gossamer wings.

Tod swallowed his consternation. Until this moment he had never suspected that other Fane, even of the most humble breed, still lingered in the south, let alone that he would find them here at Edgecott. It troubled him greatly that he had failed to sense their presence before.

The sprites obviously found his surprise a source of great amusement. "Tod!" the leader piped. "Tod the hob!"

Tod glared at her. "That is the name."

The sprites giggled. Tod remembered why he had always preferred to avoid their kind. Such creatures never appeared unless they wanted something of the one they harried.

"Why are you here?" he demanded, resisting the urge to swat them across the wood.

The sprites performed a delicate aerial ballet, twining about each other with grace and precision that even Tod could not help but admire. The leader came to a halt a dozen inches from Tod's face.

"You must come," she said. "Come to Béfind."

Tod stiffened in astonishment. "Béfind?"

"Béfind! Béfind!" the sprite scolded. "She awaits! Come!"

"In Tir-na-Nog?"

"Here, here!"

Tod shook his head to clear the buzzing between his ears. He knew the name Béfind . . . no one who had ever lived in Tir-na-Nog did not. She was one of the highest of High Fane, cousin to Queen Titania herself . . . and *she* would have few reasons to visit the world of men.

Yet she was here, and he did not for a moment consider ignoring her summons. He was only a hob, and he knew his place. But as he followed the sprites through the wood and over hill and meadow, he wondered what possible purpose such a high lady could have in demanding his presence.

The sprites led him to a lake and skimmed like darting insects across the water, aiming for a small, open building with a triangular roof supported by fluted columns. Under the roof, reclining in a thickly cushioned chair, was a lady whose silver gown matched her hair and cool, piercing eyes. The sprites gathered in a circle around the chair and assumed the shape of lovely young women, their dresses every shade of green and yellow.

Tod alighted on the marble floor and bowed, his hair falling across his face. "My lady Béfind," he whispered. "Tod is at your service."

"Rise and look upon me, little hob."

Tod lifted his head and met the lady's gaze. She was beautiful, as of course she must be; the smile that curved her lips was faintly mocking and did not reach her eyes.

"No doubt you wonder why I have come to earth, and why I have summoned you," she said, her musical voice soft and beguiling.

Tod bowed again. "It must be that my lady has business with my master," he said.

Béfind leaned forward, catching Tod's eye. "I have never met the son of Hern. How often has he come to visit his kin in Tir-na-Nog?"

"Not since . . . since he was a child, my lady."

"Since his father was banished from the Land of the Young."

Tod swallowed, suddenly uneasy. "Aye, my lady."

Béfind leaned back again, tapping one silver nail against her lip. "Do you find it incredible that my 'business' on earth might be with you?" She laughed at his silence. "Let me lay your curiosity to rest. It is neither you nor your master who brings me here, but you may be of great service to me, little hob. I believe we have a mutual interest."

203

Tod avoided her gaze and the power that coursed behind it. "I do not understand, my lady."

She signaled to one of her sprites, who produced a goblet of wine. "How many Fane walk the soil of the place humans call Edgecott?" she asked.

For a long moment Tod did not understand her, and then, with a start, he began to see a possibility he had previously failed to consider. His pulse quickened.

"There are three, my lady," he said slowly.

"You, Donal son of Hern, and . . ." She sipped her wine. "I believe they call her 'Ivy.' "

"Aye."

"A child taken from the streets of the Iron City by your master," she said, "and brought here to be educated in the ways of human society by the woman Cordelia Hardcastle."

"My lady is well informed."

"I have excellent agents," she said, waving her hand at the sprites. "They are very good listeners. And they have been watching Donal since he left the north. As they have also been watching you." She sighed. "Do not be so downcast, little hob. It is not entirely your fault that you failed to detect my servants. You have lived in the mortal world for more than a thousand human years. Even the sharpest Fane senses must suffer from constant exposure to such an abyss of Iron and death."

A chill raced up Tod's spine. "My lady," he said thickly, "my lady has some interest in the girl?"

Béfind drained her cup and tossed it into the air. It vanished before it struck the ground. "I have come to right a great injustice," she said. Her lip curled in a scowl, and a flurry of waves rose on the lake. "Perhaps you wonder how a child of the Fane should have come to be abandoned to the mortal realm, and why only now her people have bestirred themselves to find her?" The waves on the lake slapped the shore with increasing violence. "I came to this realm nearly forty earth years ago, seeking a human lover who would give me a halfling child. I was told the babe died at birth, but it was delivered to a human woman to raise as her own. Only now has this treachery been revealed."

Tod shrank away from her rage. He had thought little of Ivy's strange past, but to know she was Béfind's daughter . . . He closed his eyes, thanking the gods for their favor.

"My lady will take her back to Tir-na-Nog," he said.

"Yes." Her anger dissolved like dew beneath the warm summer sun. "And that is where I shall require your assistance."

"My lady?"

She smoothed the skirt of her gown. "You

wish to be rid of the girl, do you not?"

Tod chose his words with great care. "I bear my lady's daughter no ill will —"

"You seek to avert my anger by lying, little hob, but it is not necessary. As I said, my servants have been watching you and your master. You fear that Ivy will enchant your master, and that she will come between him and you. Is that not so?"

Tod sank into a deep crouch. "My lady . . ."

"You and the son of Hern have been together for many years. Without him, you are alone in this world." She bent and lifted his chin with her fingertips. "You wish Ivy gone, and I wish her restored to her rightful heritage. Our desires are complementary. The only thing that prevents us from achieving our aims is the amulet she wears. You have seen it?"

"Tod knows she wears such an ornament. It is bespelled?"

"It prevents any Fane from touching her, or even revealing that she herself is of Fane blood." Béfind's face darkened. "He shall not win this game. *He* —" She broke off and smiled at Tod, showing her perfect white teeth. "Surely your master has had some physical contact with my daughter."

"Aye, my lady," Tod said, remembering the embrace he had witnessed at the big house. "Perhaps he is not bound by the amulet's magic, since his mother is mortal."

"Perhaps." She stroked the locks of silver hair tumbling over her shoulder. "Tell me, little hob. Can your master be trusted with the information I have given you? Would he assist us in restoring my daughter to Tir-na-Nog?"

Tod's mouth was so dry he could scarcely speak. "My master does not know that Ivy is Fane."

"But if he did know?"

"He remembers how Queen Titania cursed and exiled his father."

"So he still bears a grudge."

"Aye. And he believes that my lady's daughter will find happiness with the Hardcastle."

Béfind frowned and stared out across the lake. "He has lived too long in the mortal world. I will not trust him. You shall do this work alone." Her gaze fixed on Tod. "My daughter has also been poisoned by her upbringing among humans. Though she cannot be told of her true nature directly, she can be prepared for the time when the power of the amulet is overcome. She must be told of the wonders of Tir-na-Nog and of the Fane, so that she will have no fear of leaving this earth behind. That is your task. You must become her friend, one she trusts implicitly."

Tod's thoughts whirled like catkins in a brook. "How shall I reveal myself, my lady?"

"That I leave to you. But she is Fane. Her spirit will surely recognize what her mind would deny."

"Shall she meet my lady?"

"In good time. I shall introduce myself in such a way that she will regard me as a true friend and ally." She bade Tod rise with a flick of her hand. "Go now. Do as I bid, and you shall have your master to yourself once again."

In an instant her sprites had taken their original forms, and Béfind rose from her chair in a sweep of silver cloth. Then she and her servants vanished, leaving Tod alone among the columns.

He made his way back to Edgecott, his stomach churning with excitement and dread. It would seem as if the problem of Ivy had been solved, or would be soon enough. Yet Tod knew it would not be an easy task to conceal his dislike and befriend the girl. And he was troubled by the fact that Donal must remain ignorant of Béfind's plans. Though Tod himself had begun to think of how he might drive Ivy away, he had not considered the consequences of such a betrayal.

For betrayal it was, no matter how he turned it about in his head. He had not yet given Béfind his word to act as her agent. He could still back away, even if it meant risking Béfind's wrath.

Spinning with frustration, Tod went in search of his master. He must decide, and quickly. Even though he could not speak of

Béfind's scheme, his heart would tell him what he must do.

"Ivy, my dear," Cordelia said, "where is Dr. Fleming?"

The girl looked at Cordelia with a blank expression, preoccupied with her own dreamy thoughts. Cordelia shook her head with mild exasperation, went past Ivy to the door and looked outside. There was no sign of the errant veterinarian.

Ordinarily she would not have considered his lack of sociability to be anything but an inconvenience. She admitted to some annoyance that he seemed so eager to escape again when he had been left alone all day, but she had only herself to blame. If she had not allowed herself to look forward to his admittedly challenging company, she would have no cause for disappointment. Nor would she have interpreted his moments of keen attentiveness — or the sparkle in his green eyes — to be anything more than grudging courtesy.

Tonight, however, it was not her foolish and groundless expectations that made her so desirous of his presence. Tonight — as the good doctor had undoubtedly forgotten — Sir Geoffrey was coming down to dine with his daughter and her guests. For such an occasion, everything must be perfect.

She changed into a plain dress and boots,

tied on her bonnet and walked briskly to the cottage. Donal wasn't there. Nor was he at the stables, where the grooms spoke of his visit and his remarkable handling of the stallion Boreas. The story left Cordelia a little breathless, as if she had witnessed the spectacle herself, and she went on to the menagerie in a state of distraction that had nothing to do with the hazards of the coming meal.

The animals were very quiet as she drew near the enclosures, and she felt a pang of guilt for not visiting them more frequently since her return from Yorkshire. Then she found Donal sitting on the bench across from Othello's cage, and every sensible thought went flying out of her head.

Donal looked up, his expression cast in brooding lines, and it seemed to Cordelia that the black pupils of his eyes nearly swallowed up the green as he met her gaze.

He got quickly to his feet. "Cordelia," he said, something very like guilt crossing his face. "Have I missed dinner?"

"I take it that you forgot about Sir Geoffrey?"

Donal flushed. "Dash it all, I —" He cleared his throat. "I beg your pardon."

His obvious chagrin disarmed what remained of her pique. "No harm has been done," she said, "but you have only an hour to dress."

Donal touched his mangled cravat, apparently aware that it was beyond saving. "I'm sorry you came so far to find me. I fear I won't be very good company tonight."

"Oh? Has it something to do with the events at the stables this afternoon?"

He glanced at her in surprise. "No. No, not at all."

A long silence followed, and Cordelia searched for a polite way of shaking him into a more satisfying response. "Will you tell me what troubles you?" she said at last.

He walked away from her and stopped before Othello's cage. "You asked me to examine your animals," he said. "I have done so."

She went to stand behind Donal, peering into the shadows of the panther's shelter. Lambent yellow eyes glowed in the darkness. "What have you learned, Doctor?"

He moved to the apes' enclosure. "These animals are not ill," he said. "Not in the way you might expect. They fail to prosper because they have been stolen from their native habitats and forced to live in unnatural confinement."

Cordelia stopped halfway between the cages, parsing his speech for the censure it must contain. "That is your diagnosis?" she demanded. "That all these animals suffer merely from the fact of their captivity?"

"Yes."

She drew in a deep breath, continuing on

until she could see Heloise and Abelard perched in their bare-branched tree. They looked as they always did . . . far too quiet for such lively creatures, their yellowish-brown coats dull in spite of the care with which they groomed each other.

"My dear doctor," she said, clipping each word as she spoke it, "your analysis may be quite accurate, but it is of little use to me since I can hardly release these animals to run wild about the countryside."

He turned to her, and there was a gentleness in his face she had hardly expected. "Theodora told me how you saved them from fates far worse than imprisonment," he said. "I was not suggesting that you had done anything of which to be ashamed."

"I shall have to thank Theodora for defending me, since I must assume that you questioned her about the circumstances of my acquisitions."

He had the grace to look uncomfortable. "I did ask her," he admitted. "It would have been difficult for me to accept if you had purchased healthy animals, or had them captured."

Cordelia ignored the tears burning behind her eyelids. "I am sorry that you think so ill of me —"

"I don't." He took a step toward her, raised his hands and let them fall again. "Cordelia, I . . . think very well of you."

She pressed her palm to the bars of the cage, working to control the emotions that weakened her knees so shamefully. "I have done what any decent person would do."

"You're wrong." He joined her, placing his hand close to hers. "Very few would take such trouble with mere animals. The horses in the stables, and the dogs . . . they think very well of you, too."

"You have this on excellent authority, I take it."

"The best."

Cordelia felt the warmth of his body and caught the faint scent of straw and horseflesh on his skin. She was acutely aware of the way the evening breeze played in his disheveled hair, and how the untidiness of his clothing only called more attention to the taut leanness of the frame beneath. What in God's name was wrong with her?

"If you recognize that my animals are better off now than when I found them," she said, "you must concede that I have their welfare constantly in mind. I know what is best for them, and —"

"*Your* animals," he interrupted. "Do you truly see them that way, Cordelia? Do you believe that you own them?"

"If I did not own them, they would have no protection. It is my duty to do everything within my power to help them adjust to their new lives here, in England."

"Some creatures will die rather than accept existence in a cage. What if they cannot adjust?"

"All they require is kindness, and they will accept the necessity of adaptation."

"Would you reason with them, Cordelia?" he asked softly, holding her gaze. "Do you expect them to think as men do?"

"Of course not. But all creatures on Earth are subject to certain principles. The laws of Nature are rational — one can see that in the perfect construction of a flower and the symmetry of a butterfly. Order will always prevail."

"You do not acknowledge chaos as an inescapable influence on all living things?"

"If there is chaos, it is not the natural state of life. When given the opportunity, Nature will seek balance and tranquillity." She risked a glance at Donal's face. His expression was flatly disbelieving. Suddenly it seemed vital that she make him understand. "The world is not as *we* would make it, Donal. Even the animals recognize this truth, and will alter themselves to thrive within it."

He cocked his head, green eyes intent on hers. "A certain malleability is beneficial to survival," he said. "But that seems contradictory to your theory of a natural order, does it not?"

"I said that all things *seek* order," she said, "that all life falls into a pattern that human eyes and minds can discern and encourage. If the world were as it should be, there would be no need for such constant struggle. But when we accept our places in the pattern, we find true peace."

"You speak of Heaven, not Earth."

"You are cynical, Donal. Have you never sought the happiness that comes with surrender?"

He turned his head, staring blankly into the cage. "Surrender to what? What is my place?"

The profound sorrow in his question struck at Cordelia's heart like a cry of pain. She reached out to touch his arm. "You would know it," she said, "if you would open your heart to the society of men in which you belong."

"Which society?" he asked, facing her again. "Should I attempt to join the sphere of the landed gentry that you inhabit? Or perhaps I should set my aim higher, and climb to Lord Inglesham's exalted circle?"

Cordelia flinched from the bitterness in his voice. "We do not choose the circumstances into which we are born."

"But you admit that we can change them, or you would not have invited Ivy to become a lady."

"She clearly does not belong on the streets of London —"

"And *she* can be tamed," he said.

Her skin went from hot to icy cold, and she

snatched her arm away. "Ivy is not an animal."

"We are all animals, Cordelia. You speak of the natural world, but you have not recognized that simple fact."

"You are wrong. We —" Cordelia pressed her lips together and swallowed her argument. "Have you any practical solution for the care of my animals?"

He sighed, running his hand up and down the bars. "Are you willing to try an experiment, Cordelia?"

"An experiment?"

"It will require you to suspend judgment and abandon your preconceptions for a short while."

"And you think I cannot do so?" She stared up at him. "What does this 'experiment' involve?"

"I would like you to sit on that bench and allow me to guide you in a foray of imagination. You will envision yourself as one of the animals in the menagerie . . . imagine the life they led before they were dragged from their homes —"

"Imagine? I can do better than that, Doctor. Perhaps in your conversation with Theodora, she mentioned my travels with Sir Geoffrey?"

"She did."

"Then it may not surprise you to learn that I have visited the natural habitats of these creatures, or regions very similar."

"You have made an effort to reproduce at least some of those conditions here, but merely 'visiting' is not enough. You must —"

"In which parts of the world have you traveled, Donal? Or are you basing your philosophy upon what you have gleaned from books and your 'imagination'?"

His eyes darkened. "I plan to rectify my lack of personal experience very soon."

A strange thrill of dread coursed through her body. "Indeed?"

"I have already begun to make plans to leave England. It is my hope to explore the wildest lands of every continent, even if it takes me the rest of my life."

Cordelia touched her throat and looked away. "You will do this . . . quite alone?"

"I have no close companions suited for such travel," he said. "But that has no bearing on our discussion. Will you indulge my request?"

"It is getting late. We must soon return to the house."

"This should not take long."

"I hardly see the point of such a game."

He leaned closer, and the warm scent of his body engulfed Cordelia in a soothing haze. "Are you afraid, Cordelia?"

She swayed and caught herself against the bars. "Afraid of what?"

"Of losing a little of your unshakeable control. Of discovering something in yourself you may not wish to find."

She stepped away from the cage. "Certainly not. I am mistress of my own mind, Doctor."

He arched a brow and gestured toward the bench. She walked to it slowly and sat, her posture as erect as if she were sipping tea in a duchess's drawing room. Subtle, treacherous unease fluttered in her chest. "What do you wish me to do?" she asked.

"Relax as much as you can," he said, taking up a position at her left side. "Empty your mind of thoughts, and envision what I describe."

She closed her eyes, but only because she didn't want to see Donal's face. She had boasted of being mistress of her own mind, yet she felt as if she were careening out of control, allowing this man, this virtual stranger, to manipulate her for reasons she didn't understand.

That is but a delusion, she told herself. *He has no power over your thoughts or emotions. And if you do as he requests now, you may ask him to be on his best behavior tonight. . . .*

"Are you ready?" Donal asked.

She released the stale air from her lungs. "Yes. You may proceed."

CHAPTER ELEVEN

Donal's voice softened to a near whisper. "It is spring," he said, "and the apes are on the hunt."

But it was an easy kind of hunting, filled with many pauses for games and grooming as she and the others ambled through the forest of oak and cedar. On her back she carried her young one, whose tiny fingers gripped her fur as he gazed in constant amazement at the world around them.

Eldest sister, who led the band, knew all the best places to find succulent roots and tender leaves. The mother ape was grateful for the plentiful food, for she was often hungry; as soon as she had her fill she stopped to feed the little one, cradling his small body in her arms as he suckled. When the meal was finished, a male she favored shyly approached and offered to groom her fur. She basked under his caresses, and watched in amusement as another male teased her youngling into a game.

Soon the joyful play spread to the other

members of the band, and the apes chased each other among the rocks, shrieking with delight. The mother ape became a youngling again, remembering the days when she, too, had ridden on her mother's back, and all the world had yet to be explored. . . .

The scene faded, the reds and browns and olives of the landscape blending and spinning like a whirlpool of earth and stone. Cordelia searched for a foothold in the chaos, but neither up nor down held any reality. The world went gray as a thick London fog. She opened her mouth to cry out, and a sun-browned hand reached from the emptiness to grasp hers.

She went where the hand led her, helpless as an infant. Gray mist gave way to the bright green of a meadow, its canvas spattered with wildflowers like dabs and dashes of an artist's paints.

She stood in the grass, trembling with excitement as the pack gathered around her. The hunt had been successful; after many days of weary tracking and gnawing hunger, they had found a white-rump weakened by illness and brought it down, each wolf doing its part to drive and trap and make the kill.

Now she and the others had full bellies, and they had slept all through the warm day. But the sinking sun brought with it the intoxicating smells of evening, and the first howls broke the silence, calling the pack to play.

A gray male of middle rank rubbed against her, inviting a friendly scuffle. They nipped at each other, basking in the familiar joys of kinship while the scent-laden breeze bathed their fur. Bodies jostled and bumped, noses touched, tails waved. Then the great black male who led the pack lifted his head, ears pricked, and the others fell in behind him as he began to run.

They ran through the forest where the trees grew tall, splashed through the stream and clambered up rocks that reached into the sky. They scattered smaller creatures before them, hearing the high-pitched cries of warning from those who knew the fear of the hunted.

She knew no fear. Nothing in her world hunted the pack, and nothing killed its members save the strongest hoofed runners or other wolves . . . and sometimes the two-legs with their long, shining arms.

As if the leader had shared her thoughts, he turned in his path and led the pack to the high place that overlooked the den of the two-legs. They did not look dangerous from such a distance, scurrying about in their nests like insects. But the pack leader ventured closer still, close enough that the foul odor of the two-legs clogged the she-wolf's nostrils. So strong was the scent that no wolf saw the intruder until it was already upon them.

In some ways it resembled a wolf, but she could not mistake its scent for anything but a creature of the two-legs. It was massive and heavily furred, and it wore a band about its neck. It seemed not to be afraid, though it was alone and the pack was many.

Her hackles rose. The pack leader advanced, his tail raised high in challenge. If he gave the signal, the pack would fall upon the false wolf in a storm of teeth and claws. But the leader stopped, deliberately turned his back on the outsider, and scraped his hind feet as if he were covering scat.

One by one the other wolves turned their backs, marking the creature for what it was: a pitiful thing, barred from the wild, stinking of the two-legs from whom it begged its food. Sad, lost creature, severed from the pattern of life and the ecstasy of freedom. . . .

Lost. Pitiful. Cordelia wandered again in the mist, searching for something she had forgotten. Surely it must be here. She had let it go in the mountains or the forest, when she could no longer bear its presence. Now she felt overwhelming urge to claim it anew, wrap it about herself like the magic cloak of a primitive medicine man who could change his shape at will. Once she had it, she would never lose it again.

But the gray light dimmed, and she found herself on a narrow track winding beneath the arched, dripping branches of an ancient jungle. Soft-winged flyers screeched from the green wall above, flitting in and out of shafts of sunlight that seldom reached the damp, fragrant earth.

She paid no attention to the denizens of the trees. She was on the hunt, and her prey was not far ahead. Her paws sank into the deep layer of fallen leaves and rotting wood. She carried her sleek body low to the ground, a shadow among shadows. So silent was she that not even the long-tailed chatterers raised the alarm.

Step by step she drew closer to the kill. Her heart beat faster. The tip of her tail lashed against her flank. Wetness flooded her mouth. The scent of the prey was hot with panic, for it knew it had little time left to live.

When she finally sprang, ravenous for the taste of flesh, the old buck was too exhausted to flee. She sank her teeth into the side of its neck, and gouts of warm blood splashed over her muzzle. The prey collapsed to its knees, but she showed no mercy.

This was life. This was her reason for existence, this sweet victory. She was already feasting before the buck drew its last breath. But then a terrible roaring swept through the jungle, and she looked up in rage, ready to defend her prize.

She had no chance to fight. The cold, hard branches crashed down around her, and she was staring through them, confined in a space so small that she could barely turn. Deafening noise beat against her ears. Flat faces stared at her, opening mouths filled with blunt, useless teeth. Paws like those of the tree-chatterers poked sharpened sticks into her body. She snarled and slashed, but never did her claws strike flesh.

Until one flat-face left part of the branch-cave open and she saw her way out. Filled with rage and terror, she ran into a clamor louder than any in the forest, voices shouting and flat-faces pointing their strange limbs. Suddenly one of them stood before her, blocking her path to freedom. She leaped, claws raking. The flat-face howled and fell writhing to the ground. She ran, and the howling ceased. For a while, for all too short a while, she was left in peace. . . .

Cordelia jerked from the dream, her face bathed in perspiration. She still felt the rampaging wildness of the leopardess, the animal's savage love of freedom and hatred for anything, anyone who would trammel her wild ways. She still heard the cry of the girl whom the panther had clawed, saw the familiar face with its hazel eyes and upturned nose.

Lydia. Oh, Lydia.

"Cordelia?"

Donal's voice brought her the final step over the threshold, back to the safe, predictable English countryside. She pressed her hand to her damp forehead, trembling too much to risk standing.

The bench creaked as Donal sat beside her. Soft, clean cloth brushed her cheek and temple. "Are you all right?" he asked.

She opened her eyes. His face was close to hers as he dabbed at her with his handkerchief — too close, too intimate after such a horrible experience. And yet a part of her wanted nothing more than to lean against him, fold herself into his warmth, beg him to remind her that she was human. . . .

Or acknowledge that she was every bit as savage in her desires as a bloodthirsty predator.

God help me.

She jerked away, raising a hand to ward him off. "I am . . . fine," she said, steadying her voice with an effort. But the anger endured, no matter how hard she fought it. "What did you do to me?"

He drew back, crumpling the handkerchief in his fist. "I . . . I did not mean to upset you. I only intended —"

"I was there, with the animals. I *felt* . . ." She looked toward the cages, half-afraid to see the creatures she had so nearly become. They were clearly as disturbed as she was. The macaques leaped from branch to branch, the wolves raced from one side of their enclosure to the other, and the panther crouched near the bars, his tail lashing with short, violent cracks.

She shuddered and took a deep breath. "It doesn't matter," she said. "We must go dress for dinner." She gathered her feet under her and prepared to rise.

"Cordelia." Donal took her arm in a firm grip and stared into her eyes. "Don't reject what you have seen, what you felt. Your mind was open to this experience because these feelings are a part of you, as they are a part of all of us. They will help you to understand —"

"Please release me," she said, gratified that her words were firmly under rational control again. "You have had your experiment. Now I will ask you a favor in return." She met his gaze and found that she could do so without a telltale shiver. "As you now recall, Sir Geoffrey is joining us at table tonight. It will be a more formal meal than we are accustomed to taking at Edgecott. I would ask you to remember that my father is easily agitated, and to avoid any provocative conversation. I will request the same of Ivy."

He let his hand fall. "I understand perfectly."

"Thank you. I shall see you in the drawing room at eight-thirty." She walked away quickly, before he could detain her with further arguments about the beast he presumed lay waiting in her soul.

She strode across the park, her skirts whipping about her legs. "These feelings are a part of you" indeed. What nonsense. Human beings were *not* animals, or they should not have dominion over the earth. And if *she,* in her youth, had been subject to uncivilized impulses, she had long since brought them under command.

If Donal had not done so — and she increasingly believed that must be the case — he had no right to assume the same of others.

Cordelia stumbled on an uneven patch of ground and forced herself to slow her furious pace. How had he managed it? How had he influenced her to concoct such incredibly detailed images? Much of it could have been derived from her own travels and imagination, and yet she had been so utterly engulfed in those worlds that she had all but lost her human consciousness.

She had *seen* Lydia injured as if it had happened right before her eyes. If she were to believe the vision, and Donal's claim that she would share the experience of her menagerie animals, then it would seem that Othello had been guilty of the attack on her sister. But she knew that was not true. And in her dream, the panther had been female.

None of it made sense. Cordelia grasped for a rational explanation and remembered reading of a Scottish doctor who had developed a technique of inducing a state of trance, which he called "hypnosis." It was not impossible that Donal had learned of this technique and practiced it on her.

She caught sight of the house through the trees and felt a jolt of relief. It was frightening to think how thoroughly Donal had suborned her mind, and what a truly unscrupulous man might achieve by the same method. But Cordelia did not for a moment believe that Donal would cause harm with such an extraordinary skill. His motives were honest, if misguided. With patience and persistence, she would make him acknowledge his errors of thought and action.

Her spirits much improved, Cordelia went into the house and climbed the stairs to her room, her thoughts turned again to the very prosaic problem of the evening meal.

"I have already begun to make plans to leave England."
The words echoed in Tod's head like the tolling of iron bells and ripped at his heart like the claws of the black beast prowling behind the bars of its cage. He made not a sound in his grief; Donal never knew he was there.

Tod flew to the grandfather oak and perched among its wide branches. He buried his face in his arms, ignoring the radiant bird-song and the gentle breezes sifting through his hair. Donal was leaving England. He was leaving Tod.

"I have no close companions suited for such travel." Donal knew that Tod could not go with him. He had been making plans, and yet he had never seen fit to tell the one who had

served him all his life. Would he have told Tod before he left, or simply abandoned him?

The knot of sorrow in Tod's belly drew tighter. *He cares nothing for Tod.* Anger swelled in a wave that set him to swaying on his branch, snapping twigs and leaves between clenched fingers.

Today Tod had been given a choice: to act for Lady Béfind without Donal's knowledge, or to remain strictly loyal to his master. Donal had made the choice for him. But Tod would never let the son of Hern see how he grieved.

Tod laughed until all the birds flew away.

Donal watched Cordelia go, his head still aching with the effort of sharing the animal's thoughts. He hardly noticed the discomfort, for his heart suffered a far worse affliction.

He knew she had *seen.* She had climbed with the apes, run with the wolves and stalked with the panther; she knew what it was they had lost when men had captured them.

And she had refused to accept what she learned. She had rejected the lesson because she feared what it told her about herself. She had rejected Donal and the small, simple gift he had tried to give her.

He sank down on the bench, resting his head in his hands. Somewhere he had gone wrong, trying to reason with her when the subject at hand had so little to do with rationality. She clung so fiercely to the superiority of her intellect and her certainty of the way things should be.

Donal realized that he still clutched his damp handkerchief and laid it on the bench, smoothing it with his fingertips. The bitter truth was that Cordelia could not bring herself to trust him. He had wanted to help her and her animals, and he had failed. When he had looked into her eyes, he'd seen only revulsion.

And as for the animals . . . He had betrayed their trust by letting Cordelia into the privacy of their thoughts. They were restive and angry, but their ire wasn't directed at the man who had disrupted their fragile peace.

Cordelia herself was its object. Not because she had mistreated them in any way. But because they sensed the anger she felt toward them, hostility she kept deeply buried. Rage Donal couldn't completely understand.

It had something to do with the girl . . . the young, fair-haired child whose image Cordelia had injected into the visions. Somehow Cordelia had twisted Othello's memories and drawn upon recollections within her own mind. But what was their significance? Who was the girl injured by the unfamiliar panther? Was this the sister of whom Theodora had spoken, lost years ago to some tragic accident?

He could be certain of only one cruel fact.

Cordelia sincerely believed these animals could be broken to docility and contentment, for at some point — in a past he could only begin to imagine — she herself had been broken of the wildness in her own soul.

Donal rose slowly, clenching his muscles to stop their trembling. He visited each of the cages with a silent and heartfelt apology, stopping last at Othello's enclosure. The leopard would not come near him, nor did he answer Donal's pleas.

The weight of a terrible sorrow hung like a yoke on Donal's shoulders as he walked back to the cottage. He washed up as best he could, changed into the freshly laundered garments Edgecott's servants had left in his clothes press, and managed to torture his cravat into yet another lopsided knot. He couldn't bring himself to care. He had promised to make himself agreeable to Sir Geoffrey, but it was not as if he were posing as anything but a temporary, if respectable, employee granted a singular but unsolicited honor.

Edgecott's senior footman met him just inside the door to the house and anxiously herded him into the drawing room. Cordelia, Theodora and Ivy stood in a stiff tableau at one side of the elegant room, each dressed in what must be her most attractive finery. Ivy's gown was white as befit a virginal young girl, but her mouth was set in a rebellious line as if she and Cordelia had just been quarreling.

She looked up and beamed at Donal as he entered. "Donal!" she cried, starting across the room at an indecorous gallop.

"Ivy," Cordelia said. Her voice was quiet and as unyielding as that of any general certain of his absolute authority. Ivy came to a halt, bit her lip, and curtseyed to Donal.

"Good evening, Doctor," she said.

Donal played along with the game. "Good evening, Ivy," he said. "Your dress is lovely. Is it one of those you purchased in town today?"

She flushed and pressed her hands to the impossibly tiny circumference of her waist. "It was altered for me," she said in a whisper. "It once belonged to Cordelia's —"

"It is not polite to whisper in company, my dear," Cordelia said, coming to join them. She smiled at Donal, an expression entirely lacking in any emotion beyond polite welcome. "Good evening, Dr. Fleming. I am delighted that you could join us."

She spoke as if not the slightest disturbance had ruffled her composure just a short while earlier. Her gaze met Donal's and swiftly moved away. "We shall be going in to dinner presently. I have reminded Cook to prepare only vegetarian dishes for you, Doctor."

Donal knew she was referring to the awkwardness during the previous evening's dinner, when he had been served a hearty slice of rare roast beef. Cordelia prided herself on being able to provide Donal with a wholly meatless diet, according to his custom, and she had been embarrassed by the incident.

"I am grateful for your consideration, Mrs. Hardcastle," he said, suppressing the desire to take her slender, gloved hands in his. "Thank you."

"I would have spared you the presence of meat on the table," she said, staring at a point somewhere over his left shoulder, "but Sir Geoffrey will have his beef and fowl. I'm sure you understand."

"Of course." He searched for a way to ease the tension that stretched between them. "I confess I have not attended a formal dinner in some time, and I find myself surrounded by so much beauty that I can scarcely recall the rules of etiquette drummed into my head so long ago. Is it to be my honor to escort you to table, Mrs. Hardcastle?"

Much to his amazement she flushed, and her gray eyes flickered toward his. "This is only a family affair, Doctor, but I should be pleased to accept your arm."

Ivy gave Donal a mournful look of reproach, but Theodora nodded to Donal as if they were old friends who understood each other without the need for words. Donal wondered if Cordelia had confided any part of her menagerie encounter to her cousin, and decided any such disclosure was highly unlikely. Yet it was clear that Theodora saw through the air of serene benevolence Cordelia imposed upon herself and expected others to accept without question.

Before he could give more thought to the matter, Croome appeared to inform them that dinner was served. Donal offered his arm to Cordelia, and Theodora and Ivy walked together behind them into the dining room.

As always, the head of the table was conspicuously vacant, though the setting left no doubt that the place of honor was shortly to be occupied. Donal saw Cordelia to her chair, removed his gloves, and remained standing until the other ladies had taken their seats. There followed a period of awkward silence while the butler and footmen awaited the arrival of the master. Ivy openly fidgeted, staring pointedly at the dishes arranged on the sideboard. Theodora made herself very small in her chair, while Cordelia sat erect and imperturbable, her eyes as reflective as twin mirrors.

Sir Geoffrey's approach was heralded by a sudden flurry of activity among the servants. A few moments later a thin and soberly dressed man of middle years walked through the door, half supporting an older gentleman on his arm.

Donal had already formed an unfavorable picture of Sir Geoffrey, drawn from what he had heard of the baronet's conversation with Cordelia and Cordelia's references to her father's many "peculiarities." He was quite unprepared for the man who paused on the threshold.

Sir Geoffrey was not a tall man, but he carried himself with the sheer physicality of a natural athlete despite the signs of recurrent illness to which Cordelia had alluded. Leashed energy vibrated from his spare frame, and he wore his well-cut clothes as if they could barely contain the coiled muscle and sinew beneath. His high forehead was crowned by a full head of thick gray hair. His handsome face was thin and there were deep shadows under his eyes, but his skin bore the weathered appearance of a life spent outdoors, and fine creases carved by sunlight stretched across his forehead and webbed at the corners of his eyes.

Those eyes were gray like Cordelia's, and every bit as piercing as they swept the room. Sir Geoffrey stepped away from his assistant, who meekly withdrew, and strode forward to brace his hands on the back of his chair.

Donal stood and waited for the baronet's acknowledgment. It was not long in coming. Sir Geoffrey hardly glanced at the women before he fixed his stare on Donal's face. His nostrils flared as if he had detected some offensive odor.

"You," he said. "You are the animal doctor."

"Donal Fleming. At your service, Sir

Geoffrey."

The baronet barked an unpleasant laugh and looked Donal up and down. "Not at *my* service. Cordelia speaks very highly of your skills, Fleming, and you are apparently not the manure-grubbing bumpkin I would expect to come out of Yorkshire, but I can see far better uses for the overly generous wages she proposes to pay you on behalf of her wretched menagerie."

Donal kept his face expressionless and glanced at Cordelia. She regarded her wine glass as if she hadn't heard a word her father had spoken.

"I have been told, Sir Geoffrey," Donal said, "that you are a naturalist of some repute. Am I to understand that you have no interest in the animals Mrs. Hardcastle brought back from your travels?"

"Interest? Perhaps if her collection included species from Phylum Arthropoda rather than the tediously inelegant Mammalia, I might find it of some small value. As it is . . ." He waved impatiently at the footman who hovered near his chair and allowed himself to be seated. Immediately the footman poured him a generous glass of sherry from the decanter on the table. Donal resumed his seat as Sir Geoffrey drained the glass.

"You, I suppose, have no knowledge of insects," the baronet said while his glass was refilled. "Why should you, when there is nothing a man of your profession can do to improve upon the perfection Nature has already bestowed upon them?"

"Dr. Fleming is a most observant gentleman," Cordelia said, her voice as low and soothing now as it had been commanding with Ivy in the drawing room. "I believe that his interest in the natural world extends to all its facets."

"Ha." Sir Geoffrey gestured to Croome, who in turn signaled the footman to begin serving the meal. "Has your latest protégé empowered you to answer for him, Cordelia? Do you already lead him about by the nose as you have attempted to do with every male of any species who has had the misfortune to cross your path?"

Cordelia's face went white. Donal pushed back his chair and prepared to rise. Out of the corner of his eye he could see Cordelia urging him to silence with the eloquence of her gaze. He pretended not to notice.

"Sir Geoffrey," he said, "I am only a guest at your table, but I respectfully urge you to employ greater restraint when you speak to a lady."

Sir Geoffrey nearly choked on his sherry, and his violent movement sent the platter-laden footman scurrying out of reach. The baronet slammed the palm of his hand on the table.

"You speak so to me, you insufferable

puppy?" he snarled.

"The gift of speech was given to only one species of the Phylum Mammalia," Donal said. "It would be a sin indeed to waste such a capability when its employment is so clearly required."

Sir Geoffrey stared, red-faced, as if he might ignite from within, and suddenly burst into gales of laughter. "By God," he said. "He gives as good as he gets, does he?"

Cordelia half-rose. "Papa, you must be careful. . . ."

The baronet's amusement ended in a fit of coughing, and his meek attendant materialized to offer assistance. Sir Geoffrey pushed the man away and gulped down the glass of water a footman placed before him.

"Sit down, Cordelia," he said, wiping his hand across his mouth. "I am not dying just yet." He ignored Donal entirely and turned to examine Ivy. "And this is the other creature you netted in Yorkshire, is it?" His eyes narrowed speculatively. "A pretty piece. She puts me in mind of someone . . ." He drummed his fingers on the table. "Of course. Lydia. The eyes . . ." He looked at Cordelia. "Is this why you took her in? So that you could have Lydia again?"

Ivy threw Cordelia a startled glance. Cordelia accepted a bowl of soup from the footman and picked up her spoon. "Lord Inglesham tells me that he brought you a number of interesting books on botany while Theodora and I were in Yorkshire, Papa. I hope that you have found them enjoyable?"

Sir Geoffrey opened his mouth to answer, but Ivy spoke first. "Who is Lydia?" she demanded.

Cordelia set down her spoon. "It is not polite to interrupt a conversation, Ivy. I was speaking to my —"

"You haven't told her about your sister?" Sir Geoffrey asked, the words edged with spite. "Hasn't she the right to know why your guilt over Lydia's death has made a common guttersnipe the recipient of such miraculous good fortune?"

Cordelia met her father's gaze. "We will not speak of such things tonight, Papa." She took a careful sip of her soup. "Cook has taken special care with dinner. Let us enjoy it." She nodded to Ivy. "Perhaps you can show Sir Geoffrey what you have learned, my dear."

Ivy's face set in dangerously stubborn lines. "Perhaps that would not be such a good idea," she said sweetly, mimicking Cordelia's tone. "Surely a 'common guttersnipe' could never perform up to the exacting standards set at this table."

Cordelia nearly dropped her spoon. Sir Geoffrey looked on the verge of apoplexy, and Theodora cringed in her seat. Donal closed his eyes. There would be no peace at this table tonight. Sir Geoffrey had poisoned

239

the atmosphere with his gibes and innuendo, driving a wedge between Ivy and Cordelia when they most needed to be allies. Had Donal been glib and clever he might have rescued them all from disaster, but the cruel undercurrents in this family's relationships were too bitter and complex for his mending.

As matters stood, he would have preferred to take his leave and find refuge among the horses in the stable or the rabbits in the wood. But leaving the women to Sir Geoffrey's odious whims was quite out of the question.

He cleared his throat. "Sir Geoffrey," he said, "I would be most interested in hearing about your travels around the world."

The baronet's eyes snapped to his. "Would you, indeed?"

"I have been considering such travels myself, and I should be glad of any advice you might —"

"Advice? My advice to you is to quit this house while you can. There is no place for you here, and when Inglesham marries my daughter —"

"Father!" Cordelia exclaimed.

"You are no longer a maid, Cordelia, nor are you young. You'll get no better offer. I'd gladly pay a fishmonger or chimneysweep to take you off my hands. And as for that horse-faced cousin of yours —"

"Sir," Donal said, struggling to control his

voice, "I have asked you to treat the ladies with respect. Perhaps you are too ill to recognize your inappropriate behavior. Shall I call a servant to escort you to your room?"

The silence was thunderous. Sir Geoffrey's sallow skin reddened as if he had been scalded. His breath sawed in and out of his throat.

"You *are* ill, Papa," Cordelia said, rising. "We shall take our meal elsewhere, so that you may rest."

Sir Geoffrey shot to his feet, toppling his chair behind him. "Cordelia," he rasped, "get that man out of my house, and have him take that miserable shadow of Lydia with him."

Ivy bolted up in her seat, her eyes shimmering with angry tears. There was a sudden commotion at the door, and Sir Reginald dashed into the dining room. He dodged a footman's grasping hands and leaped into Ivy's lap. She hugged him to her chest.

"You are a horrid old man," she said to Sir Geoffrey, "and I would not stay in this house for a thousand pounds a year."

"Ivy —" Cordelia began.

"You!" Ivy said, turning on Cordelia. "You only wanted me because you feel guilty about your sister?" She darted away from the table. "And *you* made me come here," she said to Donal. "Sir Reginald is my only true friend." She spun for the door. Cordelia hesitated, her gaze flying from Ivy to her father, and rose to follow the girl.

"Let her go," Donal said. "She will do better alone for a little while."

Cordelia's eyes glistened with humiliation. She signaled to a footman, who left the room and returned with Sir Geoffrey's attendant. He hurried to the baronet's side and spoke softly in his master's ear.

"Get out," Sir Geoffrey whispered. He pressed his hand to his chest. *"Out!"*

Donal remained by his chair, watching Sir Geoffrey as Cordelia and Theodora collected their gloves and beat a dignified retreat. Only when they were well out of the tyrant's reach did he turn to follow.

"Fleming," Sir Geoffrey said behind him. "You think yourself quite the gentleman, do you not, defending my *helpless* daughter?" He wheezed a laugh between his teeth. "D'you fancy a female who lacks every sensibility a proper lady ought to have, no matter how much she tries to ape the more delicate members of her sex?"

Donal faced the baronet. "Since you had the raising of your daughter, sir, you are hardly in a position to complain of any flaws in her character."

Sir Geoffrey took a step forward, and his attendant restrained him with a hand at his elbow. "She was born into her character," he snarled. "She would have been no different if she'd spent all her life in England."

"Indeed? You seem eager to be rid of her, yet I am under the impression that it is her very strength of purpose that efficiently manages this house, its grounds and its staff when you are indisposed. Are you quite certain Mrs. Hardcastle is so easily dispensable?"

Sir Geoffrey leaned heavily on the table, his arm trembling beneath his weight. "You know nothing of Cordelia, animal doctor. You imagine that you see strength instead of willfulness, composure in place of the constant struggle for self-control."

"Perhaps you are not the one to speak of self-control, Sir Geoffrey."

"For all her defects, you shall never be her equal."

Donal bowed. "That was never my ambition, Sir Geoffrey. Good evening."

He strode from the room before the baronet could engage him in another fruitless contest of wills, but his mind was spinning with all he had heard. More talk of the mysterious Lydia, of guilt and death. Sir Geoffrey's apparent disdain for Cordelia when he so clearly relied on her to manage his affairs. And more allusions to the passions that lay concealed beneath Cordelia's seemingly unexceptionable exterior.

"You imagine that you see strength instead of willfulness, composure in place of the constant struggle for self-control." Donal had glimpsed that struggle on more than one occasion. He

knew that Cordelia's emotions had been raging tonight, and he had been helpless to comfort her. His feeble attempts to defend her had been more than worthy of Sir Geoffrey's mockery.

Every imprudent feeling urged him to go to her now, to explain his behavior and assure her that he had paid no heed to her father's ugly remarks and veiled accusations. But she had suffered quite enough humiliation this evening, and he would be the last person she wished to see.

CHAPTER TWELVE

Tod was waiting near the great stone house when Ivy ran out the door, Sir Reginald in her arms.

She paused long enough to set the spaniel down, swiping at her face with the backs of her hands. Wetness glistened on her cheek. A moment later she was running again, up into the wolds overlooking the house and into the sanctuary of the trees.

Tod followed, his heart's wings beating hard inside his chest. He had spent the past hours making ready for this first meeting, knowing he must skillfully feign friendship for one who had been his rival. But he had not been prepared for the sight that greeted him now.

In her white dress, Ivy looked like a queen of the Fane, wrapped in cloth woven of cobwebs and morning dew. She pulled at the metal pins that confined her hair and the lush, dark tresses spilled down her shoulders and flowed out behind her like a swathe of starless night.

She was nothing less than beautiful.

Ivy flung herself down at the base of the grandfather oak. The dog sat beside her and licked her hand. She stroked Sir Reginald's silken coat with willow-slender fingers.

"She doesn't really want me," she said, her voice catching on a sob.

Tod closed his eyes, driving away the sympathy that kindled unbidden in his breast. He cared nothing for the girl or her troubles. He had enough of his own.

He smoothed his hair and walked out of the shadows, his legs as unsteady as a foal's on its first day of life.

"Who does not want my lady?" he asked.

Ivy lifted her head and stared. Her eyes widened, for she saw him at once . . . saw him for what he was, just as Béfind had predicted. Sir Reginald jumped up and wagged his tail.

The girl stilled the dog with a touch of her hand. "Who . . . who are you?" she asked.

Tod released his breath. She was not afraid. If her voice held a tremor, it was only because he had come upon her without warning, and she had been raised by mortals. She had never seen his like before.

"Tod is the name," he said. He bowed deeply, his hair brushing the carpet of grass. "Tod is at my lady's service."

"Tod." Her cornflower-blue eyes drifted from the top of his head to his bare feet. "You are . . . not an ordinary man."

He straightened and held her gaze. This was the greatest test.

"Tod is Fane," he said. "Fane of the wood and of the hidden places."

"Fane," she repeated, biting her lip. "I do not know that word."

He wrinkled his nose. "Some have called us the Fair Folk," he said, "among other things."

Her brows dipped in thought, and then suddenly her fair face lit with understanding. "The Fair Folk. You are a fairy!"

He grimaced at the corrupted mortal word and wiggled his fingers to imitate the flutter of tiny wings. "Not like *those*."

Ivy reached for the delicate chain about her neck. "My mother . . . she told me such stories when I was little."

Tod delayed his answer, fixing his gaze on the amulet. From the fine silver chain hung an intricate knot of ancient design, its center marked by a brilliant blue stone — a talisman designed to repel any being of the Fane race.

"Stories," Tod murmured. "Stories are often wrong. Fane are real."

"So it seems." Ivy brushed the tips of her fingers across her cheek, drawing Tod's gaze with them. His heart seized as if he had been struck by a bolt of Cold Iron. "I think I always knew." She met his eyes. "Why are you here?"

He wrapped his arms about his chest for fear that he might betray himself before he had won her trust. "My lady was sad," he said.

Her lips curved in a smile that had a strange and deadly effect upon his resolve. "You came because I was sad?"

He nodded, not trusting himself to speak. She gathered her skirts about her and rose, shedding leaves from shimmering cloth. "You do not even know me," she said. "Do the Fane visit anyone who is troubled?"

"Not anyone," he whispered. "Fane avoid most humans."

"Then I must be special," she said, mocking herself.

"Aye. But Tod *does* know my lady."

"Do you? What is my name?"

"Ivy."

She pressed her cheek to the oak's rough bark. "Where did I come from?"

Dangerous ground. "From another place."

"Another place." She bowed her head, hiding behind the fall of her hair. "Was I not sad in that other place, when I was alone? Why didn't you come to me then?"

The rebuke brought heat to his face, as if he had reason to feel ashamed. "Tod did not know my lady *then*," he said. "Fane stay away from the Iron cities of men."

She laughed. "That's one name for London." She sat down again, her gown settling about her in an ivory cloud. "Have you always lived here, at Edgecott?"

"No. Tod comes from . . . from many places. But now Tod is here, to serve my lady."

Her breath sighed out, curling through his hair. "Are there others like you at Edgecott, hiding from people?"

He thought of Béfind and her sprites, but he had no need yet to lie. "Most are gone," he said, "gone away to Tir-na-Nog."

She closed her eyes. "I have heard that name before," she said. "The home of the Fair Folk, where all is light."

"Aye. There my lady would be a queen."

"Me? I'm no one's queen." Her eyes darkened to the color of a summer storm. "Sir Geoffrey is as horrid as the worst men in Seven Dials. Cordelia took me in because I remind her of her dead sister and Donal . . ." She stared toward the great house as if she might gladly topple it to the ground. "I don't belong to anyone. I should go somewhere else —"

"No." Tod patted the grass near the edge of her skirt, his hand trembling. "Stay. My lady must stay."

"For what?"

"For . . ." He exhaled, letting his fear leak away with his breath. "For me."

She turned her haunted gaze back to his. "I still don't understand. Why have you come to be my friend?"

Tod thought quickly. "Fane ways are not mortal ways."

She lay on the grass and looked through the branches at the distant stars. "Then you must tell me all about them. And about Tir-na-Nog."

Tod sat beside her and drew his knees to his chest, holding his body snug as a hedgehog in a fox's den. "The chain," he said. "Who gave it to my lady?"

She grasped the knot in her fist. "Cordelia gave me the chain," she said. "Do you know Cordelia?"

"I have seen the Hardcastle," Tod admitted.

"The Hardcastle," Ivy echoed. She opened her hand, cradling the pendant reverently. "My father gave me this."

"Your father?"

She tilted her head, lost in some memory. "I told *them* I didn't remember him," she said. "But I saw him, once, when I was still living with my mother. He didn't speak his name, but I knew who he must be."

"What was his appearance?"

"Beautiful." She polished the silver knot with her thumb. "Everything about him was beautiful."

"As is my lady."

She slipped the talisman back inside her bodice. "Thank you, Tod," she said. "I believe you *will* be my friend."

"Always."

"I won't let you forget." She sat up, suddenly alert. "Someone is coming." She retreated to stand with her back against the oak. "It's Donal. I don't want to talk to him tonight."

Tod understood her reluctance all too well. "I can hide you," he said.

"He won't see me if I stay very quiet," she said, circling to hide behind the oak's broad trunk.

Tod had no chance to argue, for Donal appeared at the crest of the hill and saw him before he could disappear. Donal descended quickly, his face set in a frown.

"Tod," he said. "I'm looking for Ivy. Have you seen her?"

The hob had never directly lied to his master until this moment. It was more difficult than he had anticipated.

"Tod has not," he said in a small voice.

Donal sighed. "She took Sir Reginald with her, and he's here," he said, bending to give the dog a quick pat. "I only hope she didn't act precipitously because of an unfortunate misunderstanding." His mouth twisted in a grimace. "Perhaps it's just as well. Keep watch for Ivy, and report to me if you find her."

"Aye," Tod said, bowing to hide his eyes.

Donal looked askance at him, his frown deepening. "Is something wrong, Tod?"

"All is well, my lord. All is well."

"Good." Donal slapped his thigh, inviting Sir Reginald to accompany him back to the house. "I'll have a word with Mrs. Hardcastle and then retire to my cottage. Good night, Tod."

"Blessed eve, my lord."

When Donal had passed over to the other side of the wold, Ivy slipped out from behind the oak. She advanced on Tod, hands on hips.

"You *know* Donal," she accused, her voice taking on the hint of an accent Tod hadn't heard before. "You called him 'my lord.'"

He bobbed his head. "Tod has known Donal for many years, as Tod knew his father."

"Then Donal must know you're Fane."

"The bond between Tod and my lord's family is an old one. There were once many such alliances. Fane lingered longest in the North, near the home of the Flemings, before they left this world for Tir-na-Nog."

"But *you* did not go to Tir-na-Nog."

"Tod stayed with Donal."

"As his servant?" Tod inclined his head. "Yet you deceived him," she added.

"Only for my lady," Tod whispered. He clasped his hands. "Tod begs that she does not speak to my lord of our meeting."

Her eyes narrowed. "Why not?"

"Tod . . . wishes this to be our secret. For my lady's sake."

"Even though we've just met?"

"Tod wishes only to help my lady find peace."

"Peace." Ivy stretched out on the grass, arms spread wide. "I won't go back to the house tonight. Will Donal miss you if you stay with me?"

No, Donal would scarcely notice. His thoughts were upon more important matters than the happiness of one small hob.

Shivering with confusion and sorrow, Tod lifted Sir Reginald into his arms and sat beside Ivy. His hatred for her had vanished in a few brief moments. The world had become a strange and frightening place, and he had never felt so alone.

Cordelia almost collided with Donal as she was ascending the hill, intent on holding the satin skirts of her evening dress above the uneven ground. They broke apart in confusion, each stammering awkward apologies that to Cordelia's ears sounded stiff and cold.

Donal bowed. "I beg your pardon, Mrs. Hardcastle," he said. "Are you quite all right?"

Cordelia knew he didn't refer merely to their near-accident. She let the silence stretch too long, and Donal moved as if to continue on his way.

"Please wait," she said. He stopped immediately, spearing her with the harrowing directness of his gaze.

"About tonight," she said carefully. "It did . . . not quite turn out as I had planned."

"So I gathered," he said with no hint of mockery in his voice. "I apologize for any part I played in the evening's difficulties."

Difficulties. How simply he spoke of disaster. "It would have been better if you had not challenged Sir Geoffrey," she said, avoiding his eyes. "I warned you that he was easily upset. He is eccentric —"

"And rude, and more than a little cruel," Donal finished.

Cordelia flushed. "I asked you to say nothing that would agitate him."

"Even when he insults you and Ivy and Theodora almost in the same breath? As ill-bred and unpolished as I may seem to you, I was not taught to stand by in silence while ladies in my company are maligned . . . even by a *gentleman*."

Cordelia winced. Donal could not have been more plain in his dislike of Sir Geoffrey, and she found it difficult to defend her father under the circumstances. Donal had acted sincerely in her defense. Sincerely and gallantly. As upset as she had been when the dinner had ended so ignominiously, she was compelled to admit that his chivalry had both flustered and pleased her out of all reason.

And was that not the root of every disturbance she had felt since his coming . . . that constant inner battle between pique and pleasure, annoyance and admiration? She simply wasn't accustomed to being protected, and Donal seemed to provoke in her a mortifying defensiveness and frightening vulnerability.

"I thank you for your concern," she said, "but I am quite accustomed to dealing with my father's —"

"Hard-heartedness?" Donal interrupted. "His utter lack of consideration for anyone but himself? Is that what you and your sister had to endure while you grew up in his care?"

Cordelia choked on an intemperate reply. Donal was not blind. But he had not known Sir Geoffrey in the days when he was whole and intent on his work, when the baronet had delighted in so many varied interests and diversions that it was all Cordelia could do to get him to eat and sleep and rest the body of which he demanded so much.

"He was not always so," she admitted. "He has grown bitter since his illness robbed him of his old vigor, and has frequently kept him confined to the estate. Surely a man as active as yourself can understand that."

"I can understand the toll such an illness must take," Donal said. His voice softened. "To give up such freedom must have been difficult indeed."

His sympathy left Cordelia with no will for further argument. She lowered her head. "You must have many questions after the things you heard tonight."

"I knew you had lost a sister," he said. "I am sorry."

"It was many years ago."

"Some sorrows do not lessen with time."

She stole a glance at his face. "You speak from experience," she said.

"We have all dealt with loss," he said. He hesitated, glancing off toward the wood. "If you would find it helpful to confide in an impartial listener . . ."

He trailed off, clearly embarrassed by his offer, and she did not answer. Perhaps he believed what her father had said, that she had taken Ivy into her home only because the girl reminded her of Lydia. She would have to disabuse him of that notion, and they would have to reach some sort of understanding regarding Ivy. The girl must learn how to deal with discourtesy — especially from persons of rank — and bear it with poise and calm if she was to make a place for herself in society.

"Your offer is most thoughtful," she said. "But I believe this day has been trying enough for both of us. I shall find Ivy and bring her back to the house —"

He raised his hand. "No need. She can come to no harm here, and she needs time alone." He took Cordelia's hand in his. "I ask you to trust me again, even if I have disappointed you in the past. She'll return tomorrow none the worse for a night away."

Cordelia stared down at their joined hands, the white of her glove against the weathered tan of his skin.

"She spoke of leaving Edgecott."

"Hotheaded talk. I will see that she is at the house before breakfast."

Cordelia slipped her fingers from his. "We will speak of this further tomorrow. I thought perhaps we might ride to a place I know that has a pleasant aspect of our river. Theodora and I will provide a picnic luncheon, if that is acceptable to you."

He smiled again, a teasing light in his eyes. "Does Theodora ride?"

Cordelia found her mouth quivering with inappropriate laughter at the image his words evoked. "No. But she is quite a hand with a dog cart, and she will be glad enough to get out of the house."

"What of Ivy?"

"Provided she returns before breakfast, I shall leave her with Mrs. Priday. It won't hurt the child to learn more of keeping a country house, and contemplate her immoderate actions at the same time."

Donal's smile faded. "Are you so certain that she will marry some lord and become mistress of a grand estate?"

"Come, let us not quarrel any more tonight. If you see Ivy on the way to the cottage, please send word to Croome."

"Put your mind at ease. She'll be back by morning."

She nodded and stepped back, half afraid and half hoping that he would take her hands again. But he only bowed and offered a quiet good evening, leaving her to wonder how such an unremarkable parting could stir her heart to an ache that would stay with her through the long night.

Ivy returned early the next morning, just as Donal had predicted. Her gown was soiled with grass stains, dirt and twigs; Cordelia's maid declared it beyond recovery, but Ivy offered neither contrite explanations nor defiant excuses for her behavior.

Cordelia refused to begin the day with another quarrel. By tacit agreement, she and Ivy postponed the inevitable discussion of the previous evening's events. If Ivy was unhappy with the prospect of staying in with the housekeeper on a lovely May morning, she thought better of expressing her displeasure.

Cordelia had enlisted Cook to pack a basket of cucumber sandwiches, boiled eggs, seasonal fruits and meat pie, which Theodora was to take in the dog cart. A groom saddled Cordelia's favorite mare, Desdemona, and a handsome chestnut gelding for Donal, but when Donal arrived he declared that the gelding was out of spirits and calmly led the stallion Boreas out of his stall.

"You intend to ride Boreas?" Cordelia asked, watching as Donal took a saddle from a nervous groom.

Donal stroked the horse's arched neck and smiled. "I assure you that Boreas and I are already good friends. He's in need of a good run."

"I suppose he confided this desire to you?"

Donal tightened the girth strap and inspected each of the stallion's hooves. "Naturally."

"He has been known to throw even the most expert riders."

"And with good reason . . . as you know, having saved him yourself." He finished his work and straightened, meeting her gaze. "He's improved immeasurably since you took him from that creature who called himself his owner."

One of the junior grooms stepped forward, twisting his cap in his hands. "It's true, ma'am," he ventured. "And since the doctor came yesterday, Boreas has calmed down considerable. It's like a miracle, it is."

"I don't doubt it," Cordelia murmured. She could see that Boreas no longer fidgeted and stamped when held on a lead, and he showed no signs of attempting to bolt. She'd left him in Gallagher's care when the stallion first arrived, but the Irishman hadn't achieved as much in months as Donal had in a single day.

Encouraged by Cordelia's response, the groom pulled a handful of grain from his pocket and offered it to Boreas, who accepted it daintily. "I've seen him run, too, ma'am," he said. "Faster than lightning, he is."

"But his racing days are over . . . aren't they, my friend?" Donal said. He leaned close to the stallion's ear, cocked his head as if listening to some whispered confidence, and laughed. "Perhaps we will, at that."

"I beg your pardon?" Cordelia said.

"Perhaps we'll have a little race of our own," Donal said, a private challenge in his eyes. "Boreas would like to show your mare his mettle."

Cordelia was spared the need to respond by the arrival of the dog cart, Theodora at the ribbons. "If you and Boreas are quite ready?" she said, accepting the groom's hand. She stepped up onto the mounting block and settled into the side saddle, modestly arranging the skirts of her riding habit. Donal swung into his saddle with natural grace and gathered the reins. He held Boreas back until Cordelia and Desdemona had taken the lead.

They rode at a sedate walk away from the stable and onto the carriage road that meandered through the park. Boreas was on his best behavior; Donal rode him with a slack rein and an easy, relaxed posture. Desdemona was positively flirtatious. The mare insisted on staying close to the stallion, which meant that Donal's knees were soon brushing Cordelia's skirts.

She made several unsuccessful bids to draw Desdemona away and finally conceded defeat. The sun was gloriously warm, the breeze thick with the scent of flowers, and Cordelia remembered other days . . . days when she had been lost to the glories of nature in lands far from England's shores.

But such memories aroused thoughts of what she had imagined in the minds of the menagerie's inhabitants, so she quickly shut them away and searched for some harmless topic of conversation.

"You have never told me what you think of our park, Dr. Fleming," she said.

He tilted his head toward her with a little smile. "It is beautiful, Mrs. Hardcastle. Beautiful, peaceful and very English."

"You make the very state of 'Englishness' sound not quite desirable."

"That was not my intention. There is no impropriety in a thing being what it was meant to be."

"I'd have thought that you would prefer to see all of this island in its original, natural state."

"To achieve such a state, one would have to wipe out several thousand years of history," Donal said, "and that would hardly be practical."

"Impractical and undesirable."

"Yet the beavers, bears and wolves might not agree. Men drove them to extinction in England hundreds of years ago."

"I pity those creatures, as I do any persecuted by men," she said. "Yet if humankind had not existed in England, you would never have been born."

"That might not have been so great a loss."

"You are too modest, Doctor. You have done much good in the world."

"Would there be a need for veterinarians if men did not misuse the animals placed in their care?" He looked away. "I should very much like to find a place that no human being has ever touched."

"And if you found such a place, you would abide there in lordly solitude?" She shook her head. "It has often seemed to me that you pretend to a misanthropy that you do not truly feel."

"Do I not?" He brooded on the path ahead of them, lips compressed.

"Your work has undoubtedly given you a dim view of your fellow men, but your compassion is no respecter of species. If it were, Ivy would not be here today."

"Nor would she be at Edgecott if not for the tragedies you have suffered."

She stiffened. "If you refer to my father's comments . . ."

"I refer to the pain you would pretend does not exist," he said, looking into her eyes with an intensity that startled her. "*You* have been badly hurt more than once, Cordelia, and not only by your father. You endured the losses of your mother, your sister, your husband. And those losses have shaped you as surely as mine have shaped me."

CHAPTER THIRTEEN

Cordelia heard Donal's words, and suddenly memories she had thought long discarded washed over her like an unstoppable tide.

"But I don't want to go!"

Lydia's voice pierced Cordelia's concentration like the strident blast of a hunter's horn. She set down the dress she was neatly folding and faced her younger sister with her anger held tightly in check.

"It will do no good to whine about it," she said. "Papa has made his decision. We are to go to India, and there is no more to be said on the subject."

"You don't care because you haven't any friends!" Lydia accused. "You spend all day at the stables and kennels, getting so dirty that no one wants to be around you."

Cordelia stiffened. "Bennet is my friend . . ."

"Only because he likes horses. He doesn't think you're at all pretty."

"I should rather be a horse than an empty-headed chit like you!"

Lydia pouted, her nine-year-old face almost losing the delicate winsomeness that had made her their mother's favorite before Eveline Amesbury's death three years before. Lydia had always been spoiled, and Papa had always deferred to her wishes . . . until now.

Now Papa said he had had enough of wasting his time in England when he could be overseas pursuing his long-deferred work as a naturalist. He had remained at Edgecott only for the sake of his daughters, pressured by Mama's relatives to give them a proper upbringing.

"I've had enough of their interference," Papa had told Cordelia when he had announced his decision. "You are twelve, old enough to care for Lydia. You'll learn far more of value away from this painted prison."

Cordelia had not disagreed. Papa was hopeless in society, and Mama had said that Cordelia took after him in her refusal to accept the rules of proper behavior. Lydia was the "little lady." And that was why Lydia didn't want to go. She intended to be just like Mama, graceful and elegant and admired by everyone in the county. Everything she wanted was here.

And I shall have to find a way to make her happy, Cordelia thought. Certainly Papa would never make the effort.

No one would care if Cordelia was happy or not. That, too, she would have to do herself.

She placed the folded dress in the trunk and

sat on the edge of the bed, clenching and un-clenching her fists. She would have been glad to leave this very instant. There would be so many new things to do and see in India, and all the other places of which Papa had spoken. Perhaps she wouldn't feel so awkward and different away from Edgecott. Perhaps Papa would like her better.

And perhaps, when they returned to England, Cordelia would finally know who she was meant to be.

She stood up and made her way to Papa's rooms. Clothing was scattered over every piece of furniture. Nothing had been packed. Papa's valet had already found another position, and it was clear that Papa would never finish if he didn't have help.

With a sigh, Cordelia began to pick up the shirts and trousers and other garments, separating them into piles for folding. If someone didn't take charge, everything would come apart again. And there was no one else to do it except Cordelia.

But not forever. Someday she would be grown up and get to choose her own life. And no one in the whole wide world would be able to stop her. . . .

"Cordelia?"

She came back to herself with a start, surprised to find Desdemona still beneath her and the soft English sunshine warming her shoulders.

"Are you quite well?" Donal asked, leaning over to peer into her face.

She cleared her mind with an effort. "Quite," she said, summoning a smile. "I was merely . . . remembering."

"They must have been most unpleasant recollections."

She glanced back at Theodora and kicked Desdemona into a smooth, swift canter. But she knew she could not outrun either Donal or his questions. He was soon beside her again, holding Boreas gently but firmly as the animal tried to surge ahead.

"I offered to be an impartial listener," he said.

"Impartial?" She exhaled sharply and commanded her muscles to unlock, well knowing that Desdemona's skittishness betrayed her. "You ask these questions because of Ivy, and I am far from certain that you can be impartial where she is concerned."

"Perhaps that is an impossibility for either one of us," he acknowledged. "But I am not only concerned for Ivy."

Cordelia counted slowly under her breath, letting the irrational anger wash through her. "Has the learned veterinarian taken it upon himself to cure the terrible afflictions he has observed at Edgecott?"

Boreas tossed his head, eyes rolling. Donal reined him to a walk, and Desdemona dropped back, ignoring the firm pressure of

Cordelia's heels.

"You have said that I pretend to a misanthropy I don't truly feel," Donal said. "If that is so, am I not permitted to be concerned for the welfare of another human being?"

"I have never doubted that you care for Ivy —"

"But not only for her."

Cordelia finally looked at him, bracing herself for the pity she feared to see in his face. There was none. But the openness of his gaze, the unflinching tenderness in his eyes, was far more devastating.

She twisted the reins about her fingers. "Dr. Fleming —"

Donal reached over and touched Desdemona's neck. The mare stopped.

"It may be against all the customs of your society," Donal said, "but I consider you a friend. And it is my understanding that friends attempt to help one another in times of need."

No glib response came to Cordelia's lips. Confusion held her mute — confusion and a strange paralysis that stripped her of all defenses.

"It is . . ." She swallowed, appalled at the hoarseness of her voice. "It is kind of you —"

"Pray do not accuse me of this indifferent 'kindness,'" he said gruffly. "Can you return my friendship?"

She was vaguely aware that Theodora had

once again caught up with them, but her cousin seemed part of another, distant world. "I can," she stammered. "I do consider you a friend, Donal."

"Then you will let me help you."

"I can manage my father. I have done so since I was a child."

"I don't doubt it. But his extraordinary degree of hostility suggests that your relationship with him has never been an easy one."

Shameful tears stung Cordelia's eyes. She blinked them away. "If we are truly to be friends," she said, "then these confidences you desire must be shared in equal measure."

She was as much saddened as relieved to see the wariness in his gaze. "I doubt you will find my past to be of much interest," he said.

The dog cart rattled up alongside them. Theodora looked at them quizzically.

"We are almost to the river," she said. "Shall I go on ahead?"

"If you don't mind, Theodora," Cordelia said.

Her cousin nodded and clucked to her horse, turning him toward the grassy bank. Cordelia watched her go. In a flat, steady voice, she told Donal of her mother's death from a lingering illness and Sir Geoffrey's decision, some years later, to take his children with him to India.

Donal guided Boreas very close, the top of his boot nearly touching her skirts. "I understand that you seldom returned to England for the next several years."

"Theodora told you."

"Only in the most general terms. Sir Geoffrey saw to your education?"

Cordelia let Desdemona's smooth rhythm lull her into a sense of detached indifference. "He hired tutors when they were available, and taught us himself when he could."

"What of a child's other needs?"

"We were never without adequate food and clothing and shelter."

"And love?"

"My . . . Sir Geoffrey is not one to display overt affection."

Donal let the silence stretch for several uncomfortable moments. "He referred to me as your latest protégé, and suggested that you attempt to dominate any male who crosses your path. Why would he say such a thing, Cordelia?"

Her throat grew disagreeably tight. "My father was a brilliant naturalist, but his brilliance . . . distracted him from attention to the daily necessities. I helped him by caring for Lydia and saw to those common details of life that he was not equipped to manage."

"And he resented his dependence upon you."

She looked away. "When we returned to England, he . . . grew even more bitter at his inability to shape his own life. That is what you saw last night."

Donal tucked his chin against his chest. "What did Sir Geoffrey do when you married Captain Hardcastle?"

"Theodora told you about my husband?"

"Only that you were married but three months before he died."

The bluntness of his words slashed at Cordelia's fragile composure. "Yes. Sir Geoffrey did not approve of James, or at least not of our marriage. He left shortly before the wedding."

"But you were happy."

Happy. Cordelia had not considered happiness a necessity of life for a very long time. "James was very free with his affections. He was generous to a fault. After Lydia died . . ."

Donal's voice roughened. "I am sorry. You must have suffered greatly at his loss."

"I was fortunate," she said. "I was able to rejoin Sir Geoffrey soon after the funeral, and there were many distractions." She realized how cold her explanation sounded and glanced at Donal to gauge his reaction. His expression was grim.

"If your curiosity is quite satisfied," she said brusquely, "perhaps you might tell me something of your youth and background."

Boreas danced sideways and half-reared, snorting through flared nostrils. "What do you wish to know?" Donal asked.

"Where were you born? What is your family like? How did you come to be a veterinarian?"

Donal gently brought Boreas back under control. "I was born in Westmorland. My parents were separated when I was an infant, but were reunited by the time I was six. They still live in Westmorland, along with my younger brothers, one of whom is married."

"A most concise biography," Cordelia said dryly, "but it seems that you have omitted your entire childhood. Surely it was difficult for you if your parents were separated so early in your life?"

Boreas bobbed his head up and down. Donal sighed. "When I was born, my parents were not married."

His words fell like a thunderclap. Cordelia jerked on the reins, confusing poor Desdemona. She eased her grip and waited for her heartbeat to slow.

"I am sorry," she said. "I didn't mean —"

"I'm not ashamed of being a bastard," he said. "In your circles it may be a scandal, but it was not a matter of importance at Hartsmere."

"Hartsmere?" she repeated, grasping for a less disconcerting topic.

"The . . . village where my parents live."

Cordelia didn't recognize the name, but she had seldom traveled so far into the north. She knew that birth to unwed mothers occurred quite frequently in the countryside, in spite of stern sermons by churchmen and the disapproval of good society. Certainly she had seen plentiful examples of such circumstances in many parts of the world.

But Donal's parents must have been somewhat educated, or their child would not have been likely to harbor the ambition to become a veterinarian.

"It might relieve you to know that they had intended to be wed," he said, breaking into her thoughts. "A misunderstanding came between them, but later they rectified the error. My brothers are quite legitimate. We were all raised identically."

"Your parents are both still alive?"

"And well." He smiled with such affection that Cordelia knew he truly adored his family.

"I'm glad." Her throat constricted on emotions she dared not examine. "Did you live with your mother before their reunion?"

Boreas planted his hooves and stopped in mid stride. Donal stared at a point between the stallion's ears, and after a few moments the horse began to walk again.

"I was given away at birth, without the knowledge of my mother," Donal said. "I was fostered in Ireland, among people who were interested only in the money they received from the man who had arranged the adoption."

No expression of dismay seemed adequate

to address the rigid dispassion with which Donal spoke those words. "They were cruel to you," Cordelia said.

He shrugged. "They were poor and ignorant. One old man was kind to me when I was very young, and taught me my letters. He died when I was five, and after that I was left to do whatever I pleased."

"That is no way for a child to live," she said.

"I had friends among the animals," he said, his voice losing some of its harshness. "They understood me, and I them. When my mother found me and brought me home to Hartsmere, I was given everything I had lacked. My father soon joined her, and I was happy."

Cordelia knew that there must be far more he left unsaid, but she comprehended how difficult it had been for him to reveal so much. He was not by nature a man much given to confidences in others, and yet when he did speak it was with complete honesty.

"Now I understand why you took Ivy from the streets," she said.

"It was purest chance that I found her."

"Pray do not belittle your generosity." She smiled at him warmly. "Yet I see why you chose to heal animals. They must have seemed far more worthy than the people you had known."

"I was blessed with a natural gift," he said. "It would have been wrong not to use it. As it would be wrong for Ivy not to make use of the natural talents she possesses."

Cordelia's smile faltered. "I intend to cultivate her intelligence and spirit, each within its proper boundaries."

"And if she rejects those boundaries?"

"I see no reason why she should, if we both encourage her to accept the benefits of self-control by setting our own examples."

"Self-control is more difficult when one is afraid of abandonment."

"Abandonment? I would never —"

"Of course you would not, but Ivy must be feeling insecure about her place here after last night's revelations."

"I can assure you that I did not choose to bring Ivy to Edgecott because of my late sister."

"Tell me about Lydia."

She closed her eyes, dreading the power of her reawakened memories. It was so easy to go back to that terrible day. . . .

"She is very ill," the doctor said, rising from his chair beside Lydia's bed. "She suffers from a severe infection in the scratches on her hand and arm. I have done what I can, but her body is extremely weak."

Papa sat down heavily, his face pale with shock. "What are her chances?"

The doctor shook his head and glanced from Cordelia to the bed. "It would be best if we continued this discussion outside."

Papa followed the doctor out of the bungalow,

leaving Cordelia alone with the smell of sickness and guilt. She fetched a clean cloth, wet it at the wash stand and gently draped the cloth over Lydia's hot brow. There was nothing of beauty left in Lydia's face now; her eyes were deeply sunken, her lips cracked, her hair soaked with perspiration.

Cordelia dropped her head into her hands, wondering why the tears would not come. She should be weeping. She should be tearing her hair and beating her breast, knowing that she alone was responsible for Lydia's illness.

It had been such a small and common thing, their quarrel: Lydia complaining once again of her hatred for their life of wandering, her desire to return to a normal existence in England . . . Cordelia impatient with her sister's incessant lamentations.

"Why will Papa not take us home?" Lydia had demanded. "The longer we remain away from England, the greater chance that we shall be ruined for good society." She dragged her brush through the wealth of her honey-blond hair and examined the strands caught in the bristles. "Papa cares nothing for the proprieties. Everyone at home will think we have become complete savages!"

Cordelia was in no mood to indulge her sister's self-pity. "I have no desire to go back," she said coolly.

"That is because it's already too late for you," Lydia said. "You're eighteen. You'll never be a real lady." She smirked. "You like being a savage, running about in the forest and villages. I've seen you sneak away at night, dressed in men's clothing. Where do you go, Delia? Do you have a lover?"

"Lydia!"

"You think you can have everything you want, while I have nothing. It won't be that way forever. I despise this place —"

"Then why don't you leave?"

Lydia had flounced away, her face pale with anger. But Cordelia hadn't believed that Lydia would ever take her scornful advice. . . .

Papa burst into the room, his hair mussed and his face drawn with grief.

"What have you done?" he cried.

Cordelia rose, her legs trembling beneath her. "Papa . . ."

"I left Lydia in your care. She is only fifteen!"

Cordelia stared at the floor. He was right, of course. Lydia was her responsibility, but she had chosen to go out that night, out to the native town where she could be free for a little while, where no one knew her for anything but a local boy in loose and slightly dirty clothing. She had gone to forget how much she dreaded the prospect of returning to England, where there would be no more freedom ever again.

She had failed to anticipate that Lydia, who so disdained everything that wasn't proper and civilized and English, would defy her own convictions and flee to the market . . . that a savage wild animal would escape its captors at the worst possible moment. . . .

"She may die," Papa said, "because you abandoned your duty."

"I am sorry, Papa . . ."

"You can't be trusted. You're selfish and wild, just like —" He broke off, his body seeming to shrink before Cordelia's eyes. "I should never have taken you from England."

"No, Papa. It wasn't —"

But he fell into a chair and refused to speak again. Cordelia put him to bed and spent the rest of the night by Lydia's side.

Two nights later Lydia was dead.

Cordelia opened her eyes. Donal was gazing at her face, his lips slightly parted.

"I am deeply sorry for your loss," he said.

She worked her hands on the reins, unsure of how much she had said while she sojourned in the past. Evidently it had been enough.

"Thank you," she said.

They rode for several minutes in silence. "You said that Lydia's injuries were caused by an animal?" Donal asked.

"Yes."

He continued to stare with those shadowed green eyes, drowning her in memories of vine-clad forests and the scent of tropical blossoms. "Your father blamed you for her death."

"It was many years ago."

Donal reined Boreas close and covered her hand with his. "Then why do you punish yourself for being human?"

Cordelia snatched her hand away, dizzy with shock. Desdemona nickered. Cordelia looked up to find that they had reached the riverbank, where Theodora had already spread out a blanket beneath a spreading ash. The timing could not have been more fortunate. Cordelia let Desdemona have her head, and the mare carried her toward the blessed sanctuary of the river and her cousin's company. She dismounted beside the water.

Donal slid from Boreas's back and loosed the stallion to join the mare, watching as Cordelia feigned a single-minded fascination with a cluster of flowers growing on the riverbank. She had been strongly affected by his questions, and he could hardly blame her. His own heart was pounding out a tattoo like a shaman's drum. He had pushed too close to Cordelia's hidden pain, and his own.

Fool, he thought. *What good comes of your prying? You've done nothing but added to her unhappiness. She undoubtedly wishes you in perdition, or at least a thousand miles from Gloucestershire.*

Just as he wished himself away, in some lost and unpeopled place where this morass of human emotions had no power to entrap him.

He left Cordelia to recover her composure and joined Theodora on the blanket, making certain that his voice was quite steady before he spoke.

"You have chosen a perfect spot, Theodora," he said with a slight bow.

She smiled and offered him a plate. "How was your ride?"

"Very pleasant." The untruth came too easily for comfort, and he was certain that Theodora saw through it.

"I hope you like cucumber sandwiches," she said, sparing him further questions. "If you will fetch the wine from the river, you may have some of Cook's famous Madeira cake."

Donal did as Theodora asked. He and Cordelia avoided each other by unspoken agreement, and soon the three of them had settled down to the generous repast.

Cordelia gave her full attention to her meal, eating with exaggerated daintiness. Theodora watched both of them under her dark lashes. Donal was under no illusion that she had failed to note the intensity of his exchanges with Cordelia. He suspected that the older woman was near bursting at the seams with speculation, but she knew well how to keep her thoughts to herself.

The facade of peaceful normality continued as the cousins spoke in desultory tones of the latest fashion in bodice sleeves and the making of aromatic sachets. One might have assumed that Cordelia had never ventured beyond the confines of a typical Englishwoman's narrow sphere. It seemed that was what she would have the world believe.

"I have heard that Shapford has been taken for the summer," Theodora said, waking Donal from his half doze. "Some foreign countess . . . Russian, I believe. Have you any news of her, Delia?"

Cordelia arched a brow in surprise. "This is the first I have heard of it," she said. "Russian, you say? That is one country Sir Geoffrey and I never visited. We shall call on her once she has had a chance to settle in."

"I should enjoy it," Theodora said. "But we must be boring Dr. Fleming with all this talk of women's affairs."

Donal blinked in the dappled shade and sat up. Theodora reclined comfortably against the ash's trunk, her dove-gray skirts billowing about her like a mass of undisciplined rain clouds. Far from being relaxed by the pleasant warmth and the lazy drone of bees in the meadow, Cordelia sat stiffly upright as if some old governess were examining her for the tiniest lapse in conduct.

"I brought my volume of Tennyson's poetry with me," Theodora said, removing a pair of spectacles from a small case in her reticule. "Shall I read?"

"By all means," Donal said.

Theodora opened the well-thumbed book. "Have you a favorite?"

"My familiarity with Tennyson is not all it might be. You choose."

She frowned over her spectacles and selected a page. "I believe you will like this one," she said.

> "Oh blackbird! sing me something well:
> While all the neighbors shoot thee round,
> I keep smooth plats of fruitful ground,
> Where thou mayst warble, eat, and dwell."

She continued reading, lending pathos to the poet's complaint that the blackbird, though given the freedom to roam "the range of lawn and park," refused to sing.

> "Take warning! he that will not sing
> While yon sun prospers in the blue,
> Shall sing for want, ere leaves are new,
> Caught in the frozen palms of Spring."

Theodora set the book in her lap and met Donal's gaze. "Is it not evocative?" she asked.

Donal could see Cordelia out of the corner of his eye. She showed no sign of having connected the titular bird with herself, and yet Donal couldn't help but believe that Theodora had deliberately chosen that particular poem for a reason. Like the blackbird, Cordelia was capable of music that she would or could not share with the world, for all her works of charity. She kept her truest song locked within her heart.

"Shall I read another?" Theodora asked. She turned the pages. "*The Lotos-Eaters.*"

> " 'Courage!' he said, and pointed toward the land,
> 'This mounting wave will roll us shoreward soon.'
> In the afternoon they came unto a land
> In which it seemed always afternoon.
> All round the coast the languid air did swoon,
> Breathing like one that hath a weary dream.
> Full-faced above the valley stood the moon;
> And like a downward smoke, the slender stream
> Along the cliff to fall and pause and fall did seem."

Donal recognized the story of Odysseus and his crew's visit to the exotic land of the Lotos-eaters, where his crew ate of seductive fruit. After they had partaken of the gift,

> "They sat them down upon the yellow sand,
> Between the sun and moon upon the shore;
> And sweet it was to dream of Fatherland,
> Of child, and wife, and slave; but evermore
> Most weary seem'd the sea, weary the oar,
> Weary the wandering fields of barren foam.

Then some one said, 'We will return no
  more;'
And all at once they sang, 'Our island home
Is far beyond the wave; we will no longer
  roam.' "

Theodora closed the book and folded up
her spectacles. Donal shifted uncomfortably.
Unless Cordelia had told her, she could have
no idea that he intended to leave England,
his "island home," once he was finished with
his work at Edgecott. Was it toward Cordelia
to whom the poem was directed? If so, it was
a secret message that Donal did not yet understand.

Theodora obviously had no intention of ad-
dressing his silent questions. She began to
gather the scraps of their luncheon, repack-
ing the utensils and plates into their basket.
Cordelia got up to saddle Desdemona, and
Donal followed to assist her.

There was a brittleness to Cordelia's motions, a tension that told Donal he wasn't
alone in his reaction to the poems. He tightened the mare's girth strap without speaking
and called Boreas. The stallion bobbed his
head.

"I know," Donal said, scratching the horse
between his ears. "You've been still too long."

"Then perhaps we'll have that race you suggested," Cordelia said behind him.

He turned to see her face flushed and her

eyes feverishly bright with challenge. Desdemona gave a piercing whinny, and Boreas rolled his eyes.

"Well?" Cordelia said. "Martin said you had worked wonders with Boreas. Or have you lost your nerve?"

Donal glanced toward Theodora. "Your cousin —"

"— can find her own way back to Edgecott," Cordelia finished. She led Desdemona beside a flat stone and mounted with far more speed than grace. "Are you ready?"

Donal jumped onto Boreas's back and collected the reins, drawn into the ferment of Cordelia's extraordinary mood.

"On my mark," Cordelia said. "Ready, steady . . . go!"

CHAPTER FOURTEEN

Bennet Wintour, Viscount Inglesham, watched the dark bay stallion race up the lane at breakneck speed, its long legs flying, and did his best to ignore the rider so expertly balanced in the saddle.

"It's just as I told you, m'lord," Gallagher said. "That devil beast is as fast as they come. He wasn't worth a ha' penny when the Missus brought him here, but since the animal doctor came . . ."

The animal doctor. Inglesham scowled and slapped his gloves against his hand. He'd taken a dislike to Fleming from the moment they'd met in London, but he'd never expected to meet him again. Far less had he dreamed that the fellow would turn up at Edgecott, favored by Cordelia and eating at her table as if he were her equal.

And that wasn't the worst of it. Not by half.

It was Sir Geoffrey's scrawled letter that had brought Inglesham back to Edgecott in so untimely a fashion, but he had not found

Cordelia available when he arrived. Oh, no. She had been out with Fleming on a "picnic," of all things, and now she galloped back to the stable like an Amazon, hot on Fleming's heels.

She was *laughing.* Cordelia, who seldom had more than a formal smile for him, a friend and neighbor she'd known all her life. The man she was to marry.

"I see you don't like him either, m'lord," Gallagher said. "He's an upstart, that one."

Inglesham looked askance at the groom. "If what you say is true, he managed what you could not. He tamed that animal and made it run for him."

"Aye." Gallagher turned his head to spit and stopped at the expression on Inglesham's face. "There ain't many better with horses than me, that's certain. But Fleming . . ." He made a furtive warding gesture with one hand. "What he did with that beast ain't normal, your lordship." He lowered his voice. "I've watched him. We know *his* kind in Ireland. He's —"

Inglesham never heard the rest of the groom's opinion, for Boreas dashed into the stableyard, spraying gravel with his hooves, and slid to a halt. Fleming was smiling as he twisted in the saddle to watch Cordelia ride up behind him. Her hair had come loose from its pins and straggled about her shoulders; even from several yards away Inglesham could see that her eyes shone with excitement. She didn't notice Inglesham at all.

"Very well," she said, still laughing and breathless, "I concede the victory to Boreas. And only to him, mind you!"

Fleming inclined his head. "On behalf of Boreas, I accept your gracious concession." He bent over the stallion's neck and whispered in its ear. Boreas walked to Cordelia's horse, nuzzling the mare while Fleming gazed at Cordelia with far too much familiarity. He spoke in a voice too soft for Inglesham to hear. Cordelia's fair skin flushed with pleasure.

Inglesham tossed his gloves to the ground and strode into the yard, carefully shaping his expression to one of pleasant neutrality.

"Ah," he said, "Mrs. Hardcastle. I trust you had a pleasant ride?"

Her head snapped about in surprise. "Lord Inglesham!" Her flush deepened as Gallagher appeared to help her dismount. With hardly a glance at Fleming she began to rearrange her hair, belatedly aware of how wild she must appear to her servants and intended.

"Lord Inglesham," she repeated, smoothing her skirts with nervous hands, "I did not know you were at Edgecott."

He bowed. "Alas, I arrived after you had already left."

She attempted a smile. "I'm sorry to have

missed you. I thought you were in London.
. . ."

"My business concluded more quickly than I anticipated." He looked past her to Fleming, who had dismounted and held Boreas's reins in a white-knuckled fist. "I see that you were not without company in my absence."

Cordelia followed his gaze. "No. I . . . Theodora is returning in the dog cart. Dr. Fleming felt that Boreas might benefit from a hard run." She gestured toward Fleming. "I believe I introduced you in London. Lord Inglesham, you must remember Donal Fleming. . . ."

"How can I forget the extraordinary circumstances of our first meeting?" Inglesham said. He smiled coolly at Fleming, remembering their brief conversation outside the house when the man had first arrived. It was clear that Fleming remembered the exchange as well, for all that he had failed to heed Inglesham's advice about keeping to a servant's place. "Mrs. Hardcastle has informed me that you were working as a consultant at the Zoological Gardens."

Fleming nodded brusquely. "I was."

"And now you are here in our quiet little county. You must find it very dull, Doctor, to spend your time taming horses instead of wild elephants."

Fleming loosened his grip on the stallion's reins and shifted his weight, settling into a deceptively relaxed posture that hinted of both self-assurance and insolence.

"If you have any elephants at hand, Lord Inglesham," he said, "I will be glad to do what I can for them."

"I shall keep that in mind." Inglesham flicked a bit of dust from his lapel. "I can see that I must find you more engaging employment, Fleming, so that you will not feel compelled to fill up your hours performing tasks that are beyond the scope of your profession."

Cordelia stepped between the men with the subtlest of motions. "Dr. Fleming has been very ably looking after my menagerie," she said.

"Of course," Inglesham said. He walked around Cordelia to Boreas, stopping just out of reach of the stallion's teeth. "Yet I'm told that he has also done remarkable work with this fine fellow . . . isn't that so, Gallagher?"

The groom, who stood nearby with Cordelia's mare, cast an uneasy glance at Fleming. "Aye, your lordship."

"It was only a matter of simple kindness and respect," Fleming said. "Even so, any stallion is somewhat unpredictable. You might wish to move away, sir."

Inglesham barked a laugh. "I know horses, Fleming. They merely require a firm hand and a clear understanding of their place in the world."

Fleming's eyes darkened. Boreas arched his neck and lunged at Inglesham, teeth bared to bite. The stallion's muzzle passed within an inch of Inglesham's shoulder.

"Spirited indeed," he said, brushing at his sleeve. "But if the brute ever offers harm to Mrs. Hardcastle —"

"Boreas was a perfect gentleman with me, Lord Inglesham," Cordelia cut in. She looked toward the lane that curved away into the park, where a cloud of dust heralded the arrival of a horse and carriage. "Ah, I believe Miss Shipp is returned." She signaled to Gallagher, who edged closer to the stallion as if he were approaching a venomous serpent. "If you gentlemen will go ahead to the house, we shall follow presently."

"With your permission, Mrs. Hardcastle," Fleming said, "I'll stay to look after Boreas."

Cordelia hesitated, and Inglesham waited to see if she would insist that this ill-mannered provincial accompany his betters. Her common sense reasserted itself, however, and she merely nodded. "As you wish, Doctor," she said formally. "Thank you for your escort."

"It was my honor to be of assistance," he said, and led Boreas away without another word. Cordelia gazed after him a little too long and then faced Inglesham with an uncharacteristically bright smile.

"I am sorry to have kept you waiting," she

said, starting in the direction of the house. "If only I had known you were returning so soon . . ."

Inglesham offered his arm. "Think no more of it, my dear. I did not expect you to pine away in my absence, after all . . . though I do wonder what Fleming has done to stand so high in your favor."

She stopped abruptly. "You refer to our ride? It was all quite proper, I assure you."

"I've no doubt of it."

She searched his eyes, frowning faintly. "I told you before Dr. Fleming's arrival that I had employed him for an extended consultation and treatment of my menagerie."

"I remember."

"I can see that you do not approve —"

"Not approve?" He patted her hand. "My dear, I know how fond you are of your animals. I would not begrudge you anything that adds to your happiness." He resumed walking, tucking her arm more closely in the crook of his arm. "I am nonetheless surprised that you would choose a common veterinarian, your employee, as a companion for your leisure hours. Surely you can find company more appropriate to your position as a baronet's daughter. Lady Margaret is a most amiable neighbor, and Mrs. Kenworthy has indicated to me that she would enjoy more frequent visits to Edgecott. Julia Whitehurst sets the fashion in London, and she would be glad to advise you. . . ."

"Lady Margaret," Cordelia said with a touch of scorn, "is much too hard on her horses. I always feel as if Mrs. Kenworthy is hoping to find that I have acquired some barbaric native customs during my travels, and as for Julia Whitehurst . . . she would rather spend all her time before a mirror than with any other woman!"

Inglesham held up his hand. "Pax," he said. "If none of those ladies suit you, I can introduce you to a dozen more. You really should involve yourself in society's pleasures, my dear. There is no reason why you couldn't make a success of it. Nothing prevents you but your own stubbornness."

Cordelia fell silent for several moments. "I surmise by your speech that you deem my success in society more important than the charitable work in which I am currently engaged."

He swung her about so that she was halfway in his arms. "How many times have we discussed this, Cordelia? You know that is not so." He took her chin in his hand. "I admire your work tremendously, as I admire your intelligence and fortitude. Why else should I be so impatient to marry you?"

He saw uncertainty in her eyes, the passage of thoughts she refused to consider because they were unworthy. No, Cordelia was no fool, but he knew how much she longed to be ordinary, accepted, safe in a life of domestic contentment that would erase the irregularities of her youth once and for all.

"We will be happy, Cordelia," he said. "We are perfectly suited. You will go on with your charitable ventures in complete freedom, and I will finally have the anchor I have lacked all these years."

She gazed up at him. Her lips parted. He bent to kiss her, and for a moment he thought she responded. But then her body grew rigid and she pushed him away gently, grasping his coat sleeves with her gloved hands.

"You know that I care for you, Bennet," she said. "But I've been in England less than a year. When I am settled —"

"You will never be settled until you accept the life and position you were meant to have," he said, suppressing his impatience. "And what of this girl you have taken in? You wrote that she came from a disadvantaged background but showed great potential for reformation with the appropriate training and influence. Would such an unfortunate not benefit from the example of a suitable marriage set before her?"

Cordelia bit her lip. "Of course." She sighed. "I have not been entirely honest with you about Ivy. You have not seen her since her arrival . . ."

"No." He studied her face. "What is it, Delia? What is this talk of dishonesty?"

"I did not intend it," she said. "I simply thought it would be easier to explain if you saw her as she is now, not as you remember her."

"You speak in riddles, my dear."

She met his gaze. "Very well. To put it bluntly, the girl I have taken in is the one who attempted to steal your purse in Covent Garden."

He stared at her, genuinely startled for the space of a heartbeat. "That street urchin?"

"Yes." She took a deep breath. "The tale is rather complicated. You see, the girl was in Covent Garden because Dr. Fleming had just rescued her from Seven Dials and brought her to his hotel beside the market."

"Seven Dials?" He shook his head. "You are saying that the girl and Fleming are connected?"

"As peculiar as it seems, yes. Dr. Fleming came upon her in the rookeries while he was returning to his hotel from the Zoological Gardens." She continued with an outlandish tale about Fleming taking the girl back to Yorkshire, where Cordelia had met her again when she'd gone to seek Fleming's advice about her menagerie.

"The girl was living with him?" Inglesham asked.

She gave him a wary glance. "He tried to settle her with a local family, but she had run away from them on the day I arrived. That was when I discovered that Ivy was not at all what she had appeared to be in London. Dr. Fleming had been equally deceived. We had assumed her to be a child of no more than twelve years, but it soon became clear that she was a young woman . . . one who, at some time in her earlier life, had enjoyed a happier existence than the one she knew in Seven Dials."

"What sort of existence?"

"Ivy professed no certain memories of her past save for a few scattered images, but her speech changed dramatically when I questioned her." Cordelia's eyes lit with enthusiasm. "She is of good breeding, Bennet. She must have been born to parents who saw to her early education and taught her decent behavior before some tragedy compelled her to live on the streets."

"Remarkable," Inglesham murmured. "So naturally you saw it as your duty to restore the poor girl to something of her former privilege."

"Yes. It is not as if I do not possess ample resources for such an undertaking. When you see her . . ." She smiled. "She is extraordinary . . . graceful and charming when she puts her mind to it. She will truly blossom with care and discipline."

Inglesham almost felt sorry for the girl. "You know nothing of her parents?"

"Not yet, but I hope to conduct further

inquiries in the near future." She touched his arm. "As promising as she is, Ivy is still a bit wild. That is why Dr. Fleming's presence is helpful. He was the first to win her trust, and she regards him as a friend."

"And you, Cordelia?" he said. "Do you also consider him a 'friend,' even though you pay his wages?"

She stumbled a little, clearly taken aback by his abrupt change of subject. "I respect his skills, as I respect those of Croome or Priday or any one of our farmers. They are no less worthy simply because they must earn their livings."

They walked for a while without speaking, and Inglesham spent the time enumerating all the things that would change once they were married. Edgecott and its lands would come under his control, though Sir Geoffrey would continue to live in the house. The excess of servants Cordelia kept on out of her excessive beneficence would be pared down to a minimum so that their wages could be more suitably employed in paying off Inglesham's gambling debts and financing future bets. Her menagerie would be sold to wealthy collectors, and improvements to the village and farms would be sharply curtailed.

But none of that could occur until Cordelia accepted his proposal, which she had put off yet again. As ridiculous as it seemed, a country veterinarian had become a rival for

Cordelia's attention, and he must be got rid of as quickly as possible.

As for the girl . . .

"Ivy!" Cordelia said. Inglesham looked up to find that they had reached the house, and an apparition in pale blue satin was coming toward them on invisible feet that seemed to skim weightlessly over the ground.

The girl stopped short when she saw Inglesham, and he had ample time to study her face. For a moment he couldn't believe that this was the filthy urchin from Covent Garden. Cordelia's warnings hadn't been nearly sufficient to prepare him for the transformation.

Ivy was a rare beauty, with creamy skin and silky black hair eminently suitable as a subject for poetry. Her figure, even hidden beneath corsets and voluminous skirts, was exquisite. Her blue eyes actually deserved the old saws about bottomless pools and azure skies.

"Lord Inglesham," Cordelia said, oblivious to his fascination, "this is Ivy. Ivy, Viscount Inglesham."

Inglesham strode forward and bowed with a theatrical flourish. "Miss Ivy," he said. "I am delighted to meet you."

The girl's brows drew together, and she clutched at something hung from a chain about her neck. "You . . . you are the man who wanted to send me to the rozzers," she said.

He laughed. "You were right, Cordelia. She is charming." He gifted Ivy with his most persuasive smile. "You need have no fear of me, my dear," he said. "I can see I made a mistake."

"Because I'm wearing pretty clothes and speak like a lady?"

"Ivy!" Cordelia reproved.

"No, don't scold her," Inglesham said. "She has every right to dislike me." He dropped to one knee before Ivy. "My lady," he said solemnly, "will you not forgive this foolish knight, and accept his service?"

Ivy stared into his face. Her lips flirted with a smile. "Perhaps I will," she said. She held out one hand and he took it in his, kissing the dainty fingers. He got to his feet.

"Now that we are friends," he said, "you must tell me all about your adventures and how you came to be at Edgecott," he said.

She glanced at Cordelia. "Cor . . . Mrs. Hardcastle must have told you," she said.

"Only a very small part of the story," he said. "What is that you hold in your hand?"

She looked down distractedly and opened the fingers that still clutched the end of the chain. An intricate, knotted design made of polished silver gleamed against her bodice. Inglesham had never seen its like before.

But he had *heard* of it. . . .

"Cursed bitch had black hair — what you could see of it — and blue eyes." Kemsley smacked his lips, swollen as they were, and his voice thickened with rage and thwarted lust. "B'God, she was an armful. Never thought she'd fight back . . ." He coughed and wiped blood from his mouth.

"If you want her caught," Inglesham said, "you'd better give me a better description. She probably lives close to the tavern where you found her."

"Aye." Kemsley tried to sit up and moaned, falling back again. "Thought she was young when I first saw her . . . maybe fourteen. Up close I could see she was nearer eighteen. But still fresh enough."

Fresh enough, Inglesham thought, to suit a man who preferred his conquests barely out of childhood. "Were there any other distinguishing characteristics?"

Kemsley cursed. "After I offered a generous sum to tup her, her voice changed. She spoke just like a lady, as if she'd been raised in Grosvenor Square. Can you credit it? She said 'I'd rather share my bed with a hog.'"

Inglesham doubted that the girl's peculiarities of speech would lead him to her. "What did she wear?"

"What do any of them wear? A dress. Mostly rags, but it fit in the right places. And she had a thing around her neck."

"What thing?"

"A silver locket. No . . . a pendant. Shaped like one of them twisted Irish designs that has no beginning or end. It had a blue gem right in the middle of it." His face paled, and his breath came short. "Not something a common drab would be wearing, but she defended it the way an abbess guards an untouched virgin in a bawdyhouse."

Inglesham rose from the bedside. "I'll send for a physician, Kemsley. You stay in bed, and leave this female to me."

"See that you find her," Kemsley said, breaking into another fit of coughing. "I'll make her pay."

Inglesham snapped back to the present, knowing that only seconds had passed while he remembered his last conversation with his old friend and crony. He smiled at Ivy, murmured some compliment and moved away, still trying to make sense of the bizarre coincidence.

He had never found the girl who had inexplicably done Kemsley so much damage, and Kemsley had never made her pay. He had died the next day of apoplexy . . . brought on, the physician claimed, as a result of injuries he had received in a brawl with opponents who had obviously been much larger and stronger than himself.

Inglesham had accepted Kemsley's death with mild regret and thought no more about the irregular circumstances of his demise. He certainly hadn't connected the child in Covent Garden with Kemsley's vague description of his assailant. If she'd been wearing the pendant, it hadn't been visible.

Now it was. And while it seemed possible that there were other black haired, blue-eyed girls of indeterminate age in London who had mastered both a rookery drawl and the refined accents of the educated and privileged, Inglesham doubted that any of them possessed jewelry of the precise type Kemsley had described on his deathbed.

There was no proof, of course. The victim was dead, and even if he had lived, he would never have admitted to the authorities that a slip of a girl had hurt him so badly while he was engaged in less than respectable activities. Inglesham himself couldn't imagine how Ivy, fine-boned and ethereal, could possibly have overcome so large and portly a gentleman.

Nevertheless, incredible as it all appeared, Inglesham had a strong suspicion that he might find Kemsley's tale extremely useful in the very near future.

He turned back to Ivy and Cordelia, who were conversing with a certain stiff formality as they waited for him to rejoin them.

"I apologize, ladies," he said. "I was momentarily distracted by thoughts of unfinished business." He smiled at Ivy, who returned his smile with a subtly flirtatious lowering of dark lashes. He offered one arm to her and the other to Cordelia, and together they went into the house.

The evening meal was simple and hearty in the manner Cordelia generally preferred, lacking the finer touches Inglesham enjoyed at his own estate. Fleming failed to put in an appearance, so Inglesham amused himself by lavishing attention on Ivy under the pretext of offering recompense for his former poor judgment of her character.

She responded with increasing interest, preening at his flattery like a sleek and self-satisfied cat. If she was as vicious as Kemsley claimed, she was certainly capable of wildly contradictory behavior. And though she plainly could adapt herself to any circumstance and had been clever enough to survive where many would not, she was also prey to a very common female weakness: her head could easily be turned by a resourceful gentleman's charms.

Not long after dinner Inglesham excused himself and strolled out to the stables. He found Gallagher smoking in the stable yard, chatting with the other grooms. Gallagher straightened and tossed the cigarette away when he saw Inglesham. The other men scattered.

"We never did finish our conversation today, Gallagher," Inglesham said, pulling a pair of cigars from a silver case tucked in his coat. "You were about to tell me something about Fleming."

Gallagher scratched his ill-shaven chin. "I don't seem to recall, your lordship."

Inglesham offered a cigar to the groom, who took it quickly enough. "Allow me to remind you. You said that what he'd done with Boreas wasn't normal. You said you'd been watching him, and that you knew 'his kind' in Ireland." He struck a match and lit Gallagher's cigar. "You never told me exactly what 'kind' he is."

Gallagher took a long pull on the cigar and shuffled his feet. "I . . . it's somethin' only an Irishman could understand, your lordship."

"Why don't you let me be the judge of that?"

"Well . . ." Gallagher looked right and left and hunched his head between his shoulders. "I've seen him talkin' to the horses, me lord, as if they was people. They do things for him they won't for anyone else, not even me."

"Eccentric, to be sure," Inglesham said, "but hardly inexplicable."

Gallagher stubbed out the cigar with an angry jerk. "I couldn't get near Boreas, but *he* tamed him like the beast was a newborn lamb. And today, after you left . . ." He wet his lips. "He talked to the horses again. He was talking about you, your lordship."

"He was gossiping with the horses about me? How very mortifying."

"He was . . . he was casting spells on them, to make them do whatever he commands."

He met Inglesham's eyes with half-cringing defiance. "He ain't human, me lord. He's born of the Fair Folk, or my name ain't Brian Gallagher."

"Are you telling me that he is a fairy? Is that the word?"

"The Tuatha Dé Danann, we call 'em. They say there ain't many left, even in Ireland. But some can take on any shape, even that of a man, and —"

Inglesham shook his head. "I've no time for children's stories, Gallagher. If this is all you have . . ."

"No, your lordship." The Irishman's face twisted with cunning. "If you'll come with me. . . ."

He set off for the stable block, and with a sense of keen disappointment Inglesham followed. Fairies, indeed. That was what he got for listening to the ravings of a superstitious Irishman.

He waited impatiently while Gallagher entered one of the stalls and came out with a chestnut gelding Inglesham often rode when he visited Edgecott. The groom quickly saddled the beast and stood near its head.

"Try it, your lordship," he said softly.

"What are you playing at now?" Inglesham snapped.

"You've ridden Bumblebee a hundred times," Gallagher said. "You should have no problem now."

Scowling in annoyance, Inglesham approached the gelding. It shied away, ears flattened. Inglesham snatched at the reins and tried again. Bumblebee jerked up his head and lashed out with his hind legs, narrowly missing Inglesham's arm.

Inglesham swore. "Give me a crop," he said. "I'll teach the cursed nag its manners —"

Before he finished speaking, Gallagher was up on the gelding's back, neat as you please. The horse didn't so much as twitch, but when Inglesham came near it bared its teeth in pure malice.

"Shall we try another mount, your lordship?" Gallagher asked, sliding to the ground. "Betsy is our gentlest. Even a child in leading strings could ride her."

Without waiting for Inglesham's reply, the groom took Bumblebee back to his stall and returned with a sleepy dun cob. The instant she saw Inglesham, she lifted her head, rolled her eyes and began fighting Gallagher's grip on her lead like an unbroken filly.

"You see?" Gallagher said, breathless from the struggle. "Visit the stalls, Lord Inglesham. None of the horses will let you near. Fleming did this."

Snorting with disgust, Inglesham did as the groom suggested. Gallagher was right. Whenever he drew near a stall, its occupant shied and reared as if its very life was threatened. His fingers were nearly bitten off by the fat little pony in the loose box, and even the stable cats hissed and arched their backs.

"He's fey, Fleming is," Gallagher muttered when they returned to the yard. "If he can bespell animals, your lordship, why not people?"

Inglesham hardly heard him. "It shouldn't be possible," he murmured. "But if it is . . ." He grabbed Gallagher's arm. "Fleming made Boreas run again. He made these horses turn against me."

"Aye, your lordship."

"What else could such a man do, Gallagher? If animals listen to him, can he understand them?"

Gallagher cast another glance about the yard. "He knew how Rajah had that bad case of colic last month. He knew that Molly's colt was turned in the womb before it was born. The beasts . . . *whisper* to him, your lordship."

Gallagher fell silent, and all at once the clutter of facts and thoughts that had been spinning about in Inglesham's head coalesced into a single, incredible idea.

"You're a gambling man, Gallagher," Inglesham said, "and so am I. I think it's time to put this notion of yours to a real test."

"And what would that be, your lordship?" Gallagher asked warily.

Inglesham only laughed.

CHAPTER FIFTEEN

Viewed from behind the bars of the cage, the world was an endless nightmare of alien smells, frightening noises and scornful prey forever out of reach.

Donal perched on the thick branch of the dead tree in Othello's cage, breathing in short puffs through his nostrils. He was only half-aware of his own body with its overlong limbs and flat monkey's face; Othello's senses filled his mind with their wordless pain and brutal longings, and it was all he could do to remember his purpose on this cold and empty summer morning.

His true life's work was healing, or so he had always believed. He had come out to the menagerie today as he had done every day during his weeks at Edgecott, opening himself to the animals, seeking a way to ease the bitter hurt of their captivity.

But though the animals accepted him now, let him move about their cages and gave freely of their thoughts and feelings, Donal knew he had failed them. Failed to remedy the malaise that trapped them in bonds of stillness and sorrow; failed to do anything more than share the burden of their grief and keep them alive when they might have simply faded away.

He moaned softly, a sound of despair that no ordinary human throat could shape. The panther crouching beside him blinked golden eyes and took up the chorus, repeating the plea that Donal could never answer.

Let me go.

Donal turned on the branch and pressed his face to the warm, sleek black coat. A great velvet paw came to rest on his shoulder, razor claws barely pricking the linen of his shirt.

Let me go.

Donal drew back, letting the tears coarse unheeded down his face. *I cannot,* he said. *Forgive me.*

The panther sighed, exhaling memories that tasted of rich earth and dripping leaves. He laid his head between his paws and closed his eyes. Enduring the unendurable. Retreating into a world that not even one half-Fane could enter.

Donal jumped down from the branch, his muscles still resonant with a leopard's power. Teeth bared, he stalked to the cage door and opened the latch.

Tod settled lightly on the bench across from the cage, his body almost invisible in his half-materialized state. He studied Donal's face with a worried frown.

"It's not my lord's fault," he said, his voice rough with emotion. "Do not be sad."

Donal sat on the bench and massaged his aching temples. "I don't know what more I can do, Tod. There is only one cure for what ails them."

Tod sat beside him, kicking his child's legs. "Freedom," he said.

"Yes. But even if I had the power to give it to them, it may be too late."

"Never too late," Tod said with such vehemence that Donal looked at him with greater attention than he had done in many weeks. He knew he'd neglected the hob, who relied so much on his friendship. Both of them lived suspended between the Fane and mortal worlds, but it was far worse for Tod. He could never be accepted as human.

"I'm sorry, my friend," Donal said. "I've been too caught up in my own concerns of late. What troubles you?"

Tod looked up in extravagant surprise. "Why, nothing, my lord. Nothing troubles Tod."

All Fane had a gift for deception, but Donal knew Tod too well. "You've been lonely here," he said. "That *is* my fault. I —"

His words were interrupted by the rhythm of hoofbeats approaching on the gravel path. Tod flitted up from the bench, fading from sight as the horses came near.

"Good morning," Inglesham said, smiling down from the back of a long-legged gray stallion. "Hard at work, I see."

Donal looked beyond the viscount to the horse and man who followed him: Boreas, his coat brushed and glossy with health, and the groom Gallagher. Gallagher stood as far from the bay stallion as the lead would allow. Inglesham's mount sidestepped nervously at the scent of the predators behind the bars, but Boreas stamped with barely contained excitement, his mind filled with memories of wind rushing past his ears and the heady triumph of victory.

Donal shook off his distaste and met the viscount's hooded eyes. "To what do I owe this singular honor, Lord Inglesham?"

Inglesham dismounted, tossed his horse's reins over the back of the bench, and ambled closer to Othello's cage. "Did I just see you inside with that beast?" he asked.

"Yes. If you would care to make a closer acquaintance with my friends, I can certainly arrange it."

Inglesham glanced at him, an edge of hostility cutting through the veneer of good humor. "Oh, no, Doctor," he said. "Wild animals are far too unpredictable, particularly when they have 'friends' such as yourself."

Donal raised a brow. "Surely you don't believe that I have any control over these poor creatures' behavior."

"It's most appropriate that you ask that question, Fleming, because that is precisely what I have come to find out."

A sharp sense of foreboding stopped Donal's breath. "I'm afraid I don't understand you." One again he caught the restless intensity of Boreas's thoughts. "Why have you brought Boreas here?"

Inglesham strolled alongside the cages, pausing to peer into each one with a semblance of interest. "I am by nature a man who enjoys a good wager, Fleming . . . and when an intriguing possibility presents itself, I am not one to stand on formality in matters of rank or station."

"How very egalitarian of you."

"Indeed. I believe that every man has a right to prove himself, even one who prefers kennels and pig wallows to civilized society."

"I didn't realize that you spend so much time among animals, Lord Inglesham," Donal said.

Inglesham paused in the act of picking up a stick, his muscles tightening beneath his expertly tailored coat. "I didn't realize you were such a wit, Fleming," he said. He slapped the stick against his thigh. "I suppose you have a great deal of time to practice with such an undemanding audience."

Donal longed to snatch the stick from Inglesham's hand and beat him about the head with it. "I regret that I haven't the time to engage in 'civilized' repartee with you, Lord Inglesham," he said, "but as you noted earlier, I have work to do."

Inglesham clucked in disapproval. "A man who devotes all his time to labor has little chance of winning his fair lady," he said, casually approaching the apes' cage. The animals shrank back and then cautiously crept up to the bars, drawn by the sight of a new face. "What repulsive creatures. Poor Delia must sometimes wonder if you truly prefer the company of these dumb brutes to hers."

The sound of Cordelia's pet name on Inglesham's lips filled Donal with loathing. "It is not a question of preference, Lord Inglesham," he said coldly. "Why are you here?"

The viscount recoiled as Heloise pressed her face against the bars. His mouth curled in disgust. "While I may not fully appreciate every aspect of your profession, Doctor," he said, "I am an admirer of fine horseflesh. I've observed with some interest the work you've done with Boreas, restoring him from a broken-down nag to a semblance of the competitor he might have been under more fortunate circumstances."

"I simply brought him back to good health. It was never my intention to make a racer out of him."

"Perhaps not, but I was with Mrs. Hardcastle when she purchased him, shortly before he was due to be led off by the knackers. I saw what he was then, and you have wrought no less than a miracle."

Donal shrugged. "It was no miracle. Only patience."

"You do take pride in your labors, do you not?"

"Easing pain is my job. If I've succeeded in that, I am satisfied."

"Such modesty, Doctor." Inglesham walked away from the cage, still tapping the stick against his boot. "Surely you must, on occasion, take some satisfaction in displaying the products of your skill for the admiration of others."

"I see no purpose in such exhibitions."

"And yet your animals commonly show off their assets in order to attract a mate. Will you ignore the lessons of nature?"

The hair at the back of Donal's neck prickled in warning. "You are too obscure for my poor understanding, Lord Inglesham. If you will excuse me —"

"I propose a race, Fleming," Inglesham interrupted. "A private race between my Apollo and your Boreas, with you and me as the riders."

Donal almost laughed, but then he glanced toward Boreas and was overwhelmed by the horse's emotions: tension, exhilaration, a near-frenzy of anticipation for the chance to test his strength and speed against a rival.

The big gray Apollo, Boreas's match in size and conformation, was equally aroused, but his mind was full of the complacent hauteur that came with the presumption of superiority. Like master, like mount.

"I'm sorry you've gone to so much trouble, Lord Inglesham," Donal said, "but I am not interested in wagers or races, nor have I a limitless access to funds that can be thrown away on games of chance." He touched the brim of his hat. "Good day, sir."

Inglesham stared at him, a half-smile curving his lips. "Do not be so quick to dismiss me, animal doctor. I have my heart quite set on this match, and I know that every man has his price."

"Oh? Then perhaps you will enlighten me as to mine."

The viscount hurled his stick at the apes' cage, striking the bars. Heloise and Abelard shrieked and leaped up into the branches of their tree, upset by this sudden and unexpected cruelty. The wolves raced back and forth across their pen.

Donal took a step toward Inglesham, fists clenched. Inglesham never lost his maddening smile. "Now, now, Doctor," the viscount said. "I know perfectly well that you would like nothing better than to engage me in a bout of fisticuffs, and I confess I would not be averse to it myself. But such a contest would be not only premature, but also inadvisable given the present state of affairs."

"What state of affairs?" Donal growled.

"Why, your ridiculous notion that you are my equal . . . and that you are in love with Mrs. Hardcastle."

Shock stabbed under Donal's breastbone and seized his lungs. After a frozen spell of stunned silence he found his voice again. "I have no wish to be your equal, Inglesham," he said. "And as for your second assertion —"

Inglesham laughed. "You should see your face, Fleming. One would think I had suggested that your mother had enjoyed an intimate relationship with one of those apes." He leaned forward, making a tempting target of his noble chin. "Can it be that you haven't yet acknowledged your true feelings?"

Donal didn't move. If he did, he would flatten Inglesham with a single blow. "You speak nonsense," he said. "Mrs. Hardcastle is my employer —"

"Who also fancies herself in love with you."

Arjuna the sun bear, who almost never stirred from his nest in the shady part of his cage, gave a low grunt and heaved to his feet. Abelard found a melon rind and threw it at the bars. Boreas nearly jerked the lead rein from Gallagher's hand.

"Viscount Inglesham," Donal said, "I strongly advise that you put yourself under the care of a physician as soon as possible.

You have apparently taken a fever that's addled your brain."

"I'm not the one who's addled." Inglesham sat down on the bench and stretched his long legs. "Whether or not either one of you admits it, Cordelia has contracted an infatuation with you, doubtless due to her unconventional upbringing, and you are not making much of an effort to discourage her."

"What proof —"

"An emotion as delicate as love requires nothing so vulgar as proof. I've heard you speak of Cordelia, and her of you. I've seen you together. You may be a keen observer of animal life, Doctor, but I am a practiced student of *human* passions."

"Mrs. Hardcastle has spoken of marrying you."

"Of course. Her father desires the match, and she finds it difficult to flout his wishes."

Donal's heart surged into his throat. "You, too, wish to marry her, even though you don't love her."

"Don't I?" Inglesham crossed one leg over the other and inspected the heel of his boot. "I am certainly fond of her. We grew up together, as she's doubtless mentioned. We would be a . . . comfortable couple."

Donal turned his back on Inglesham, afraid his face might reveal too much. "If you cared at all for her happiness, you would abandon your suit."

"Spoken like a true lover."

Donal let several minutes of silence elapse before he risked speaking again. "Since you are obviously convinced of this remarkable fantasy," he said, "and it is your intention to marry Mrs. Hardcastle, I presume you've come here to either bribe or threaten me into leaving Edgecott."

Inglesham chuckled. "Nothing of the kind, my good fellow. Nothing of the kind. As I said earlier, I intend to let you prove yourself worthy of Cordelia, here and now."

Donal snorted in disbelief. "With a race?"

"Admit it, Doctor. As much as you attempt to remain detached and above the fray, there is nothing you would like better than to test yourself against me, man to man." He got to his feet. "Apollo has never been beaten in any match race in which I've entered him. He is the superb product of impeccable breeding and the best training wealth and influence can obtain. Your beast, on the other hand . . ." He cast a disdainful look at Boreas, who continued to dance with impatience. "He is rather like you, is he not? A creature who aspires to heights he will surely never reach."

Anger such as Donal generally reserved for the abusers of animals and children took hold of him like a storm, drawing his muscles so tight that they vibrated with the strain. He opened his mind again to Boreas, felt the stallion's desperate yearning for the ultimate freedom, the need to strive against all rationality or hope. Only when he ran was he truly loosed from the bonds of his captivity. Only then did he become one with the ancient ancestors who had ruled the plains before the coming of man with his ropes and whips.

Boreas cared nothing for the very real possibility that he might be defeated. He didn't think of the future. The present was all, and the present demanded that he run as if his life depended upon it.

Donal closed his eyes, no longer able to separate himself from his patient's primal desires. No longer wishing to do so.

"Where will we have this race?" he said through clenched teeth.

Inglesham nodded with smug satisfaction. "Just over that rise is a long meadow bounded by stands of wych elms on either side. We shall start at one end and finish at the other."

"And what are the stakes?"

"Given your limited funds, Doctor, I shall not strain your purse. If I win, you will formulate a convincing excuse, pack your bags and leave Edgecott within the week."

Donal's blood seethed in his veins. "And if Boreas wins?"

"I shall not speak to Sir Geoffrey about your inappropriate affection for his daughter." His face sagged in a parody of regret. "How unpleasant it would be if she is forced to choose between placating her fragile father and keeping you . . . employed."

Donal knew exactly how he should reply to such an outrageous threat, but his mouth refused to form the words. He had become as mute as Boreas, capable of showing his emotions only through the actions of his body and the resolution in his heart.

He turned and strode past Apollo to Boreas and snatched the lead from Gallagher. The groom stepped back as Donal swung onto the stallion's back. Man and beast became one in that moment, perfectly attuned and intent on only one goal.

Boreas set off for the meadow at a trot. Tod flickered over the stallion's neck, his face split in a devilish grin.

"Shall Tod knock that man off, my lord?" he asked. "There are nettles in the meadow."

Boreas tossed his head. Donal shook his. "No, Tod. No magic."

Tod shrugged and settled in for the ride. Inglesham and Apollo soon overtook them, Gallagher trailing at a breathless jog. Within minutes they were gathered beneath the elms at the south end of the meadow, gazing across the smooth expanse of sheep-cropped grass.

"Are you ready?" Inglesham asked Donal with a supercilious grin.

Donal nodded, his attention absorbed by the irresistible force of Boreas's need. He hardly noticed when Gallagher took up the starter's position and raised his cap. He gave no command when the cap fell. Boreas plunged forward like an eagle stooping after its prey, and Apollo was only a hand's-breadth behind him.

The working of legs like powerful pistons, the thrust of hooves that tore the sod and sent it flying, the flare of nostrils sucking in air to fuel lungs and heart and blood and bone . . . all these sensations became Donal's world. He bent low over Boreas's back, exulting in the sheer love of the race, the single thing this brave soul had cherished in an existence of abuse and neglect.

But the glory couldn't last. A pale blur appeared at Boreas's right side, its elegant form marred by the figure who clung to its back. Donal bared his teeth and whispered a rhythmic chant of encouragement, even as he recognized that Boreas's courage was not enough. Even as he felt the pull of tendons and the grinding of bones as an old injury dragged the stallion back to earth.

The horse began to labor, his breaths coming short with pain and determination. Apollo surged ahead. Despair washed through Boreas . . . despair so terrible that tears of grief welled in Donal's eyes.

And then, as he passed, Inglesham twisted in the saddle and looked into Donal's eyes. He grinned and waved with a jaunty toss of his hand.

That was when Donal forgot every rule of human honor and fair play that had been drummed into his head as a boy. He severed his union with Boreas and bent his thoughts on Apollo. Not to coerce; that he would never do, no matter how sorely tempted. But he asked, he begged, he pleaded as humbly as he knew how. And Apollo chose to listen. His gallop slowed. Boreas drew level with him and gradually pulled ahead.

Tod laughed from his invisible perch atop Boreas's forelock. The hiss of Inglesham's curse cut through the rumble of hoofbeats. A crop appeared in his hand. He lashed at Apollo's flank.

With a flick of his finely sculpted ears, Apollo stopped short. Inglesham flew over his head and crashed to the ground, rolling out of the horses' path. Boreas crossed the last stretch of meadow and pulled up among the trees. He favored his right foreleg and his chest heaved with exertion, but his joy encompassed Donal in a warm glow of triumph. Tod peppered the stallion's damp nose with jubilant kisses.

Donal dismounted and bent to examine the injured limb as Inglesham scrambled to his feet. Apollo stood some distance off, regarding his owner with a look of disdain. The viscount started toward his mount. Apollo backed away. Inglesham circled the stallion. Apollo trotted in the opposite direction.

"Fool," Tod crowed. "Fool, fool, foolish human!"

Donal smiled and ran his hands over Boreas's fetlock. "I'll put a poultice on this at the stable," he said. "But no more racing for a while, my friend. I fear we both lost our heads . . ."

"But not the race."

Donal straightened to meet Inglesham's gaze, expecting a scowl of rage and insinuations of cheating that the viscount could not possibly defend with any rational explanation. But Inglesham was not frowning. To the contrary, there was a peculiar glitter in his eyes that Donal would almost have called satisfaction. Or vindication.

"You did it," Inglesham said.

Donal looked out at the meadow, where Gallagher had finally managed to catch Apollo. "Boreas deserves full credit, not I."

"*You* made Apollo . . . do what he did."

So much for conceding gracefully. This inevitable argument was no less than Donal deserved for his lapse in judgment.

"That is hardly possible," he said. "I didn't touch him, and I certainly had no access to him before you arrived."

"Of course not. You didn't have to." Inglesham pointed toward Gallagher. "He told me, and I didn't believe it. Why should I? But I saw your face just before Apollo threw me." To Donal's amazement, he smiled. "I've ridden in a hundred match races, and won most. Apollo has never disobeyed me before. He is a born competitor. There is no logical reason why he should suddenly misbehave . . . unless you spoke to him."

Donal concealed his wariness beneath a blandly inquiring mask. "Spoke to him, Lord Inglesham?"

"Ah, you play the innocent so well. But I know your secret, Fleming."

"We all have our secrets, and you have had your race." Donal took Boreas's lead and brushed past Inglesham. "If there is nothing more . . ."

Inglesham grabbed his arm. "But there is. Did you think this was the end of it?"

Donal stared at the viscount's hand and slowly met his gaze. "Go to Sir Geoffrey if you wish, Inglesham. I am through with your games."

Inglesham released him and stepped back to lean against the nearest tree, one leg crossed over the other. "How fond are you of little Ivy, Dr. Fleming?" he asked.

Donal dropped the lead. "What?"

"A straightforward enough question, I believe." Inglesham stifled a yawn behind his hand. "Cordelia told me all about your dramatic rescue of the child from the rookeries in London. I was quite surprised to learn that Delia's pretty new protégée is one and the same as the ragged waif who robbed me in Covent Garden."

A breath of wind circled Donal's head, reminding him of Tod's presence. The hob's agitation seemed to match his own. Thoughts of stinging insects and an avalanche of bird droppings filled Donal's mind.

"I understand that Ivy lived with you for a time, before Delia so graciously gave her a home here at Edgecott," Inglesham purred. "Of course you could not have realized that she was in fact a young woman. . . ."

"I did not," Donal said. "Not until Mrs. Hardcastle came to offer me employment and saw her again." He gritted his teeth. "Naturally, once I learned the truth, I agreed that it would be best for Ivy to reside elsewhere."

"Naturally." Inglesham gouged the tree trunk with his bootheel. "I am most impressed with your benevolence toward one so much less fortunate. I expect such liberality from Cordelia, but in a man of your station . . . what motivated such largesse, I wonder?"

Boreas snapped at the air with broad yellow teeth. Donal retrieved the lead and started in the direction of the stables. He had gone only a few feet before Inglesham fell into step beside him. "How much *do* you know of the girl's years on the streets of London?" the viscount asked.

Donal felt the toothed jaws of a trap waiting to be sprung. "Only what she remembers of them," he said in a flat voice.

"The poor child must have found it difficult to maintain her innocence, especially as she grew to womanhood."

"She disguised herself very well, as you noted."

"Indeed. But perhaps she didn't always maintain the masquerade. Perhaps she was occasionally driven to . . . desperate acts."

Donal refused to grant Inglesham the satisfaction of a response. Inglesham sighed. "Cordelia has such high hopes for the girl," he said. "It would be a great pity if she were to be disillusioned, don't you agree?"

"And you plan to create this disillusionment," Donal said.

"That will hardly be necessary. Ivy will do it herself. The question is whether it will take a mild or painful form." He stroked his riding crop. "You care too much for Cordelia to wish her pain, just as you care for Ivy. Doubtless you would do anything to protect them."

Donal stopped. The grass under his feet began to boil with the movements of hundreds of tiny creatures. He sent them away with an effort. "Protect them from you?" he asked.

Inglesham placed his hand on his chest in a mockery of affront. "From me? Not at all. From Ivy's unfortunate past. You see, your innocent little ward is a murderess as well as a thief, and if you do not do exactly as I tell you, I shall see that she spends the rest of her life in a cage from which she will never escape."

CHAPTER SIXTEEN

Nearly mad with rage, Tod buzzed about Inglesham's head like a wasp making ready to sting. He had come to Donal this morning in spite of his desire to avoid his master, knowing that he must behave as if nothing had changed between them. When Donal had apologized for his neglect, Tod had come very near forgiving him for concealing his plans to leave England.

But then Yellow-Hair had interrupted with his threats against Donal and Ivy, and incongruous emotions had possessed Tod like some powerful enchantment — not only the familiar desire to protect Donal from mortal treachery, but anger that Ivy should be in danger . . . Ivy, who was nothing to him save a responsibility he had never wanted.

It didn't matter. All he wished now was to punish Yellow-Hair . . . if only Donal would permit it. But Donal only stared at his adversary, calm and cold as a still, deep lake.

"What is this lie?" he asked quietly. And he

listened with equal dispassion as the bad man spoke of incomprehensible things: of some other mortal in the Iron City, of dark places and darker feelings, of an unprovoked attack by a thief who carried the same pendant that protected Ivy from the wrong enemies.

"What proof?" Donal asked when the man was finished. "All you have is the word of this dead acquaintance."

"Proof?" Inglesham said, snorting through his mouth like a nasty troll. "*My* word is enough against a nameless thief whose actions led to the death of a titled gentleman. Sir Geoffrey will gladly support me in my accusations."

"Against his own daughter?"

"He will naturally desire to protect her. I truly fear for her state of mind if she learns that this girl she has taken into her heart is capable of such savagery. She would be placed in an untenable position." His face grew long. "Delia is much more delicate than she would seem, you know. That is often the case with women who appear unusually strong-willed."

His face still expressionless, Donal drew Boreas closer to keep the horse from kicking Yellow-Hair across the meadow. His anger reached so far that even the beasts in their cages roared and howled.

"What do you want, Inglesham?" he said at last.

The man examined the tips of his fingers. "Very little, actually. Nothing that you will find unduly taxing. I have told you that I enjoy betting, and flat racing is my particular sin." He smiled. "Have you ever been to a race meeting, Fleming?"

"No."

"No matter. I will instruct you, and the rest you'll learn quickly enough. You will accompany me to various meetings, and you will advise me as to the physical state of the entries and the accuracy of the odds placed on each horse. If I am happy with the results . . . that is, of course, if your picks win and I obtain a useful profit . . . little Ivy's secret will remain so."

Donal's nostrils flared. "You expect me to determine which horses will win each race?"

"Surely that is not beyond your capabilities. I've seen proof enough of that. And if ever there is any doubt in your mind as to the final outcome of any race, you can certainly provide the necessary encouragement — or discouragement — to the appropriate animals to see that the desired results are achieved."

Tod hugged himself, trying with all his might to remain invisible when he wished more than anything to pelt Yellow-Hair's head with every bit of filth he could find. Donal had the power to make Boreas, even Apollo, turn and trample Inglesham to death. But that was not his way.

"How long is this agreement to last?" Donal asked.

"If you do your work well, through the end of this racing season should be sufficient for me to accumulate a respectable pile. And when I have adequate funds . . . why, it will not seem quite so necessary to seek other sources of income."

Donal stared at the grass beneath his feet. The narrow blades still trembled with the frenzied activity of the creatures that lived in and on the earth, but he did not send them against the one who threatened him and Ivy.

Do not trust him, Tod thought furiously. But Tod's master was no fool. He would have a scheme for dealing with this horrid human.

"I'll give you my answer tomorrow," Donal said.

"A delay will win you nothing," Inglesham said.

"Tomorrow," Donal repeated.

"Tomorrow by sunset, Fleming. No later."

Donal stood very still a moment longer and then turned, leading Boreas away. Tod waited until they were passing through a dense grove of trees before he materialized.

"My lord!" he cried. "Let me go back. Let me punish this mortal."

"No, Tod. We live in a human world, and I will not resort to Fane methods to defeat a low scoundrel like Inglesham."

"But he lied, my lord. He said . . . he said that my lord loves —" Tod almost choked on the terrible word "— loves the woman Hardcastle."

Donal's skin flushed red. He didn't answer.

Tod hovered before him. "Remember, my lord. Remember the Black Widow —"

"Inglesham is a fool," Donal said sharply, "and that is why he won't win this contest. Think no more of it, my friend."

"And what of the girl? She is in peril."

Donal cocked his head. "So you no longer dislike her, Tod? You are concerned for her welfare?"

Tod squirmed. "She does not deserve to suffer such harm."

"No. And I have no intention of obeying Inglesham any longer than is required to counteract his blackmail. The first thing I must do is talk with Ivy."

"My lord will explain the danger?"

"I see no need to upset her or Mrs. Hardcastle at present. This is between me and Inglesham." He frowned in the direction of the big house. "Please find Ivy for me, Tod, and return at once."

Tod obeyed, skimming high over the treetops and looking down upon the groomed human landscape with an eagle's eye. He found Ivy sitting under a broad-canopied horse chestnut. Her dress was torn and muddied at the hem, her hair tangled with bracken, but to Tod she looked strangely beautiful. His whole body shook with anger — not only at Yellow-Hair, but at himself for his own jumbled emotions.

He led Donal to the horse chestnut and found a seat on a high branch to eavesdrop on the conversation. He scarcely listened to the dull pleasantries man and girl exchanged as they sat together under the tree. He watched the play of sunlight and shadow on Ivy's silken skin and found himself succumbing to the musical lilt of her voice as if she had cast a spell upon him. A spell he was losing the will to resist. . . .

"I know there are things about your past you didn't tell me," Donal said. "I understand why you were reluctant to trust anyone with the story of your life. But now that you are to live with Cordelia on a permanent basis, I think it only right that you keep no secrets from her."

Ivy glared at him from beneath the dark arch of her brows. "What of the secrets *you* keep from her?" she demanded.

"I beg your pardon?"

"Never mind." Ivy pulled a bit of bramble from her hair. "What do you want me to tell her?"

"Everything you remember about your childhood and your time in the rookeries until I found you." He plucked at a blade of grass. "I thought you might feel more comfortable speaking to me first."

"Even though you hardly ever talk to me anymore?"

Donal glanced aside. "For that I apologize. I have always tended to . . . fall short where my human connections are concerned."

Ivy drew her knees to her chest. "Where should I begin?"

"Why don't you start with what you remember of your early childhood?"

Tod hung on every word as Ivy began to reveal the secrets of her past. "My mother's name was Estelle," she said. "Estelle Naismith. Her father was a diplomat for England in Russia. That was where Estelle met my father."

Donal leaned forward, and Tod mimicked his motion, nearly tumbling from his perch. "Then you did know your father."

"Only what my mother told me. She spoke of him only when she was . . . when she had taken her laudanum."

Tod glanced at Donal. He did not know all the strange substances humans ingested in the belief that they would improve their health or happiness, but he had heard this word before. The look on Donal's face confirmed his suspicions.

Ivy also noticed Donal's expression. "Mama was . . . often ill just before . . . before everything was lost," she continued, the defiance in her eyes belying her stammer. "She needed the medicine."

"Go on," Donal urged softly.

"My father was a gentleman of the Russian nobility," she said, recovering her confidence. "He was smitten with Mama as soon as he met her at a palace ball. But her parents did not approve of him, and he was too highly placed to marry a mere diplomat's daughter."

Tod edged closer, turning her words about in his head. Béfind claimed that Ivy was her daughter, given to a mortal woman in an act of treachery. But who was Ivy's father? Was this Russian the mortal lover of whom Béfind had spoken?

"In spite of the obstacles between them," Ivy continued, "they found ways to meet in secret. And in time —" She glared defiantly at Donal. "Estelle had a child."

Donal held Ivy's gaze. "You think that I'd be shocked to learn that your parents were not married when you were born?" He shook his head. "Ivy, my own parents had not yet married when I was conceived, and they were separated before the legal union could take place. I am like you."

Ivy unfolded her legs. "Truly?"

"Truly. I see no shame in it, if your parents loved one another."

"They did. But . . ." She dropped her eyes. "Something happened. My father had to go away, and when Estelle's parents learned that she was with child, her father arranged her marriage to an old man who was paid to take my mother as his wife."

Donal closed his eyes, and Tod knew he was remembering the similar arrangement his own mortal grandfather had made to save his mother's reputation. "You were born in Russia?" he asked.

"No. The old man died soon after their marriage, and Mama's parents were to bring her back to England. But they were killed on the journey. My mother would have been lost, except that she had the jewels my father had left her . . . the ones she had hidden from my grandparents. They were enough for her to take a house in London. Her father's connections enabled her to establish herself in society. She was considered a great beauty." Ivy tossed her head. "Men were always pursuing her."

"And what of you?" Donal asked.

"I had books and pretty dresses, and every night I watched Mama go out to routes and balls in her beautiful gowns."

"She spent little time with you."

Ivy shrugged. "I could do whatever I wanted, and I liked to watch the people who came to the house to see her. But after a while, the jewels started to run out. We had to move to another part of London. Estelle still went to parties, but less visitors came. The servants left. That was when she started taking the laudanum and talking about my father."

"How old were you then?"

"Ten, I think. I don't remember." Her voice was light, as if the events that had shaped her young life were meaningless to her now. "Mama went out less and less, and our maid never had enough money to buy the food we needed. So I looked for ways to help. I went out into the streets and found out how other people lived."

"That was how you learned the speech of Seven Dials."

"Oi'm very good at copyin', Oi am," she said in a thick accent. "I was good at hiding, too. And I found out that I could sneak in and out of people's houses without their noticing. So I went to the houses of my mother's friends and took things they wouldn't miss, so I could sell them for food and medicine. For a while that was enough. But then Mama got very sick, and no medicine would help her. I don't think she could go on living as we had to live then."

Tod gripped the tree branch, suddenly and inexplicably desperate to comfort Ivy with assurances that she need never suffer so again. But Donal was still in the way. He said, "I'm very sorry, Ivy."

"I think Mama was glad to die. But then men came to take the house and everything in it, and they would have taken me away, too. So I went to live in the streets. I was fine until . . ." She touched the chain of the pendant that rested against her heart. "I knew what men could be like, so I stayed a child."

Donal reached for her hand and cupped her fingers in his. "It must have been very hard for you."

"It wasn't so terrible. At least I was free." She looked from his hand to his face. "But I was glad to go with you, once I knew . . . once I was sure you were safe."

Donal squeezed her hand and released it. "Did you always dress as you did when I found you, Ivy? Sometimes you must have wished to act and look your own age."

"Sometimes."

"And you had trouble with men when you did."

Her blue eyes sharpened. "Not often." She gathered her skirts to rise. "I must go now —"

"Ivy."

She paused at the quiet but irresistible authority in his voice. "I've told you all I know," she said.

"Are you quite sure?"

Leave her alone, Tod wanted to shout. *Leave her alone, leave her —*

"Was there a particular man," Donal asked, "one who might have approached you not long before we met? Perhaps when you'd decided to be yourself, your true age, for just one night?"

338

Between one moment and the next Ivy changed from a rebellious young woman to a terrified child. She fell back against the tree trunk, her fingers driving hard into the bark.

"I didn't mean to hurt him," she whispered. "He wanted to . . . he was going to . . . and I didn't want him to. I was so angry . . ." She covered her face with her hands. "I only hit him a few times, but he screamed so dreadfully, and fell. I ran . . ."

She broke off on a sob, and Donal quickly rose to stand beside her. She turned into his arms with a soft cry. Tod moaned with her anguish and his own.

"It's all right," Donal said. "You were the one who was attacked. You had a right to defend yourself."

She lifted a tear-streaked face. "I . . . don't know what happened. He was so much bigger than I. It was as if . . . as if all the anger I felt went into my hands when I hit him."

Tod understood at once, though Donal could not. The anger of a Fane was no ordinary rage. With enough force and passion, it could even kill.

Ivy had reason enough for anger; anger against the cruel twist of fate that had left her to suffer, ignorant of her true heritage, in an uncaring mortal world.

"Why didn't you tell me these things in the beginning?" Donal asked. "It would have made no difference to me, or to Cordelia."

Ivy trembled, her body poised on the brink of flight. "How did you know? You weren't there. No one saw . . ."

"I heard rumors," he said. He stroked her hair. "I wished to hear the story from you."

She drew away, her fingers clutching the lapels of his coat. "Please don't let the rozzers take me. Please —"

"Hush. No one will come for you. You're safe here."

"Oh, Donal." She strained upward, her neck arched like a swan's, her lips ripe as summer berries. Her fingers crept up to tangle in his hair. "I know you will always protect me."

Her mouth pressed to his. He stood utterly still. Tod clenched his teeth on a cry of protest, and a crow burst upward from the chestnut with a caw of distress.

Donal set his hands on Ivy's shoulders and gently pushed her away. "I care for you, Ivy," he said, "and I will protect you to the best of my ability. But this —" He touched his fingertip to her lips. "This is not for you and me. You'll find someone you can love with all your heart, if you will only give yourself time. . . ."

She broke free, hair whipping about her face. "Love?" she cried. Her laughter sparkled and spiraled skyward, silvering the leaves like a rime of frost. "Poor dull, serious Donal.

Don't you recognize a game when you see it?"

Donal frowned. "Ivy . . ."

But she caressed his cheek with a drift of her hand and left him, trailing bubbles of mirth and mockery. Donal stared after her.

"Tod," he murmured, "have I grown so old that I have forgotten what it is to be young?"

Tod did not answer. He was shaking, his thoughts blurred with shock and bewilderment. He had considered Ivy a danger to his master, to the bond he and Donal had shared for so many years. But *Donal* was not at risk from the girl he had rescued.

At last Tod understood the source of the malady that had afflicted him since he had first spoken to Ivy beneath the grandfather oak. He no longer despised her as a rival. He looked upon her now and felt emotions quite different but every bit as powerful: admiration. Affection.

Desire.

Tod's heart swelled with joy and terror. He abandoned the tree and pursued Ivy, racing beside her as she ran to the river and immersed herself in its healing waters. She emerged with her face washed clean of all fear and sorrow, her supple body sleek as an otter, all the heavy layers of her underskirts abandoned to the current like the cast-off casings of a butterfly.

"Tod," she said in surprise.

He swept her a gallant bow. "Tod has come to bear my lady company, if she will have him," he said.

She smiled and settled beneath a willow, patting the ground beside her. "I am sorely in need of amusement. Tell me another tale of the Fane. Let me forget this world for a little while."

And so he did, though he burned with humiliation and dreadful longing. He might worship at Ivy's feet, but his adoration could never be returned so long as he remained trapped in this stunted and ridiculous body.

He remembered the day when the priest of the White God had laid the curse upon him. . . .

He walked upon the beach on the shores of the island men called Eire, listening to the cries of the gulls and the lap of water on the sand. He lingered in the mortal realm, for he, unlike so many other High Fane, still found some pleasure in the world his people were slowly abandoning. The company of mortals amused him, and on occasion he paid court to their females.

His thoughts touched briefly on the girl he had lain with eight months before. She had resisted him at first; she had wept and claimed loyalty to the man she was to marry, as if some silly mortal custom could stay him from taking what he desired. In the end she had surrendered. He'd had his pleasure and left her, seeking

342

other entertainments.

Yet still he thought of her. He even considered returning to the cottage she shared with her sire and dam to see how she fared. It was possible she carried his child. He might leave her with a few trinkets to pay for the rearing of the brat. Mortals could not simply pluck their food from trees and vines as did the Fane in Tir-na-Nog, and she —

The sound of heavy human feet grinding in the sand diverted his attention. He turned, surprised that any mortal should dare approach him in his solitude. But when he saw the creature's long robes and the wide silver cross that hung about his neck, he stiffened with foreboding.

The man stopped, clutching the cross in one broad, callused hand. His face was stained red with anger.

"You are the one they call Aodhan?" he demanded.

Aodhan took a single step back, his boots only a handbreadth from the tide. "Who are you to question me, mortal?"

The priest lifted the cross. Sunlight glared from it, casting spears of light that pierced Aodhan's eyes. "Speak, spawn of wickedness. I know what you are, and you cannot harm me."

Ire rose in Aodhan's heart, and he lifted his hand to call up an enchantment that would put the mortal in his place. But the words failed him, and his power shriveled like the skin of an overripe fruit.

"I am Aodhan," he said, meeting the priest's insolent gaze. "Why do you disturb my peace?"

"You are the one who lay with the maiden Cliona eight months past?"

"And if I did?"

The priest closed his eyes, his hand upon the cross white about the knuckles. "She died," he said. "She died giving birth to the child you sired when you raped her."

For an instant Aodhan felt the pull of regret. Surely it was no coincidence that he had been thinking of Cliona this very day. He would never have condemned the girl to such suffering. It was easy to forget that mortals lived with pain and death every day of their short lives.

"I regret this occurrence," he told the priest. "I shall recompense her mother and father for their loss."

"Recompense?" The priest opened his eyes, and his chest heaved with his passion. "Yes, creature of the Sidhe. You shall pay. Too long have your kind wandered our land and taken what you wish with no thought to the evil you do. Your time is nearly ended."

Aodhan laughed. "Shall you drive us away, little priest?"

"I am not so powerful, but He who is my Master will claim this island for all time. As for you . . ." He held the cross high, and his lips began to move in some silent incantation.

Aodhan turned to walk away, but some invisible force held him captive. A strange tingling began in his feet and worked its way up into his legs and hips. He looked down and saw, to his horror, that his boots flapped on feet far too small, his trousers pooling about his ankles. His hands were lost in the sleeves of his tunic. The ground was far too near.

He lifted his hands to his face. His lips, his nose, his eyes were all in the correct position, but they had changed. And when he opened his mouth to speak . . .

"What have you done?" he croaked.

The priest looked down upon him, all the anger gone from his eyes. "It is not I who have punished you," he said. "Hear me, you who were once known as Aodhan. You shall wear this shape and spend the rest of your days in service, until you learn what it is to be human."

Tod sat up, the taste of fear in his mouth. Ivy slept beside him, unsullied by his memories.

So long. So long it had been since that meeting upon the shore. He remembered returning to Tir-na-Nog, begging Queen Titania to lift the curse, knowing that only she might have the power to counter the White Priest's magic.

Titania had laughed. Instead of raging that a mere mortal had so violated one of her own, she had mocked him and bid him accept his new condition. And so he had fled to the forests and mountains in the north of the

English isle, where he had become servant to Hern, the Forest Lord.

A thousand mortal years had passed, but neither Hern nor his son had ever learned of the curse. Tod had finally accepted that he would always be a hob and nothing but a hob. Until today.

Now there was reason again to approach Titania . . . if one of exalted blood could be found to plead on Tod's behalf. Donal would never understand, but there was another who might.

Tod gazed upon Ivy's face, his fingers aching to touch her. This torment must end. No matter what he must do from this moment on, no force in the two worlds could keep him and Ivy apart.

CHAPTER SEVENTEEN

"It simply will not do," Cordelia said, holding on to her temper by a thread. "The state in which you returned to the house yesterday is not acceptable, Ivy. You cannot run about the countryside — no, not even Edgecott — missing half your petticoats and your shoes. You are not a child to let your hair become a bird's nest, and tear your gowns among the brambles . . ."

She broke off, dismayed at her own anger and the rebellious look on Ivy's face. The girl knew better. She had once enjoyed the comforts of an ordinary home. She was bright, far brighter than most. And yet, in spite of all the work Cordelia had done with her, all the weeks at Edgecott, Ivy was still wild. Wild and completely unrepentant.

Indeed, Cordelia's own, once-predictable existence had taken a chaotic turn, and she no longer knew what to expect from one hour to the next. Her quarrels with Sir Geoffrey, previously mild and quickly settled, had become strident in tone as he grew more erratic with every passing hour. He shifted rapidly between days of lethargic melancholy, when nothing at all could pry him from his bed, to periods of extreme emotion when he complained of bizarre, terrifying dreams. Only this morning he had shouted himself hoarse with half-mad ravings Cordelia had barely understood. His insistence upon her marriage to Lord Inglesham took on the violence of obsession, while his dislike of Donal, with whom he'd had almost no dealings, bordered upon irrational hatred.

As for Inglesham himself, he remained a constant and solicitous visitor. Too solicitous by half, though the pressure he brought to bear was of a much subtler variety. She could no longer turn to him as a friend when her emotions were so vexedly disordered.

And then there was Donal. Donal, so quiet and sure, always watching her, looking into her very soul. Distracting her from duty with the mere fact of his presence.

He was certainly no help with Ivy. How could he be, when he refused to admonish her for behavior that must surely undermine all Cordelia's plans for the girl? He wanted no part of society's rules. How could he do anything but inadvertently encourage Ivy to break them just as he did?

Cordelia calmed her thoughts with an effort and distractedly poured cooling tea into her half-empty cup. "Do you understand me, Ivy? If you are to succeed in this world, you must learn to compromise a little of your freedom. There is no other way." She sipped the tea, suppressed a grimace, and set the cup down again. "Will you not try a little harder, my dear?"

Ivy thrust out her lower lip in a deplorable but all-too-effective pout. She scuffed her feet under the sofa. "What if I don't wish to succeed in this world?" she demanded.

Cordelia's heart rattled against her ribs. "You cannot return to what you were. This is your home now."

Ivy said nothing. After a while Cordelia realized that further conversation was pointless, and she was weary to death of constant disagreement.

"You may go to your room, Ivy, until dinner."

Ivy got up and strode for the stairs. "Flounced" might have been an apt word for any other young girl, but Ivy was far too light on her feet to be anything but graceful even in the throes of revolt.

"She is still very young for her age, in spite of what she has experienced," Theodora said from the drawing room doorway. She took a chair across from Cordelia, her plain face drawn in lines of rueful sympathy. "It has not been so very long since she lived on the streets of London."

Cordelia rang for a maid to replace the cold tea with a fresh pot. "If she had been born in Seven Dials, I should hardly expect anything of her. But Donal has told me what she remembers of her past . . . information she declined to share with me, I might add . . . and though my inquiries in London have failed to turn up any living relatives, it is clear that Ivy's mother was respectable enough to teach her daughter the essentials of polite society. I believe Ivy's refusal to cooperate is deliberate." She paused, monitoring her voice for any trace of self-pity. "I can only conclude that I am failing with her."

Theodora did not leap to reassure her but gave Cordelia's words thorough consideration before she spoke. "It seems to me," she said, "that you are far too severe upon yourself."

"In what way?" Cordelia asked. "I have provided everything I judged that Ivy requires. I have striven not to place undue restrictions upon her activities here at Edgecott, and yet . . ." Her throat tightened, and she felt the treacherous prickle of tears behind her eyes. "What have I done wrong, Theodora?"

Her cousin reached across the small table between them and touched her hand. "Nothing. Nothing but expect too much of yourself."

Cordelia was temporarily relieved of the necessity of replying by the arrival of the tea.

She poured for herself and Theodora, making quite sure that her hands were steady.

"When I was young," she said, "I . . . witnessed the consequences of such wild behavior. I will not see Ivy subjected to the unhappiness that must inevitably come of her present attitude."

"Do you think Ivy is unhappy now?"

"She must be, or she would not —" She looked at Theodora more closely. Her cousin was not one for idle conversation, and her questions were seldom trivial. "Do *you* think she is happy, Theodora?"

"I do not know her as well as you, of course. But . . ." She sipped her tea and carefully set down the cup. "I do not believe that her emotional state is the cause of your dilemma."

"If you have advice, cousin, I would be happy to hear it."

"May I speak frankly, cousin?"

"Of course."

Theodora met her gaze. "I believe that *you* are unhappy, and that your unhappiness stems from denying your own feelings."

"I have just told you my feelings, and you discounted them."

"I do not speak of your concerns about Ivy and your relationship with her."

"Indeed?"

"It seems to me that you have been placed in an untenable position, Cordelia, and you will have to make a choice. Sir Geoffrey makes no secret of his wishes for your future, but you neither refuse nor accede to his requests. Why?"

Cordelia blinked in mild surprise at Theodora's uncharacteristic bluntness. "A second marriage is not a thing to be rushed into. I hardly expect my father to understand, but —"

"It isn't that you fear the institution of marriage, though you may have convinced yourself that that is so. You simply will not admit that you do not love Inglesham . . . and that someone else has stolen your heart."

Cordelia bolted from her chair, darting across the drawing room with no aim or purpose. "I never knew you to be such a romantic, Theodora."

"One in my position must be pragmatic, but that does not put an end to dreams." She looked down at her hands, small and neat and as ordinary as her face. "And if you will not allow yourself to dream, my dear, then I must do it for you."

Cordelia completed her meandering circuit of the room and gripped the back of her chair. "I need not ask whom you believe has 'stolen my heart.' "

"Sir Geoffrey has recognized it in spite of his illness. So has Ivy, and Inglesham is not entirely a fool." She gazed unflinchingly into Cordelia's eyes. "You have no wish to marry

Inglesham. You never did, but now there is a clear reason for putting an end to any expectations."

"Why should I not marry one who has been so kind to me and so good to Sir Geoffrey?"

"Now you are being foolish," Theodora said with surprising sternness. "You will never marry without love." She smiled sadly. "I know that you loved Captain Hardcastle during your short time together."

Cordelia felt her way into her chair, uncertain that her legs would continue to support her. "Yes. I loved him very much."

"And you were very young. You still blame yourself for not saving him, as you blame yourself for Lydia. Delia, don't you see . . ."

Theodora's voice faded, thinning to the sound of a scorching wind blowing through the trees.

The night was hot. Even the punkawallahs with their ever-moving fans could not chase the heat away.

James was still drinking. He had begun early that evening and had not stopped since, though Cordelia had begged him to moderate his consumption. Her pleas fell on deaf ears, as they had so often done of late.

She sat on the cane chair at her dressing table and stared into her own hollowed eyes. She had thought little enough of Captain Hardcastle's habits when she had married him. He was charming, amusing, unfailingly generous

. . . so very unlike her father that she had found herself in love with him almost the hour they met. Everyone else loved him, too: his men, his fellow officers and every unmarried lady in the cantonment.

James had never caviled at her unconventional upbringing. He held her in his arms when she spoke haltingly of Lydia's death. And when he had asked her to become his wife, it had never occurred to her to refuse. At last she might have her own life again.

But things had begun to change . . . when? A week after their marriage? Two? She had begun to realize that James drank more than the other officers. She began to see how it affected him . . . how he spent so much of his time in a stupor, lost in a world she could never enter. She realized that charming, amusing, generous James wrestled with demons even her love could not exorcize.

That was when she realized that it was her duty to save him.

Cordelia rose from the dressing table and walked slowly into the drawing room, where James was pouring himself another whiskey. He looked up as she hesitated in the doorway.

"Well, Delia?" he drawled, lifting his glass in a genial salute. "Come to lecture me again?"

She swallowed her instinctive apology and attempted a smile. "Come, my dear . . . is it any wonder that I am jealous of anything that diverts my husband's attention away from me?"

He laughed, tipping the glass this way and that. "Always my plain-spoken Delia." He drained the glass and moved to set it on the sideboard. It crashed to the floor. He picked up the empty bottle, held it up to his eyes and swore under his breath.

" 'Scuse me, Delia. Not for a lady's ears." He opened the sideboard door, peered inside and gave a deep sigh.

"Now where'd I put it? Got to be around here somewhere. . . ."

Cordelia gathered her courage. "Won't you come sit on the verandah? At least the air is fresh."

"You go outside, sweetheart. I'll be along in a moment." He staggered into the small kitchen. "Where are they?" he muttered, turning in a clumsy circle.

There was no retreating now. Cordelia lifted her chin. "I had them destroyed."

"Beg . . . pardon?"

"They are gone, James." She reached for his arm. "You must see that it is better this way. Without the constant temptation —"

James shook his head, profound sorrow in his eyes. "Won't work, sweetheart. I'll find another."

Cordelia closed her eyes, very close to panic. "My dear," she said, "I know you. I know what you're capable of, what you might achieve if you were not beholden to the bottle. I will not see you ruin your life before my eyes."

He laughed. "Would have been ruined already if not for you." He cupped her face in his hands. "Mistake, getting married. No good for you. Can't save me. You should go. Now. Go far away."

"I love you, James. I shall never abandon you." His hands shook as he dropped them. He lurched away, crashing into the horsehair sofa. "Have to go out. I'll be back . . . before supper."

"Please, James . . ."

He waved to her jauntily and stumbled through the door. For a moment Cordelia stood frozen, unable to think or feel. Then she sat stiffly on the sofa until her maid found her there near dawn and chivvied her off to bed.

Anjali woke her well after sunrise, when they brought Cordelia the report that James had made a reckless, unauthorized foray from the cantonment in pursuit of a dacoit band that had been raiding the local villages. He had found the bandits. He had fought heroically. But that had not been enough.

She knew then that he had killed himself rather than cause her pain. She had not saved him. She alone was responsible. . . .

"He would not have changed unless *he* wished it. Over that, my dear, you had no control."

The gentle, familiar voice brought Cordelia back to the cool safety of Edgecott's drawing room. Her hands were icy cold in Theodora's grip. Tears leaked from her eyes.

"You don't know," she whispered. "You can't understand —"

"I understand this much," Theodora said. "You made yourself responsible for Lydia, James, Sir Geoffrey, now Ivy. You believe you failed to save them. But there is a man here at Edgecott who does not require salvation . . . one who has the strength to stand beside you as your perfect match, who shares your honesty and your courage. And it is because of this that you love him."

Cordelia stood up so quickly that her skirts caught on the tea tray and sent it crashing to the carpet. "There is no further point to this discussion," she said hoarsely, "and I would ask you not to mention it again. Kindly remember that you are a guest in this house —"

She stopped, suddenly aware of the cruelty in her words. Theodora had shrunk in on herself, her eyes dark pools of hurt and chagrin.

"I . . ." Cordelia began, looking away from her cousin's humiliation. "I know you meant well, but I . . ."

Theodora rose shakily to her feet. "I am sorry to have disturbed you, Cordelia. I think I shall go up to my room and rest."

Before Cordelia could offer an apology, Theodora was rushing out the door.

With a curse far more vulgar than those she normally permitted herself, Cordelia charged from the drawing room and out of the house. Afternoon sunlight struck her eyes, reminding her that the better part of the day remained . . . a day that should be filled with writing letters, making calls and administering to the affairs of the several charitable organizations to which she belonged.

Instead of turning back to her private sitting room and the desk with its neat stack of unanswered missives and reports, she ran up the stairs, shed her morning gown, and put on her riding habit. With her trailing skirts looped over one arm, she strode out to the stable and asked a groom to saddle Desdemona. Her thoughts kept up a constant dialogue, arguing among themselves like quarrelsome jackdaws.

You had no reason to speak to her so, she chided herself as she reined the mare toward her sanctuary beside the river. *Theodora deserves better from you, and she meant only the best. . . .*

But I do not love Donal Fleming. She kicked Desdemona into a gallop, and they flew across the grass. *I am not afraid of marriage. I am certainly not afraid of marrying Inglesham.*

Yet you don't love him.

You don't, you don't, you don't. Desdemona's hooves beat out a muffled cadence.

With a sharp pull on the reins Cordelia set Desdemona in the direction of the menagerie.

Much to her shame, she had not visited it since her strange experience with Donal there four weeks ago. She had been afraid that the painful emotions of that day would be repeated.

Now she faced that same risk again. Donal might be there. It was imperative that she face her fears head-on.

Perhaps we are attracted to one another, she thought with painful honesty. *It is human as well as animal nature to seek out the opposite sex. But* we *can control such instincts. . . .*

She flushed as she thought of Donal's strong, sunbrowned hands, his direct and fearless gaze, the coiled energy hidden beneath his unfashionable and ill-cut clothing. Surely *he* would laugh at Theodora's claims. He was too sensible not to recognize the barriers to any bond beyond the most polite friendship between them.

A friendship that included confidences she had never shared with anyone but, on rare occasions, the very cousin who claimed to know her mind and heart so well. She had never told Inglesham so much. She could not imagine ever doing so.

But I have known Inglesham since childhood. He is of an amiable nature, indulgent with his friends, popular in society. He possesses the influence that could further my work. And though he is prone to the bad habit of gambling, I know I could help him, give new purpose to his life.

While Donal Fleming, her other self mocked, *is merely a working man of indifferent background, stubbornly independent, indifferent to convention, careless of how his blunt speech might be received. A man who respects your talents and intelligence without condescension, who cares nothing about the peculiarities of your childhood and youth. A man who would doubtless give his life for the weak and oppressed, be they animal or human. . . .*

Cordelia pulled up as she crested the hill above the menagerie, scanning the row of cages. Donal was there, speaking to a child dressed in a motley collection of ragged clothing in shades of brown and green. The boy had the appearance of a beggar or perhaps a Gypsy, yet Cordelia knew of no such vagrants in the vicinity of Edgecott.

Curiosity drove her down the hill, and as she reached its foot both Donal and the child looked up. Donal's eyes widened in surprise, but it was the boy's gaze that seized Cordelia's attention. Those eyes — brown and slightly tilted in a face that seemed all pointed chin and red hair — did not belong to a child, not even one of Ivy's harsh experience. It was as if the boy were really a man of unusually short stature, a man unlike any Cordelia had ever seen.

Just as she had reached that conclusion, the little man began to spin until he was a blur of motion, shooting skyward in an impossible leap. Then he vanished. Cordelia swayed in the saddle, pressing her fingers into her temples.

"Cordelia!"

She opened her eyes to find Donal regarding her quizzically, his hand on Desdemona's neck. "Are you ill?" he asked.

"Only a little dizzy," she said. She accepted his help in dismounting, tested the steadiness of her legs, and sat on the bench. "Who was that child you were speaking to?"

"Child?"

"Perhaps a particularly short-statured young man, with rather ragged clothes and red hair."

Donal rose up on his toes and settled back again, his expression blank. "I've been here alone all morning."

"I see." She let the matter drop, arrested by the shadows under his eyes and the haggard droop of his mouth. "Have you been sleeping, Doctor?"

"I beg your pardon?"

"You appear somewhat fatigued." She hesitated. "Is something troubling you?"

He smiled, too quickly. "Not at all. I have a deplorable tendency to remain awake long after most sensible people are in bed, and I prefer to rise early. Such odd hours come from spending so much time with animals."

And not enough with people, she thought.

People who would see that you do not wear yourself to the bone . . .

"I do not believe you are telling the whole truth, Doctor."

He paused just long enough that she thought he was about to confide some terrible and long-held secret, one that would bind them together irrevocably. But he only shrugged.

"It's nothing." He glanced toward Desdemona. "Where are you riding today?"

"Out to the river." She stood up and strode toward the mare. "Since you are not in a mood for conversation —"

"Cordelia." His soft footsteps padded behind her, and the small, loose hairs stirred at the back of her neck. "I have missed your company."

"I have hardly been far away, Doctor. I believe I saw you at the dinner table last night."

His breath glided along her temple. "May I join you?"

Cordelia knew how she ought to respond. She ought to escape his influence as often as possible, relegate him once again to the position of trusted employee, nothing more.

But that in itself would be a mistake, for it would prove that she had something to deny to herself, to him and to Theodora.

"If you wish," she said, gathering up the reins. "You will find me along the river path."

Cordelia had nearly perfected an air of cool detachment by the time Donal arrived on Boreas. They rode side by side along the river, and a feeling of contentment stole over Cordelia in spite of the day's unpromising beginnings. She told herself that she had come to terms with Theodora's assertions. She simply had to prove them wrong, but with grace and moderation, not anger.

She was just composing some innocuous conversational gambit when Donal halted Boreas and pointed toward a thicket of goat willow crouched at a bend of the river.

"Do you see him?" he asked.

Cordelia peered in the direction he indicated. "Him? Oh!"

It was a fox, sleek and beautiful, its triangular ears pricked toward the intruders. Emerging from among the low-hanging leaves and branches were a trio of kits — round, miniature replicas of their parent, each one intent upon these strange new creatures who had ventured so near their den.

Donal edged Boreas closer. "Did you know that both male and female foxes share the work of raising their litter? The dog fox grooms and plays with his children."

"That is most admirable."

"Yes." He dismounted and walked a little way toward the vulpine family. They made no attempt to flee. "The male and female remain together until the kits are able to hunt for themselves."

"And then the male abandons them," Cordelia said.

"Not exactly." Donal crouched, and the adult fox sat on its haunches while the kits began to play in the rough-and-tumble manner of young creatures everywhere. "It's usually the vixen who sends him away . . . until the mating season comes again."

Cordelia shivered. "It must be gratifying for the vixen to have such power."

"Females have a great deal of power in the animal kingdom, Cordelia. Much more than you might imagine. In a majority of species, it is they who choose with whom they will mate."

"Like the peahen with the peacock, selecting him for his brilliant plumage," she said with an attempt at lightness. "Among the birds, it is the male who wears the brightest colors."

"And among mammals, it's most often the strongest and fittest who win the right to reproduce. Even then, the female usually has the final say."

"And do you believe this rule extends to human beings?" she asked.

Donal helped her to dismount again. The warmth of his bare hand penetrated through the kid of her gloves. "I believe that women possess more power than they realize."

"Perhaps in some distant land I have never

visited, but not in England."

"Perhaps not," he conceded, shedding his coat and laying it on the grass. "Yet *you* are free to make your own decisions."

She stared at the foxes, who stared back. "Am I?" she murmured.

"Others may attempt to influence you, but you have the strength of will to set your own course." He indicated his jacket. "Please, sit."

"I shall ruin your coat."

He chuckled. "You've never mentioned it aloud, but I feel certain that you regard my current wardrobe as sadly lacking in style. This might compel me to purchase a coat that will meet with your approval."

She sat down gingerly. "You certainly have no need of that!"

He sat beside her. "Yet it is true that I am a rather plain beech owl compared to Lord Inglesham's splendid peacock."

Cordelia adjusted her skirts over her riding boots. "Fortunately, I am no peahen."

"Far from it." He cocked his head. "A peregrine suits you much better."

"Nor am I a hunter," she said tightly.

"I remember that you did not enjoy sharing Othello's memories."

She rubbed her upper arms, though the early afternoon was far from cool. "You know they were not memories, Donal . . . only images your skill with hypnosis placed in my mind. And no, I did not enjoy them."

"That was my fault. I should have known better. The animals in the menagerie had experienced too much pain, and you were forced to share it." He touched her shoulder with the tips of his fingers. "It's not too late to try again."

"No, thank you. Once was quite enough."

"But there's so much more to learn, Cordelia. So much you haven't seen." He looked toward the foxes, who had been joined by another adult. "I can show you what *they* feel . . . not as hunters, but as they are now . . . a family."

"I hardly see what purpose —"

"The more you understand of the animals, the better you will be able to care for your own when I am gone."

Her heart climbed into her throat. "Gone? Are you planning to leave us, Doctor?"

"That was always the arrangement, was it not?" He plucked a blade of grass and rubbed it between his fingers. "I have a little more work to do, and then . . ."

"And then you'll be off to find that place where no human being has ever trod." The anger in her own voice startled her. "I'm sorry. You're quite right — that was our arrangement. Do you anticipate an imminent departure?"

"Not imminent. I do not believe that . . . Ivy is ready."

Cordelia bit the inside of her lip, wondering if Donal regarded her as much a failure with the girl as she did. "She is not making as much progress as I had hoped."

"You have an unfortunate tendency to hold yourself too much accountable for the well-being of others," he said, "and care too little for your own."

"I took responsibility for Ivy of my own free will."

"But has caring for her made you happier, Cordelia? Would you surrender the responsibility if you could?"

"Never." She held his gaze. "I am more than fond of her. She needs me, and I should not know what to do without her."

"Is it enough just to be needed?"

"What greater calling can there be, especially for a woman?"

Donal plucked a blade of grass and twirled it between his fingers. "What of your own needs, Cordelia?"

"An austere life suits me well enough, especially when it leaves more resources for those who are less fortunate, human or otherwise."

"And your dreams?"

She gazed at the river, letting the sparkle of sunlight on water carry her away from the dangers of emotion. "My dreams are for Ivy, for the wonderful life she will have when she . . . when she finally realizes . . ."

"Promise me you will not marry

Inglesham."

She blinked, certain she had not heard him correctly. "I beg your pardon?"

He looked up, and she saw that his eyes had gone dark and strange. "He doesn't merit your trust in him, Cordelia. And your father does not have your best wishes at heart."

Cordelia struggled to stand, tangled her feet in her skirts and snatched the trailing fabric away with a ferocious sweep of her hand. "I know perfectly well that you do not like the viscount, Doctor, but —"

"You must trust me in this," he said, his voice hoarse, pleading and demanding at the same time. "Please, Cordelia."

She took a step away from him. "Why?" she asked. "Why do you so despise a man you hardly know?"

"You may have little faith in instinct, but I must rely on mine."

"That is the best explanation you can provide for such vague accusations?"

He gave a helpless shake of his head. "I have no other."

"You may think that my father wishes to be rid of me, but I assure you . . ."

"No." He drew his hand across his face. "No. I spoke out of turn. Forgive me."

His genuine contrition disarmed her completely. The tightness in her chest receded. "Perhaps we should find another topic of conversation."

"Yes." He glanced at the thicket of goat willow. Cordelia was surprised to see that the fox family was still there, apparently fascinated by the inexplicable human antics.

Donal rose and gazed into Cordelia's eyes. "Let me make amends," he said. "Let me give you something beautiful."

She knew at once what he wanted of her. She had been so determined to avoid any further intimacy with him, and yet what he proposed was the most extreme form of closeness imaginable.

"Only this one last time," he said, "and I shall never suggest it again."

One last time before he leaves us, and then these upsets and arguments will be over. My life will be normal again. . . .

Just as she wanted it. Just as Lydia had yearned for her own life to be, in the weeks before she died.

"Very well," she said. She settled again on Donal's coat and let the tension flow out of her arms and legs. "What shall I do?"

"Only relax, and think of the foxes. I'll do the rest."

Cordelia could not help but try to remain alert as Donal began to speak, but his voice was like the gurgling river or the soughing of wind in the treetops, and soon she was drifting, anchorless, in the world he built with his words. It was as if the animals themselves spoke in her mind, and she began to see through their eyes, feel what they felt.

Joy. Not the fear she might have expected in animals so often mercilessly hunted by men, nor the ceaseless focus on obtaining food. Instead she felt the boundaries of her body dissolve, replaced by a supple, red-coated form ideally shaped for its life and environment.

She raised her muzzle, broad ears catching every sound and movement from shrubbery, meadow and river. The water sang to her, and each breath of wind brought some new, fascinating odor that stirred the hairs on her back with a kit's restless excitement.

A sharp yip from one of her two little vixens brought her back to the thicket. She nosed at each of the younglings in turn, admonished them to remain close, and then turned her gaze upon the two-legged ones across the meadow.

She knew they were harmless, these creatures; they carried no pain-sticks, offered no threat. One of them was so different from most two-legs that the vixen was confused at first; to her it smelled almost like a fox. She nuzzled her mate, who reassured her with a wave of his handsome brush.

Male and female, he reminded her. She coughed in amusement, remembering the way the two-legs had bristled and circled one another like vixen and dog fox at their first meeting, each testing the other's worthiness. She could not tell which had gained dominance.

Both were still, almost as still as a hunter awaiting the reckless dash of a mouse from its nest in the grass, but the eyes of the male were upon the vixen, eyes the color of summer leaves. . . .

She shook her head and bent again to her young ones. They rolled about in mock battle, all three strong and thick-coated with health. This territory the vixen had chosen was abundant with game and hiding places where the kits could rest in safety; it seemed likely that the entire litter would survive the season. She caught the young male under her paw and licked a patch of mud from his coat while he protested and squirmed, only half as indignant as he pretended.

Her mate rubbed his cheek against hers, his contentment as warm as sunlight playing among the branches overhead. He was as proud of his litter as if he had borne them himself. Proud of his mate's beauty, her grace, her cunning.

She leaned into him, anointing herself in the musky scent of his coat, his compelling maleness. Images flitted like butterflies through her memory: the redolent crunch of last autumn's leaves under her paws as they met again after a long season's parting; the dance of approach and retreat, flight and pursuit; his hot breath misting about her face as he sang to her of the most delightful joining to come. Her tail trembled with need of him, with the exaltation of their reunion. . . .

Cordelia swayed, her mouth flooded with unfamiliar tastes, dizzy with the smell of inexorable masculinity. Donal was pressed close, his skin radiating heat through the thin muslin of his shirtsleeves, his face mere inches from hers. The pit of her stomach throbbing with a need she recognized and could not resist.

Donal cupped her face between his strong countryman's hands and kissed her. Her mouth opened under his, thawing and blossoming beneath the healing warmth of his caress. He gentled her as he might gentle a frightened, wounded animal; his lips were firm but never invasive, giving far more than they took. She melted into him, arms stealing about his waist, hands splayed over the hard, shifting muscles of his back and shoulders.

He groaned softly, echoing the cry trapped in her own throat. She welcomed the erotic memories he called out from the depths of her mind where she had hidden them for so long: sensual visions of swaying branches and broad leaves slick with moisture at the end of a sultry day; a resplendent jungle flower luring her to its quivering petals with the sheer, carnal seduction of its perfume; the pungent aroma of exotic spices and sweetmeats dripping with honey; the silky laughter of veiled women and the flash of a brown hand, painted with henna in ancient designs; a drift of strange, enticing music that slid over her skin like silk.

And then she was naked, her entire body taut with anticipation of the ecstasies to come. But it was not James she envisioned lying beside her amid a wanton tangle of sheets and coverlets. It was *him* . . . this man, this lover, Donal Fleming with his other-worldly magic and jungle-dark eyes. . . .

"Cordelia," he whispered.

The sound of her name broke the spell. She jerked, her fingernails tearing into his shirtsleeves. Reality plunged her into a well of icy comprehension. Shame brought her to her feet and guided her to Desdemona's side when her vision was too blurred to show her the way.

You have not changed. Oh, God, you have not changed at all. . . .

"Cordelia!"

She dragged herself into the saddle, her skirts flying above her ankles, and lashed Desdemona into a startled run. The foxes disappeared in a streak of red, and Cordelia prayed with all her heart that she would never see them again.

CHAPTER EIGHTEEN

The first race meeting was everything Donal had feared, and a thousand times worse.

The course had been laid in a fallow field just outside the market town of Chipping Milborne, not twenty miles from Edgecott, and though it was a modest event in comparison to venues such as Newmarket and Ascot, the sponsorship of the local earl had attracted a sizeable contingent of county society as well as farmers, shopkeepers and laborers from the surrounding counties. The lure of sport and money attracted people of every occupation, from seasoned "turfites" to amateurs hoping for a few guineas' profit.

The din of the crowd beat on Donal's ears like the pistons of some great, many-legged machine, and the sour smell of human sweat compounded the nausea Donal felt every time a greedy, gape-mouthed turfite rubbed against him on the way to place his next bet.

Lord Inglesham paid not the slightest attention to Donal's discomfort. He was in his element; his grin drew men to him like flies to a carcass, and he flashed banknotes as if they were so much confetti. He carried the *Racing Calendar* and *Ruff's Guide to the Turf* under his arm, elevated to the ranks of the "knowing ones" through no skill or merit of his own.

He had already led Donal on an early morning inspection of the race entrants, making use of his unctuous charm and well-calculated bribes to gain admittance where it would ordinarily be denied. And he had been exultant when Donal provided him with the subtle details of each horse's condition, giving him an edge that no other turfite or even the cleverest tout could hope to duplicate.

"Excellent work, my friend," he said, slapping Donal on the shoulder. "Of course we'll know more when you see the nags at the starting line. I have a comfortable arrangement with one of the best bookmakers in the south; he'll make any necessary adjustments for me if new information becomes available."

Donal had said nothing, his stomach roiling with the thought of what he had been forced to do, and why. What he hadn't known of the track and its sordid world he had rapidly been compelled to learn: how the form of poor horses could be "puffed up" to deceive all but the most well-informed betters; how even the best animals could be made to appear lame or listless with various drugs; how owners commonly bet against their own horses, pulling their entries at the last possible moment. And though many of the horses with whom Donal had spoken were high-strung with excitement at the prospect of the coming contests, he knew how completely they were subject to their owner's cruel whims.

"I cannot read the minds of men," he warned Inglesham again as they threaded their way through booths and wagons manned by thimbleriggers, card sellers, and vendors of every sort of food and drink. "If an owner chooses to withdraw his entry or instructs his jockey to hold the horse back, I will not know."

Inglesham paused at a stall, paid for a mug of ale and inhaled the brown liquid with all the gusto of a laborer on holiday. "That can't be helped," he said, wiping the foam from his lips with the back of his hand. "And I know most of the owners, anyway. I'm familiar with their tricks." He grinned at a voluptuous young woman whose manner hinted at the pleasures to be found beneath her low-cut bodice. "Come along, Fleming. We've more work to do."

Donal followed, powerless as a beaten dog at the end of his master's chain. Anger seethed in him, but he kept it under strict control. If he let it escape it might affect the horses. They had burdens enough of their own, and no means of freeing themselves from this bondage that made them the disposable playthings of avaricious men.

Try as he might, however, Donal could not calm his troubled heart. He and Inglesham had left Edgecott two days after his perilous encounter with Cordelia by the river . . . two days after she had fled the estate, bound for some purported business in London. They hadn't spoken again after the kiss; Donal had deliberately stayed away from the house that evening, and by morning Cordelia was gone.

He had been relieved at first. He had called himself a hundred kinds of fool for breaking that fine, fragile thread of propriety that still lay between them, knowing that he'd severed it beyond repair. Knowing that he had not only brought himself one step closer to disaster, but that he had betrayed Cordelia's trust, perhaps even made her believe that a lasting relationship was possible when he knew it could never be.

Yet even as he wondered how he could have lost his human will so completely — how he had let the foxes' emotions and his own banked desire so cloud his reason — he recognized that his fears were almost certainly exaggerated. Cordelia was far too intelligent, too *sensible,* to read more into the kiss than a moment's error in judgment. The suppressed part of her nature, the part she refused to acknowledge, would slink back into the darkness of her memories.

And therein lay the real, tragic consequence of their fleeting lapse of discipline: that Cordelia would turn her back on her feelings once more, convinced that they could not be trusted, and remain a prisoner in her cage of conformity and self-denial . . . simply because Donal hadn't the courage to help her escape it. He had attempted a healing he couldn't hope to complete.

You are not to blame, Cordelia. All the mistakes have been mine, from the moment we met. I knew I could never give up my gifts, or my freedom. And yet I believed I could make you see. . . .

"Fleming!"

Inglesham dragged Donal from his grim thoughts with a firm tap on his shoulder. "Methinks your mind ain't on the business at hand, eh?" he said, his words slightly slurred from the effects of several drinks. "The first race is about to begin. I've a place in the grandstand, and of course you'll be my . . . guest." He leaned close, his breath sour in Donal's face. "I expect a reasonable profit in at least two of the races, Fleming . . . as a sign of your good faith. Less than that and I'll know you're shamming."

Donal wrapped his fingers around Inglesham's wrist and pulled his hand away. "You'll get your money," he said. "And then we'll renegotiate this agreement."

Inglesham laughed. "Re . . . negotiate? Naturally, Doctor. Wouldn't want to kill the goose that lays the golden egg, would we?"

But Donal knew he was lying. Once he saw his bets pay off, he'd only want more, and there was a whole season of races ahead of him. Eventually it would no longer be enough for Donal to pick likely winners. Inglesham would expect him to influence the horses directly. As long as he threatened Ivy's exposure to the authorities, he would seem to have the upper hand.

Tod was convinced that the only solution to Donal's dilemma was another, more malignant use of Fane power . . . one that would leave the viscount incapable of threatening anyone ever again. A horse breaking free of its handler at just the right moment could remove the mortal "problem" in a matter of seconds.

"I am a healer, not a murderer," Donal had argued. And he wouldn't subvert any animal to injure a human. There must be another way.

Donal climbed the steps into the grandstand constructed for the wealthy who had paid for the privilege of viewing the race apart from the common rabble. The four horses that had not been withdrawn from the race approached the starting line, where the starter waited with his hand poised near the brim of his hat.

"Well?" Inglesham said.

Donal studied the horses, opening his mind to the nervous thoughts of the colts dancing under their jockeys' firm control. One of the animals was chafing at the bit more than the others, and through his body Donal felt the jockey's tense posture and the grip of his thighs on the colt's barrel.

"Johnny's Cavalier will be held back," he said to Inglesham.

The viscount hissed through his teeth and jotted a note in his small black book. "And the others?"

Donal closed his eyes. A blood bay colt sidestepped and winced at a slight, deep-set pain in his left rear fetlock. "Tuesday's Child will finish the race, but not first."

"Excellent." Inglesham snapped his book closed and stood up. "Enjoy yourself, Fleming. I'll even place a small bet on your behalf."

He was gone before Donal could protest. Hunching low on the bench, Donal imagined himself far from this place and the filthy miasma of human rapaciousness. He ran and leaped with gazelles on the open veldt. He splashed in the wide rivers of Sheba's infancy. He padded through Othello's jungle, relishing the rustle of fallen leaves under his bare feet. Flowers in fantastic hues nodded at the ends of sweeping vines. The water in the streams was a flawless cornflower blue, and the butterflies were as large as Donal's head.

Butterflies. Donal held out his hand, and one of them perched on his fingers, fanning enormous wings that sparkled like rubies. The forest opened up into a meadow carpeted in blossoms of astonishing variety, some in colors Donal had no words to name. Sunshine unmarred by a single cloud bathed the meadow in golden light.

Donal bent to touch an azure petal, and the flower quivered with joy. That was when he knew he was not in Othello's jungle, or anywhere else on earth.

Tir-na-Nog. He shook his head, bewildered by the substantiality of the Fane realm his imagination had conjured up from Tod's description and his own deficient memories. The vision held him captive with its beauty, its calm, its sublime tranquillity. There were no fences or cages in the Land of the Young. Nothing ever truly died in Tir-na-Nog; suffering was all but unknown. Freedom was an unquestioned birthright.

Freedom from pain, from want — from love.

But that was only part of Tir-na-Nog. There was also vanity, indifference, casual cruelty to the humans who fell under the Fanes' spell. There was no such thing as perfection. . . .

Donal opened his eyes. The crudeness of the mortal sphere wiped all traces of Tir-na-

Nog from his thoughts. Acrid scents of horse dung and perspiration wafted through the grandstand. The hairs on the back of his neck bristled with the sensation that someone was watching him.

He turned in his seat, half-expecting to find Tod hovering at his shoulder. But the eyes that met his were not the hob's smokey brown, nor did he recognize the face to which they belonged. The fair-haired lady was lovely, exotic . . . and bold as a Newmarket doxy. Her dress was cut in an unfamiliar style, hinting of faraway lands, and her ice-blue eyes laughed at Donal as if they shared some secret jest.

Donal raised his hand to tip his hat, but the lady had already turned away, her silver laughter cutting through the buzz of conversation as she exchanged some witticism with her handsome male companion.

"A pretty piece, that one," Inglesham said, taking his seat beside Donal. "A Russian countess. She's taken Shapford, near Edgecott . . . well above your station, even if she is a —"

He broke off as the crowd suddenly hushed in anticipation of the starter's signal. The horses fretted and stamped. Inglesham raised his field glasses to his eyes, and then the horses were off in a blur of flexing muscle and flying hooves.

The race ended in victory for a gray by the

name of Archangel, and a tidy profit for the viscount. His bets paid in two of the remaining three races. As Inglesham summoned his carriage for the return to Edgecott, Donal once again broached the subject of renegotiation.

"There must be a limit to this agreement," he said, sitting as far from Inglesham as the carriage seats would allow. "I have shown my good faith. Now you prove yours."

Inglesham chuckled. "Don't be so anxious to end such a successful partnership, my friend," he said. "You, too, could be a wealthy man . . . and there is little in this world that wealth cannot buy."

"It can't buy honor," Donal said.

The viscount's smile turned sour. "It may, however, secure your little maid's future."

Donal dug his fingers into the leather of the squabs. "Do you think this game you play is without consequences, Inglesham?"

"Ah. The inevitable threats at last." He gazed indifferently at the passing scenery. "It might interest you to know that I have not entirely overlooked the areas in which your resistance to our bargain might prove inconvenient. I have already written a letter addressed to certain influential friends in London. Should Cordelia ever learn of this arrangement, the letter will be sent immediately. And if I should fall victim to an accident of any kind . . ." He shrugged. "I have left evidence that will send the authorities directly to you."

Donal laughed. "Evidence? That I have some magical power only a fool would credit?"

"I trust it won't come to such dire circumstances. And while you may wish to do me harm, Fleming, I don't believe you have it in you."

The remainder of the afternoon's drive passed in silence. When they reached Edgecott in the early evening, Donal demanded that Inglesham set him down some distance from the gate. Inglesham leaned out the window to make some final comment, but Donal had already started through the park at a hard, fast stride.

At the last moment he turned off the road to the house, unable to bear the prospect of meeting Cordelia if she had returned from London. His cottage, caught between lowering sunlight and deepening shadow, presented the illusion of a safe refuge, and Donal thought only of sleep. But when he reached the door he found that peace was to elude him once again.

Theodora sat on the weathered bench beside the door, hands clasped tightly in her lap. She stood as he approached, and Donal saw the tension of some pressing concern on her pleasant, homely face.

"Dr. Fleming. Donal. I am so glad you are

returned."

Donal felt an entirely irrational thrill of alarm. "What is wrong, Theodora?"

"I am sorry to disturb you . . . perhaps it is nothing. Indeed, I cannot be certain —"

"Come inside." He opened the door and gestured her to precede him. "I have little to offer you, but if you would allow me to put a kettle on the fire . . ."

"No. No, thank you." She sat in the plain wooden chair near the hearth and regarded him anxiously. "It is about Cordelia."

Donal closed the door and perched on the edge of the bed. "What has happened?"

"As I said, it may be nothing, but . . ." She squared her shoulders. "This afternoon, Cordelia quarreled with Sir Geoffrey again. It has happened lately with greater and greater frequency, and the effects upon Cordelia have been . . . painful to observe."

"Yes." Donal's ribs pressed in on his lungs. "This quarrel was a particularly bad one?"

"I . . . overheard some part of it." Her cheeks reddened. "Afterward, Cordelia was quite agitated. She rushed about the house as if she could find nowhere to turn."

And I was not here, Donal thought bitterly.

"I hoped she might confide in me about her difficulties," Theodora continued, "but she went into her sitting room and did not come out again until one of our local farmers arrived and asked to speak with her on urgent

385

business. Shortly afterward she left the house, dressed in a heavy cloak. Her behavior was such that I became worried for her, and I followed the farmer until I overtook him." She swallowed. "He told me that Cordelia had a longstanding arrangement with several farmers and villagers, men she trusted, to inform her when certain events occurred in the neighborhood. It seems that a dogfight was to be held near Charlcombe this very evening, and —"

Donal shot to his feet, his thoughts hardening to crystal clarity. "Cordelia has gone to stop it," he said.

"It is what I feared." Theodora held Donal's gaze, her own dark with misery. "She has been reckless in such matters before, as you saw in London. But I do not believe that she has ever attempted such a thing without first contacting others who despise such sport as she does. She is but one woman, and the sort of men who would force animals to fight each other for their own amusement . . ." She shuddered. "Even now I can scarcely credit that she would be so foolish."

Unless she has been driven to the point of desperation, Donal thought. *Desperation to take action, to fight adversaries who can be openly opposed and defeated, unlike the enemies she faces in her own home and heart.*

Enemies she could never acknowledge: her father, Inglesham, the societal conventions that kept her bound to rigid duty and an endless quest for perfection that remained ever out of reach. . . .

"I asked Croome to send our footmen after her," Theodora continued, "but Cordelia had given the servants an afternoon's liberty. I considered calling the constable, but feared he would arrive too late. That was when I thought of you."

"You were right to do so. Do you know specifically where this fight is to be located?"

"Only what I told you. Such fights are illegal, and so its patrons are careful to keep the details secret from outsiders." She rose, clutching at her skirts. "There must be dangerous men there, Donal. You should not go alone."

"I won't be alone." He clasped her hands. "You did well to come to me, Theodora. It will be all right."

"I will pray for you both."

He nodded, collected his bag and strode for the door, his thoughts reaching out for two he could count as allies. Tod was nowhere to be found, but Sir Reginald had found his way out of the house and was waiting for Donal in the drive.

He picked up the spaniel and ran for the stables, breathing deeply to calm his dread. Reggie licked his chin and whined.

"I would prefer not to take you at all, my friend," Donal told the spaniel, "but once we reach Charlcombe I may need your admirable nose to help me locate the fight."

Sir Reginald shivered, catching some part of the dark images that spilled from Donal's mind. Donal hugged the dog close. "I won't take you anywhere near that place," he said as they approached the stable. "You'll remain safely with Boreas once I know where to go."

He raced past a startled groom to Boreas's stall, where the stallion was already splintering the walls with his hooves. Donal untied the horse, carefully balanced Sir Reginald on Boreas's withers, and mounted bareback.

"Now, Reggie," he said, "we shall find Cordelia."

The byre stank of filthy straw, unwashed bodies and animals pushed to the very edge of their endurance. The cloak Cordelia wore did nothing to insulate her from the horror of the sounds and smells, the avid faces of the men who shouted out their bets as they prepared to send innocent animals to pain, mutilation and death.

There were no women here to witness this atrocity. The rough shirt and trousers Cordelia wore might disguise her sex at a distance, but if any of these human monsters discovered who hid in the shadows they would have cast her out with neither courtesy nor compunction.

Shivering with disgust and rage, Cordelia

edged her way to the corner of the byre where the dog crates were kept, most so small that their occupants — many missing ears or marked with horrible, half-healed wounds — had no choice but to lie in their own excrement. The stench was unbearable, yet one of the dogs, a brindle terrier, crept up to the bars and whimpered, begging for some comfort in this canine hell.

Cordelia pushed her fingers into the cage and stroked the scarred nose, nearly weeping at the gentle touch of the animal's tongue on her skin. Other dogs pressed toward her, some wagging their tails in defiance of their ghastly plight.

Aware that her opportunities were severely limited, Cordelia kept her ears and eyes open while she examined the cage latches. As contemptible as the dogfighting patrons might be, their shared vice evidently led them to trust each other to some degree. None of the cages was locked.

Cordelia sank back on her heels and measured the distance from the crates to the guarded byre entrance. It would seem nearly impossible to free the dogs and get them before their owners stopped her . . . and many of the poor beasts would be too poisoned with fear or excitement to escape.

That was the tragedy of it. A number of the dogs could never be allowed to run loose, for they had been repeatedly forced to attack weaker animals, cruelly punished for failure and praised for each sordid victory. But Cordelia refused to give up hope. If even one animal could be saved, she would not regret the risk or effort in coming. And if she could actually stop the fight from proceeding . . .

For just a moment her resolve weakened, and she thought of Donal. He would understand why she had felt compelled to come here, foolish as it might seem. He would gladly stand beside her, and if she had been thinking a little more clearly she would have seen the wisdom of asking him in spite of the dreadful awkwardness of their last meeting.

If awkwardness were all it was. If only she had used the sense she so often berated Ivy for failing to employ. If only she had acknowledged the volatility of her feelings before it was too late. . . .

"Just what d'you think yer doin' there?"

Cordelia stiffened at the suspicious voice and surreptitiously pulled the hood of her cloak lower over her face. The man came closer, close enough that she could see the black stubble on his chin and smell the liquor on his breath.

"You hear me?" the man growled. He caught hold of Cordelia's cloak, jerking her away from the crates. "No one gets near the dogs before the fight." He thrust his face close to Cordelia's. "Got somethin' to hide, boy? Maybe you was plannin' on swingin' the odds in yer favor?"

Cordelia shrank back in pretended fear. "I weren't doin' nothin'," she protested in her deepest voice. "Just wanted to see what they looked like."

The man spat into the rotting hay. "This yer first time, boy? It'll be yer last if you don't get back to the ring." He aimed a kick at Cordelia's legs, which she dodged easily enough. But her hood slipped from her forehead with the suddenness of her movement, and before she could turn her head the man had seen her face.

He uttered a foulness in perfect keeping with his depraved nature and seized her shoulder. "A female," he sneered. She fought him as best she could, but he twisted her arm behind her back and dragged her into the circle of lamplight that flooded the makeshift ring.

"Look what we have here, my lads," he said. "A little lady come slummin' to share our entertainment."

Chapter Nineteen

The clamor of male voices fell silent. Two men on either side of the ring yanked on the chains restraining their snarling, snapping bull terriers. Shadowed faces turned to Cordelia with snickers and scowls, muttering curses patently unfit for a lady's ears.

"What's a female doin' 'ere?" someone demanded.

"Must've come to entertain *us*," another suggested with a laugh.

Cordelia stood very still and looked slowly about the ring, searching for a familiar face. Though she had taken pains to disguise her normal appearance with a severe coiffure and well-placed smudges on her face, she knew some of the men might recognize her, and others would simply not wish to be identified by an outsider. Several men in clothing of considerably better quality than the rough garb of the majority hurried toward the entrance and slipped out.

"Well?" Cordelia's captor said. "She can't

stay 'ere. Anyone claim 'er?"

"Let her go, Joe," one man said from the rear of the throng. "We don't want no trouble."

"What if she tells?" a harsher voice asked.

Joe shook Cordelia impatiently. "Who are you, girl?"

Cordelia pushed her hood all the way back to her shoulders and stepped into the brightest pool of light. A bettor, his fingers wrapped around a heavy bag of coin, gasped in surprise and scuttled deeper into the crowd. Joe released Cordelia and stepped away.

Cordelia smiled, her heart nearly bursting with fury. "It does not matter who I am," she said. "I have come to stop this foul perversion you call a 'sport.' "

The silence stretched for a dozen measured heartbeats before the mob broke into a chorus of furious denials. Threats shot at Cordelia like missiles. A half-dozen men slipped out the doors as the "gentlemen" had before them.

"Others know of this," Cordelia cried above the torrent of voices. "They will be coming soon. Leave the dogs here, and you may —"

Something struck the side of Cordelia's head, knocking the words from her throat. She felt wetness trickling into her eyes. But there was no fear, even when she realized that her life might be in danger. She turned to face one of the men who held the chained terriers, knowing that the very animals she had come to save were entirely capable of tearing out her throat.

"Give them to me," she commanded, holding out her hand.

The handler stared at her with disbelieving eyes. "Get out," he hissed. "Get out while you still can." His gaze flickered over her shoulder, and Cordelia almost had time to prepare herself before the blood-matted blanket descended over her head in a choking shroud.

The next few minutes were a chaos of rough, groping hands and muffled arguments as the men debated what to do with her.

"I tell you, I know her. If you hurt her, there'll be hell to pay."

"That's *yer* problem, laddie. You should've put up a better watch."

"She saw some of us."

"Well, then, she can't testify against you if she ain't here, can she?"

Cordelia tried to speak, but the fetid cloth filled her mouth. Just as the men's sinister debate reached its crescendo, the dogs began to howl. The noise rose to a deafening pitch, provoking more curses from the men, and then stopped as suddenly as it had begun.

"Release her."

Donal's voice was a miracle, strong and firm and commanding, and even the harsh sawing of the men's breathing stilled. One of them lost his grip on Cordelia, and she slipped to the ground.

She had no clear sense of what happened then. As she untangled the cloth from about her head, a new sound rose in the byre, eerie and harrowing. Men began to scream. They screamed as if they were drowning in boiling oil, as if they were being flayed alive . . . as if they had fallen into the very pits of hell in which they so richly belonged.

For a single, nauseating instant Cordelia felt a sensation unlike any she had ever endured: debilitating pain; the nightmarish illusion of jaws closing about her neck, her face, tearing flesh and muscle; a dread and rage so indescribable that she could do nothing but lie frozen in shock. Then it was over, and she could move again.

Cordelia pushed to her feet, searching blindly for Donal. He stood in the center of the ring, his hands fisted at his sides, his head thrown back in strange and terrible exultation. The fighting patrons had fallen in various contorted positions about the ring, writhing, clawing at their faces and clothing, whimpering and shrieking all the while.

"Donal!" Cordelia cried.

A shudder racked his body, and he released his breath in one long sigh. He lowered his head and opened his eyes. The horrible cries began to subside, the men collapsing into exhausted, shivering lumps wherever they came to rest.

Donal met Cordelia's gaze, his own still veiled and distant. "Are you all right?" he asked in a rough whisper.

She touched the cut on her forehead, knowing that she could never properly describe what she had just experienced. "Yes. I am unhurt." With a grimace of loathing she stepped around the men sprawled at her feet and cautiously approached him. "What happened?"

He passed his hand over his eyes. "I . . . don't know. Perhaps they ate something that didn't agree with them."

His theory was preposterous, though he clearly did not intend it as a joke. Something uncanny had struck these men down, and Cordelia suspected she had felt some small part of what they had suffered. But her own thoughts were far too muddled to propose a more logical explanation for the men's singular behavior and their present state of prostration — or why Donal's arrival had seemed to precipitate it.

As for Donal himself . . . she would have sworn that he, too, had undergone some bizarre transformation and was only just emerging from it. Cordelia took a firm grip on her reason and clutched Donal's rigid arm. "Whatever the cause of their illness," she said, "it cannot last forever. Help me gather the dogs. I have a wagon hidden in the wood across the pasture. We'll take them back to the house . . ."

He tossed brown hair out of his eyes with a shake of his head. "You've done enough, Cordelia. Go to the wagon, and wait. I'll bring the animals."

"No. This is my battle as much as it is yours." With a final swift glance at the men, none of whom seemed inclined to stop her, she hurried to the cluster of cages.

Now that she no longer needed to hide, Cordelia had a much clearer view of the animals she had set out to help. While some were on their feet, alert and even wagging their tails, a number lay unmoving, soaked in their own blood. Donal joined her, crouching with his palm pressed hard against the nearest crate.

"Murderers," he snarled. "Savages."

Cordelia covered his hand with hers, and discovered that both were shaking. Somehow she understood that she must be the one to keep them focused on their purpose.

"Help me get them out," she said. "Quickly, Donal."

He roused himself and began to open the cages at one end while she started at the other. It was soon evident that some of the dogs would attack each other if given the opportunity; Donal seemed to know which ones required special handling and spent a few extra moments with them, speaking in soothing tones that promised peace and rest. A few dogs he left in their cages and carried the crates outside the barn.

When they had collected and secured a dozen dogs who were capable of walking on their own, they went back for the sick ones. Five animals Donal eased from their cages, holding their limp bodies against his chest as if they were his beloved children. A spotted terrier, ravaged by countless deep lacerations, feebly raised its head and licked his chin. Another snapped at Donal's hands until his touch calmed it into submission.

"Will they recover?" Cordelia asked, sick with anger.

"I'll do what I can as soon as we're back at Edgecott," he said. He glanced at the nearest men with something very like hatred in his eyes. Had any of them moved even a little, Cordelia had no doubt that Donal would have pummeled them to within an inch of their lives.

One by one he carried the wounded animals out to the wagon and laid them on a pile of blankets in the bed. Sir Reginald and Boreas were waiting, tied to a nearby tree. Donal gave the spaniel to Cordelia and placed the dogs in the wagon, with the caged dogs at the rear. He ministered to the anxious animals while Cordelia drove home, Boreas trotting along behind. If any of the dogfighters had recovered from their ordeal, none made any attempt at pursuit.

Once at the house, Donal drove on to the kennels and Cordelia stopped to look in on Theodora and Ivy, who had remained awake and greeted her in the drawing room with a dozen worried questions. She left Sir Reginald with Ivy, changed into an old dress, and promised to give both women a complete report the next morning. She ran all the way to the kennels.

She found Donal with the most seriously hurt animals in a run carpeted with straw and blankets, his shoulders hunched as he worked with his instruments and bandages. Cordelia hung back, not wishing to interfere, until Donal hoarsely asked for her help.

Together they tended the animals through the night, their clothing smeared with mingled blood and perspiration as they struggled to save their patients. The spotted terrier fought gamely, but as dawn broke Donal met Cordelia's eyes with a look she could not misinterpret.

"No," she whispered. She bent over the dog and tried to lift it in her arms, feeling its life seeping away even as she willed it to fight a little longer. "No. There must be something more you can do . . ."

"He has lost too much blood," Donal said, his voice cracking. "He is ready to go, Cordelia."

"Oh, no." She pressed her face to the matted coat. The terrier whined deep in its chest, begging for release. Her tears dropped onto his muzzle, and she gently stroked them away with her fingertips.

Donal reached out and laid his palm on the terrier's heaving side. "Go, now," he said. "Sleep, my friend. You have earned your rest."

Cordelia could have sworn that the dog looked directly at Donal with gratitude and acceptance. She seemed to feel an odd sense of relief in her own heart, fading memories of pain and fear that lost all their power with the sweet threnody of Donal's voice.

The terrier let his head fall to the blankets, gave a final deep sigh, and lay still.

The heaviness of death descended on Cordelia like a choking cloud, filling her chest with unendurable grief. She rocked the terrier in her arms, swallowing her sobs.

"Don't grieve for him," Donal said. "He is free of a terrible existence. He is at peace."

"Peace? Peace for one out of thousands?"

He touched her cheek with such tenderness that she could feel the ramparts of her control — the walls she had built so high and so well — begin to crumble. She laid the terrier down on his bed and turned her face away.

"I wanted to save them."

Donal dropped his hand. "You have, Cordelia."

"A handful. A drop in the ocean."

"You are but one person. You cannot save

the world."

She slammed her fist against the wall. It had been years since she had felt such rage, such black despair. "If I had had a weapon," she said, "I believe I could have killed those men. I would have seen them all dead, even the ones who —" She gasped at the power of her fury, the liberating joy of setting it free with images of violence and destruction. It lifted her to her feet like a hot, fierce wind.

"Even now," she said, "even now I could hunt them down. Just like Othello." She laughed. "What does that make me? As bad as those men. As savage as any wild beast."

Donal got up and clasped her arms in an unbreakable grip. "It makes you what we all are," he said, his green eyes blazing. "Human and animal. A creature of this earth."

She began to tremble. "Of this earth," she repeated. "Is that truly what *you* are, Donal?"

His muscles tensed, though he did not release her. "I don't understand you."

"That day at the menagerie . . . again with the foxes, feeling what they felt . . . I thought it was only a form of mental suggestion. But then, tonight . . ." She paused, knowing that her supposition was as mad as her bestial emotions. "Tonight I *knew* what it was to be one of those dogs, to fight and die and live in terror. And I think the same thing happened to the men."

Donal dropped his gaze. "How could that

be possible?"

"Because you made it happen." She bared her teeth in a smile. "*You* punished those murderers, just as they deserved."

He opened his mouth for a denial, but his face had never learned how to lie. "Cordelia —"

"It's more than a doctor's skill, isn't it? You know what the animals think, what they feel." She snatched at the front of his half-open, bloodstained shirt, her nails catching in the fine, curling hairs that dusted his broad chest. "Can you do the same with people?" She leaned into him. "Do you know what we think, Donal? Have you seen everything . . . everything we try to hide? Is it so easy for you, to sit in judgment. . . ."

"No." He grasped her wrists, holding her as if he feared she might fly into a madwoman's frenzy. "Please, Cordelia. You have endured too much. Let me take you to the house."

"Oh, yes. By all means, make certain that the delicate female is protected from herself." She wrenched free. "Who sent you to my rescue tonight? Was it Theodora? She always looks at me as if I am about to . . . about to —" Her voice tripped in midsentence, stumbling over emotions that seethed like a South Atlantic storm, like lava spilling from a volcano believed long extinct.

Carefully, so carefully, she stepped back until she could retreat no further. She knew that if she moved from that spot, even to leave the kennels, her body would shatter and the fragile edifice she called her strength, her courage . . . her soul . . . would crumble into dust and nothingness.

"Please, go," she whispered.

He searched her face with eyes that gave no quarter. "I will not leave you here alone."

"Damn you." She closed her eyes. "Go away, go away, go away. I don't want you to see. I don't want . . ." A current of dizziness swept over her, and she could not remember what she had been about to say. She slid her foot to the side, desperate to keep her balance. Her skirts dragged her down, down and down into a swirling vortex of darkness.

Donal moved an instant before she fell, scooping her into his arms and letting her weight lie against his chest. For all her fitness and vitality, her bones seemed as light as a bird's, her flesh no more substantial than the wings of a butterfly.

"Cordelia," he said, caressing her pale, drawn face. His fingers came away wet with her tears. The fine skin of her throat quivered, but she did not waken.

Donal carried her into a clean, unused run and laid her on a bed of straw, leaving her just long enough to see that the rescued dogs were resting and needed no further care. Then he gathered her up again and started for his cottage. It was much closer than the house, and he knew that Cordelia would rather face questions later than allow members of her household to see her as she was now. No mortal doctor could cure her of this illness.

And that, he reflected grimly, was his doing.

He reached the cottage as the sun broke over the horizon and set her down on his bed, drawing the coverlet up to her chin. Though the evening had been warm, he shoveled fresh coals into the grate and started a fire. Cordelia would need tea when she recovered, and he intended to provide her with every comfort.

Feeling angry and helpless, he drew a stool up beside the bed and took one of her limp hands in his, chafing it gently.

"I'm sorry," he said. "Pitiful words, aren't they?" He laughed. "It's just as well you can't hear them, or you would fix me with your most scornful gaze and tell me I have nothing to be sorry for. You would hide behind your pride, Cordelia, because you would be ashamed. Ashamed that I have seen what you would call weakness."

Cordelia didn't stir, and Donal knew he was the true coward for speaking to her when she couldn't hear him.

"I should have known that you would guess the truth, sooner or later. Perhaps I wanted you to know." He lifted her hand to his lips and kissed it, first her fingers and then her palm, stroking his thumb along the lines that the Gypsies claimed could foretell a man or woman's future. "When you wake, you'll blame yourself for having fallen beneath your own exacting standards. For maudlin sentimentality and pointless anger. For being merely human. But it was I who drove you to it, *a stór.* I opened your mind to the part of yourself you did not wish to see. And then . . ."

He swallowed and set her hand back down on the bed, tucking it under the coverlet. "I lost myself as well, Delia. I wanted you. I have from the beginning. I wanted you, but I also wanted my freedom. So I took just a little of you, and that little was enough to upset all the rules by which you live your life."

The coals shifted in the grate, and he rose to jab at them with a poker. The hapless coals tumbled this way and that, and the nascent flame nearly went out.

He turned to her again, his throat tight with longing. "I've lived *my* life outside those rules, Cordelia. Neither human nor Fane . . . trying . . . trying to set myself apart from both. I believed myself above the cruelty of mankind. But last night I became what I most despised. I made those men feel what the dogs felt, every last drop of agony and fear. And I enjoyed it."

Cordelia's head moved on the pillow, rolling toward him, but her eyes remained closed, her breathing soft and steady. Donal resumed his seat beside the bed and touched the brown hair so severely drawn back from her face.

"I did not mean for you to suffer, for you to know . . . You were not ready. It was more than you could bear."

He gazed down at her face — fair and vulnerable, stripped of the unyielding mask she showed the world, finally at peace. He went to the washstand, poured fresh water from the pitcher and dampened a cloth to bathe the dirt from her skin. Half-afraid of waking her, he wielded the cloth with utmost care, his arm trembling from the effects of her nearness and the misery of his confession.

He trudged back to the washstand and stared at his shadowed face in the mirror. The ache of loneliness weighed on his heart like a casing of lead, loneliness he hadn't felt since Susannah Stainthorpe had dashed his youthful dreams of romance. Tod, it seemed, had abandoned him. Ivy didn't need him, in spite of her youthful belief that she was in love with him. He had come to enjoy Cordelia's company, her uncompromising nature, her courage; he had become almost dependent upon it.

"Can it be that you have not acknowledged

your true feelings?" Inglesham had mocked him. Now he looked into his own eyes and accepted the truth. He had come as close to loving Cordelia as he ever could. If things had been different — if their needs and ambitions were not so thoroughly incompatible — he might even have found a way to stay.

"I have never known how to ask forgiveness, Cordelia," he said. "I have always avoided the necessity. But I must learn, for soon my work here will be done, and I cannot leave you if I —"

"Donal."

Her voice was hardly a whisper, but it shattered his soliloquy like a bellow. He spun about and knocked the stool aside in his haste to reach her . . . in his fear that she had heard too much.

But her half-lidded eyes held no accusation, no judgment. She moved her hand beneath the coverlet and he took it, resisting the urge to raise it to his lips.

"How are you feeling?" he asked.

She smiled in a way that left him breathless. "Much better."

"No dizziness? No discomfort?"

She curled her fingers about his. "I am still . . . grieved. But I am no longer out of my senses."

"Don't blame yourself for that, Cordelia. You were —"

"I know how I must have sounded. Wishing

407

to kill those men. Accusing you of . . . such ridiculous things that you must have thought me quite mad."

Tell her the truth, Donal thought. *That is the very least you owe her.*

But the moments passed, and he could not bring himself to overturn the accommodations she had made to rationalize the past few hours' events.

"I never thought you mad," he said. "Only . . . perhaps a little overwhelmed."

"Yes. And worse than that if you had not been there."

He glanced away. She pushed back the covers and touched his face, fingers stroking his cheek. "You do not need to ask my forgiveness," she said. "There is nothing to forgive."

He shook his head, held mute by the explanations and excuses dammed behind his tongue. Cordelia let her hand drop to his chest, pressing her palm over his heart. Her gaze roamed about the room. "I have not been in this cottage since you took possession. It is very pleasant."

"I . . . brought you here because I thought you would prefer it, at least until you regain your strength." He did his best to ignore the heat of her skin burning through the fabric of his shirt, but his mouth went dry and his pulse began to race. "I took the liberty of loosening your stays. I hope you will not take offense."

She flushed deeply. "I quite understand. You are, after all, a doctor of sorts."

"Of sorts." He cleared his throat. "You should go back to sleep. I'll visit the house and tell them . . . I'll ask Theodora to come, so that the proprieties will be maintained." He attempted a smile. "I'm sure that no one will think —"

"To the devil with the proprieties," she said. She curled her fingers into his shirt, pulling him down with startling force. Her breath caressed his lips. "Do not send for my cousin, Donal."

He froze. "Cordelia . . . you are not yet recovered from your ordeal. You should —"

"Should. *Should.* How weary I am of that word!"

"I understand, but . . . you are not yourself."

"I am more myself than I have been in a very long time." Her nails scraped his skin. "I know what I want, Donal. Do not deny me."

Donal closed his eyes, fighting for control over the desire running hot in his blood. "There is no greater stimulus for the urge to . . . to procreate than the proximity of death."

"Procreate?" She laughed. "Ah, yes. You insist that even we human beings are animals." She stared into his eyes, her own blazing with hunger and conviction. "Do you truly think that I am driven by mindless, bestial urges, lost to all reason?"

"I think you are suffering, Cordelia. You'll

feel differently tomorrow, and regret —"

"I'll regret nothing." She seized his hand and drew it to her bodice. "You once told me that I have little faith in instinct. You were wrong." She released a shuddering breath. "I know this is what we both need. I have never been so sure of anything in my life."

Donal locked his muscles, bracing himself to dash her illusions once and for all. "I cannot stay with you, Cordelia."

Fleeting bewilderment crossed her face. "What has that to do with —"

"Whatever comes of this, whatever happens between us, I will be leaving Edgecott."

Comprehension replaced the hesitation in her eyes. "Do you think I do not know that? Did you believe that I would demand that you love me?"

He went hot and cold by turns, stunned by the implacable clarity of her question, the fearlessness of her honesty. "If I could stay," he said, half choking on the words. "If I could be what you wanted —"

She covered his mouth with her fingertips. "You are what I want. Here and now. Nothing else exists." Her lips formed the ghost of a smile, the faintest trace of uncertainty. "Is it that you do not want me?"

"God. Cordelia . . ." He took her face between his hands, no longer caring if she felt how badly he trembled. "I want you. I always have."

"Then let us both take what we want." She reached up. "Come to me, Donal."

Chapter Twenty

The battle was over.

Donal came to her at last, his arms strong and sure, his lips gentle as they found hers. For the span of a heartbeat she remembered other times, other kisses . . . a fumbling experiment with a planter's son in Brazil, stolen meetings with a young subaltern in India, her first encounter with James, Inglesham's eminently civilized pecks . . . and then all thought of other men fled her memory, and there was only him.

She pressed against him, doing her best to make him understand that gentleness was the last thing she wanted. She slid her fingers through the thick, loose curls of his hair and shamelessly begged him to devour her. He opened his mouth, still hesitant, but when she nipped his lower lip he groaned, a deep rumble of surrender, and pushed his tongue inside.

A liquid flood of warmth rushed through Cordelia's body. She arched her neck as

Donal began to remove the pins from her hair, letting the locks tumble free about her face and shoulders. She felt the complete wanton, and yet there was no shame, only growing excitement.

Without words she guided his fingers to the tiny buttons at her bodice, eager to feel his hands on her skin. His breath came hard and fast, matching her own, yet he took his time, opening her bodice and helping her remove the bulky garment. But she was by no means freed of her cage; the stays he had already loosened rested like a weight of steel over her breasts.

She lifted her hair and turned. "Unlace me," she said. She felt his fingers tremble as he pulled the laces free. Cool air swept beneath her chemise, the final layer that stood between her and the touch she longed for.

He reached around her and cupped her breasts in his big hands, stroking his thumbs over her nipples through the thin fabric. The feeling was indescribably erotic. James had never taken his time with her in bed; even when he was sober he was boyish in his impatience, and though he was never rough he assumed she enjoyed her pleasures as perfunctorily as he did.

Donal did not. He brought her to aching readiness without ever touching her flesh, and only after she was near to crying out with frustration did he turn her about in his arms, lift the chemise over her head and lay his hands on her body.

"You are beautiful," he whispered. She almost believed him. She accepted his worship as he weighed her breasts in his palms, lowered his head and took her nipple in his mouth, laving it with his tongue. She gasped and trembled as he laid her back upon the bed, suckling her gently and then with hungry intensity, giving thorough attention to one nipple before moving to the next. Her gasps and moans were the only sounds to break the silence.

He lifted his head and looked into her eyes, his gaze warm with admiration and desire. "Your petticoats," he said. "They are . . . rather inconvenient."

"Yes," she said, her voice unsteady. "Most inconvenient."

She sat up, her hardened nipples stroking the linen of his shirt as he undid the fastenings at the back of her skirt. He lifted her from the bed, and she wriggled free of the skirt with a little laugh of self-consciousness. He caught her laughter with a kiss as he undid the petticoats one by one and let them fall about her feet.

She stood before him in her cotton drawers, fighting the urge to cover herself with her arms. He looked at her as if she were a goddess, a creature out of myth and legend that no man dared touch.

He cupped her face between his hands. "Are you afraid?" he asked.

"No. Not of you. It is just that I am so very plain."

"Plain? You?" He chuckled and drew her against him. "You are magnificent in every way."

"Oh, Donal . . ."

He quieted her again with his mouth on her lips, her throat, her breasts, and then he carried her back to the bed. He stood before her without embarrassment and removed his shirt, revealing a well-muscled torso with a dusting of coppery hair from chest to hard stomach. She had only moments to admire his breathtaking masculine beauty before he began to unbutton his trousers. She could not look away, and when he had shed his drawers she saw that he was fully, and impressively, aroused.

"I do not believe," Cordelia said softly, "that I have ever beheld such a fine male specimen of the species Homo sapiens."

Donal's cheeks reddened, but her compliment only seemed to fuel his desire. He joined her on the bed, stretching out beside her, and resumed his caresses, stroking her skin from breast to belly, gliding over hip and thigh as he removed her drawers and left her naked to his gaze. His fingers circled her navel, moving lower to dip between her thighs in delicate exploration.

She closed her eyes and gasped. "Donal . . ."

"Hush," he said. His finger skimmed over her slick, tender flesh, finding the tiny bud where all sensation gathered. He teased it with small, circular motions as he suckled her breasts and kissed her throat, bringing her closer and closer to the mysterious and magical moment of completion.

But it was not enough to experience that moment alone, no matter how unselfishly Donal might wish it. Cordelia pressed her face to Donal's chest, flicking his nipple with her tongue. He froze. She reached down between them and found the hard length pressed against her thigh, stroking it with her fingertip.

"I want you inside me," she whispered into the hollow of his shoulder. She shifted her legs, resting her thigh over his hip, and guided him against her.

If there had been a moment when Donal might have broken free, when his mind might have overcome the needs of his body, that time had long since passed. He felt Cordelia's velvet warmth opening to him, heard her low moan of approval as he slid inside, and he was lost. Lost as she wrapped her legs about his hips to pull him deeper, lost beyond all recovery when she gasped his name in time to the rhythm of his thrusts. When he would have been gentle she dug her nails into his back and demanded his ferocity, and soon there was nothing but the dance of their bodies and Cordelia's sighs of pleasure.

Still Donal held himself back, waiting for Cordelia to reach her peak before he let himself find his. But she would have none of it. She arched up against him, her fingers tangled in his hair, and played him like a fine instruments in the hands of a master. Just as he felt himself begin to lose control she bucked and shuddered beneath him, and with a groan of triumph he surrendered.

With their bodies still linked he rolled Cordelia to her side, cradling her head in the crook of his arm. His heart was so full that he couldn't speak for fear of the words he might say. Instead he stroked the damp hair from her face and kissed her forehead, content beyond all reason.

She pulled back and kissed his chin, her face still flushed with passion. Tears shimmered in her eyes.

He leaned over her, stricken. "Why are you weeping? Did I hurt you?"

"No." She smiled and wiped at the tears with the back of her hand. "I do not believe I've ever been so happy."

"Céadsearc," he said hoarsely, hating himself, "you have made me very happy, too."

She rose up on her elbow, her hair spilling over her shoulders, and smiled at him tenderly. "How strange that I can almost hear your thoughts," she said. "Right now you are wondering how best to remind me that this is but a temporary pleasure, and that it would be a mistake for me to rely upon you for my future happiness."

"Cordelia . . ."

"You need not say it, for I already know." She caressed his lower lip with her fingertip. "Be at ease, my lord Enkidu. I shall not demand anything of you, save perhaps a few more nights like these. I am willing to take what pleasure we can steal . . . today, tomorrow, for as long as you remain at Edgecott."

For all her brave words, Donal heard the quiver in her voice. He was more than grateful to accept the temporary liaison she offered, but to speak of it now seemed crass and vulgar.

"Enkidu," he said, grasping at a less painful subject. "Where have I heard that name before?"

"It was the name I gave you in my mind when first we met at the Zoological Gardens. You have heard of the Epic of Gilgamesh, the great Babylonian hero? His dearest companion was Enkidu, who was lord of the beasts and could speak their tongue."

Donal shivered. "I know the story." Just as he knew that Enkidu, the wildest of wild men, was tamed when he lay with a woman sent by Gilgamesh, and thus lost his mystical bond with his animal brothers.

That would not happen to Donal. He might

lie beside Cordelia a thousand times and never lose his abilities . . . unless he slipped over the deadly border from friendship and desire to love.

"I hope I have not offended you?" Cordelia asked, smiling shyly.

"How could you? At least you found me worthy to be lord of something."

"Worthy indeed." She stretched up and kissed him lightly. "But if you feel you have not yet earned your title, I should be more than willing to give you another chance."

Donal groaned and pulled her against him. Her mouth was hot and wet, and her heart beat strongly against his chest . . . so strongly that it seemed to shake the very walls of the cottage.

Someone was knocking at the cottage door.

Donal lifted his head, aiming a savage thought at the one who so cruelly plunged him and Cordelia back into harsh reality.

"What is it?" Cordelia asked.

Donal rose and threw on shirt and trousers, buttoning up in haste as the knock sounded again. Cordelia sat up, her gaze losing its softness as she looked toward the door.

"Stay where you are," Donal warned her. "I won't allow them to know you're here."

She pulled the coverlet up to her shoulders. "Do you think such a thing can be kept secret?" She tossed her hair. "I am not ashamed."

Donal admired her spirit, but he knew that soon she would begin to consider the consequences of their joining. When she did, she would realize that it was ill-advised to allow either Ivy or her father to learn what had happened.

He tucked in his shirt, pulled on his boots and carefully opened the door. A nervous footman stood on the threshold. He bobbed his head at Donal, attempted to look over Donal's shoulder, and retreated several steps when Donal fixed him with a withering glare.

"I am sorry to disturb you, Doctor," the boy said, his Adam's apple bobbing with his words. "I am looking for Mrs. Hardcastle."

"And you expected to find her here?"

The footman stared at Donal's disheveled hair. "I . . . er, we were told she was with you at the kennels. She wasn't there." He straightened. "It is a matter of some urgency, Dr. Fleming. Sir Geoffrey has taken quite ill, and Miss Shipp directed that Mrs. Hardcastle be found at once."

Donal winced inwardly, certain that Cordelia had heard the young man and would shortly be at the door, heedless of her reputation.

"Mrs. Hardcastle assisted me in caring for the animals she rescued last night," he said, willing Cordelia to keep quiet a little longer. "It was a most trying experience. She mentioned taking a walk by the river when we parted early this morning. I would advise you to seek her there."

The footman hesitated, unprepared to question Donal's statement and yet clearly not convinced. "Miss Shipp fears for Sir Geoffrey's life, Dr. Fleming. If you would assist me in locating Mrs. Hardcastle . . ."

"Of course. If you'll go on to the river, I'll join you presently."

He closed the door in the footman's face and quickly turned to Cordelia. She was already up, buttoning the bodice he had so recently taken such pleasure in removing.

"I heard," she said before he could speak. "It must be urgent indeed if Theodora sent servants to fetch me." Pink tinged her cheeks. "Don't worry about the servants, Donal. There will always be gossip. It can't be helped." She heaped her hair atop her head and inserted pins here and there to secure it in place. "I must return to the house at once."

"Of course." He fetched her cloak from the stand behind the door and draped it over her shoulders, allowing his hand to linger at the angle of her neck. It seemed likely, even certain, that he would never touch her this way again. "Don't berate yourself because you were not at the house. If you must blame someone, blame me."

Cordelia shook her head, one brief jerk of denial, and Donal knew that no plea or demand would convince her that she was not at fault for her absence when her father had taken ill. She would punish herself again and again for having dared to consider her own needs, if only for a single hour in a life of selfless responsibility.

She hurried to the door, tying her bonnet under her chin, and paused to glance back. Already she had difficulty in meeting his gaze.

"Will you come?" she asked, her voice thin with fear barely held in check. "If my father is as ill as John claimed . . ."

"I'll follow you within the hour," he said. He took a step toward her, aching to give her comfort and knowing she would not accept it. "Cordelia —"

She smiled sadly, opened the door and slipped out into the harrowing light of morning. Donal stood in the doorway and watched her stride away, his eyes straining after her diminishing figure as if she might vanish forever. His vision blurred.

A slight, familiar weight came to rest on his shoulder. "My master weeps?" Tod asked softly.

Donal raked his hand over his eyes. "Tod," he said, clearing the roughness from his throat. "Where have you been?"

Tod flew up, hovered a few feet above the earth, and landed on the broad-leaved stalk of a yellow hollyhock. "My master called for me?" he asked, evading Donal's question.

Torn between relief and annoyance, Donal

sat on the bench beside the door. "Yesterday," he said, "I could have used your help in dealing with a particularly unpleasant case of mortal wickedness."

The hob looked at Donal from beneath his shaggy brows. "The dogs?" He ducked his head. "Reggie told me. He said the Hardcastle helped them."

"She did, and she could have been hurt if I hadn't —" He paused, knowing that Tod didn't deserve his anger. "I'm sorry. I have seen more of man's inhumanity to his fellow creatures in the past weeks at Edgecott than I witnessed in a year at Stenwater Farm." He knotted his hands together. "At the races, with Inglesham . . . I looked for you there. It was a nasty business."

"Did you punish the Yellow-Hair?"

"No. But when I was there, I dreamed of Tir-na-Nog. It seemed as if I were a thousand miles and a world away from the cruelty of man."

Tod bent his head and industriously rolled one of the hollyhock leaves into a narrow tube. "You wished to escape this world."

"If only it were so simple."

Tod was silent a long moment. "My lord, your father left the Land of the Young forever because he loved. In mortal love he lost his powers."

"I haven't forgotten. Why do you mention it now?"

"The Hardcastle was here."

The peculiar tone of Tod's words engaged Donal's full attention. "Yes, she was."

"My lord . . . mated with her?"

Donal shot up from the bench, banging his elbow against the wall of the cottage. Once he would have laughed at such a question, but not now. Not after Cordelia.

"That, my friend," he said firmly, "is a matter between the lady and myself."

Tod flinched, tearing the rolled leaf in two ragged pieces. He stared at Donal with wide, mournful eyes, and Donal was reminded that, after all the years Tod had been with him — through childhood scrapes and adolescent misery and the adult life of solitude he had chosen — he still didn't know the hob as another true Fane might, didn't fully understand the sometimes alien thoughts that lived in that red-thatched head. But he could make an educated guess.

Tod, like Inglesham, believed that Dr. Donal Fleming had fallen in love.

Donal turned his back, deeply disturbed at Tod's assumption. It was only natural that the hob should feel concern, wrong though he might be in his suppositions. He had witnessed Donal's near-loss of abilities before, when Donal had believed himself in love with Mrs. Stainthorpe. Donal had confided in no one else at the time, not even his parents, but the horror of that experience —

of being cut off from the thoughts of the animal world — had left its mark.

"You have nothing to fear, Tod," he said heavily. "Mortals, especially those of the half-Fane variety, can be just as trifling in their affections as any of the Fair Folk. I will not be remaining at Edgecott. But now the lady's father is ill, and I must go to the house."

He started into the cottage and found his way blocked by Tod's darting form.

"Come away," the hob said, his little body humming with anxiety. "Come away now, my lord. We will take Ivy back to the farm. We will be free again."

"What has Ivy to do with —"

"She is not happy here, my lord. She is Fane."

Donal stopped in mid-stride. "What?"

"She is Fane," Tod whispered. "Like my lord. Like Tod."

Donal sank down on the bed. "Are you certain?"

"Very certain, my lord."

"But how is this possible? How could I not have known?"

Tod alighted on the clothes press. "My lord is *half*-Fane," he said. "Perhaps —"

"Perhaps that's why I failed to see." Donal glanced up sharply. "How long have you known this, Tod?"

Tod averted his gaze. "At first, Tod thought it made no difference."

"But it explains so much . . . why the dogs behaved as they did. Why she trusted me from the beginning. Why she finds it so difficult . . ." Donal closed his eyes. "She must not realize what she is. I've seen no evidence of other Fane talents. Perhaps the ability to survive the most abominable conditions is a gift in itself."

"Mayhap she unknowingly summoned my lord to save her."

"Anything is possible, and yet . . ." He pinched the bridge of his nose. "Assuming her mother was an ordinary woman, her father . . . the one she never knew . . . must have been Fane. But it makes no sense that a half-Fane child should come to be living on the streets of London. Unless —"

"She was lost," Tod said. "Lost even to those who would gladly take her from this earth."

Donal studied the hob with heightened interest. "You said you didn't believe it made any difference if Ivy was Fane. What did you mean?"

"My lord brought her here to make her happy. As long as there was a chance that she could be happy in a mortal life . . ." He stopped, tugging at the ends of his hair, and insight struck Donal like a stinging slap.

"Tod. You . . . *care* for Ivy, don't you?"

The hob hunched lower on the clothes press. His mobile, expressive face gave Donal all the answer he required.

"When did this happen?" Donal asked. "How?"

"Since she came here. Since I . . . we —"

"Has Ivy *seen* you, Tod?"

Tod hung his head. "Aye, my lord."

"And she knows what you are?"

Tod nodded.

Donal rubbed his eyes. "You haven't told her about her Fane blood?"

"No, my lord. Only stories of the Fane, and Tir-na-Nog."

"She doesn't know what *I* am?"

"Not that. But should she not be told the truth?"

Donal groaned. "I'd thought Ivy's situation complicated enough, but now . . . Good Lord, any mortal girl would find it daunting to face such enormous changes in her life. But a Fane . . . she must be driven by instincts and compulsions she has no way of comprehending."

"Alone," Tod sighed.

Donal got to his feet, his shoulders bowed with weariness. "Cordelia wants what's best for Ivy, but she works in ignorance. If she should lose Ivy now . . ."

"She would keep Ivy prisoner," Tod said fiercely.

Donal shot Tod a piercing look. "You've been at the house, haven't you?"

"Tod has heard how the Hardcastle speaks

to Ivy, how she makes Ivy unhappy —"

"You're wrong, Tod. Cordelia loves the girl, and Ivy hardly knows her own mind. I won't separate them without good reason."

"When Ivy knows the truth, why should she stay here?"

The hob's defiance was startling in its intensity. Tod had changed in the weeks that Donal had neglected him, and Donal had only himself to blame.

"What would you suggest, Tod?" he snapped. "Where would she find a better home? Stenwater Farm is out of the —"

"There is a place for all Fane," Tod interrupted. "A country where she would always be among her own people."

"Tir-na-Nog." Donal dragged his palm across his face. "A place where everything is perfect and unchanging, love is forbidden and Ivy would grow as cold and hard as Titania herself."

Tod hopped down from the clothes press. "Why would my lord force Ivy to become human? Should she not make her own choices?"

Donal turned away and stripped off his shirt, selecting a clean one from the clothes press. "Such decisions cannot be made in haste," he said. "I need more time to think."

"You would choose the Hardcastle," Tod accused, his mouth bared to show sharp white teeth. "You think only of *her.*"

"*Enough.*" Donal splashed water on his face,

combed his hair and buttoned on his second-best waistcoat, hardening his heart to Tod's distress. "You will say nothing to Ivy. Is that clear?" He shrugged into his coat and retrieved his bag. "I'll inform you of my decision as soon as I have made it."

Tod buzzed past him in a black cloud of anger, spinning furiously out of sight.

The house was still and silent when Donal reached the door. The footman who answered his knock seemed to be walking on tiptoe; even the usual creaks and groans to be heard in any settled building seemed absent.

Croome met Donal in the drawing room, where the butler informed him that Mrs. Hardcastle was awaiting him in the east gallery. If Croome gave Donal a particularly long and speculative look, Donal had no leisure to contemplate the salacious thoughts that might already be at work behind the servant's expressionless face. His own mind was already fully occupied.

Donal took the stairs two at a time. He met Theodora on the landing as she was leaving the east wing with a tray of tea things; she nodded briefly to Donal but did not detain him.

He found Cordelia pacing back and forth in front of the long line of ancestral portraits. She had changed into an austere, dove-gray gown and her hair had been tamed with the skill of an able maid, but to Donal's eyes the plain and sensible clothing was no more than protective coloration. Her shoulders sagged in relief when she saw Donal.

"How is he?" Donal asked, curbing his urge to take her in his arms.

"Not well." She twisted an already well-wrung handkerchief between her fingers and shook her head. "According to his valet, he suffered a seizure of some kind just after dawn, and then relapsed into a state of insensibility. I have sent for the local physician, of course, but I fear Sir Geoffrey's condition is . . . is . . ."

Donal cupped his hand around her elbow and steered her to the nearest chair. "He has not had similar symptoms before?"

"Not such as Chartier describes. He said that my father reported strange visions late last night, and began to cry and strike out as if he had seen something monstrous. Malarial fevers occasionally bring on mild hallucinations, but none of such violence." She pressed her palms to her cheeks. "I fear he has lapsed into a coma. When I visited him, he did not show any signs of regaining consciousness."

Donal walked to the window overlooking the drive, cursing his impotence. "When is the doctor to arrive?"

"He was out on another call, but his housekeeper expected him to return within the hour." She followed him to the window. "Sir

Geoffrey asked for Inglesham before he lost consciousness. Do you think I should send for him?"

It was a measure of Cordelia's disquiet that she asked his advice on such a subject, especially when she must know his answer beforehand.

"I don't see how the viscount can help Sir Geoffrey," he said, "unless you would take some comfort in his presence."

"No." She rubbed her arms and shivered. "Will you look in on my father?"

Donal could hardly keep from touching her, here where any passing servant of moderate intelligence could perceive their relationship. "I have some skill in healing animals," he said, "but I have never attempted to cure a human ailment."

"I ask only that you see him."

Refusal was out of the question. Donal followed her to Sir Geoffrey's suite and entered a room that smelled of sickness and desperation. The baronet's valet, Chartier, sprang up from his seat when Cordelia entered and gave a slight bow.

"No change?" Cordelia asked him.

"No, *madame.*"

She went to the bed and bent over her father, gently touching his forehead. "He is so quiet," she said, her voice breaking.

Donal set down his bag and took the chair beside the bed. "It would be best if I were left alone with him," he said.

"Of course." She gestured for Chartier to precede her from the room. "Only tell me if there is anything you require."

He nodded, already considering what he might possibly do to ease Cordelia's fears. The difference between human and animal consciousness was astronomical, and he could think of few mortal minds he would less rather share than Sir Geoffrey's. The best he could hope to achieve was some slight sense of the severity of the baronet's condition.

Donal closed his eyes, allowing his thoughts to dissipate like mist, and opened his mind. At first all he felt was the grayness of limbo. He ventured a little deeper, wary and poised for retreat.

The blast of sensation struck him in a blinding wave, overwhelming his ability to regulate its flow into his brain. He bore it for a few seconds and then jerked free. His head throbbed with the complexity of the scrambled thoughts and images he had caught from Sir Geoffrey's mind, but amid the chaos he gleaned a single thread of understanding.

He got up, testing his balance as he leaned on the chair, and then began to search the suite. As expected, he found no incriminating evidence in plain view, or in the clothes press, dressing table or desk in the adjoining rooms.

But when he found the locked cabinet in the dressing room, he knew he need search no further.

Chartier waited outside the door, his features aligned in a semblance of devoted concern. Cordelia was nowhere in view.

"If you would come in, Chartier," Donal said, "I have a few questions to ask of you."

The valet clasped his hands at his chest and entered the suite. Donal closed the door firmly behind him and held out his hand.

"The keys, if you please," he said.

"I beg your pardon, *monsieur?*"

"The keys to the locked cabinet in the dressing room."

The valet's expression shifted from surprise to cunning in an instant. "I do not have access to that cabinet, *monsieur.* It is Sir Geoffrey's private property."

Donal seized the valet by the lapels of his coat. "I have no time for your prevarication when Mrs. Hardcastle is in distress," he said. "I must see what is in that cabinet, and if I am compelled to bother her about it, I am afraid you will not like the consequences."

Chartier regarded Donal with the eyes of a man who knew better than to test another man's propensity for violence. "There is no need for this rough behavior, *docteur,*" he sniffed. "If you will kindly release me. . . ."

Donal let him go with a little push. "The key."

"Very well." The valet smoothed his coat with long, deliberate strokes of his fine-boned hands. "Follow me."

He led Donal directly to the clothes press and ran his fingers behind the scrollwork that concealed its upper edge. "Here it is, *monsieur,*" he said, handing the small bit of metal to Donal. "Now, if you will permit me to wait outside —"

"No. You stay here until I'm finished."

"But —"

Donal clenched his fist, and the valet subsided, taking a seat at the far side of the room. Donal returned to the dressing room, fit the key in the cabinet's lock, and opened the door.

The shelves within were stacked with countless bottles of several shapes and sizes, none of any great age, all empty, many marked with labels in both French and English. The smell that came out of the cupboard was distinctly that of alcohol mingled with other components both chemical and herbal, overwhelming in their potency.

Donal picked up the first bottle that came to hand and examined it carefully. He recognized the nature of the contents at once, and remembered what he had heard and read of the effects on those who overindulged in these particular spirits.

But that was not all he discovered. The smaller, unmarked bottles had carried an even more potent brew, for Donal recognized the brown stain at the bottom of the glass and identified the scent associated with tincture of opium.

Sir Geoffrey had not only been heavily indulging in the strong liquor known as absinthe, but he had clearly become dependent upon laudanum as well. Such substances would in no way improve his physical state; they would only exacerbate and gradually worsen his condition until such devastating symptoms as hallucinations, convulsions and even coma became the inevitable consequences.

Donal replaced the distasteful stuff, closed the cupboard door and went to confront Chartier.

"You knew of Sir Geoffrey's hidden vices, did you not?" he asked without preamble.

The valet shrugged his shoulders. "I am but a servant, not a physician. It was not my place —"

"Mrs. Hardcastle knew nothing of this. If she had, she would never have permitted her father to consume such potentially dangerous substances."

"Sir Geoffrey is my master," the valet said with a show of defiance.

"And your master now lies there, perhaps near death, with a long recovery almost certainly ahead of him. Since you abetted Sir Geoffrey in reaching this condition, I would venture to guess that your position in this household has become somewhat precarious."

Chartier's face went blank. "What would you have me do, *monsieur le docteur?*"

"Sir Geoffrey was not mobile enough to acquire such a stock on his own. Who supplied it?"

"Surely I do not know, *mon—*"

"Oh, you know. And you will tell me."

The valet glanced toward Sir Geoffrey's bed and shifted in his chair. "He will see that I never find employment again."

"And I'll do far worse. Who is 'he,' Chartier?"

But Donal already knew, though he had no obvious facts to back up his supposition. When Chartier finally provided the name, Donal laughed.

"Now I understand why Sir Geoffrey has been such an enthusiastic advocate for the viscount," he said. "How long has this been going on?"

"Since Sir Geoffrey's return to England," Chartier admitted. He lowered his voice, his crafty eyes shifting from side to side. "It was always Lord Inglesham's plan to marry Mrs. Hardcastle . . ."

". . . and by supplying the bedridden baronet with such illicit amusements, which a man in the viscount's position would have no difficulty in obtaining," Donal said, "he guaranteed Sir Geoffrey's support of his suit."

"Sir Geoffrey developed a strong need of these gifts," the valet said, "one might even say a fanatical dependence. He became most upset when he could not acquire them in a timely fashion. He has not had his cache restocked in several days."

And that was hardly surprising, Donal thought, when Inglesham had become obsessed with his new plan for acquiring a fortune at the races. Satisfying Sir Geoffrey had no longer seemed quite so important. But from the baronet's perspective, keeping Inglesham happy would seem an absolute necessity. No wonder he had demanded the viscount's presence before he had lapsed into unconsciousness.

"Very well," Donal said. "Listen carefully, Chartier. You are to say nothing of this to Mrs. Hardcastle, or anyone else in the household. Lord Inglesham is not to be admitted to these rooms. Nor will you accept any further 'gifts' from Inglesham on your master's behalf."

"But how can I refuse the viscount?"

"I doubt Mrs. Hardcastle or the doctor will allow visitors, but I'll trust to your natural cleverness . . . and your desire to keep your position."

Chartier weighed Donal's words, his expression as prudently neutral as that of any practiced politician. "Considering Sir Geoffrey's condition," he said, "this surely cannot remain secret for long."

"You've kept it quiet for months," Donal said grimly. "You'll continue to do so until I have dealt with the problem at its source. I will not have Mrs. Hardcastle involved in any capacity, do you understand?"

"Oui, monsieur."

"When the doctor arrives, I'll speak to him myself. There is nothing more to be done until then. Keep Sir Geoffrey as comfortable as you can."

Chartier bowed with an air of derision, but Donal cared nothing for the man's opinion of him as long as the valet obeyed his instructions. He picked up his bag and left the suite, preparing himself to face a worried Cordelia.

Much to his relief, she still had not returned. Presently he heard voices at the foot of the stairs, Cordelia's and one belonging to an unfamiliar male, and he guessed that the doctor had finally come. He waited in the gallery until the physician reached the top of the stairs and, finding the man alone, introduced himself. The doctor, one Phillip Brown, listened without interrupting as Donal recounted his observations and repeated his request that nothing be said to the patient's daughter.

"I quite agree," Dr. Brown said, prodding at the nosepiece of his spectacles. "There is no need to upset the ladies." He glanced toward Sir Geoffrey's door and sighed. "I am only a country doctor, but I have seen such cases before . . . both overreliance upon opiates and the condition known as absinthism. The only cure is time and complete separation from the offending substances."

"As I suspected, Doctor," Donal said. "I hope that I may be of some use in assuring the latter."

"As you are a friend of the family, and obviously understand the situation better than I, I will leave you to do as your judgment dictates." He smiled. "I believe the world of medicine may have lost a worthy practitioner when you chose to treat animals instead of people, Dr. Fleming."

"Thank you, Dr. Brown." Donal escorted Brown to Sir Geoffrey's suite and returned to the staircase. The path was clear, and so he hurried outside, desperately in need of a safe place to vent his rage.

Tod appeared as soon as Donal had rounded the corner of the house and found a quiet space in the shadow of a rose arbor.

Donal tossed down his bag. "I should kill him," he said.

"The Yellow-Hair?" Tod asked. He swooped beneath the arbor and hung one-handed from a vine-covered arch. "Aye, my lord. Kill him."

Tod's bloodthirstiness effectively dampened Donal's own. He sucked in a deep breath. "Murder is no solution," he said. "But Inglesham must be dealt with, and soon. The man won't give up . . . not until he's had the fear of God put into him."

"Fear of Fane," Tod said. "Fear of the Forest Lord's son."

Donal was in no mood to smile. "My father was ruthless enough in his time," he said, "but I was born in this world, and my powers have never been great." He raised his fists. "If I have to use these two hands —"

"Make Yellow-Hair suffer," Tod urged. "Punish, and then go."

"Go," Donal whispered. He looked up at the house, remembering how much like a cage it had seemed when he had first arrived at Edgecott. It was still a cage, but now it held a new prisoner: his heart. And no matter what he did to Inglesham, no matter how many lies he told himself about freedom and the manifold dangers of love, he would not escape without forcing Cordelia to pay the price of his cowardice.

CHAPTER
TWENTY-ONE

For a moment — as long as it might take for a dragonfly to beat its wings — Tod thought he had won. In that glorious instant he was certain that Donal had recognized the futility of his mortal scruples and accepted that he had no future here, prey to the constant and ruthless demands of human emotion. He had seen the truth at last. He and Ivy and Tod would leave this place, Tod would convince Donal to enter Tir-na-Nog and Queen Titania would lift Tod's curse.

All this Tod envisioned, like a glorious dream, and then his hopes withered beneath Donal's wretched and disconsolate gaze.

There would be no victory, now or ever.

With a silent cry of rage Tod burst upward, ignoring the cruel scrape of thorns on his skin as he fled the rose bower and the treachery of his lord. He fixed his thoughts on the one who could restore his joy and flew up to her bedchamber window, which stood open to the late morning breeze.

She lay on the great, soft bed, her dark hair loose upon the pillows. Tod perched on the window ledge and was about to enter when he saw that Ivy was not alone.

"I am sorry that I have spent so little time with you these past few days," the Hardcastle said from her chair at the foot of the bed. "I did not wish to neglect you, my dear, but circumstances . . . have been most trying of late. I hope you can understand."

Ivy sat up against the pillows, and though Tod could not see her face he knew that she had been weeping.

"I know about the dog fight," she said, her voice husky with uncertainty. "Why didn't you tell me, Cordelia?"

Donal's lady gazed down at her hands. "I told no one, Ivy, and that was foolish of me. I should not have gone alone."

"Are the dogs all right?"

A smile transformed the Hardcastle's features, making her appear almost beautiful. "Most are recovering nicely. We lost one . . . but Donal tells me that his passing was painless."

"Oh." Ivy dropped her head, the silky veil of her hair falling across her face. "What about your father?"

The lady's smile faltered. "He is very ill. At the present time he remains unconscious, but the doctor has every hope of his recovery."

"I'm sorry." Ivy twisted her coverlet between her fingers. "I said nasty things about Sir Geoffrey. I wished that he . . . he . . ."

"Nonsense." The lady rose from her chair and sat on the edge of the bed. "You must never believe that your wishes had anything to do with it. We all have unpleasant thoughts about others, but that does not make them come true."

"Sometimes," Ivy said, "not even our greatest wishes come true."

The Hardcastle leaned forward and took Ivy's hands. "What have you wished for, Ivy? Only tell me, and I will do my best to help."

Ivy looked away. "You've given me so much already."

"But I fear I have not made you happy." The lady touched Ivy's cheek. "Nothing means more to me, my dear, than making a good home for you, and that we should become the best of friends. If only you would confide in me. . . ." She stopped and seemed to withdraw, both physically and emotionally. "I am sorry for disturbing your rest. Perhaps we can have tea when the house is not so much at sixes and sevens."

She started for the door, but Ivy called after her. "Did you mean it when you said . . . I could confide in you?"

The lady turned back, her eyes bright with hope. "Of course." She resumed her seat. "What is it, Ivy?"

Tod pushed his head halfway in the open

window, keeping himself invisible while he studied Ivy's face. The girl was obviously weighing an important subject, and Tod sensed that it was not unrelated to her tears. Her mouth set in a determined line.

"Is it true," she began slowly, "is it true that you and Donal spent the night alone in his cottage?"

It was obvious from the Hardcastle's reaction that she had not been prepared for the question. She half rose, skirts rustling, and then sank back again. Her features smoothed into an expressionless mask.

"Where did you hear such a thing, Ivy?" she asked.

"Is it true?"

The lady gazed toward the window, though her eyes saw nothing. "I was with Donal in the kennels, helping him to care for the dogs. Afterward —" She sat up straighter, shoulders thrown back as if she were about to confront a deadly enemy in pitched battle. "Yes, Ivy. I was with Donal."

Ivy sank into her pillows like a hunted animal seeking its nest. "Please," she said. "Go away."

"Ivy . . ." The lady held out her hand and lowered it again. Tod saw that it was shaking. "What occurred between Donal and me was private. It was not meant to hurt you in any way. I —"

"You have told me to be 'good,' " Ivy said,

the words edged with scorn. "You said I was too wild, that I had to think of my reputation as a lady. But you don't care about *your* reputation, do you?"

The Hardcastle rose, brittle as a mullein stalk in winter. "I am a widow," she said, "and an independent heiress in my own right. While some would castigate me for my actions, they would certainly judge an unmarried girl far more harshly for the same behavior. That is simply the reality of our world."

"Then your world is mad."

"It may not seem fair, but —"

"You can do whatever you like, and all your rules don't mean anything."

"You're wrong, Ivy. They are important. I . . ." She swallowed audibly. "I made a mistake, because I was distraught over what had happened that night. Donal was a perfect gentleman. It was entirely my fault."

Ivy gathered a fat pillow to her chest and wrapped her arms around it tightly. "I don't think you're sorry at all," she accused. "And Donal . . ." She buried her face in the white cloth. "Oh, go away. Go away!"

The lady stood there a few moments longer and then turned, moving with a heavy tread. The door closed with a click. Tod slipped into the room.

Ivy was weeping again, her sobs muffled by the pillow. Tod alighted on the table beside the bed and patted at her tangled hair.

"Do not weep, *a chuisle.* You are not alone."

Ivy raised her head, sniffed, and met his gaze with red-rimmed eyes. "Tod," she said. "Where have you been?"

He ducked his head guiltily. "Tod heard the Hardcastle's speech," he said, eager to mend her misery. "Is this why you mourn?"

Ivy tossed the pillow aside and laughed. "I mourn for all that can never be." She scraped her hair away from her damp face. "I don't belong here, Tod. That becomes more and more clear to me every day."

Tod's heart leaped with happiness. "Because of what the Hardcastle told you?" he asked.

"Oh, how can you possibly understand?" She faced him, her legs crossed under the thin gown that clung so enticingly to her body. "If it were only that. . . ."

Only that. Tod clenched his fists. He hated Donal for causing Ivy such pain, and yet he rejoiced in knowing the girl had begun to accept that he could not love her. Donal's mortal woman had done Tod an unexpected good turn by telling Ivy the truth of her mating.

Oblivious to his thoughts, Ivy sighed. "It is all so useless. I have tried to fit in. Cordelia would never believe it, but I have tried. And I know she's done so much for me, given me so many beautiful things . . ."

446

"Has she not been cruel?" Tod whispered close to her ear. "Has she not wrapped you up in heavy clothing that ties you to the earth, and bound you with laws even she does not keep?"

Ivy's eyes filled with tears. "Yes. She thinks she needs me, because of her sister. But I only upset her. And Donal . . ." She bit her lip. "I can't be good the way they want me to be. I want to go where I please and do what I please, not follow their silly rules. Sometimes I get so angry, and I think that no one in the world should stop me from getting what I want."

"Aye," Tod said. "You should have what you want, *a ghrá mo chroí.*"

"But I don't know what that is. I only know . . . I want to go away, to a place where I can't disappoint anyone, where there are no rules to be broken."

Tod leaned as near as he dared. "What if Tod could find such a sanctuary," he said, "where his lady need never be unhappy again?"

Ivy closed her eyes. "I would bless you forever, my friend."

Only friends now, a chroí. But when we are in the Land of the Young, together . . .

A thrill of awareness raced through Tod's blood, drawing him back to the window. A carriage drawn by a pair of silver-white horses was rolling up the drive. Lounging amid the velvet luxury of its squabs was an exceedingly beautiful woman, so lovely and perfect of feature that even a mortal might guess that she was more than human.

Ivy joined Tod at the window. She caught her breath.

"I wonder who she is?"

Tod shivered. There was no reason in the world why Ivy should recognize the woman. Only Tod knew why she had come to Edgecott, and what he hoped to gain from serving her.

He had been forced to choose, and he had chosen. The lines were drawn. There would be no turning back.

Cordelia woke in confusion, her mind awash with fading dreams of sensual pleasure and unbearable sorrow.

She sat up on the bed, pushing loose hair from her face. The angle of the sun through the window told her that she could not have slept more than a few minutes, but she knew she should never have allowed herself to rest while her father's condition remained so uncertain.

With a soft groan she hobbled to the washstand and bathed her face, conscious of little aches and twinges in parts of her body she seldom had reason to notice. Even this morning's turmoil, and the upsetting conversation with Ivy, could not erase the memory of what she and Donal had shared. Already she wondered where he was, what he was doing, if he lingered near the house to see how she fared.

She forced her thoughts into more suitable channels and dragged a brush through her hair, haphazardly pinning it up without regard for her appearance. She put on a plain dress whose severe and restrictive lines served as a reminder of who and what she was. Ignoring her first impulse, she went to Sir Geoffrey's rooms, where Dr. Brown had settled in a comfortable chair to watch over his patient. He assured her that no more could be done until her father awakened, and that he had all he required for the time being.

Reminded by the rumbling in her stomach that she had not eaten in many hours, Cordelia took the servant's staircase down to the kitchens in hope of finding bread and cold meat to stave off her hunger. She nearly collided with Sir Geoffrey's valet at the bottom of the stairs.

"*Pardon,*" he murmured, slinking away toward the door that led to the kitchen gardens. His furtive bearing immediately drew her attention, and she saw that he was attempting to hide a large valise behind his body.

"Chartier," she said sharply. "Why are you carrying your bags? Are you leaving us?"

He stopped, his thin frame hunched like that of a child caught in an act of mischief. "I, er . . . *madame,* it is not what you —"

Cordelia advanced on him, fists clenched. "Perhaps it has escaped your attention that your master is extremely ill?"

Chartier threw down his bag and folded his arms across his chest, cold fury distorting his pointed features.

"Mrs. Hardcastle," he said, "I have had enough of this house and the fools who dwell in it, and I will tell you why. For months I have endured Sir Geoffrey's abuse and kept his secrets because the viscount paid me well for my silence. But I also have my pride, *madame,* and when a mere animal doctor presumes to threaten me, even a man in my position must reach the limits of his patience."

"*Who* threatened you?" Cordelia demanded. "Why should you provoke the viscount's anger?" She took another step toward him. "What have you done, Chartier?"

He laughed. "Ah, *madame,* I pity you. So much goes on in this house that you know nothing of. Your tyrant of a father was no more than a puppet in Lord Inglesham's hands, and yet you trusted the *vicomte,* did you not?" He shook his head in mock pity. "And as for *monsieur le docteur* . . . he is so desirous of protecting you, as a good lover should be, and still he deceives you."

450

The blood drained from Cordelia's face. "Either speak clearly, Chartier, or I shall see that you never hold another position in England."

The valet made a rude gesture. "I care *that* for your little island. But I will tell you everything, *madame,* and then you may see how well you have managed the affairs of your house."

He spoke then, with precision and obvious satisfaction, explaining how Inglesham had rapidly worked his way into Sir Geoffrey's favor after the baronet's return from the tropics; how he had plumbed Sir Geoffrey's weaknesses by plying him with opium to ease his discontent and absinthe to stimulate his senses, knowing full well that Mrs. Hardcastle would strenuously disapprove. Soon Sir Geoffrey cared for nothing but his illicit pleasures, and they began to take their toll on his precarious health and already volatile disposition.

Once Sir Geoffrey was dependent upon the substances and demanded ever-higher doses, Inglesham warned him that he could not guarantee a continuous supply unless he won Cordelia's hand . . . and her fortune. The baronet increased his pressure on his daughter to marry the man of his choice, regardless of her personal wishes.

"So you see, *madame,*" Chartier said, "*Le vicomte* was also aware of your weaknesses, and of your desire to appease your father. He was certain that you must eventually surrender to Sir Geoffrey's commands, since he had no difficulty in making you believe that you would retain control of your fortune after you were wed. Was he not, after all, an old and trusted friend?" He snickered. "Sir Geoffrey surely knew that Inglesham would never keep his word to you, since *le vicomte* borrowed from your father often enough to feed his own vice of gambling."

Cordelia ground her teeth together, biting off the instinctive protest that rose to her lips. She knew in her heart of hearts that Chartier wasn't lying. Sir Geoffrey's reliance upon the alcohol and opium explained much about his increasingly erratic behavior, and his wild insistence that she marry Inglesham immediately.

But how could she have been so thoroughly deluded in her judgment of Inglesham? How could he have changed so much from the boy she had known for so many years? Yes, he had always been somewhat self-indulgent — fond of fine clothing and horses, accustomed to getting his way — but to use an old friend so callously, to deliberately make him ill in order to acquire his daughter's money . . .

"It is sad, *n'est-ce pas,* to discover that one has been a fool?" Chartier said.

Oh, yes. Yes, indeed. But Cordelia had discovered that long ago, when others had paid for her folly.

"What has Dr. Fleming to do with this?" she asked, her voice remarkably steady.

"He was most gallant, *madame.* When you sent him to attend Sir Geoffrey, he discovered the cabinet where your father kept his 'medicine,' and I was compelled to tell him the rest. He feared, however, that this information would be too great a burden on you, and so he ordered me to hold my silence." Chartier snorted. "He seemed most enraged at *le vicomte's* activities. Or perhaps it was not concern for you which prompted his threats . . . after all, only yesterday he attended the races with Inglesham and did not tell you. Perhaps the doctor and *le vicomte* are greater friends than they pretend, *non?*"

"Dr. Fleming would never attend a race. He despises such entertainment."

"Even so, *madame,* I heard Inglesham inform your father that he expected to derive great benefit from Fleming's cleverness with the horses, and that if he regained his wealth through such gambling he would no longer require Sir Geoffrey's influence upon you." Chartier picked up his bags and opened the garden door. "And now I shall take my leave of you, *madame,* and of your vulgar lover. Good day."

The door slammed. Cordelia winced and pressed her hands to her face. Everything Chartier had said seemed too fantastic to credit, yet the valet had never once flinched from meeting her eyes as he related his story. She could think of no reason why he should prevaricate simply to upset her, especially when he was abandoning an excellent position and any hope of references. Despicable he might be, but he had spoken the truth.

Strangely enough, it was not the revelation about Inglesham's treachery that most disturbed her. If not for the harm he had done Sir Geoffrey, she might almost have felt relief . . . relief to know that she was absolved of the need to marry him. But the fact that Donal had learned of it and did not tell her . . . and that he'd actually attended a race with a man he so bluntly claimed to despise . . .

There must be a rational explanation. And it did not shock Cordelia that Donal would think to "protect" her by withholding damaging information about her father and Inglesham. He was, after all, a man, and she a mere woman who must inevitably founder under the weight of too much responsibility.

Cordelia turned blindly back toward the stairs. If this business of the race was an unrelated anomaly — Chartier's insinuations to the contrary — then it seemed probable that Donal intended to deal with Inglesham himself. That was not only foolish and dangerous, but entirely inappropriate. The only one entitled to confront Inglesham was the daughter of the man he had betrayed.

But first she must face Donal.

Strengthened by her resolve, Cordelia climbed the stairs and strode for Sir Geoffrey's suite. Croome met her before she reached the door.

"I beg your pardon, Mrs. Hardcastle," he said, "but a visitor has arrived — one Countess Pavlenkova — and has asked to see you." The butler's mouth twitched with elegant distaste. "I attempted to inform the lady that you were not at home, but she would not leave."

Cordelia glanced distractedly toward the staircase. "Countess Pavlenkova? I have never heard of her."

"Apparently she has recently taken a house in the neighborhood. One must assume that she is not familiar with English customs." He sniffed. "She is presently in the drawing room, sampling Mrs. Jelbert's teacakes. Shall I make another attempt to . . . dislodge her?"

Cordelia resisted the urge to tear the pins from her hair and flee the house. "No, Croome. Please tell the Countess than I shall join her presently, and send Biddle to my room."

"Very good, Mrs. Hardcastle."

"Would you also be so kind as to locate Miss Shipp and Dr. Fleming, and ask Miss Shipp to join me in the drawing room. Dr. Fleming is to wait for me in the morning room."

"Yes, madame."

"And Croome . . . under no circumstances are you to admit Viscount Inglesham to the house."

The butler raised a brow but offered no comment. As he hurried off to fulfill her requests, Cordelia returned to her room. She asked Biddle to arrange her hair in a style that could be managed in a few minutes, ignoring the girl's dismay over the state of her tresses. Once her coiffure was in place, she briefly examined herself in the cheval glass, shrugged off her dull appearance and descended the stairs.

She had not known what to expect of her inconvenient visitor when she entered the drawing room. That the woman might be somewhat exotic seemed likely, since her name was of Russian origin. But Cordelia wasn't prepared for the vision that rose to meet her in a froth of ice-blue skirts and sparkling laughter.

"So you are Mrs. Hardcastle," the countess began, hardly waiting for Cordelia to clear the doorway. She floated across the carpet, extending an exquisitely gloved hand like a princess accustomed to the most enthusiastic adulation. "I do so hope I have not inconvenienced you, but I could not wait to make the acquaintance of my nearest neighbor."

Cordelia took the offered hand and stole a

moment to collect her thoughts. Her first impression of the Countess Pavlenkova was of pure, crystalline beauty . . . beauty so rare and brilliant that it seemed anyone who looked too long at her face must surely be blinded by her radiance. Her face was cream brushed with rose, her eyes blue as a mountain lake, her hair silver as the coat of an Arctic fox. Her figure in the outlandish but striking gown was exquisite, and she exuded an air of otherworldliness that reminded Cordelia of Ivy in a way she could not define.

"I am glad to make your acquaintance, Countess," Cordelia said, the polite fiction coming with practiced ease. "You are welcome at Edgecott."

Pavlenkova looked her up and down without a change of expression, released Cordelia's hand and made a graceful circuit of the room, touching this figurine or that memento with a polite show of interest. "I understand that your father seldom leaves the house, but that you manage his affairs," she said. "I am delighted to see that not all Englishwomen creep about in the shadows of their men."

The sheer rudeness of the countess's comments momentarily stunned Cordelia to silence. She took a stand in the center of the room and straightened her shoulders.

"My father," she said, "is ill, which is the reason I cannot properly entertain you this afternoon, Countess. And I fear you have somehow received a mistaken impression of my countrywomen. You may have noticed that our ruler is female."

Pavlenkova paused, halfway turning toward Cordelia. "But of course, your Victoria. She is indeed much to be admired." Her eyes darkened with sympathy. "I did not know about your father. I am so sorry."

Once more Cordelia was at a loss, bewildered by the foreign woman's sudden changes of mood. She seemed to shift from insouciance to effrontery to commiseration in the blink of an eye.

Theodora appeared as Cordelia was formulating a reply, and she gave an inner sigh of relief. At least now there would be two to face this troublesome guest, and Theodora was a steadying influence in any company. She cast Theodora a warning glance and took her arm.

"Countess Pavlenkova," she said, "may I introduce my cousin, Miss Theodora Shipp."

Pavlenkova drifted toward them, examining Theodora with the same dispassionate thoroughness that she had scrutinized Cordelia. "Miss Shipp," she said, failing this time to offer her hand.

Cordelia felt her temper begin to rise again. "Would you care to be seated, Countess? I will refresh your tea." She nodded to Theodora, and they took seats opposite the one

Pavlenkova had occupied while the maid brought in a fresh pot of tea.

"Cousin," Cordelia said formally, "Countess Pavlenkova has taken Shapford for the summer, and wished to make our acquaintance."

"Indeed?" Theodora smiled at Pavlenkova. "I had heard that the house was now occupied. It is pleasant to know that we have been blessed with such agreeable neighbors."

Pavlenkova sipped her tea, made a face and set down her cup. "Yes," she said. "Most pleasant." She looked at Cordelia. "It is very quiet here. Do you live alone, you and your father?"

"We have a guest, a young lady who has recently come to us from Yorkshire. Small as our family may be, we seldom find ourselves suffering from loneliness."

The countess fluttered her fingers before her mouth as if to stifle a yawn. "And will I not see this young lady?"

Theodora caught Cordelia's eye, clearly mystified by the Russian's behavior. "Ivy is resting," Cordelia said. "Perhaps she will have the pleasure of meeting you at another time, Countess."

"Oh, I am certain of it." Pavlenkova crumbled a bit of cake on the tray and brushed her hands across the expensive fabric of her gown. "I shall invite you all to Shapford for dinner. We shall get to know each other very well indeed. I —"

She stopped abruptly as Ivy flew into the room, dressed in her best gown, her dark hair barely contained by its pins. Her spaniel trotted along behind her. Close on their heels came Donal, who had obviously failed to heed Croome's instructions to await Cordelia in the morning room.

"Ah," Pavlenkova exclaimed, rising to her feet. "This must be Ivy."

"Yes." Cordelia rose, pretending an ease she was far from feeling. "Ivy, make your curtsey to Countess Pavlenkova, our new neighbor."

Ivy slowed her headlong rush, belated wariness tightening her features. Sir Reginald continued past her, skidded to a halt, and stared up at the countess. He growled softly, the hair rising along the back of his spine.

"Reggie!" Ivy hissed. The dog ceased his growling, but his hair remained on end and his tail tucked flat against his hindquarters. He slunk to a refuge behind the sofa.

"I am sorry," Ivy said, making a pretty curtsey. "I don't know what's come over him."

The countess shot Sir Reginald a look of distaste and pinned Ivy with her glittering smile. "It is of no importance." She clapped her hands. "But what a lovely young lady you are! Come, child, and let me look at you."

From that moment it was clear that Ivy was

thoroughly caught in the countess's spell. She gazed at the Russian with wonder and admiration, and Cordelia was struck again by the indefinable similarity between girl and woman.

Ivy edged closer, her eyes locked on the countess's face.

"You are so beautiful," she whispered.

The countess laughed. "How charming, my dear." She reached out as if to touch Ivy, hesitated, and let her hand fall. "I am told you are from Yorkshire, but is that not a barbaric land of barren rocks and hills? Surely you cannot have been born in such a place."

"I . . . I . . ." Ivy stammered and blushed. "I was not born there, my lady."

"As I guessed." Pavlenkova glanced at Cordelia with a strange look that was almost triumphant. "You are surely an orphan, born of royal blood. Is it not so?"

No sound escaped Ivy's lips, but her eyes were full of abject worship. Cordelia tried to remember when she had seen the girl so flustered. It was absurd that Ivy should be so taken in by a glamorous appearance and facile allure, but Cordelia wasn't amused.

Why did the countess show so much interest in a girl of unknown origins whom she had never met? Why should their bond be so immediate, so powerful that no one could mistake it?

And how can she succeed in an instant where I have failed in weeks of effort and care?

She forced a smile. "Ivy's parents are deceased," she said, "but she has a new family in us."

The countess seemed not to hear. "We must be certain that you are treated as befits your obvious quality," she said, holding Ivy's rapt gaze like a spider intent on a fly. "We will start with your clothing. I shall show you how to set off your hair and eyes, and —"

"I beg your pardon," Donal said, his voice booming over hers. "Have we met before, Countess?"

Pavlenkova glanced up, startled, as if she had not noticed that Donal had entered the room. Cordelia hastily corrected her own dereliction.

"Countess Pavlenkova, may I present Dr. Donal Fleming?"

The countess looked directly at Donal and smiled. "I do not believe we have ever met, Doctor," she said, "for surely I would remember such a handsome face."

Cordelia watched for Donal's reaction to the Russian's peculiar charms, feeling the knot of foreboding tighten beneath her ribs. Donal's face revealed nothing but cool, distant courtesy. He inclined his head.

"If you say it, Countess," he said, "it must be so."

Pavlenkova flashed her teeth at him and returned to Ivy, but Donal's gaze never left the woman. Like Ivy, he appeared to be caught in her web, even if he refused to acknowledge it.

Cordelia studied Theodora out of the corner of her eye, wondering if even her cousin had taken the lure, but Theodora was staring into her cup of tea with the blank gaze of one who would prefer to be anywhere else. Suddenly she set down her cup and rose, excusing herself with words so soft that no one but Cordelia heard her.

There was no rational reason for Cordelia to feel abandoned. She had agreed to meet with Pavlenkova; she alone was responsible for the disturbance the countess had wrought. And, indeed, whom *had* the woman disturbed? Ivy hung on the Russian's every word, Donal showed no emotion at all, and Theodora had simply walked away. Only Cordelia was troubled by this powerful, almost nauseating aversion to the Russian noblewoman.

But it is not simply aversion, is it? she asked herself. *You blame your visitor for your own failures. Your own . . .*

She never completed the unbearable thought. Theodora reappeared, her face very grave.

"I am sorry to interrupt you," she said to Cordelia, "but Sir Geoffrey is asking to see you, and Dr. Brown feels that you should come at once."

CHAPTER
TWENTY-TWO

Torn between relief and fear for her father, Cordelia quickly rose from her seat. "Countess," she said, "I must beg you to excuse us. Sir Geoffrey requires our presence."

Pavlenkova, who had been interrupted in modeling her gown for Ivy's admiration, allowed a scowl to mar her features before she smoothed them into bland regret. "I hope that your father is improved, Mrs. Hardcastle."

"I am sure all that he requires now is rest, and perfect quiet." She began to herd Pavlenkova toward the door. "I have enjoyed our visit. Perhaps, when Sir Geoffrey is fully recovered, you will call again."

"Most assuredly." She beamed at Ivy. "We shall see each other very soon."

Though it seemed to take an eternity, the countess finally reached the front door and swept off to her waiting carriage. Ivy stared after her until the door closed, and then she went upstairs without speaking another word.

Cordelia felt Donal standing behind her, silent and remote. Before Pavlenkova's visit, she had been prepared to question him at length about his reasons for concealing the cause of Sir Geoffrey's illness and attending the race with Inglesham. She was cravenly grateful that Sir Geoffrey's summons had put off the inevitable confrontation.

"I . . . I should go upstairs," she said awkwardly. "If you would be so good as to remain at the house while I speak to my father. . . ."

Theodora joined them, her eyes downcast. "I am sorry, Cordelia," she said. "I spoke as a ruse to rid you of that . . . that woman." She met Cordelia's eyes. "Can you forgive me?"

The strength drained from Cordelia's body in a rush. "Of course, my dear." She closed her eyes. "I confess that I . . ." She remembered Donal's presence and opened her eyes again. He was gone.

Theodora took her arm and led her into the morning room. It was cool and dark and private. Theodora made Cordelia sit down, left the room and returned a moment later with a dampened cloth.

"Put this over your eyes," she said. "I know you haven't slept in over a day, and that woman alone would be enough to drive anyone mad."

Cordelia obeyed, despising her own vulnerability even as she blessed her cousin's thoughtfulness. "You did not care for the countess?" she asked.

"I found her quite odious," Theodora said. "But I could have borne her if not for your distress."

Cordelia pressed the cloth against her eyes. "Was it so obvious, then?"

"Only to me."

"But I had no reason to dislike her as . . . as strongly as I did, Theodora. It is wholly irrational to so mistrust a woman I have just met."

"Not wholly." A chair creaked as Theodora sat beside Cordelia. "Her constant flattering of Ivy was most inappropriate. I have seldom witnessed such objectionable manners in any person of rank."

And did you see how Donal stared at her? Cordelia wanted to ask. *Does our distaste arise only from our sex? Is she truly so beautiful, so fascinating that any man will instantly become her slave?*

She held her tongue and let the cloth fall from her eyes. "But Ivy should be exposed to all manner of people, including those from other countries. She has been very isolated here. In my desire to groom her for society, I have failed to provide her with sufficient and appropriate companionship." She swallowed. "Clearly that has been one of my many mistakes with her, and why she was so taken by the countess."

"If Ivy had been at Edgecott for a year, or half so long, I might agree," Theodora said. "But she has gone from the streets of London to Yorkshire to this house in only a few months. It is no wonder that her head is easily turned."

"Nevertheless —"

"Once Sir Geoffrey is well again, you can devote more time to Ivy," Theodora said. "Perhaps you will even permit me to take on a few more domestic responsibilities, so that you will not face so many competing demands."

Cordelia looked away. "I have failed you as well. Your life here must seem very dull."

"Oh, never dull, I assure you. You doubt yourself too much. I am very fortunate, and so is Ivy."

Cordelia took Theodora's hand. "It must seem as if I hardly care for her," she whispered. "We so often quarrel. But if I were to lose her —"

"You will not . . . certainly not to *that* pale creature."

Suddenly the room seemed brighter. Cordelia's shameful self-pity began to release its grip.

"I know we cannot avoid the woman entirely," she said, "but we shall not encourage a closer acquaintance than is strictly required by courtesy."

"And," Theodora added, "you will show Ivy

that she has far more to gain from your care and instruction than from an ingenuous stranger, however alluring she may be."

"Then I must set a better example than I have done thus far," Cordelia said. "My actions must be beyond reproach in every way. I will become a confidante that Ivy can trust without demur." She smiled at her cousin. "I am grateful for your wise advice, Theo."

Theodora opened her mouth as if she would speak, gave a slight shake of her head, and sighed. "I am always here, Delia," she said. "Only tell me how I can help."

Cordelia rose and started for the door. "If you would look in on Ivy and Dr. Brown? I must find Dr. Fleming. We have an important matter to discuss that cannot wait."

As Theodora murmured agreement, Cordelia told herself that it would not be so terribly difficult to say what must be said. *You will compel his honesty with your own. You will deal with Inglesham. And when it is over, nothing will be lost but the lies.*

Nothing at all.

The Lady Béfind, known in the world of mortals as Countess Pavlenkova, smiled as she leaned back on the squabs and gazed at the house from which she had been so firmly ejected.

How foolish they were, these humans, to think that they could so easily be rid of her.

469

She had visited the girl's guardians for the sheer amusement of it, not because it was in any way necessary for her plans to succeed. Indeed, she supposed she had given them some warning by her treatment of Ivy. But Cordelia Hardcastle's suspicions only made the game more enjoyable.

Adding to her delight in the proceedings, Hern's son had been there as well, glaring at her as if he had surmised what and who she was. Of course they had seen each other once before, at the race where Béfind had made her first public appearance as Pavlenkova. But they certainly had not "met" . . . and even if they had, it was clear that Donal Fleming had not known she shared his Fane blood.

Perhaps if Tod hadn't warned her of Fleming's blindness, she might not have risked meeting him here. But it was all too delicious . . . that Hern's son, recluse and misanthropist that he was, had fallen in love with Ivy's would-be guardian. . . .

Béfind laughed. Donal was half-Fane, however much he denied it. He might play at loving a human; he might act the gallant and scorch an unwelcome visitor with the green fire in his eyes, as he had done in his lady's drab little drawing room. Yet he would never truly belong among mortals. That fact gave Béfind an advantage no common female could ever hope to match.

Béfind signaled to the coachman, who circled the horses around the drive and away from the house. She glanced back, hoping to see Ivy at a window, but what she saw instead stopped the breath in her throat.

A man stood behind a large window on the first floor, his face distorted through glass and glare. The eyesight of a mortal could never have discerned his features, but Béfind recognized him at once.

Geoffrey.

Béfind sank down in her seat, all good humor fled. She had considered many possibilities when she prepared for her visit to earth, but this was not one of them.

Her sources, Fane and otherwise, had informed her that the Hardcastle woman lived with her invalid father. How could they know that the mortal female's sire was none other than Sir Geoffrey Amesbury? He would be old, now . . . old in human years, so fleeting and brief. The youth she had met far in the north of this island existed only in her memory. And yet old man and young were one and the same.

She urged the coachman to a faster pace. It was highly unlikely that Geoffrey had seen her. Even if he had, surely he would not *know* her. Humans saw what they expected to see. Though he'd known she was Fane when they became lovers, his mind wouldn't accept that she was still young and beautiful when he was wizened and gray.

With a scowl, Béfind reminded herself again of the reasons she had come, and how much she stood to gain. Already she had achieved excellent results. Her servants had confirmed that the hob, Tod, had obeyed her commands and plied Ivy with tales of the Fane and Tir-na-Nog that could not fail to turn her head. They had also reported Ivy's belief in a noble Russian father, which gave Béfind the perfect guise in which to approach the girl and win her favor.

Nevertheless, obstacles remained. Like Tod, Béfind could not touch Ivy as long as she wore the amulet, let alone take her through the Gate. Yet if no Fane could remove the charm, one who was *half*-Fane might do so. And if Béfind could seduce or trick Donal into returning with her and Ivy to Tir-na-Nog . . . why, there was no telling what marvelous form Queen Titania's gratitude might take.

Good spirits restored, Béfind shook her hair loose and laughed all the way home.

The animals were restless.

They paced back and forth in their enclosures, leaping up and down on the branches, growling or grunting or chattering as their various natures decreed. Sitting on the bench opposite the cages, Donal feared that their agitation was a direct result of his own.

Sir Reginald sat on the bench beside him, watching the captive beasts with alert and wary eyes. He, too, was still shaken by the encounter with Pavlenkova.

Donal scratched the spaniel in his favorite spot behind his silky ears. "She was certainly unpleasant enough," Donal conceded, continuing the conversation that had begun in his own mind. "But that hardly explains our antipathy, does it?"

Reggie growled and placed a paw on Donal's thigh. Othello paused in his endless pacing and glared at dog and man, coughing deep in his throat.

"I know," Donal said. "She is not to be trusted, that's clear." He glanced skyward, half hoping to see Tod appear with belated apologies for his absence. But Donal no longer knew what to expect of the hob. No more than he knew what to expect of himself.

Yet his instant and instinctive loathing of Countess Pavlenkova was not really that difficult to explain. Her behavior toward Cordelia and Theodora had been discourteous at best. And as for Ivy . . .

"Whatever that woman's intentions," Donal said, "they can't be beneficial to the girl. Yet I'm certain that Ivy will want to see more of her —"

"And that," a feminine voice said, "I shall not permit."

Donal rose from the bench as Cordelia

came to join him. He offered no welcome, for he could see that she was in no mood for pleasantries. Her mouth was set, her brows drawn, and her eyes were as dark as a storm over the Pennines. She planted herself before Donal, spearing him with her stare. Sir Reginald cowered at Donal's back.

"I see," Donal said cautiously, "that you did not care for the countess."

"Most observant of you, Dr. Fleming." She cast a glance at the animals. Her frown deepened. "It appears that all of Edgecott lies under a cloud today."

Donal gestured toward the bench. Cordelia ignored him. She gazed unseeing at the weathered wood, and only Reggie's sorrowful whimper broke her trance.

Her attention snapped back to Donal. "Countess Pavlenkova," she said, "is my concern, not yours. But you may be of assistance in another matter."

"Anything, Cordelia."

"Anything." She drew in and released a sharp breath. "Even lying in order to protect my delicate sensibilities."

Reggie rolled himself into a ball of red and white fur. Donal held Cordelia's gaze.

"This is about Sir Geoffrey," he said.

"Yes, among other things."

"Did Dr. Brown tell you?"

"No. If you arranged for him to keep your secret, he abided by your agreement. But

Chartier was under no such compunction."

Donal thought longingly of the Frenchman's face under his fist. "What did he tell you?"

"Everything about my father's dependence on Inglesham's 'gifts,' and the blackmail in which the viscount engaged to attain my hand and fortune."

Donal sighed and ran his hand through his hair. "I am sorry, Cordelia. I only recently discovered the viscount's role in Sir Geoffrey's illness, and I —"

"You thought it best to conceal this discovery from one who might find it too great a burden. Or perhaps you had some other motive for such prevarication?"

"Prevarication?" Donal felt his temper begin to stir. "I did not lie, Cordelia. I simply withheld certain information, until —"

"Until I was fit to hear it, or until you had fully prepared a suitable story?"

Donal stared at her in bewilderment. "Story? You can't believe that I had anything to do with Inglesham's activities. I despise the man, even more so now that I know what he's done to your family."

"Indeed. Then why did you attend a race with him, apparently to aid him in winning his bets? You, who strives to protect animals from such exploitation?"

Donal heard the anger in her voice and knew that she did not truly believe he had been in league with Inglesham. She was confused, resentful, perhaps a little frightened by what seemed like betrayals on every side, but she was not foolish. They had shared too much for her to reject all their hard-won trust.

And yet, for her sake, he must lie.

He lowered his voice to a soothing, reasonable tone. "I can understand why learning of this would concern you," he said. "But there is an explanation, Cordelia. Inglesham was under the impression that my skill with animals, particularly Boreas, would enable me to pick winners at the races with greater accuracy than most turfites. I agreed to accompany him to one race so that I could watch him." He cleared his throat. "You see, I had already begun to suspect that he was deceiving you in some way that I could not yet ascertain, and I hoped to learn more by feigning an interest in his . . . diversions."

Cordelia studied his face, sifting his words for truth or falsehood, and the tension began to drain out of her body. "Yet you felt you could not tell me."

"How could I accuse your . . . fiancé of transgressions I could not even name?"

"And did you learn anything of value?"

"No. But my suspicions were not allayed, and when Chartier admitted to me that Inglesham had been supplying the opium and absinthe to your father . . ."

"I see." Cordelia sat down on the bench, fingers buried in the folds of her skirts. "And you wished to shield me from this painful knowledge."

He covered her hand with his. "You drive yourself too hard, Cordelia. It isn't wrong to allow someone else to take part of the burden."

She smiled humorlessly. "Theodora said much the same thing."

"Then you can forgive me for my interference."

Slowly she withdrew her hand from beneath his. "Yes, if you will answer another question. Do you intend to punish Inglesham yourself?"

Her bluntness gave him no room to maneuver, no time to consider the right evasion. His hesitation betrayed him.

"You *do*," she said, "even knowing that assaulting a viscount would be extremely foolish for a man in your position."

"A commoner?" he said with a twist of his mouth. "A simple country veterinarian?"

"A man without the connections the Wintours have had for many generations," she said. "Do you believe he wouldn't have you thrown in gaol for any transgression against him?" She seized his arm. "Donal, you must put all such thoughts out of your mind. Inglesham and his odious schemes are my problem, and I shall deal with him in my own way."

"You cannot turn your back on him, Cordelia, not even for an instant. He'll become like a cornered rat if he feels trapped, and he won't balk at making your life a living torment if he can."

She lifted her shoulders. "I know Inglesham. I can handle him. You must swear not to interfere."

"Don't ask me to let you face danger alone."

"I do ask. I demand it."

Donal stalked toward the cages, the growls and grunts of the animals beating against his ears. His heart slammed in his chest, demanding action, violence, vengeance. He was a wolf on the scent of its prey, Othello stalking his next hapless victim.

"There is something more, Donal," Cordelia said behind him. She drew near but not close enough to touch, allowing an invisible barrier to stand between them. "What we . . . what happened in your cottage . . . it will not be repeated."

He began to turn and stopped himself, sucking breath through his teeth. "Why, Cordelia? Have you grown to hate me so much?"

"No." Her voice cracked. "No. It has nothing to do with Inglesham or my father. It's only that I have come to realize . . . such liaisons are not advisable, not when I have Ivy in my care, and Theodora . . ."

"I never demanded anything of you," he

said, cursing the unsteadiness of his words. "We both knew there would be no future in it, but we agreed . . . there would be a little time. . . ."

"I know. I was too intent on my own pleasures, you see. It has happened before. But you must understand . . . Ivy hears the servants' gossip, and she can only wonder why her guardian breaks the very rules she imposes on her young ward. I cannot expect her to maintain propriety when I do not."

"Then Ivy is the reason you'd deny yourself — deny both of us — a little comfort?"

"She is more important than either of us, Donal. And since we will not . . . be together in the future, it can only make the situation more difficult if we continue." Her fingers brushed his shoulder and slipped away. "Please try to understand. From now on we must return to what we were before."

"Employer and servant?" he asked, making no attempt to hide his bitterness. "Baronet's daughter and lowly animal doctor?"

"Never lowly, Doctor. I shall always hold you in the highest esteem . . . and affection."

"Cordelia —"

But she was already walking away, steps uneven and head bowed.

Reggie crept along the bench, his body drooping with sadness. Donal scooped the spaniel into his arms and pressed his face into the warm, soft fur.

"It seems we've both been abandoned," he said hoarsely.

The spaniel licked his chin. Reggie's simple thoughts were filled with shapeless dread, for he had no means to discover what had aroused his fears.

But Donal was half-human. He looked into his soul and saw clearly, for the first time, the specter that most terrified him. He envisioned a life without Cordelia . . . never to see her again, spar with her, hold her in his arms.

Oh, yes, *he* had been the one to tell her that they had no future together. But now she had deprived them both of the weeks they might have shared, days of companionship and nights of rapture where the future did not exist. And she had done it because she still denied the passion within herself, refused to accept her own needs and desires, feared she might pass her shameful "weaknesses" on to Ivy like some infectious disease.

If she knew what Ivy was, she'd be forced to accept that the girl she sought to protect existed only in her imagination.

Donal set Reggie down, afraid that his anger would further upset the little dog. His fury was building to fever pitch: rage at Inglesham and Sir Geoffrey, at Ivy for her fickle Fane blood, at Cordelia, at himself most of all. Such anger must find an outlet, or it would fester and burst like an overripe boil, poisoning every animal within reach of his mind.

With a deep, deliberate breath he expelled the tightness from his muscles. He might not have a cure for all of his present dilemmas, but at least one would yield to direct and ruthless action. He had every reason now to take the drastic steps that Tod had advised, without guilt or hesitation.

Tod was not here to enjoy his triumph. The responsibility would be Donal's alone. And when it was done, nothing would impede Cordelia's freedom save her own stubborn heart.

CHAPTER
TWENTY-THREE

"So," Béfind said, "it would seem that you have fulfilled your task with admirable efficiency, little hob."

Tod didn't answer, his tongue tied in knots, his thoughts torn between longing and terror while the lady bestowed her deceptively benevolent gaze upon him from among the pillows heaped on her velvet couch. He had never thought this moment would be easy, but now he found the very prospect of venturing his request daunting beyond all his imaginings.

"Come, come," Béfind said, selecting a ripe peach from a tray held aloft by a giggling sprite. "You have done well. You have earned your reward, and soon I shall take Ivy away from your master, just as you desired."

Tod bowed deeply. "Yes, my lady. But . . . there is . . ." He swallowed and closed his eyes, his mouth too dry for speech.

Béfind leaned forward to study Tod's face with pale, emotionless eyes. "Is there something more you would tell me, hob? Something else you would ask in return for your labors?"

Tod's heart began to speed like Epona's horses. "My lady . . . Tod was not always as you see him now."

"Indeed?" Béfind yawned and snapped her teeth together with a click. "And what were you before, pray tell? A god, perhaps? A king?"

Tod winced at her mockery but held his ground. "Even in the world of men, there is magic . . . curses of great power . . ."

"Ah. You speak of curses." She rested her chin on her hand. "Now that I think of it, I do recall a tale of a young Fane lord cursed by some mortal a thousand years ago. He was condemned to live out his life as a hob . . . or was it a troll? I cannot recall. . . ."

"A hob, my lady," Tod said. "This hob standing before you."

She flashed her diamond-bright smile. "Yes. How remiss of me not to have noticed." She stroked her lower lip. "As I remember, the curse was laid upon you by a mortal holy man, a follower of the White God. Such a curse is powerful indeed. Only one of equal power might break it . . . one such as Titania, perhaps?"

Tod inclined his head. "My lady is wise."

"But you were banished from Tir-na-Nog with your first master, Donal's father, many years ago."

"Aye, my lady. But one of the High Fane might carry Tod through the Gate, and speak for him before the queen."

"So one might." Béfind examined her ivory nails. "I wonder, little hob, why you did not make this request when I first approached you."

Tod averted his gaze. "Tod is accustomed . . . he did not think . . ."

"Did not think? Did not think that my servants continued to observe you, even after you agreed to do my bidding? Did not think that I should object to your telling Donal that Ivy is Fane . . . or that I would not know that you desire her?"

Tod struggled with a rush of choking fear, fighting the urge to abase himself or creep under the nearest piece of furniture. "Tod did not intend to do it," he whispered.

"You are not worthy to touch her feet," Béfind said. "Not as you are now."

"But as Tod might be again . . ."

Béfind clucked softly. "Perhaps . . . if you continue to serve me well."

Tod's feet rose above the floor, lifted up by his joy. "Anything, my lady. Only ask, and it will be done."

Béfind was silent for a long moment, her gaze distant with thought. "What of your master, little hob?" she said at last. "Do you still bear him some loyalty?

"My lady?"

"It seems he has fallen prey to the same affliction as his father." She shuddered. "Such a horrid creature, with that crow's plumage and sour face."

Tod hunched his shoulders. "My lady speaks of the Hardcastle."

Béfind snorted with derision. "Even in a single meeting I could see that Donal fancies himself in love with her, and she with him . . . is this not so?"

"Aye, my lady."

She shook her head. "Poor child. He has been driven mad by the company of mortals. Titania has long desired her grandchild's return to the Land of the Young; she would be most pleased with the Fane who brings him back." She held up her hand. "Yes, I know he thinks ill of Tir-na-Nog because of his father. Perhaps he can be persuaded to change his mind."

"Would my lady tell him who she is and what she plans for her daughter?"

"You do not advise such honesty?"

"My lord does not wish to separate Lady Ivy from the Hardcastle."

"I see." Béfind frowned darkly. "It occurs to me that removing Hardcastle from the picture may solve several problems at once." Her eyes gleamed like Cold Iron. "She took Ivy in with good will, and so I shall not punish her unduly."

"My lady is gracious."

"I have always been too soft-hearted." Béfind struck at a sprite that had pulled her hair while brushing it, and the creature tumbled head over wings across the room. "Tell me . . . has the female any suitors besides our Donal?"

"My lady would induce her to seek another mate?"

"It might amuse me to work a love charm upon her . . . or, better yet, on a man for whom she has no liking." She smiled, showing the edges of her teeth. "Do you know of such a candidate, little hob?"

Tod carefully considered his answer. Now that he had made his decision and cast his lot with Béfind, he wished no ill upon Donal's lover, especially Fane mischief that would cause Donal pain. If he spoke of Inglesham, there was no telling what Béfind might do.

"You *do* know," Béfind accused. "You are concealing something from me." Her voice deepened, and a thrill of terror drove Tod to his knees. "Speak, hob, or I swear by the Morrigan's tits that your curse shall bind you for eternity!"

A hideous wailing shrieked in Tod's ears, a cry of unendurable mourning. In an instant he suffered the torment of endless years separated from Ivy, exiled to a life without purpose, cast out of Donal's service like a shirt that had grown too worn for wearing.

There would be nothing left for him but the final death.

He fell prone upon the cold floor.

"I beg of you, my lady," he gasped. "Be merciful."

"Speak!"

Tears pooled beneath Tod's cheek. "There is a man," he said, "a mortal lord who would wed the Hardcastle, but she does not favor him."

"Ah." Béfind leaned back among her pillows. "This man must be very desperate, very ugly or very blind to choose a female such as Hardcastle."

"He wishes to seize control of her fortune, my lady."

"And what would he give to obtain what he desires?"

Tod climbed to his knees. "My lady would save Donal from the humans?"

"If it will turn him toward his father's people again."

"This man, Lord Inglesham, gambles at the races. He compels my master to increase his wealth by choosing the horses that will win."

Béfind started. "A mortal knows of Donal's abilities?"

"Aye, my lady . . . but only that he has a gift with animals, not that he is Fane."

"Fool," Béfind muttered, though Tod did not know if she referred to Donal or the viscount. "How is it that any mortal can compel even a half-blood Fane to do his will?"

"Inglesham knows of Lady Ivy's former life in the City of Iron. He claims that she killed another mortal, and he would tell those who enforce human law if Donal does not aid him."

Béfind rose with a curse. Her servants scattered with cries of dismay. "This Inglesham threatens my daughter?"

"Aye. But my lady Béfind is wise. She knows a way to use the Yellow-Hair for her own purposes, and free Donal from his bondage."

With a swish of her skirts, Béfind strode across the room. "Yes," she hissed. "I shall use and punish him with one stroke." She spun to face Tod. "Go. Return to my daughter, but say nothing. When all is arranged, I shall inform you of my will."

Tod abased himself again. "Tod is my lady's servant."

"Yes. And do not forget it, little hob."

She dismissed him with a flick of her fingers, and Tod walked all the way back to Edgecott, his heart too heavy for flight.

It was a simple matter to learn the location of Viscount Inglesham's manor, for it lay close to Edgecott and there was no mortal in the county who did not know his name.

Béfind rode alone, leaving her attendants

behind. The work that must be done today required no host of sprites or troublesome hobs. No one was better suited to it than Béfind herself.

She rode her silver mare along the winding drive, catching glimpses of the grand house as she passed among hills and stands of oak and elm. For grand the house was . . . by the standards of men. Inglesham was hardly poor in either land or domicile, yet Béfind had no trouble believing that he desired more wealth than he would ever require in a brief mortal life. Greed was a driving force in human nature, and she meant to exploit that vice to its fullest.

The drive straightened to a wide, tree-lined lane in the last quarter mile, and it was at the final curve that Béfind saw the other rider. He sat quietly on his horse behind a particularly thick copse of elms, his gaze intent on the house.

Béfind chuckled. *Ah, son of Hern,* she said to herself. *What brings you here? Are you also bent on revenge?*

As if he sensed her presence, Donal turned his head. His expression, already grim, set in ominous lines. He touched his heels to his bay mount's flanks and the beast swung about, gliding away into the trees.

Béfind clucked to her mare in mocking regret. "It seems he does not wish to further our acquaintance."

With a laugh she kicked the mare into a trot, and soon she was at the porticoed entrance of the house. An alert servant opened the door before she could dismount. The man immediately recognized her quality, sent a lesser servant to find a stableboy, and ushered her into a luxuriously appointed drawing room.

"Whom may I say is calling, madame?" he asked with a deeply respectful bow.

She smiled, amused at his stammer and fascinated gaze. "You may tell the viscount that Countess Pavlenkova has urgent business with him."

The servant backed away, nearly colliding with a table in his haste. "At once, my lady," he said.

Béfind looked for the chair with the greatest command of the room and assumed an imperious pose. It was a measure of the servant's obvious infatuation with her that the viscount appeared before she could become annoyed.

"Countess Pavlenkova," he said, favoring her with a most charming smile as he straightened from his bow. "It is a very great honor to receive you in my humble home. I but recently learned of your arrival in the neighborhood, or I would have placed myself at your service the very moment your shoes touched English soil."

Béfind considered her best approach as she

studied him. He was a handsome fellow, with his tumbled golden locks and smooth features. Though she knew little of the cost of mortal goods, she guessed that his exquisitely fitted jacket, waistcoat and trousers were far from inexpensive. He was obviously accustomed to beguiling the ladies; with one of his type she might dance around the subject at hand for hours, simply trading compliments and flirting with innuendo and sly glances. But she had no time for such games.

She offered a faint smile and extended her hand.

"I thank you for your welcome, Lord Inglesham," she said, permitting him to kiss the air above her fingers. "If you knew of my arrival, then perhaps you also heard of my call at Edgecott this morning."

He released her hand with some reluctance and took a seat opposite hers. "I have, Countess. Did you find your visit enjoyable?"

" 'Enjoyable' is not the word I would employ, Viscount."

"Indeed?" He raised a finely-shaped brow. "I regret to hear it. Were you perhaps so unfortunate as to meet that vulgar animal doctor Mrs. Hardcastle employs to look after her beasts?"

Béfind tapped her riding crop against the heel of her boot. This mortal was far from discreet in his conversation with a stranger, but that was all to the good. *She* had no intention of revealing more than he needed to know.

"You might say," she said, "that Dr. Fleming is the very subject of my visit here today. He . . . and Mrs. Hardcastle." She fixed him with her most seductive gaze. "I have come to you to request your assistance in a matter of some delicacy. I hope that you will not object to a serious discussion on such short acquaintance."

"A serious discussion, Countess?" A frown twitched at the corner of his mouth. "Naturally all my humble resources are at your command, but —"

"Excellent." She rose, compelling him to stand as well. "Will you be so kind as to escort me to your garden?"

His look of sheer perplexity gave her great satisfaction, but he overcame his bewilderment and offered his arm. The garden to which he led her was modest and somewhat overgrown; it was clear that he preferred to spend his money on his personal pleasures rather than on groundskeepers who would cultivate the beauty of his surroundings.

Yet Béfind found what she sought: a sprawling, unhealthy looking rosebush with a handful of sickly buds. She strolled over to it and cradled a bud in her palm.

"Are you fond of flowers, Countess?" Inglesham asked, coming up behind her.

She laughed. "What lady is not fond of

flowers? Alas," she said, casting an eloquent glance about the garden, "it seems that you are not."

He gave an apologetic smile. "If I had known you were coming, Countess, I would have filled your arms with blossoms."

She stroked the bud with the tip of her finger. "Perhaps I can rectify your oversight."

"Indeed?" He moved closer. "What can I do to please you, Countess?" The back of her neck prickled at the touch of his breath. "Only name it, and I shall fulfill your every wish."

"That, sir, is a most dangerous promise." She closed her eyes and called upon her powers. The bud trembled. The rosebush stirred from root-tips to crown. And then it began to grow — branches lengthening, leaves springing from bare twigs, new buds bursting forth in sprays of blushing pink.

Inglesham gasped. Béfind ignored him. She coaxed the little bush to its full glory, feeding it with her own spirit, until the buds unfurled and the entire shrub was a blazing mass of lush blossoms.

"There," she said. "Did I not tell you that I would correct your negligence?"

He stared at her, his mouth opening and closing like a fish out of water. "You . . . What did you do?"

She stepped back to examine her handiwork. "Surely not even a mortal is as blind as that. Do you not admire my performance?"

"Performance?" The creases in his face deepened and then relaxed. "Of course. It is an illusion." He clapped his hands with more vigor than sincerity. "Brava, Countess. Your talent is most prodigious. Did you learn it in your mother country?"

Béfind snapped off a blooming branch and thrust it toward Inglesham. "Hold it, Viscount. Smell the flowers, and tell me if it is illusion."

Gingerly he accepted the branch from her. A moment later he dropped it, blood dripping from his thumb where he had pricked it on a thorn.

"It . . . it is impossible," he said. "That bush has not bloomed in years. You made it . . . but that is . . ."

"I see that your usual fluency has deserted you," Béfind said. She flicked her fingers toward the fallen branch, and it flew up into her hand. "Are my small abilities so astonishing, then, when you have seen what Dr. Fleming can do?"

Inglesham felt his way to a bench and abruptly sat down. "Fleming . . . What has he to do with, with . . ."

"Did I not say that he was the subject of my visit?" She sauntered to the bench, leaned close to Inglesham and brushed one of the roses across his face. He flinched. "Have you not guessed, my little lord? Did you not already suspect that Donal is more than human?"

His astonishment had clearly reached its limit. "I don't understand you."

"Let me make it very plain, then. I know that you have blackmailed Dr. Fleming into aiding your bets at the races because you believe that he has a particular gift with animals. Is that not so?"

Inglesham sputtered. "Blackmail? I have no idea what you are talking a —"

"You weary me, Viscount. I see that I shall have to provide additional proof of my sincerity."

Béfind spun lightly on her toes, stared at the rosebush and thought of death. In seconds the shrub had shriveled to a blackened stalk, and then that, too, disintegrated into ash as if it had burned up from within.

She turned back to Inglesham. "What I did to that unfortunate plant," she said, "I can do to other mortal things. Would you care to experience personal evidence of my power?"

Inglesham's face had gone gray. "You killed it."

"Yes. But it was already dying, so you have not lost too much . . . yet."

"What are you?"

"I am not human." She smiled gently. "And neither is Donal Fleming. But that is not so great a revelation, is it?"

The viscount covered his eyes with his

hand. "You and Fleming . . ."

"Are the same . . . or nearly. He is a halfling, for his mother was mortal." She sat on the bench, amused when Inglesham scooted aside so as not to touch her. "We are of the Fane, whom you mortals have called the 'Fair Folk,' among other epithets."

"F-fairies?"

She rolled her eyes. "Such a horrid word."

The viscount plumbed the depths of his soul and found a scrap of courage. "Why are you here?"

"I think it is time for that serious discussion." She tore an inch from the hem of her silk gown and fashioned several fat pillows, which she arranged about herself. Inglesham only stared. "Let me begin by explaining your situation in words even a mortal can comprehend. You are a man constantly in need of money. You desire to wed Cordelia Hardcastle for her fortune."

A narrow, sly look came over Inglesham's face. "You know a great deal about me, Countess. Or should I still call you that, my lady?"

"It will do." She rested her hand on his thigh. "I can almost admire your low human cunning in manipulating one of the Fane, even though you did not know what he was. However, he is one of my race, and therefore it is my intention to protect him . . . both from you and from that creature he believes he loves."

"Cordelia?"

"Yes. Most unfortunate. While we Fane are not averse to dallying with mortals on occasion, what you humans call 'love' is quite another matter. I would free Donal of this debilitating sickness."

"Sickness," Inglesham repeated with a snort. "Cordelia believes she loves *him*."

"But she does not know what he is. Such knowledge might be enough to repel her — your race is hardly known for accepting what it does not understand — but I haven't time to wait for the situation to take its natural course." She tightened her fingers on his leg. "And that, my dear viscount, is where you may be of service to me."

"How, Countess?"

She reached inside her bodice and withdrew a tiny crystal vial, radiant with its own inner light. "You want Mrs. Hardcastle. I want Donal. The best means to achieve both our aims is to see that Cordelia finds a new object for her devotion . . . you. This potion is the means by which you shall win her love."

Inglesham regarded the vial with suspicion. "You wish me to drug her?"

"Oh, this is nothing so crude as what you call a 'drug,' Viscount. Its workings are subtle, but a certain crudity is required to initiate its effects. Here, take it."

He obeyed, holding the vial between his

thumb and forefinger. "A love potion?" he asked.

"In a manner of speaking." She ran her fingers up his leg, pausing just short of his bulging male member. "First you must contrive to get Hardcastle alone, where you will not be disturbed. Then you pour the contents of this vial evenly into two glasses of wine or some other beverage strong enough to conceal its mild flavor. You must both drink; a few swallows should be sufficient."

Inglesham gazed hungrily into her eyes. "And then?"

"For the potion to begin its work, you must then lie with the woman you would bind to you."

"Lie with Cordelia?" He laughed. "Not her. Not before marriage. She might as well be wearing armor under her skirts."

"Are you so certain that Donal has not already enjoyed her favors?"

His upper lip drew back from his teeth. "*I* have no magic to entice her."

Béfind withdrew her hand from his leg. "Do you think so little of your seductive abilities?" She clucked sadly. "Perhaps I have chosen the wrong man."

She had struck the right chord, for he drew up and glared as if he had entirely forgotten the peril she represented. "I believe I can *convince* her," he growled.

"Very good. Once you have joined your

body with hers, the potion will be activated, and Cordelia will be helplessly in love with you. She will agree to anything you propose."

"And this love will endure?"

"Oh, yes. At least until you have her wed."

He sank into a brooding silence. "I pray that you will forgive my frankness, but this is all very sudden. If only you will allow me time to think . . ."

She jumped up, scattering the pillows, which vanished before they touched the ground. "There *is* no time, mortal. Either you do as I ask, or I shall see to it that you never win another bet, that no woman will ever favor you again and that you die in abject poverty."

"How do I know that you can —"

She swept her arms outward, withering every plant within a hundred feet. "Shall I show you again?" she cried. "Shall I take your manhood now, and allow you to 'think' on that?"

He hunched over, crossing his arms protectively across his lap. "No," he whispered. "No, my lady. That is not necessary."

"I am glad to hear it." She sighed and smoothed her skirts. "I suggest you arrange to entice Cordelia away from Edgecott very soon . . . within the next few days. I have a little more business to conduct in the mortal realm, but when I am finished, I expect Mrs. Hardcastle to be your eager servant." She smiled. "Are we in accord, Viscount Ingle-sham?"

"Yes." He coughed. "Quite."

"Then I shall show myself out."

She left him, her thoughts already skipping ahead to her next target. Donal would not be nearly so easy to control, but in the end he, too, would surrender to her will.

CHAPTER
TWENTY-FOUR

Donal did not return to Inglesham's estate that evening. He contented himself with dreams of vengeance throughout the sleepless night, and paced the cottage floor as he pondered Countess Pavlenkova's inopportune arrival at Inglesham's estate.

Given what he had observed of the woman at Edgecott, he did not for a moment believe that her visit had been the casual call of a stranger. She seemed exactly the sort of female with whom Inglesham would be well acquainted, and Donal's instincts told him that her interest in Ivy — whom Inglesham had threatened — was no mere coincidence.

Ironically, one of Inglesham's footmen had been waiting for Donal at the cottage when he returned from his thwarted punitory expedition. The man had informed Donal that the next race was to be held near the village of Woolhampton in three days' time, and that the viscount would meet his "partner" outside Edgecott's gates at dawn that morning.

Donal had dismissed the footman and immediately began to formulate new plans for Inglesham's downfall. At least he wouldn't have to find an excuse for his absence from Edgecott; Cordelia was fully occupied with her father, who was recovering from his illness under Dr. Brown's diligent care. Donal still felt the sting of her rejection, and that anger would serve him well when he was about to forsake all the tenets by which he had lived his life.

It had become very clear to Donal that he no longer had good reason to linger at Edgecott. The animals suffered from his proximity when he failed to control his emotions. Ivy hardly benefitted from his presence, and even Tod had turned against him.

He needed no further proof that his attempt to reside and work in the company of humans was a dismal failure. The distant, untamed lands across the sea still called to him; if their voices were muted by the yearning in his heart, he knew they would not be so forever. Grief, like love, held no lasting sway in those of Fane blood. He would lose himself in the wilderness, and learn to live alone again.

And if he solved the mystery of Pavlenkova's purpose in Gloucestershire, he could end Inglesham's menace and be free to leave Edgecott before Cordelia learned what he had done.

Just after sunrise, Donal fetched Boreas from the stables and rode out across the park, following a groundskeeper's directions to the manor house now occupied by the Countess Pavlenkova. Shapford had obviously seen better days; its grounds were neglected, and at first glance the house looked sadly in need of repair.

Donal's first impressions were borne out when no servant appeared to take his mount or meet him at the door. He knocked, waited several minutes and knocked again. At last a woman opened the door . . . a very peculiar servant, whose dress had the same outlandish quality as the one the countess had worn during her visit to Edgecott. She regarded Donal with wide eyes, as if he were the one out of place, and suddenly vanished, leaving the door open behind her.

Donal entered, too vexed to stand on ceremony. He heard raised feminine voices at the end of the hall and pursued the sound to its source.

The large drawing room might have been elegant once. Certainly the countess had done little to improve it during her residence; half the furniture was still in dust covers, and the mantelpiece and tables were bare of the usual trinkets and lady's miscellany.

One might have said that so beautiful a woman had no need of ornaments, and as

Donal paused in the doorway he was momentarily nonplused by Pavlenkova's startling allure. She held court in a large chair placed in the center of the room, her gown a rich gold velvet more appropriate to a palace function than an early morning at home. Her "servants," of which there were at least a half-dozen, had the appearance of ladies-in-waiting. Donal doubted that any of them had done a day's work in their lives.

The countess looked at Donal with mild interest as she plucked ripe strawberries from a silver tray. "My, but you are early, Dr. Fleming," she said, licking juice from her full lower lip. "Is it quite the thing in England to pay visits before the sun is up?"

Donal didn't bother to bow. "I would not think that English customs are of much concern to you, Countess," he said.

"Oh! It seems that this is not a social call." She gave him a sly look under her long, pale lashes. "Have I done something to offend you, Doctor? Did I commit some terrible faux pas at Edgecott?"

Donal entered the room. The ladies bobbed and whispered as if he might attack them, their skirts fluttering like wings. "I am sure if we were in your country, Countess," he said, "your behavior would be entirely appropriate."

The servant holding the tray let it fall with a clatter. Strawberries rolled in every direction across the parquet floor. A flash of annoyance crossed Pavlenkova's face, and then she smiled.

"I do apologize, Doctor, for any misbehavior. I am very new to this country, it is true, and my business here is of a certain urgency, which may have led me to . . . an unwitting neglect of the social niceties."

Donal studied the countess with unwavering attention. In anyone else, such an apology might have seemed sincere, but Donal was more interested in her explanation.

"Might I ask, Countess," he said, "the nature of your business in the county?"

She hissed a command to the servants, who hurriedly gathered up the fallen berries and fled the room. "Please make yourself comfortable, Doctor. We cannot have a decent conversation while you loom over me like a hungry bear."

Donal located an uncovered chair and sat down. "Thank you," he said gruffly.

She waved off his thanks. "May I guess that you are here because of our . . . encounter at Viscount Inglesham's estate last night?"

He flushed, remembering how much at a disadvantage he had felt when she caught him, even though she couldn't know the reason for his presence. "I had been riding for some time," he said, "but I hadn't realized that I'd gone so far as Lord Inglesham's park."

"Then you were not on your way to see him?"

"No. But I was surprised to see you there, Countess. Are you acquainted with the viscount?"

"Only by reputation. I felt it would be wise to become known to the people of stature in this county, so that my purpose here would be accepted."

"And what is that purpose?"

She sighed. "I see no reason why you should not know. I feel that I can trust you, and that you will not reveal my secret until I give you leave to do so."

Donal was not in the least deceived by her flattery. "Does your business have something to do with Ivy?"

The countess pressed her hand over her heart. "But that is remarkable! How very astute of you, *mon cher docteur.* It is precisely because of the girl that I have traveled from my country."

"Why?"

"As strange as it may seem, Dr. Fleming, I believe I am her cousin."

"I beg your pardon?"

"I could not be sure, of course, until I had seen her. And even then . . ." She retrieved a fan from a small side table and snapped it open. "Many years ago, my cousin Prince Aleksei courted a young Englishwoman whose father was a diplomat at the Tsar's court. Aleksei was very much in love with Estelle and intended to marry her, but alas . . . his parents would not permit such a match, and arranged to have him sent away before he could offer the lady a proposal. He sent her a small fortune as an apology for his desertion, but he did not know she was with child until some time had passed. By then he had married in Russia and could not go to her."

In amazement, Donal remembered Ivy's confession about her mother Estelle, her Russian father, and her own birth out of wedlock. Her story matched Pavlenkova's account. But it made no sense at all if Ivy's father was Fane, as Donal had always believed.

Unless her *mother* had been the one of Fane blood, raised as human and unaware of her heritage just as Ivy had been. Such mistakes were rare but not unknown.

"Dr. Fleming?" Pavlenkova said, raising an inquiring brow.

"I'm sorry," Donal said. "Please go on."

"My cousin assured himself that Estelle was comfortably situated and returned to his own life," the Countess continued. "It was only many years later, when his wife had died and he himself was ill, that he resolved to find Estelle and their child again."

"Estelle is dead."

"So we discovered." Pavlenkova face assumed mournful lines. "Aleksei died six months ago, but he left his entire fortune to Estelle's daughter. He entrusted me to find her and restore her to her heritage."

Donal rose from his chair and paced a circle about the room. "You're saying that she is an heiress?"

"*Évidemment.* She will be a very wealthy woman. All I need do is prove to my cousin's solicitors in London that she is indeed his daughter."

"And how do you propose to do that, Countess?"

"I have met her, and *I* am convinced. But there is another means of verifying her identity. Aleksei sent her a pendant, a unique design made especially for her. If she still has it . . ."

Donal stopped short. "If she does?"

"Then I will take it to the solicitors as evidence, and they will surely accept her true identity."

His head spinning, Donal clasped his hands behind his back. "This is all very sudden," he said. "If it's true —"

"You so readily doubt my word, Doctor," Pavlenkova said with a pout. "How have I earned your dislike?"

"How did you locate Ivy? She lived for years in the rookeries of London —"

"I am aware of that sad circumstance. I hired men of particular skill to seek her out, and they traced her from her mother's previous residence to Seven Dials and then to Yorkshire." Her crystal eyes warmed. "They learned what you had done for Ivy. I was filled with much admiration for your kindness."

Donal waved her compliment aside. "Then these men of yours followed us to Gloucestershire," he said, "and you arranged to meet with Ivy. Why didn't you reveal your purpose then?"

"Because it would be premature to announce my intentions before I have collected the necessary proof to satisfy the solicitors. To raise the girl's hopes, only to dash them . . ." She shook her head. "I am not capable of such cruelty."

Raise the girl's hopes. Donal resumed his pacing, trying to imagine how Ivy would react to such a fantastic tale. Would she rejoice at knowing her father had remembered her in the end? Would she forget Cordelia in her excitement at obtaining her own fortune and a chance at complete independence? Who would guide her, help her manage her new wealth and all the responsibilities it brought with it?

Who indeed?

"Your interest in Ivy is strictly a matter of uniting her with her inheritance?" Donal asked.

"And to fulfill my cousin's wishes. Ivy would have made him very proud." She lifted her chin. "She also is *my* cousin, and I wish to see that she receives everything to which she is entitled. Is that so difficult to understand? Would you not wish the same for your relations?"

"Naturally, but —"

She stood and swept toward him. "Your desire to protect Ivy is laudable, Doctor, but it does not serve her in this case. You can take an active part in her future if you will help me to obtain her pendant without alerting her to the reason for my presence here."

Donal stared at the countess for a full minute of silence. "To my knowledge," he said, "Ivy never removes the pendant. If I'm to borrow it, I'll have to give her a good reason."

"I am certain that a man of your resources can find one that will not arouse her suspicions," Pavlenkova said. "Will you help me, Dr. Fleming?"

He closed his eyes, weighing his irrational dislike of the countess against the chance that she was speaking the truth. "Very well," he said. "I'll obtain the pendant and bring it to you."

"*Merveilleux.* Prince Aleksei would thank you if he were here, as I do."

Donal turned to go and paused in the doorway. "I'm trusting you, Countess, for Ivy's sake. But if you are playing a game of deception —"

"I would not dare," Pavlenkova said softly. "I have no doubt that you are a very dangerous man."

She saw him to the front door with all due courtesy, but Donal could not help but feel that he'd missed something vital in their exchange. He comforted himself with the thought that if he made himself an essential part of this drama, he could ensure that Cordelia had some say in Ivy's future.

Tod did precisely as Béfind commanded. Keeping himself invisible to mortal and half-mortal eyes, he observed as Donal spoke to Ivy about her pendant, suggesting that he might be able to use it to obtain further information about her father. Tod followed Donal when he delivered the pendant to Béfind and returned to Edgecott. And when next the dawn threw its brilliant veil across the world, Tod secretly delivered Béfind's letter to Ivy's room.

He sat on the windowsill and studied Ivy's animated features as she read the letter. He timed his appearance to the exact moment when she finished, her eyes alight with excitement.

"Tod!" she exclaimed. "I am so glad you've come. Something wonderful has happened."

Tod pretended surprise as he jumped down from the window. "What is it, my lady?"

Ivy hurried to her clothes press and flung

open the doors. "A woman came to visit yesterday . . . a woman such as I've never seen before." She whirled about, hugging an apricot gown to her chest. "I knew as soon as I met her that she understood me the way no one at Edgecott ever has."

Tod sat cross-legged on the bed, mesmerized by the radiant joy on Ivy's face. "How is this lady called?" he asked.

"Countess Pavlenkova. Isn't it a marvelous name?" She stepped behind a folding screen and began to undress. "She came all the way from Russia, can you imagine it? The same country where my own father was born."

"This countess came to see my lady, then?"

"No. That's the most wonderful thing about it." Ivy flung her dress over the top of the screen and wriggled into the apricot gown. "She didn't know anything about me before she arrived at Edgecott, but she felt the same way I did . . . as if we'd met before. After she left she realized why she had been so drawn to me." Ivy laughed. "I look just like a man she knew in Russia long ago." She stepped out from behind the screen and snatched up the letter, her eyes skimming over it eagerly. "She has no idea that my father was Russian, but I am sure that there must be a connection. She wants me to come and speak with her, tonight."

"And my lady is not permitted to go."

"Cordelia hates her. I don't know why, but

she doesn't want any of us to see the countess again." She sat down on the edge of the bed and knotted her hands in her lap. "I don't *want* to make Cordelia unhappy. She's been so good to me. I . . . care about her. But nothing is turning out the way I thought it would. She's so busy with Sir Geoffrey, and Donal . . . I don't think she'd even notice if I left Edgecott." She scraped a hand across her face and turned to Tod. "I'm going to see the countess tonight. Will you keep watch while I sneak out of the house?"

Tod placed his hand over his heart. "Tod is always at my lady's command."

"Then I shall leave as soon as dinner is finished, when Cordelia is with Sir Geoffrey."

Ivy paced out the hours in her room, feigning a headache when Cordelia came to inquire after her. She made a dramatic show of going down to dinner, as if the mere attempt to join the others cost her a great deal of effort and would result in an evening of utter prostration. As a result, Mrs. Hardcastle left her alone after the meal, and Tod helped Ivy slip from the house with no one the wiser. Sir Reginald joined them in the park, his soulful brown eyes swimming with apology for his bad manners with the countess. Ivy reluctantly permitted the spaniel to tag along.

Since it would attract too much attention to borrow a horse from the stables, Tod and Ivy walked the two miles to Shapford. When they reached the house she paused to catch her breath, smoothing her skirts with nervous fingers.

"Do I look well enough, Tod?" she asked.

"My lady is always beautiful."

Ivy smiled, but her eyes seemed to look right through him. "We must say goodbye here. I doubt that the countess would know what to make of you."

Tod bit hard on his lower lip. "Perhaps she would not be so shocked, my lady."

But it was clear that Ivy no longer heard him. She started for the house, her steps hesitant now that she was so near her goal. Sir Reginald crept behind her, his ears flat and his tail tucked against his hindquarters.

Tod made himself invisible and followed. The front door opened as if by magic, and Ivy stepped inside. Reggie slowed as he approached the door, stopped and whined anxiously.

"Don't fear, little one," Tod said, dropping down to pat the beast's trembling shoulder. "Your mistress but regains what she has lost. She'll come to no harm."

But the spaniel backed away, hair bristling, and would go no farther. Tod left the dog and entered the house.

Béfind had already greeted Ivy by the time Tod approached the room where she had taken up temporary residence. They sat side by side while Béfind's sprites, who wore the forms of human ladies, clustered about Ivy with much cooing and exclaiming over her beauty and charm.

"I am so delighted that you could come," Béfind was saying. "I do hope that you did not suffer undue difficulties in your journey here."

Ivy flushed. "No, Countess. They think I have gone to bed early. No one knows I left Edgecott."

Béfind smiled approval. "You have done very well, my dear. There is so much we must discuss tonight. Much of great import."

Ivy leaned forward eagerly. "I have so many questions to ask you, Countess. You said you knew a man in Russia who looked just like me. My father, who left my mother before I was born —"

"— was Russian," Béfind finished.

Ivy's eyes widened. "You knew?"

"*Certainement.* And that is only the beginning." Béfind drew closer to Ivy, her pale eyes working their magic. "Essential information has been kept from you, information that may very well change your life forever." She snapped her fingers, and one of her ladies stepped forward, cradling a bejeweled case as if it contained Queen Titania's most precious treasures.

Béfind opened the lid to reveal a pendant that lay cushioned in black velvet, its exotic blue stone winking in candlelight. Ivy gasped.

"My pendant! But Donal asked to borrow it —"

"Because I confided to him something of my hopes for you. Something of them, but not all, for what I am about to say must remain a secret between us." Her voice fell to a hush. "Do you agree, Ivy?"

There was no question of her doing otherwise. Tod could see that she was prepared to believe anything Béfind told her.

"Please," Ivy whispered, "do you know my father? Is he still alive?"

"Very much alive." Béfind closed the lid of the case and returned it to her servant. "I asked to see the pendant because he told me he had sent such a jewel to his daughter many years ago, and I wanted to be sure that you were indeed the right person."

Ivy frowned. "A man gave me the pendant when I was very young. He was not my father?"

"One of your father's servants," Béfind said gently. "Do not be downcast, dear one. I did not wish to raise your hopes only to dash them again if I was wrong. But I was so certain when I saw you . . . and now my faith is justified."

"My father didn't forget me," Ivy said.

"Never. But he cannot come to you, Ivy. You will have to go to him."

"Where? Oh, Countess, where can I find him?"

Béfind took Ivy's hand. "Are you certain, my dear? Are you sure this is what you wish, even if it means separation from those who have given you a home here?"

Ivy hesitated for the span of a heartbeat. "Surely I can tell them, can't I? Cordelia didn't want me to visit you, but she didn't know about my father —"

"She did, *ma chérie.*" Béfind touched Ivy's cheek in sympathy. "Mrs. Hardcastle made inquiries into your past, and her search led her to the Russian embassy in London. She discovered that your father was alive, and she chose not to tell you."

"She —" Ivy's bright gaze blurred with tears. "Why wouldn't she tell me?"

"Who can say? You know the woman far better than I."

Ivy stood and wandered about the room, her movements almost clumsy with the turmoil of her emotions. "She wanted to keep me for herself, even though she cares so much more about . . . about . . ." She scrubbed the tears from her face and jerked up her chin. "I won't go back to Edgecott, no matter what happens."

Béfind beckoned Ivy back to the chair. "Be at ease, my dear. Your time of trial is almost ended." She waited until Ivy sat down and then clasped the girl's hands in her own. "Your father was once a man of high standing in our country, but he made mistakes.

One of them was leaving you and your mother. Though it took many years for him to learn the truth, he sent me to look for you as soon as he knew that your mother was dead. Now he is paying for his earlier lapses of judgment. He is here in England, hiding from enemies he dares not provoke."

Ivy shivered, her face pale with excitement and worry. "Is he in very great danger?"

"Only if he shows himself. That is why *you* must go to him . . . if you can forgive him for his long absence."

"Forgive? Yes, of course I forgive him."

Béfind drew Ivy into her arms. "My dear cousin, you shall be restored to your rightful heritage, as a true lady of superior birth and fortune."

"But if my father is in hiding . . ."

"Never fear. The situation is far from hopeless. We have allies who shall assist us, and in time all this will be forgotten." She rose, pulling Ivy up with her. "We must prepare to leave as soon as possible . . . tonight, if you can manage it."

Ivy pulled away. "What if Donal comes looking for me?"

"Dr. Fleming? Has he any reason to suspect that you are here?"

"No." Ivy folded her arms across her chest. "He should have told me he was coming here. He's just like Cordelia, thinking I'm a child who can't be trusted with the truth."

"And a child you are not, my dear." Béfind glanced at her ladies, and a pair of them rushed from the room. "What will you require before we depart?"

"My things are at Edgecott, but I don't need them. I would like to bring my dog. I left him outside. . . ."

"My servants will fetch him for you."

"Then I'm ready."

Béfind expressed extravagant approval for Ivy's courage and cleverness, and the two ladies put their heads together as they plotted their escape. Never once did Béfind glance up at Tod, or in any way acknowledge his presence. At last she finished with Ivy and put the girl in the care of her servants.

"Ah, Tod," she said, affecting surprise. "All has gone as I planned. Now we must be sure that no mortal or halfling interferes." She tilted her head in thought. "The nearest Gate to Tir-na-Nog lies no more than fifteen miles south of this place, in a circle of standing stones long abandoned by men. We shall easily reach it by dawn. You shall go to Edgecott tonight and find some suitable means of distracting its occupants so that none will have time to think of Ivy until she is through the Gate."

Tod shivered. "What does my lady have in mind?"

"Burn the village down if it pleases you. Only make sure the son of Hern and his

mortal lover are well occupied until dawn."
She smiled. "As an added precaution, I shall
send my servants to create a false image of
Ivy that will linger until the sun rises."

"Aye, my lady."

"Go, then. And remember, little hob, that
the answer to your dreams is almost within
your grasp."

CHAPTER
TWENTY-FIVE

Cordelia propelled her weary body from Sir Geoffrey's rooms, her skirts dragging about her feet like the chains of Dickens's Christmas ghost. Her hair hung limp to her shoulders, and her eyes were gritty from lack of sleep. Yet there had been a victory of sorts today; her father had been alert for the first time since his illness was discovered, alert enough to argue and complain . . . albeit in a far more subdued manner than was his wont.

He was well on the way to recovery, Dr. Brown assured her, so long as he was denied access to the fiendish substances that had brought about his sickness in the first place. And so Cordelia had forced herself to sit at the dinner table with Theodora and an out-of-sorts Ivy, taking an hour's hiatus before she returned to Sir Geoffrey's bedside.

Now it was near midnight, and she had reached the limits of her endurance. The only thing she could think of, with the crisis finally passed, was Donal.

Donal, whom she had rejected. Donal, whom she hadn't seen for two endless days, who might very well believe he had no further reason to stay on at Edgecott. Who might be gone forever.

The grief of that final thought choked the breath in her throat, and she had to pause on the way down the stairs to catch her balance. Everything, her entire carefully-constructed life, seemed to be falling apart. Her father's collapse, Inglesham's betrayal, Ivy's resentment — her own realization that she could no longer continue in an illicit relationship with the man she had grown to care for so very deeply . . . to . . .

Her heart thumped and fluttered wildly, compelling her to sit there on the stairs. She covered her face with her hands.

Oh, God. It is true. Theodora was right. She was right.

With great effort Cordelia pulled herself up by the banister, though her legs continued to feel like rubber even when she reached level ground. She walked unseeing into the drawing room, stared about in confusion and slowly turned for the kitchen. She had tasted very little at dinner; she knew she needed to eat and drink and rest, or neither her physical condition or state of mind would be likely to improve. But she wasn't hungry, and the thought of lying still in her dark, quiet room made her ill.

Donal, she thought helplessly. *Donal, I need you.*

But of course she did not. She didn't need anyone. Donal certainly didn't need *her,* however much he might desire her body.

She pushed open the kitchen door and stepped into the warm, familiar room. Mrs. Jelbert was out, having completed her evening's work, and the kitchen maid had finished the cleaning. Cordelia searched listlessly for a crust of leftover bread or a bit of cheese in the larder. She took a plate from the china cupboard and immediately dropped it, staring in shock as the plate shattered into a hundred pieces.

"Cordelia! Are you all right?"

Theodora rushed in, cast a quick but searching glance at Cordelia, and hurried to fetch the broom. She made quick work of the mess, took Cordelia's hand, and sat her down on one of the plain oak chairs at the kitchen table.

"You look wretched, my dear," she said, peering into Cordelia's eyes. "You have not slept again, that's plain." She tucked a loose strand of Cordelia's hair behind her ear. "How is your father?"

Cordelia blinked and focused on her cousin's gentle face. "Much better. Dr. Brown says he is on the mend."

"But that is wonderful news." Theodora jumped up, busied herself about the kitchen and returned with a platter of bread, cheese and fruit. "Eat this at once."

Cordelia attempted a smile. "You are too good, Theodora."

"Not very," Theodora said dryly. "But we are as the world sees us, are we not?"

"My head aches too much for philosophy," Cordelia said, cutting a slice of bread with care.

"It is not merely philosophy when your life and happiness are at stake."

Cordelia swallowed a too-large chunk of bread. "Are you about to lecture me about my feelings again, Cousin?"

The corner of Theodora's mouth lifted in a wry smile. "Perhaps you will wish to send me packing . . . but, yes." Her smile faded. "I have watched you these past days, Cordelia. You have driven body and mind to exhaustion looking after Sir Geoffrey, you continue to blame yourself for Ivy's unhappiness, and all the while you have endured an unnecessary separation from Donal. I do not know why you broke with him, and you might say that it is none of my business. Nevertheless —"

"What makes you think that I 'broke' with him?" Cordelia asked stiffly.

"Simple observation, Delia, and a few vague words from Donal when I asked him why he had not come to dinner —"

"Then he has not left Edgecott?"

The moment the words were out of Cordelia's mouth she would have given anything to take them back, but it was too late. Theodora's mild gaze sharpened.

"I have seen him on the grounds," she said, "and at the menagerie during my walks."

"What did he say to you?"

"Only that he thought it best to remain away from the house . . . that you had enough to occupy your thoughts and had no desire for his company . . ."

"And from that you concluded that I have . . . that we . . ."

"I saw his face when he spoke. I have seldom seen a man more despondent."

Cordelia released her breath through clenched teeth. "I am sorry that circumstances prevented me from explaining the situation earlier, but you are right. I have decided that my friendship with Donal is not beneficial to either of us, and especially not to Ivy, who requires a spotless example if she is ever to become —"

A spotless example." Theodora rose and strode from one end of the kitchen to the other, her long and angry strides entirely out of character. "What rubbish." She gave a short laugh. "You must forgive my temper. It is just . . ." She whirled to face Cordelia. "It is just that I cannot bear to see someone throw away a chance at love and happiness when it is within her grasp."

Cordelia stared at her lap, unable to meet Theodora's blazing eyes. "I have . . . not done anything without careful consideration. When I saw how distraught Ivy was over my . . . my connection with Donal —"

"You mean when she heard the rumors that you had spent the night at Donal's cottage."

Fire scorched Cordelia's cheeks. "Theodora!"

"It isn't true, then? Was it all no more than servant's gossip?"

Theodora's mockery shocked Cordelia into sudden anger. "Yes, it is true," she retorted. "Are you angry because I failed to confide in you, Theo?"

"I can understand why you kept it to yourself. What I cannot understand is why you let a girl's selfish complaints determine the course of your personal life."

"But it is *not* my personal life!" Cordelia shot up, her blood surging in her veins. "Ivy looks to *me* to serve as an example of what she may become. Whatever I do will be judged . . . by society, by the people who will be important in Ivy's life, who will determine her future, whom she must learn to —"

"— to ape and flatter and wait upon in 'proper' humility, as you have done all your life?"

"I beg your pardon?"

"I am sorry. That was meant as sarcasm." She passed her hand across her face. "You are a woman of vast contradictions, Delia, not least of all that you try so hard to conform when everything in your innermost nature rebels against it." She laid her hand on Cordelia's shoulder. "Listen to me. In nearly every way you have succeeded in becoming a part of the thoroughly English sphere of good breeding and afternoon tea and noblesse oblige, so well that in a few more years you might forget that you ever had another life. You believe this is what you want. But it is not *you*, Delia."

"Theo —"

"You are not and can never be a conventional Englishwoman, my dear, no matter what face you show the world." She tightened her grip on Cordelia's shoulder. "You cannot continue to base your entire existence around caring for Sir Geoffrey, or Ivy, or the animals and people in this county. You have a right to live for yourself."

Cordelia stepped from under Theodora's hand and leaned heavily on the table. "It is not merely because of Ivy or Sir Geoffrey that I ended my relationship with Donal," she said, "nor out of concern for my reputation. He betrayed me."

"What?"

Cordelia explained how Donal had discovered the cause of Sir Geoffrey's illness and withheld the information from her.

"I can scarcely credit it," Theodora said.

She went very still, her forehead creased in thought. "Inglesham. Is this to do with Inglesham?"

Cordelia surrendered all hope of keeping the details from her cousin. "Bennet was supplying Sir Geoffrey with absinthe and narcotics, and using my father's dependence upon the substances as a means of blackmail."

"Of course. And why do you suppose Donal concealed this information from you?"

Cordelia pushed away from the table, balling her fists so tightly that her nails broke the skin of her palms. "He assumed that I would be unable to accept the implications."

"And that is what truly disturbs you, is it not? Not that Ivy is jealous of your friendship with Donal, but the fact that Donal tried to protect *you* — Cordelia Hardcastle, who needs no one."

"I don't know what you're talking about. Please —"

Theodora slammed her hand on the table. "You know perfectly well what I'm talking about, Delia." Her voice shook with barely controlled emotion. "Since Lydia's death you have believed that you must be willing to make any sacrifice for others — even to make them completely dependent upon you — simply to be worthy of love."

Cordelia pressed her arms against her stomach, doubling over with phantom pain. "No."

"The life you've led has divided you into two people — one who needs to be needed, no matter what the cost to herself, and one who yearns to be free. The very qualities you love in Donal are the things you fear most. He is your match in every way, and yet he can survive without you. And if *he* can love you without depending upon you for his very existence, then all your self-denial is for naught. . . ."

With a gasp of mortification, Cordelia ran blindly from the room. She fled down the servants' corridors, through the green baize doors and out into the cool night, sucking air as if she had been drowning. She slowed her pace and found her way by moonlight to a sanctuary beneath the swaying leaves of a weeping willow, letting the slender branches close about her like a curtain.

Theodora is right.

Her throat tightened, and she squeezed her eyes shut to hold the tears inside her lids. Whether Theodora spoke the truth or not made no difference in the way of things. Was she expected to set aside all duty and live only for herself and her own pleasure? Did Theo think that was a better way to earn the right to be loved?

But was that not her accusation . . . that you believe love must be earned?

Cordelia rocked back and forth, her thoughts writhing like a mouse caught in a trap. If she were to go to Donal now and tell him of Theodora's assertions, would he agree? Would he claim that she regarded love as no more than a martyr's reward? Oh, God. Would he *pity* her?

Far, far better that she never see him again than to think that she had made herself so ridiculous in his eyes. That she could have been so dreadfully, horribly wrong about human nature.

"And if he can love you without depending upon you for his very existence, then all your self-denial is for naught. . . ."

Cordelia sprang up just as she heard a distant, high-pitched barking from the direction of the wood. She recognized fear in the spaniel's voice, and her first thought was of Ivy.

She was halfway back to the house when Donal stepped into her path.

"Cordelia," he said. "You must go into the house at once, and advise your family and the servants to remain inside."

The urgency in his words chased the self-consciousness from her heart. "What is wrong?" she demanded. "Why is Reggie barking?"

He took her arm and marched her toward the door. "The animals have escaped."

"What?"

"Someone unlocked the menagerie doors. The wolves, the apes, Arjuna, Othello . . . all of them are gone."

The blood drained from Cordelia's face. "How is this possible? You and I have the only keys —"

"Nonetheless, it has happened. There is no sign that they were stolen, only let loose." He shook his head, but his eyes burned with rage. "Arjuna isn't likely to go far, and the animals will be more frightened than anything else, but there's a full moon out tonight. It won't be long before some farmer or villager catches sight of one of them and raises the alarm."

"I don't believe any of them would hurt a human being."

"Perhaps not, but men will certainly not hesitate to injure or kill them to protect their livestock and families."

"Then we must find them immediately."

"Not *we*, Cordelia. They are my responsibility. I want you safe inside."

Cordelia pulled her arm from his grip. "They are and have always have been *my* responsibility, and I shall help you bring them in."

"Attending the dog fight was one thing, Cordelia," he said, "but this is quite another."

She planted her hands on her hips. "You may try to stop me, Dr. Fleming. You may even succeed, temporarily. But I will not neglect my duty."

"You'll only get in my way."

"And you are only one man. There will most assuredly be panic if I alert the groundskeepers and grooms, but you cannot do this alone."

He hesitated, staring into her eyes. "What if you're wrong, Cordelia? What if they are dangerous?"

The fluttering sickness returned to Cordelia's stomach. "I will not believe it. I have cared for them. They know me. I will not be harmed."

She turned and strode into the house, calling for Croome. After she had informed him to instruct the other servants and carry the message to Dr. Brown and Theodora, she stripped out of her dress and pulled on a boy's shirt and trousers similar to those she had worn to the dog fight.

Donal was still waiting for her outside. He broke off his furious pacing and thrust something into her hand. "Do you know how to use this?"

She stared in surprise at the shotgun. "Where did you get this?"

"I borrowed it from Mr. Perkins, without explaining my real reason for the request."

Cordelia almost dropped the shotgun. "I know how to use it, but I detest such things. I would rather —"

"You will carry it at all times, and you will defend yourself."

"I will not kill."

Donal grabbed the barrel of the gun and pushed it against her chest. "Take it, or I'll lock you in your room myself."

"And how will you defend yourself?"

"The animals won't harm me."

"You are so certain."

"In this, yes." He lifted his head as if to smell the air. "There's no more time to lose. Come. Stay close."

He set off, following some inner sense with a sureness that made him seem as much a beast as the creatures they hunted. They entered the woods, which looked not at all like the ordinary place Cordelia knew by day but had somehow been transformed into an alien, magical world. Cordelia felt no fear. She was lulled by Donal's unquestioning competence, so caught up in the night's peculiar spell of unreality that she didn't realize she'd fallen behind until she heard the warning cough from the shrubbery at the edge of a small clearing.

The panther moved with absolute silence, his belly to the ground, his tail lashing his flanks as he glared at her from hot yellow eyes. Cordelia froze.

"Othello," she said softly.

The animal's tail stilled. He lifted his lips to expose dagger teeth. There was no friendliness in his manner.

"Easy, boy," she whispered, swallowing her foolish fear. This was a creature she knew, who knew her. He must recognize her as one who wished him only the best.

But he showed no sign of acknowledging her good will. To the contrary, he sank even lower to the ground, rumbling deep in his throat, and his eyes looked upon her as if she were an enemy. An enemy who had done him irreparable harm.

"Would you reason with them, Cordelia?" Donal had asked her. *"Do you expect them to think as men do?"*

He had implied that her animals were impossible to understand, but she didn't believe it. Donal's view of the world had been distorted by his own bitter prejudice. Othello was an intelligent being, not a mindless assemblage of flesh and bone. He owed her his very existence. He would *not* attack her. She would wager her life on that conviction.

"It is all right, my friend," she said, moving to lay the gun down. "You will see. When this is over —"

But she never completed the sentence, for Othello chose that very moment to spring.

Thunder boomed in the clearing, the wordless cry of a man's voice shaking the ground beneath Cordelia's feet. Othello twisted in midair and brushed by her, his claws raking empty air. In a heartbeat Donal stood between woman and cat.

"No," he said, half breathless with fear and anger. He thrust out his hand, fingers spread, and Othello cringed, ears flat to his broad skull. He snarled and lashed out with one paw, claws extended.

"No," Donal repeated. He took a step toward the leopard, who backed away, shaking his head from side to side. Donal swayed, and for a moment Cordelia feared he would fall. She reached for him just as he turned to her, his gaze terrible in its passion.

"You fool," he said. "He would have killed you."

Cordelia found her voice, harsh and rough as a raven's croak. "You're wrong. He would never —"

Donal's arms closed about her, stopping the words in her throat. The pounding of his heart carried into her own body, impressing upon her the terror he felt for her, forcing her to understand that her danger had been real.

"You fool," he repeated. "You little fool. I told you . . . I tried to make you understand —"

"Donal. Donal, my dear." She pressed her face to his waistcoat, smelling the maleness of him, the wonderful scent she had missed so dreadfully in her self-imposed isolation. It was impossible to feel fear in his arms, impossible to feel anything but joy, and astonishing hope. . . .

He pushed her away before she was ready, and she made a low cry of protest. But he took her face between his hands, holding her still with the sheer power of his gaze.

"Do you know what happened, Cordelia?" he asked.

"Of course. Othello was half out of his mind with terror and confusion. He —"

"Yes, he was frightened. But it was more than that. It was the very thing I was afraid would happen if you met with him or any of the others."

"I do not understand you. He did not hurt —"

"But he would have. He would have torn your flesh without a second thought. I *know*." He drew in a deep breath. "I feel what he felt. He hated you, Cordelia . . . as you hate him."

CHAPTER
TWENTY-SIX

Donal saw that Cordelia heard only part of what he had said, and that part she refused to believe.

"Hate him?" she repeated, her face pale with shock. "How can you say such a thing?" She wrenched free, ripping at his heart with claws sharper than any cat ever possessed. "I have cared for him, fed him, given him the finest shelter —"

"And you have resented him every moment since you saved him."

She stared at him as if at a stranger. "Why, Donal? Why should you say something so designed to wound me, when you know . . . know that I have done everything within my power to help creatures such as Othello?"

Donal closed his eyes, despising himself for what he was about to do. He seized Cordelia's shoulder and swung her about to face the panther, who lay panting on his side, ears flattened to his skull in wary submission.

"Do you wish to understand what such a

creature truly feels?" he demanded.

She stared at the panther. "We have played this game twice before. You showed me —"

"I showed you only a shadow of the truth," he said harshly. "Do you wish to see what *he* sees when he looks at you?"

She trembled. "If it were possible . . . of course, I would give anything —"

He dragged her against him, enfolding her in his arms so that she would not fall. "Look, then," he said. "Look through a panther's eyes."

And he opened himself to Othello, to the leopard's memories, to the moment of his meeting with the human female who had imprisoned him with her hatred. Hatred of him, of herself, of the freedom she had lost and would never have again. Hatred that made of Cordelia a demon, a deadly foe who aroused an unspeakable terror in the breast of a hunter who understood only one law: kill or be killed.

Cordelia gave a soundless cry and slumped in Donal's hold. He commanded the panther to stay, lifted her in his arms and strode for the house, shaking with self-contempt. He had been compelled to make her *see*, or she would never agree to remain safe in the house. And he would not risk her life again. Not when he had nearly lost control.

Croome and Theodora met Donal in the entrance hall. For the first time since he had met her, Theodora appeared on the verge of a swoon. But she took herself in hand and faced Donal with icy composure.

"Is she hurt?" she asked.

"No. She has only fainted, but she should be put to bed and remain there as long as she feels unwell."

"I shall see to it." She studied Donal's face. "You are going back out alone?"

"I must. No one else is safe with the animals."

"Safe from them, or for them?"

"Both." He carried Cordelia up the stairs and laid her in her bed. Indifferent to who observed or what anyone might think, he knelt beside her, stroked the damp hair away from her face and kissed her forehead.

He left quickly, before he could obey the dangerous impulse to remain by Cordelia's side. Once he was alone again, he could finally face the horror of that first instant when he had stared into Othello's eyes and heard . . . nothing. Felt nothing. Knew that his connection to the beast had dried up like a river in a terrible drought, leaving him thirsting and weak and helpless.

And all because of Cordelia. Because, when he had realized her peril, he had finally recognized the depths of his feelings for her . . . understood that he could no longer escape what had become the one abiding certainty in his unpredictable existence.

When Othello had leaped at Cordelia, the full weight of Donal's love for her had struck him so fast and hard that he had scarcely had the power to quiet the panther's fury. He had reached for Othello's mind, for the sturdy web of union that had always come so naturally, and found it spun out to a weak and fragile thread. He heard nothing: not the sleeping birds in the trees, not the mice in the grass nor the horses and cats in the stables.

Othello had nearly defeated him. Love had stolen his power, just as Tod had always foretold; it had made him no more than a common mortal, blind and deaf, cut off from the vital gift he had never believed he could lose again.

His love had nearly cost Cordelia her life. But with the sheer force of his will he had reclaimed his power for a few brief minutes, subdued the panther, made Cordelia see through Othello's eyes. Now, as he ran into the shadowed woods, he listened again for animal minds, aware that he hung on to his Fane-born gifts by the merest breath. But the voices were faint, so terribly faint that he understood how close he was to losing them forever.

He looked for Othello where he had left him, but the panther was gone. Driven by fear for both the menagerie inmates and the local farmers, Donal cast about for any sign of the missing beasts. The first one he sensed was Arjuna. He followed the slender cord that still connected him to the animals and discovered the sun bear snuffling in a copse of beech down by the river.

The bear was more bewildered than rebellious. He stared at Donal, uncomprehending as Donal tried to reach his mind. But Donal heard just enough of Arjuna's thoughts to know that the bear had no desire to face this alien world. In the end he was able to approach the animal and lead him back to the menagerie with little more than his trained veterinarian's skill.

Heloise and Abelard proved more difficult. They had not wandered far and were still in the park, scampering among the trees. They were like unruly children, eager to make the most of their freedom.

Donal stood beneath the trees and called to the apes with all the focus he could muster. He felt his thoughts bounce into nothingness. The woods wore their silence like a shroud.

Struggling with the beginnings of despair, Donal fought to clear his mind of all doubt and fear. He stood unmoving beneath the trees. The night closed in around him. And he waited.

A small, clever hand patted his sleeve. Another tugged at his coat. He opened his eyes to find the apes beside him, staring up into his face with solemn curiosity.

Somehow he made them understand, though he wasn't sure if they followed him because they heard his inner voice or because they had learned to trust him. They returned to their cage and gazed out at him mournfully, captive and safe once more.

He found the wolves by the sound of their howls echoing across the wolds. By the time he caught up to them they had already crossed Edgecott lands and had ventured into the fields of a neighboring farmer. The bleats of frightened sheep rose from the pasture.

Donal ran, praying that enough of his gift remained to guide him. He stumbled into the farmyard on unsteady feet. A single lantern lit the tableau of a farmer facing a wolf, his hands clutching an ancient Brown Bess. He looked up as Donal came to a stop.

"Don't fire," Donal said. "Please."

The farmer shifted his grip on the rifle, his face white as chalk. "My sheep," he croaked.

"These animals belong to Mrs. Hardcastle, at Edgecott," Donal said quickly. "Let me capture them and take them back."

The farmer's throat worked. "How . . . how can you . . ."

"Let me try. If I fail, you still have the gun."

Licking his lips, the farmer nodded. Donal approached the wolf with great care, crouching low. The animal turned to face him, growled with hackles raised, and spun away.

Donal followed, clinging to the traces of awareness that had not yet deserted him. Grass whipped about his boots. His breath sawed in his throat. He climbed the wold, straining to hear beyond the pounding of his heart.

The wolves had come to rest on a cluster of rocks overlooking the pasture, moonlight gleaming on their silver coats. They stared at Donal, contemptuous of the two-legs who thought to run them down.

Donal fell to his knees. He could never compete with the wolves in either strength or speed; their even, steady pace could carry them many miles away in a matter of hours.

You will die, he told them. *The two-legs will kill you. Come with me.*

Ears twitched and tongues lolled, but the wolves gave no answer. He knew that the deepest part of their natures commanded them to pursue freedom at any price. Donal's only hope was to seek that most fundamental instinct and counter it.

As he done before when Othello had threatened Cordelia, Donal reached inside himself for the flickering light of his power. It came back to him with aching slowness, with pain that seemed to tear at muscle and bone like barbed iron hooks. He let the pain consume him, and out of the agony he gathered the fragile fragments of his gift.

With a groan he plunged into the wolves'

memories, those he had shared each time he entered their shelter, and deliberately shed his humanity as a snake sheds its outgrown skin. The world changed before his eyes. He sat back on his haunches, raised his head and howled.

The wolves raised their heads. They leaped from the rocks and came to him, circled him with ears flat and tails held low. The male growled a challenge. Donal answered, green eyes meeting gold. The battle was silent and arduous; blackness whirled in Donal's head, threatening to pull him under. But he held fast, and when the war of wills was done the wolves ran at his heels all the way back to Edgecott.

Donal dropped onto the bench, his body aching as if he had been beaten to within an inch of his life. The effort to hold on to his power pounded through him like some lethal disease, blurring his vision and scorching his skin. But it was not yet time to rest. He must find Othello.

Heaving himself to his feet, Donal trudged away from the cages. He was certain that Othello had not wandered far from the place he had left him, so he returned to the wood and worked his way outward, examining the terrain with all his senses.

He came upon the panther less than a quarter mile away, where the river wandered nearest the trees. Yellow eyes glared balefully out of the darkness; Othello's low growl warned Donal that this final capture would be by far the greatest and most dangerous challenge.

He sought the panther's consciousness, knowing he dared not reveal a single sign of weakness. Othello snarled as he approached, his very being pulsing with hatred of everything human.

But I am not human, Donal told him. He bared his thoughts and spread his hands wide, showing himself unafraid.

Othello crouched, lashing his tail. Donal caught a glimpse of sweltering forest and a whiff of blood just before the panther sprang.

Donal rolled with Othello's weight, letting his body go limp. Claws pricked his jacket. Othello's jaws opened above his face, bathing him in the panther's hot breath. He could hear nothing but rage, a cacophony of mingled thoughts and emotions that left no room for negotiation.

His heart beating wildly in his throat, Donal worked his hands from beneath Othello's tense body and slid his fingers into the sleek black fur. "Perhaps you can't hear me," he said, closing his eyes, "but know this, my friend. I won't raise a hand against you, not even to save my own life."

Othello coughed, his fangs grazing Donal's cheek. Claws drove into Donal's skin. He ceased his efforts to communicate and thought with regret of the things he had left undone: telling Ivy of her Fane heritage, seeing the world beyond this little isle.

Admitting to Cordelia that he loved her.

All at once the weight was gone from his chest. He sat up and scanned the darkness, terrified that the panther had escaped him. With the dregs of his strength he grasped Othello's mental signature and trailed after it, his brain burning in his skull like hot coals in a grate. He raced down the hill overlooking the menagerie and came to a halt before the last empty cage.

Othello was inside, pressed against the rear wall.

Shaking with relief, Donal retrieved the last padlock and secured the cage. He made a final visit to each of the animals, hoping they could feel his gratitude. Only then did he creep to the house and drag himself through the door.

Theodora rose from a chair in the hallway, her face blanching with alarm. "Donal!" she said, reaching for his hands. "You are hurt!"

Donal squeezed her hands and pulled his away. "Minor lacerations, nothing more."

"You're trembling. I shall call Croome and have him send for the doctor. . . ."

"No. Please."

Theodora opened her mouth as if to protest and subsided. She herded Donal into the drawing room and made him sit. "I'll send for food and drink. Is there anything you need?"

Donal lifted his head with an effort. "How is Cordelia?"

"Resting quietly."

"I wish to see her."

"After you have rested." She rang for Croome, and presently a drowsy maid brought a platter of bread, cheese and fruit. Donal picked at the food for Theodora's sake, and then retreated to the spare room Cordelia had saved for him. He washed the blood away as best he could and went to find Cordelia.

She was, as Theodora had promised, resting quietly, eyes closed, breathing slow and steady. Donal took a chair across the room and simply watched her, grateful for this moment of peace, for the luxury of a brief respite from the pain that must come.

He leaned his head on the chair back and drifted, fighting sleep.

"Donal?"

He opened his eyes. Cordelia was sitting up against the pillows, her eyes fixed on his face. "Donal, are you well?" she asked. "Is it finished?"

He pulled the chair to the side of the bed and sat down again. "Yes," he said. "The animals are home and safe."

"Thank God." She leaned forward with a frown. "But you are *not* well. Your face. . . ."

Her gaze fell to his chest. "Your coat is torn!"

"It is nothing —"

She pushed the coverlet aside and reached for the bellpull, jerking on it almost frantically. Hardly a minute later Croome appeared at the door.

"Croome, Dr. Fleming is injured," Cordelia said, her voice tight with fear. "Send for the doctor at once. And bring me hot water and clean cloths."

Croome bowed and retreated before Donal could protest. He knew the cause for Cordelia's strong reaction, and that nothing would be likely to calm her except for a doctor's assurance that he would survive the night's adventure.

"Please, Cordelia," he said. "I'm not badly hurt. They are only scratches —"

"Only . . ." She covered her mouth. "Was it Othello?"

"Yes. But he stopped, Cordelia. He went back to his cage. You mustn't blame him for acting according to his nature."

"Lord," she whispered. A tear leaked from the corner of her eye.

Donal cursed himself for her suffering. He had already caused her so much pain. "Cordelia," he said hoarsely, "I must ask your forgiveness —"

"For putting yourself in such horrible danger?"

He shook his head. "For the . . . earlier matter with Othello."

She bit her lip and looked away. "Donal . . ."

"I should never have forced you to endure —"

"The truth?" She laughed softly. "To know how Othello sees me — That . . . thing . . . so filled with anger and envy, so —" The tear trickled down her cheek. "All these years, when I thought I was helping them —"

He raised his hand and lowered it again. "You must never think your acts of kindness meant nothing," he said. "But animals do not think as we do. They sense emotion in a way we can scarcely comprehend. They see beneath the surface we show to our fellow men . . . even the secrets we hide from ourselves."

"I am trying . . . trying to understand, but I —" She swiped her palm across her cheeks. "I expected my animals to love me because I saved them, and when they could not . . ." She swallowed painfully. "The fault was in me, Donal. All in me, and yet I blamed them."

Donal ached with her humiliation, the shame she had never before acknowledged. "It is not a matter of love," he said gently, "not as we know it. If you could walk among the animals, as one of them . . ."

"As you do?" She searched his eyes, her own wet with tears and yet implacable in their conviction. "I thought I was delirious the night of the dog fight, when I claimed that you punished the men by making them feel what the dogs felt. But I wasn't, was I? What you did in the menagerie, and tonight . . . it was never just a conjurer's trick, or even some new form of hypnosis. It was real." Her voice quivered. "You knew the animals' thoughts, and you made me share them."

He averted his gaze. "Yes."

"But how? How can this be?"

He struggled to find an explanation that would allow her to maintain her logical comprehension of the world she knew, but he knew that would never be possible. Just as it wasn't possible to admit to the emotions that had torn his world asunder.

When he'd thought himself on the verge of death, he had regretted not telling Cordelia of his feelings for her. Now he knew that regret had been no more than a moment's madness. His gifts had all but deserted him because of love, and the loss was still an open wound. One that might never be healed.

Even if Cordelia could set aside her own fears and love him in return, he wouldn't give her half a man, half a soul. He would not become another cause for her pain. If she could not believe the truth about him, it would make his leaving that much easier.

"You may have difficulty in accepting what I tell you," he said slowly.

"Nothing you say is likely to be stranger

than what I have already experienced."

He stared at her hand clenched on the coverlet. "Have you ever heard of the Earl of Bradwell?"

"I have heard the name."

"He is my father. And he is not human."

It was, of course, quite impossible.

Cordelia heard him out calmly, never interrupting his bizarre tale of fairy folk who called themselves "Fane" and some otherworld named Tir-na-Nog; of the Forest Lord who had wooed and won an earl's daughter and lost his immortality for love of her; of the child born before their marriage who had inherited his sire's gift with animals but chose to make a life as an ordinary veterinarian among the Yorkshire moors.

She did not doubt that Donal was an earl's son, or that he was illegitimate; that last fact he had revealed to her some time ago, and without shame. Nor did she question that he had a remarkable gift with animals that defied intellectual analysis.

But the rest . . . the stories of Fair Folk and little flying men and immortality . . . about those tales Donal was correct. She could not accept them. Especially when he began to speak of Ivy.

"She is half-Fane, as I am," he said, no longer looking at her face as he spoke. "I did not know this at first, for I haven't the sight for Fane blood. But Tod . . . the hob I spoke of . . . he warned me that she was no ordinary girl."

"I see." She purged her voice of any hint of accusation. "Is this why you were so averse to my applying the usual discipline and guiding Ivy's behavior?"

"Fane are different. They are far less disciplined than humans. They must have freedom to survive, but they can be capricious and cruel. Their ways must often seem inexplicable to mortals."

"But your ways have never seemed so utterly strange, Donal."

"I, too, am half-Fane." He cleared his throat. "I was waiting for the right time to tell Ivy what she is."

"As you were waiting to tell me."

"Yes."

"Is there . . . anything more you need to explain?"

He gave a brief laugh. "Isn't this enough?"

"It does give me a great deal to think about."

"You don't believe me."

His voice was flat and heavy, and she felt a stab of concern. "Of course, I . . . will need time. . . ."

He rose, backing away from the bed. "I should let you rest."

She noted with alarm the paleness of his face and the unsteadiness of his walk.

"Croome will return shortly with the bandages —"

"I can treat myself, if I may use the room you assigned me."

Cordelia sensed that he was eager to escape and at the end of his strength. She was half afraid that she might lose what remained of her composure if she looked directly upon his wounds. She could hardly be rational under the circumstances.

"This house is yours," she said, "but you must promise me that you will lie down and wait quietly for the doctor."

"I —"

"Promise!"

"Yes." He gave her a long, grave look and fled the room. Cordelia gathered the bedcovers against her chest and buried her face in their folds like a child who has had one too many nightmares. But this, as she well knew, was no dream.

She was composed again by the time Croome came to her. She sent him to Donal's room with the hot water and bandages. Shortly afterward Theodora arrived, carrying a tray of eggs, toast and hot tea. She set the tray down and sat on the edge of the bed, her expression drawn with worry.

"What is it, Delia?" she asked. "You're white as a ghost. Are you worried for Donal?" She smoothed the blankets over Cordelia's legs. "The doctor will be here soon, and

Donal is strong. You have no reason to fear."

Cordelia met her cousin's gaze. "I know. It's only that I —" She lay back, her own strength sapped beyond its limits. "Theo . . . Donal is mad."

"What?"

Cordelia closed her eyes. "Perhaps 'mad' is too strong a word. Of course he is incapable of doing anyone harm, or even of harming himself. But he —" She plucked at the sheets and stretched them flat again. "You know he has an extraordinary skill with animals. He used it tonight when he saved my life."

"Of course, but what has that to do with —"

"I could never find a way to account for Donal's preternatural abilities. Tonight Donal offered an explanation."

"What did he tell you?"

Cordelia recounted Donal's story, pausing now and again when the words seemed too preposterous to speak with a steady voice. Theodora listened intently.

"And you consider this madness?" she asked when Cordelia had finished.

"What else can one call it? *Fairies,* Theo. Fairies and immortal gods of the forest. They are absolutely real to him, I am certain."

"And if they are?" Theodora touched Cordelia's shaking hand. "Where is the harm in such fancies? Donal has done only good at Edgecott. He saved Ivy from a life on the streets and improved the lives of the animals. He has even brought us a little happiness." She dropped her gaze. "I am sorry, Delia, but if this is only another excuse to reject him . . ."

"Reject him?" Cordelia squeezed Theodora's fingers. "Oh, no, Cousin. I made a terrible mistake when I tried to end my friendship with Donal. Now it is clear that he badly requires our help."

"Because he is mad."

"Because he cannot overcome these delusions alone. We must help him in every way we can . . . help him to feel safe enough here that he will eventually be able to face the world as it really is. We can cure him, with affection and firmness —"

"As we have 'cured' Ivy?"

Cordelia refused to be goaded. "Time is the key, Theo. Time and patience. With my father free of his dependency, we can devote ourselves fully to Ivy and Donal."

Theodora freed her hand from Cordelia's grip and rose from the bed. "Is this how you escape the burden of emotion, Delia? By finding yet more excuses to ignore your deepest feelings?" She hugged herself and stared at the canopy over Cordelia's head. "If Donal is mad, he cannot truly love you. And if you must care for him as you would a child or a wounded animal, you cannot love him as a woman loves a man." She started for the door. "I do not believe that Donal is mad. No, I'd sooner accept that every word he speaks is the unvarnished truth."

"Theodora!"

"You're tired, Cordelia. You must rest."

Cordelia shoved at the coverlet. "Please, Theo. I only wished . . ." Her heart gave a sudden thump. "Can it be that . . . that you love Donal?"

Theodora stopped with her hand on the doorknob. "How ridiculous," she said faintly. "Donal could not love me, and I do not trouble myself with unrequited passions." She met Cordelia's gaze. "But you had best realize what you have, Cordelia Hardcastle, for it will never come again." She opened the door.

"Wait," Cordelia said, catching her breath on a wave of incongruous relief. "I have not seen Ivy since dinner. How is she?"

"Fast asleep, I'm sure. You remember that she did not feel well at dinner."

"Of course." Cordelia reached for a bit of cold toast and crumbled it between her fingers. "I will speak to her in the morning, then."

"And I will see to the doctor when he arrives," Theodora said. "Perhaps he can recommend a madhouse." She left the room and closed the door behind her.

Sick with the feeling that she had betrayed Theodora, Donal and herself, Cordelia rose and paced the room as night gave way to the first light of dawn. What had driven Donal over the edge? He had always been a little eccentric, to be sure. Perhaps the challenges he'd faced at Edgecott had proven too much for a man of such solitary character. His formerly peaceful existence had certainly undergone a radical change.

Somehow she must find a way to ease his burdens. With regard to Ivy, there was little she could say to set Donal's mind at rest. Nor could she free Donal of responsibility for the animals he loved so dearly. But there was one thing she *could* do, something she should have done days ago.

After she had consulted the doctor and was assured that Donal's wounds were not of a serious nature, Cordelia rang for Biddle and donned her best riding habit. She refused Croome's offer of breakfast and left the house just as one of the stableboys brought her mare round to the drive.

Had this been an ordinary call, she would never have presumed to visit Inglesham's estate so early. But the viscount had long since forfeited any right to courteous behavior. She would catch him unaware, before he had time to compose any glib excuses, and have it out with him. When she was finished he would never dare presume to show his face at Edgecott again.

Brimming with righteous fury, Cordelia set

out in the half-light of dawn and savored the prospect of the battle to come.

CHAPTER
TWENTY-SEVEN

Tod recognized the Gate as Béfind drove her carriage from the rutted wagon road into a broad field bordered on two sides by a wood. The field was dominated by a rough circle of massive stones, some standing twice the height of a man and others lying fallen on their sides, overgrown with wildflowers. The place sang with ancient mystery, and no one with a drop of Fane blood could mistake the stone circle's purpose.

No one but the girl who remained ignorant of the wild magic running through her veins. Ivy sat forward in her seat with Sir Reginald in her arms, staring at the stones with a look of sheer bewilderment.

"This is not the road to London!" she exclaimed.

For a fraction of an instant Béfind's beautiful face turned ugly, though Tod was the only one to see. He spun in distress, half afraid that Béfind would strike Ivy silent and whisk her through the Gate before the girl knew what was happening.

But Béfind was not yet quite so desperate. She smiled at Ivy, drew her out of the carriage and led her to one of the flat boulders that marked the perimeter of the invisible Gate.

"You are quite right, my dear," she said. "This is not the road to London. We have come to a far better place."

Ivy frowned, her gaze sweeping over the cluster of tall stones. "Where are we?"

Béfind cupped Ivy's chin in her palm, ignoring Sir Reginald's almost voiceless growl. "This, too, is a road, child," she said. "But it is one that few are privileged to find, and even fewer to travel. It is more ancient than any path built by the Celts or the Romans or those who came after them. It is as old as time itself."

"Where is my father?"

"You will find what you seek beyond the Gate . . . *this* Gate . . . in a world you can scarcely imagine."

"I see no gate."

Béfind stepped back and turned to face two upright stones that dominated the sacred circle. She fluttered her fingers, and a shimmering light filled the space between the stones, a rainbow of color made up of hues mortal eyes were hardly equipped to discern.

"There it is," Béfind said. "The Gate that will lead you to your heritage."

Ivy set Sir Reginald down and rose from the boulder. She peered into the flickering light, shook her head, and turned to meet Béfind's gaze.

"You lied to me," she said. "You said we were going to London, that my father was in hiding there."

Béfind sighed impatiently. "It was necessary to simplify explanations, my girl, or we should never have left in time."

"In time for what?" Ivy's eyes narrowed in suspicion. "What else did you lie about, Countess? Who are you?"

"You shall know all these things once we have passed the Gate." Béfind glanced at Tod, her eyes cold as a snake's. "Make yourself useful, hob. Tell her that we must go through before she can comprehend the great gift I offer."

Ivy looked up to where Tod hovered, astonishment in her face. "You can see him?" she demanded of Béfind. "You can see Tod?"

"Of course I can see him. He is of a lesser breed, scarcely worth your notice, but he has on occasion been useful."

Ivy backed away, staring at Béfind with the beginnings of fear. "Tod, what is she saying? How does she know you? What *is* she?"

Tod drifted to the ground, sick at heart, and bowed at Ivy's feet. "She is Fane, my lady," he said. "Fane, as you are Fane, as Tod is . . . though of a *lesser* breed."

"Fane?" Ivy pressed her hand over her mouth. "Like in the stories you told me? And I am . . . But I can't be —"

"You *are*," Béfind said. She moved closer to Ivy, graceful hands extended. "Did you never wonder why you felt so discontented with mortal ways, why you spent your time in wood and meadow rather than in the cold, stifling rooms of Edgecott? Did you not ask yourself why you are so much swifter and lighter than any human, how you could survive in a world where most mortal children would perish?"

Ivy continued to retreat. "My father is Fane?"

"You were born to a Fane mother, who with all your kin eagerly awaits your return."

"Return to where?"

"Tir-na-Nog, my lady," Tod said. "The Land of the Young."

Ivy stared at him, her eyes begging for truth. "You're saying that Tir-na-Nog lies somewhere beyond those stones?"

"Aye, my lady."

She gathered Sir Reginald against her, hugging him close. Girl and spaniel shivered. "If you knew what I was," she said, "why didn't you tell me long ago?"

Tod ducked his head, his flesh going hot and cold by turns. "Tod . . . it was not his place . . . Donal was Tod's master. . . ."

"What has Donal to do with this?"

"He, too, is Fane."

Ivy laughed bitterly. "Is everyone I know of the Fair Folk?"

"No, my lady," Tod whispered. "Donal is halfling, like you, but he chose to live in the mortal world. He did not know you were Fane until you came to Edgecott. He would . . ."

"Enough of this prattle," Béfind snapped. "Fleming would have prevented you from rejoining your true kin, just as Hardcastle would bind you to her in mortal sorrow and misery." She held out her hand. "Come. It is time."

Ivy's jaw tightened. "Donal doesn't know I am here."

"I told you he would interfere —"

She turned to Tod again. "Why?"

"He does not know that the countess is Fane," he said, defying Béfind's wrathful stare. "He thought only that she would help you find your father, not that she would take you to Tir-na-Nog."

"And why wouldn't he want me to go to Tir-na-Nog?"

"Silence!" Béfind cried. "Foolish child . . . did you not wish to escape him and your captors at Edgecott?" Béfind clenched her fist. "I can compel you to enter. The only thing that kept me from you was the amulet."

Ivy snatched at her bodice as if she had forgotten that the pendant was gone. Panic flushed her skin.

"What have you done with my necklace?" she demanded.

"You have no need of it now, or ever again."

"But it was my father's . . ."

"Your *father* never gave you anything but his mortal blood."

Ivy pressed her hand to the base of her neck, and there was in her eye a look of both fear and determination.

"Tod," she said, her voice shaking, "if you were ever my friend, answer me truthfully. Do you trust this woman?"

Tod understood that his entire future, and Ivy's, hung on his answer. He opened his mouth to speak. Béfind laughed.

"How much can you trust your little friend, my dear?" she asked Ivy. "He not only deceived you when he knew of your true origins, but he bargained with me . . . bargained for your affections. You see, Tod is under a curse, and he knows you cannot care for such a creature as he until that curse is lifted."

Ivy licked her lips. "You love me, Tod?"

Tod shivered. "I do . . . I do not . . ."

"Tod . . . if you care for me, even a little . . . find Donal. Bring him here."

"No!" Béfind cried. "If you do as she asks, hob, you will never know your true form again."

Tod flung himself skyward, his heart so full of emotion that he feared it would split asunder. Blood roared in his ears. No matter what he chose, he would lose: betray Béfind and lose Ivy, or ignore Ivy's plea and forfeit what little self-respect remained in his hob's feeble soul.

He glanced again at Ivy's face and knew what he must do.

"I will bring Donal," he called down to her, and darted away in a burst of speed. But Béfind was to have the last word. Before he could fly beyond her reach he felt the blow, the dizzying gust of enchantment striking him out of the air. His limbs began to change, beyond his control, and rough-woven clothing turned to russet fur.

As a fox he ran, his voice trapped in the throat of a beast. On four swift feet he skimmed over the earth, his legs pumping tirelessly beneath him. He reached the borders of Edgecott just after the sun had crested the horizon, casting long shadows like cage bars across his path.

He found Donal at his cottage, tightening the straps on his traveling bags. Donal looked up briefly, glanced down at his bags and turned again to stare at the fox panting on his threshold.

"Tod?" he asked. "Is it you?"

Tod yipped and waved his tail, desperate to make Donal understand. Donal left his bags and crouched before Tod, cupping his hand beneath the fox's muzzle.

"What is it?" he asked, frowning. "Why don't you change, so that we can speak?"

Tod whined in his throat and pawed urgently at Donal's knee. He conjured up pictures in his head . . . moving, speaking images of Béfind as the countess, of Ivy at Shapford, of their arrival at the stone circle and the revelatory conversation that followed.

Donal pressed his fingers to his temples, his eyes squeezed shut. "It's nearly gone," he said. "I can barely hear you. Try again."

It was hard for Tod to remember human words with his fox's brain, but he ran through the memories a second time, pushing them at Donal with all his might. When he was finished he knew he had succeeded by the look of horror on Donal's face.

"My God," Donal whispered. "The countess is Fane, and Ivy's mother? She's taken Ivy to a Gate?" He seized the ruff of fur at Tod's neck. "Why didn't you tell me? How could you permit this to happen?" He pushed Tod away and strode across the cottage floor. "But I fell into her trap as well, when I brought her Ivy's pendant. Damn it, I believed that Ivy had a right to choose her own future. But Béfind's manipulation will make any real choice impossible. And Cordelia . . ." He swore brutally. "How can I save Ivy if Béfind has the means to force her through the Gate?"

Tod covered his face with his paws and

whimpered. It was a blessing that he could not explain his betrayal, or the shameful ambition that had led him to trust Béfind. He had failed everyone.

Donal laughed. "The irony of it is that I was to see Inglesham for a race this morning, and I intended to follow your advice and silence him for good. His threats pale in comparison to the one Ivy faces now."

He shrugged into his jacket and ran for the door. Tod fell in behind him, but Donal waved him off.

"I know of the stone circle where the Gate lies," he said. "You go to the house and stay with Cordelia. I don't care how you manage it, but stay with her."

Tod had had enough of the fruits of disloyalty. With a bark of acknowledgment, he dashed across the park. The sun had risen another hand's width, but the house still cast deep shadows when he reached the garden gate.

With judicious use of a fox's paws and teeth, Tod slipped through an unlocked door and sniffed the air for Cordelia's scent. It lingered throughout the house, but nowhere was it stronger than up the broad staircase.

Running close to the ground, Tod darted up the stairs and followed the scent trail to a room near the end of the hall. It was empty. The smell of anger still lingered, hinting at the woman's strong emotions, but she had left the room sometime within the hour.

Casting a wider net, Tod traced the many interwoven threads of her movements along the hallway and came to another room whose door bore the mark of her scent. The door was open a crack, wide enough so that he could open it with a flick of his muzzle.

The room was very large, much more so than the one in which the woman denned. A man lay in the immense, canopied bed, propped up amid a fortress of pillows. Tod guessed at once who the man must be: the tyrant called Sir Geoffrey, Cordelia Hardcastle's father, of whom Ivy had so often spoken with such vivid dislike. Tod shook his head, sneezing at the smell of long illness, and was about leave the room the old man opened his eyes.

Any mortal might well have been surprised at the presence of a wild beast in his house, but Sir Geoffrey merely stared, his pale blue eyes locked on Tod with a strange intensity.

Tod could not have said why Béfind's enchantment chose that very moment to wear off. Perhaps it had not been meant to last more than the time she would need to convince Ivy to pass through the Gate; perhaps she had been too preoccupied to shape it properly. Whatever the reason, Tod felt his body change again, and the old man's eyes widened in astonishment.

"Fane," he said hoarsely. "Did *she* send

you?"

The mortal's question was so eerily apt that Tod almost fled in consternation. But Sir Geoffrey sat up, his arms extended in a gesture of entreaty, his wrinkled face a mask of yearning.

"You come from Béfind," he said. "You must. You are one of *them*."

Tod backed halfway out the door. "You . . . you know Béfind, Mortal?"

"Know her?" The man barked an ugly laugh. "I loved her, Fane creature . . . loved her as one of her own kind never could. I saw her from the window the day she came to Edgecott . . . not that I dared tell anyone." He cast the blankets away from his thin legs. "Where is she?"

Tod thought quickly, considering what this amazing turn of events could portend. He moved cautiously closer to the bed.

"You were Béfind's lover?" he asked.

"You must know that, if she sent you," the old man said. His eyes narrowed to slits. "What are you doing in this house?"

Tod smiled. "It is but a test, Mortal . . . to see how well you remember your time with my lady Béfind."

"Remember? Is that what you wish of me, to prove my devotion?" The man gave a great sigh and fell back among the pillows. "Forty years, and she hasn't changed. Just as beautiful as she was then, when I was hardly out of boyhood. I had just begun to make my way in the world, full of confidence and vigor . . . how simple it all seemed."

Nothing, Tod thought, could ever be simple with Béfind, especially where mortals were concerned.

Forty years. Perhaps Béfind had taken more than one lover in her time among humans, but if she had not . . .

If she had not, then Sir Geoffrey's own half-Fane daughter had been living under his roof, and he had never known.

"How old I must seem to her now," Sir Geoffrey said, oblivious to Tod's feverish speculation. "But she did not find me so then." He met Tod's gaze. "I gave her my heart, Fane creature . . . and I never took it back again, even when she left me, even when I was compelled to take a wife I could not love."

The mortal wife who must be Cordelia Hardcastle's mother. A loveless mating . . . which was ordinary enough among Fane, but a great sorrow among humans, as Tod had begun to understand.

"Your lady wishes to know if I am still worthy of her?" Sir Geoffrey asked, his voice breaking. "Of who else am I worthy now? I despised my wife. I neglected my children. All my life I have waited for Béfind to call me back."

"And would you give anything to hold her?"

Tod whispered.

"Anything." The old man clutched his bed-covers until it seemed that his knuckles must burst through his flesh. "Only tell me what I must do."

"Can you rise from this bed, Mortal?"

"For Béfind, I can race the sun across earth."

"Then prepare yourself for swift travel, and when I return I shall lead you to her."

As Sir Geoffrey rose from his bed with a groan and a curse, Tod sped from the house as fast as his will would carry him. There was but one more thing he must do before leading this desperate mortal to his lost beloved.

Once he found Cordelia Hardcastle, he would take both father and daughter to the Gate, for Ivy was not the only one in peril. Donal must not face Béfind alone, or he might very well become her next victim.

Cordelia had ridden nearly all the way to Inglesham's estate when she met his carriage on the lane leaving the park.

Burning anger had sustained her throughout the four-mile ride, and it did not falter as she reined Desdemona alongside the brougham. Inglesham poked his head out the window, brows arched in surprise, and instructed his coachman to stop.

"Cordelia!" he said. "How delightful to see you on this fine morning. I was just on my way out, but if I had known you were coming . . ."

"You have not been expecting me?" Cordelia asked, bristling at the sight of his smiling, ingenuous face. "I should not be surprised, since you obviously never considered that I might discover your scheme to gain my fortune."

Inglesham's smile tightened. "I beg your pardon?"

"You know perfectly well to what I refer, sir. Would you rather discuss it here, or in a more private situation?"

The viscount glanced up the lane, his face drawn in an excellent approximation of bewilderment. "Of course, Cordelia. I should not wish you to remain upset with me when we can so easily resolve this matter with a little conversation."

"I doubt that very much," Cordelia said. She urged Desdemona into a trot and rode ahead while Inglesham's coachman laboriously maneuvered the brougham back toward the house. No servant appeared to greet her; she dismounted and tied the mare to a shrubbery while she waited for Inglesham to join her.

He was all humble reassurances and courtly bows as he ushered her into the drawing room. Cordelia tried, and failed, to remember why she had ever found him so charming and attractive, or when he had changed from the spirited boy she had known to this deceitful cad.

"Please, make yourself comfortable," Inglesham said, indicating his favorite chair. "I fear most of the servants are out today, as I expected to be away, but Mrs. Gazard should still be on the premises. I shall send for tea —"

"Pray do not trouble yourself," Cordelia said, declining the offered seat. "I shall get right to the point. Your plot has been uncovered. It has been brought to my attention that you —" She paused, her anger seething white-hot, as Inglesham tugged the bellpull and faced her again with a faintly condescending smile. "I know what you've done, enticing my father with poisonous substances and threatening to withhold them if he did not actively support your bid for my hand in marriage."

Inglesham showed no dismay and not the slightest remorse. "Who told you such a farrago of lies, my dear? Is it too audacious to speculate that your friend Dr. Fleming had something to do with these allegations?"

"The manner in which I learned of your treachery hardly signifies," she said sharply. "I saw the evidence of it, and my father has been suffering to rid his body of the poisons you forced upon him."

"No one forces anything upon Sir Geoffrey," Inglesham said. "I am sorry if he has become dependent upon these 'poisonous substances,' as you call them, but I assure you —" He glanced toward the door, where his thin and fragile-looking housekeeper had appeared with a tea tray. "Will you pour, my dear? A little refreshment will do us both good."

Cordelia wanted to laugh at his brazen insolence, but her nerves were so tightly strung that she feared for her own self-control. She thanked the housekeeper, sat and poured out the tea, grateful to find that her hands were not shaking.

Inglesham picked up his cup and sniffed it with appreciation. "As you were saying?"

"What more is there to say? You have offered no explanation for your behavior, only pretended ignorance and denials which I do not credit in the least." She raised the cup to her lips and drank as if the liquid were some potent liquor by which she might supplement her courage. "I know you are guilty. I know that you are greatly in debt, and that you would have broken your promise to allow me continued control of my fortune after our marriage." She drained the cup. "You may dismiss any hopes you may have nourished regarding our marriage. I should sooner wed one of our footmen."

"Or a country veterinarian?" Inglesham said dryly. "Oh, no, my dear. I doubt that you will lower yourself."

"Dr. Fleming is a man of impeccable honor. If he should offer —" her cheeks burned "— I should accept, with pleasure."

Inglesham chuckled. "That would be a most amusing scene. I almost wish I could witness it. Unfortunately, such a circumstance is very unlikely to occur."

Cordelia jumped up. "You may be surprised to learn how little you know Dr. Fleming's mind . . . or my own."

"I know you well enough." He watched Cordelia curiously as she swayed on her feet and touched her hand to her forehead. "What is it, my dear? Have the morning's hyperbolic passions quite overwhelmed you?"

She braced her feet, not daring to move lest she fall. "I am done with you, Inglesham. You shan't be welcome at Edgecott, now or any time in the . . ." She fought off another wave of dizziness and stared at the teapot. "What have you done?"

"It is not what I have *done* that should concern you." He signaled to someone standing in the doorway behind Cordelia. Before she could turn, she felt her arms being grasped by strong, burly hands and inhaled a stream of malodorous breath.

"Careful, Fawkes," Inglesham said. "Bind her gently. We would not want anyone to find suspicious marks on my little bride-to-be."

"You're mad!" Cordelia snapped, her resistance ending in a painful twist of her elbows.

Her captor grunted in satisfaction and finished knotting the rope at her wrists. "What do you think to achieve by this?"

"Only your temporary cooperation, my dear," Inglesham said. "Soon such restraints will no longer be necessary."

"You have no power over me or my family," Cordelia said. "Release me at once, and I may not lay charges of assault against you."

Inglesham strolled toward her and took her chin in his hand. "Why should a loving wife wish to lay charges against her devoted husband?" He kissed her full on the mouth, stabbing his tongue inside, and it was all she could do not to retch in disgust.

"Take her out to the carriage," Inglesham instructed his brutish servant, "and keep her quiet."

"Right, your lordship." The man spun Cordelia around and half dragged, half carried her from the drawing room and out the front door as if he had nothing in the world to fear. No one else witnessed Cordelia's struggles, and when she opened her mouth to scream her captor stuffed a bit of filthy cloth in her mouth and pushed her into the carriage.

A few moments later Inglesham joined Cordelia, though he seemed disinclined to explain himself further. The shades were drawn over the windows, so Cordelia could see nothing of their progress as the carriage bumped and rolled from the relatively smooth gravel of the drive onto a deeply rutted road. After perhaps twenty minutes of travel, the carriage stopped and Inglesham's henchman let down the steps. Together he and his master lifted Cordelia out and allowed her to study her surroundings.

They had come to a dense patch of woodland with a narrow footpath leading among the trees. Cordelia caught a glimpse of a half-hidden cottage, and then Inglesham grabbed her elbow and pulled her along the path. Inglesham's servant remained behind. Soon the cottage, a well-kept dwelling with an overgrown garden, came into full view.

"Our little love nest," Inglesham said, pushing the door open with his foot. "It may not be what you expected, my dear, but once this is finished you will have no cause to complain."

Cordelia's heart beat frantically in her throat. She locked her knees and would not move until Inglesham overpowered her and threw her down on the bed in the smaller of the cottage's two rooms. He wrenched up her arms, cutting the bindings from her wrists with a small boot knife, and pulled the gag from her mouth.

"I shall put it back in if you scream," he warned her. "You might as well resign yourself, Delia. I shall have you."

"You intend to —" Her mouth refused to form the crude words. "Whatever you do, you cannot compel me to marry you. Shame will not break me, for I and my family will know that I fought you with all my strength."

He shrugged and began to unbutton his coat. "It's entirely up to you whether this will be painful or pleasant. I can make it enjoyable for you, but I shall not waste my time." He draped his coat over the back of a chair and started on his waistcoat. "It will be easier if you remove your petticoats. I would prefer not to tear your habit."

Cordelia pressed against the wall, curling her fingers into claws. "I won't insult my animals by calling you a beast," she said.

He set aside his waistcoat and knelt on the edge of the bed. "Think of your Lord of Beasts if it comforts you," he said. "Perhaps your imagination will supply the means to lessen your pain."

Cordelia smiled. "I need not rely on my imagination," she said. "You are not the first to touch me since my husband's death."

Inglesham froze as he reached for her, his expression briefly lapsing into shock. Slowly his mouth curled in contempt. "So," he said, "you took him into your bed. Somehow I am not surprised that you have played the wanton. What else would one expect from one of your upbringing?"

"No more than from one of yours. And I assure you, Viscount, that your skills will never match those of a 'lowly veterinarian.' "

Inglesham growled and struck like a serpent, seizing Cordelia's shoulders and yanking her to him. His mouth ground into hers, his teeth cutting her lip, his tongue obscene in its violent thrusting. She bit down, hard. He yelped and threw her back against the wall. While her head was still spinning from the blow, he pulled her flat onto the bed and flung himself on top of her. She kneed him in the groin. He cursed and struck her across the face.

"Bitch," he snarled, clawing at her skirts. "You'll have nothing when I'm done with you. Nothing."

She heaved against him, and he struck her again. She knew then that he would win. Sooner or later he would beat her into a state of semiconsciousness and slake his lust on her helpless body. She had no allies. No one would come until it was much too late.

With a silent prayer she bunched her fists and braced herself for another blow. Her nails raked at his face. He pinned her arms above her head with one hand and fumbled between her thighs with the other. His weight pressed against her, pushing and probing.

Forgive me, Donal. I should have listened to you from the beginning. I should have followed my heart, not my head. . . .

A sharp, high buzz like the whirring of wings swooped over Cordelia's head, and a small shape that looked absurdly like a miniature man darted directly between her and Inglesham, hovering at the tip of the viscount's nose. Inglesham stopped, staring in disbelief.

"Wicked," the tiny man said, shaking his fist. "Wicked, wicked mortal!"

Inglesham reared back. Cordelia clutched at the bedclothes and lurched against the wall. She had scarcely begun to accept that the fey little creature was real when she heard the thumping of boots on the threshold.

"Inglesham!" a familiar, shockingly unexpected voice snapped. "I should've known you'd try such a craven trick. Get away from my daughter, or I'll blow your head off where you stand."

Chapter
Twenty-Eight

"You say you are . . . Donal's friend?"

The Hardcastle's voice was strained and uncertain, but Tod knew that she was not a female to disbelieve what her own eyes told her. Nor did Inglesham show the expected astonishment, and it was no wonder; the whole room stank of magic that carried Béfind's indisputable signature.

Béfind had threatened to punish Inglesham for blackmailing Donal, but Tod had no doubt that she had arranged an equally unpleasant fate for Donal's mortal lady. Unless Tod was very much mistaken, the magic he smelled was a love potion of a particularly disagreeable type. Doubtless it would have bound mortal to mortal once the Yellow-Hair had forced himself upon the woman, but with consequences the human lord would not have anticipated.

Whatever fell purpose *he* had intended for Donal's mate, Inglesham now sat well bound under Sir Geoffrey's watchful eye and the weapon of Iron that Tod was most careful to avoid. The elder mortal had every reason to be angry. After Tod determined that the lady Cordelia had left Edgecott, a persistent instinct had warned him that she, like Donal, was in imminent danger. He had summoned Sir Geoffrey to accompany him, and as Tod tracked the lady to Inglesham's house and then this place, he had explained to her father something of the intricacies of his relationship to Béfind and Donal, Béfind's true purpose at Edgecott, and Cordelia's involvement with the Fane. He had only withheld his speculation that Ivy might be Sir Geoffrey's own daughter.

Sir Geoffrey had cursed and wept to learn that his beloved Fane lady had not come Edgecott to find him, but he had followed Tod with great determination in spite of his lingering weakness. And when he had found his daughter in danger, his cold fury had been almost as impressive as that of a true Fane lord. Tod would not have wished to be in the Yellow-Hair's shoes.

Tod bowed to Cordelia. "Tod serves my lord Donal Fleming," he confirmed, "but Tod has made terrible mistakes and seeks to make things right again. It was my lord who sent Tod to find you . . . before Tod learned that your father was already acquainted with Béfind, a powerful lady of the Fane, who plotted with this mortal to harm you and seeks to take Ivy away."

She started. "Take her away?"

"Béfind posed as the Countess Pavlenkova, deceiving even my lord Donal, and enticed Ivy with false tales of finding her father in London. Now they stand before the Gates of Tir-na-Nog, the passageway between your world and the world of the Fane. Once they pass through, Béfind will ply Ivy with the delights of the Land of the Young, and she will never return to this earth."

"But why does the countess . . . this Béfind . . . want Ivy?"

"Béfind is Ivy's true mother."

The lady trembled like one who has taken too much ambrosia. "Then Ivy, too, is . . ."

"Fane. Like my lord Donal."

"Good God." She turned to her father. "You knew Béfind?"

Sir Geoffrey bent his head. "Long ago. We were lovers, before I met your mother."

"Then you knew about the Fane."

"I had not seen Béfind in forty years. I didn't know why she'd returned until Tod came to me."

Cordelia released a long breath and focused her attention on Inglesham. "Béfind had something to do with this kidnapping?"

The Yellow-Hair sneered. "She wanted you out of the way, and I wanted your fortune. It was a most convenient alliance."

"And now it has failed."

"But it almost succeeded. Do you remember that tea I gave you? A very useful little Fairy potion spiced just for your delectation. Once I'd taken you, you would have been bound to my will until death. *That* was worth the risk."

Sir Geoffrey struck Inglesham's cheek with the muzzle of his pistol. "No one will blame me if I shoot you in defense of my daughter," he growled.

"And when did you acquire such an interest in protecting your kin?" Inglesham laughed. "All you've ever done is think of yourself."

Sir Geoffrey's face twisted in anguish. "Do you think I don't know it? How I curse myself for being like you, Inglesham . . . caring for nothing but my own wishes and comfort?"

"But now you have *changed*," Inglesham mocked.

"I'm free of the opium and liquor, thanks to Cordelia," the baronet said in a low voice. "I see more clearly now than I have in years. Perhaps it is not too late."

"If you know anything about Béfind, old man, then you also know you have no hope in thwarting her plans."

Sir Geoffrey touched the pocket of his coat with an expression of stubborn resolve. "Let me go after Béfind, Cordelia. You take the pistol and remain here with Inglesham. Shoot him if he gives you any trouble."

"That will not be necessary," a steady female voice said from the doorway. The mortal known as Theodora walked into the room dressed in a plain wool riding habit, bringing with her a strangely calming air. "I can handle a pistol, Uncle, and I am more than happy to guard the viscount until you and Cordelia return."

"Theo!" Cordelia said, taking her cousin's hands. "How did you come here? What did you —"

"I heard most of the little man's explanations," she said. "You see, after you left Edgecott in such an impassioned state, I worried about what you might do. As I considered pursuit, I saw this creature in the hallway —" she indicated Tod "— and knew that something very strange was occurring. So I waited, and when Sir Geoffrey left with his fey companion, I followed them here."

Tod hovered to Theodora's eye level and regarded her with approval. "You are not a silly mortal."

Theodora curtseyed. "I thank you, Tod of the Fane."

Cordelia scraped her hands across her face. "There is no more time for talk," she said. "We must go to Ivy at once."

"And to Donal," Tod reminded her. "Tod fears that she may somehow trick him into entering Tir-na-Nog as well."

"Would he . . . would he wish to go

there, Tod?"

"He has had many chances, and has never chosen that path. But he has found much hurt in the mortal realm, and the Fane would welcome him."

"But would he be happy?"

Tod touched the lady's hand. "Once Tod believed my lord would find happiness there. But Donal is too much like his father, too unlike the Fane who have so long distanced themselves from Man. He must love and be loved. You must not let him go."

She laughed softly. "You have more faith in me than I do in myself."

"*I* have faith in you," Theodora said.

"And I," Sir Geoffrey said gruffly.

Cordelia stared at him, and slowly the expression in her eyes changed from one of despair to fragile hope. "Tod, are there any weapons that will be of use against the Fane?"

"Cold Iron," Tod said, shuddering. "All Fane avoid it when they can."

"The pistol must stay with Theodora." Cordelia looked about and found a poker leaning against the meager hearth. "This will have to do."

Sir Geoffrey's face creased with worry. "You and Theodora should —"

"I will not stay behind, Father."

With a grunt of resignation Sir Geoffrey handed his pistol to Theodora. "As I told Cordelia," he said, "shoot Inglesham if he gives you any difficulty. I shall take full responsibility."

Theodora met Inglesham's gaze with a faintly scornful smile. "I doubt that we shall come to such straits." She tucked the pistol under her arm and gave Cordelia a quick kiss and embrace. "Go to your loved ones, Delia. I shall be praying for you all."

Cordelia squeezed her cousin's arm and turned to Tod.

"Lead us to this Gate, my friend. And hurry."

The Gate stood open. The sweetest melodies of Tir-na-Nog drifted through to the mortal world: the silvery refrain of bright-plumaged birds, the rustle of golden leaves . . . even the rush of the fragrant breeze carried its own promise of perfect joy. And Ivy, who sat on one of the fallen stones, lifted her head and listened in wonder.

"Do you hear it calling?" Béfind whispered, circling round and round her daughter in a dance of seduction. "How can you resist such music? All you need do is step through, my dear one, and all will be revealed to you."

Ivy clutched her little dog closer to her chest, throwing off Béfind's subtle weaving with a toss of her shoulders. "Not until Tod returns," she said for the hundredth time. "Not until I see Donal."

"Donal," Béfind spat. "*He* has no right to

decide your future."

"But you do?"

"More than anyone else in this or any other world. I am your mother."

Ivy shot up from the stone, her mouth working in astonishment. "You? *You* are my mother?"

"It was I who bore you," Béfind said triumphantly. "I who was to raise you among your own people . . . until another stole you from me and gave you to a mortal female."

The spotted dog whined and licked Ivy's face. Ivy sat down again, her fingers buried in her pet's thick fur. "But . . . if this is true, why didn't you tell me before?"

"Because she was afraid."

The voice rang clear and strong, and Béfind cursed her own stupidity. The hob had done as he promised, fox or no, and sent his master to interfere in his betters' business.

Donal Fleming strode among the standing stones as if he were a high lord of the Fane instead of a troublesome half-blood, his jaw set in implacable anger. The dog in Ivy's lap wriggled free and ran to him, leaping up into his arms.

Donal stroked the beast, spoke softly in its ear, and set it down at his feet. "Are you all right, Ivy?" he asked

"Yes." She rose, starting toward him. "Tod found you?"

"He did. And he reported to me every lie

this lady told to lure you here."

"Watch your tongue, halfling," Béfind snapped, "or I shall silence it."

"As you silenced Tod?"

Béfind curled her fingers, longing to put Donal in his place but well knowing that such an act would hardly win Ivy to her side. This must be handled with finesse . . . and there was still a chance she might lure Donal himself through the Gate.

"Peace," she said, smiling. "Now that you are here, Ivy will have no cause to believe that any truth is hidden from her."

Donal's nostrils flared. He looked toward the Gate.

"He hears it, too," Béfind said, resting her hand on Ivy's shoulder. "Behold his face, how he longs to enter the Land of the Young."

Donal shook his head sharply. "What has she promised you, Ivy?" he asked. "A perfect life of endless pleasure? An existence without pain or struggle or death?"

"She will have all these things, and more," Béfind purred, "as you can, Donal son of Hern."

Ivy shrugged off Béfind's hand. "Son of Hern," she echoed. "Why didn't you tell me, Donal?"

"Because *he* was afraid," Béfind mocked.

"Yes," Donal said, holding Ivy's gaze. "I should have told you long ago, but I thought you could be happy . . . that Cordelia . . ."

He faltered, betrayed by his very human weaknesses. "I should have trusted you, Ivy. I should have helped you understand what you are, what you can be. But it isn't too late."

Ivy looked away. "Béfind . . . my mother was right when she said I don't belong here."

"Is that what she said? Did she also tell you why she waited so long to claim you from this terrible human existence?"

Ivy turned on Béfind. "No," she said. "She didn't."

"That is a simple question to answer," Béfind said. "I but recently learned that my child was made a changeling in the mortal world."

"And what of the woman who raised you, Ivy?" Donal asked. "Does she count for nothing?"

Confusion passed over the girl's face. "No! She was my . . ." She shivered and edged out of Béfind's reach.

"If she had lived, would you have turned your back on her now?"

Ivy pressed her palms to her eyes. "But she isn't alive. No one wants me —"

"Cordelia wants you."

"She wants me to be like her."

"And what does Béfind want? She makes many promises, but she is also capable of great deception. Who is your father, Ivy? Does he, too, wait for you in Tir-na-Nog?"

Ivy stared at Béfind. "Where is my father?"

Fury boiled in Béfind's chest. "He was mortal, and thus of no consequence."

"You are half-mortal, Ivy, like me," Donal said. "And that means you *do* have a choice." He crouched before her. "Béfind claims to want you. Is it a mother's love that impels her to save you from a mortal's fate?"

Ivy's lips trembled. "I . . ."

"Few Fane feel love such as humans understand it. Those who do are banished from Tir-na-Nog, as my father was exiled when I was a child."

"Exiled for betraying his duty to his people!" Béfind cried.

"Because he refused to surrender me up to the life he had chosen to leave behind. The Fane as a race are fading, and they will do anything to acquire offspring. That is why Béfind would do anything to win you, Ivy . . . because you are a precious object she can't afford to lose again."

"Now *he* lies!" Béfind flung a hand toward Donal, and he staggered, buffeted by the merest breath of her power. "Look at him . . . a creature who belongs in no world, among no people. Whom will you believe — a man who rejects both his human and Fane blood, one who has failed miserably in his own attempts at human emotion, or the one who gave you birth?"

Ivy took a step toward Donal, tears glistening in her eyes. "I . . . I don't know . . ."

"Perhaps you have no reason to trust me," Donal said, catching his breath. "I have failed in many things. But there are other voices." He raised his hand, and the spotted dog ran to him. "Sir Reginald is incapable of deception. He came with you because he wanted to protect you, because he knew you would face a terrible choice. The animals in the menagerie would tell you that there are many kinds of cages. Cordelia, who loves you, knows that no happiness is gained without struggle."

"But I'm so tired," Ivy whispered. "So tired of struggling."

"And you need never struggle again," Béfind said. "All you need will be yours. . . ."

"And what of those here who need *you?*" Donal asked Ivy. "I brought you to Edgecott because I thought that you could benefit from what Cordelia had to offer. But she needs you as well. Edgecott needs your spirit . . . yes, the very things that make you different. You have so much to learn, Ivy, and so much to teach —"

"She owes nothing to humanity," Béfind said. "She has the right to choose!"

"Once you step through that Gate," Donal said, ignoring Béfind, "you will surrender any chance of determining your own fate. Do you think Béfind would take so much trouble only to let you go?"

"Enough!" Béfind said. "Your arrogance

knows no bounds, halfling. For Ivy's sake, I shall not punish you as you deserve. Instead, I offer you a challenge. Pass through the Gate with us. I will hold it open, and if either or both of you then choose to leave Tir-na-Nog, I will not prevent it."

"A trick," Donal said.

"You have no other choice," Béfind said, "for I will surely not abandon my daughter until she has seen what I offer, and you know that I can vanquish you whenever I choose."

Ivy stepped between them. "I don't want to go alone, Donal. Please, come with me."

Donal lowered his head. The little dog slunk whining between his feet.

"Very well," he said.

Béfind concealed her triumph. She faced the Gate and passed her hand from left to right. The air eddied and swirled like water in a pool. Birdsong and lilting Fane melodies spilled into the circle of standing stones, painting the dull mortal world with a tinge of brilliance.

Ivy gazed into the shifting light and started forward. Donal gave the dog a final caress. A Fane and two halflings stepped into the Gate, and the human realm vanished.

The colors were a thousand times richer than Donal remembered, the smells sweeter, the very air so crystalline that the distant mountains seemed only an hour's walk away.

Intricately carved glass towers captured the sunlight and cast it out again in a flashing prism. Brooks like blue silk sashes tumbled through the lush green grass. Across the perfectly groomed meadow, embroidered with flowers, handsome Fane lords strolled with glorious ladies, golden-horned deer grazed unafraid, and birds with tails like rainbow-hued fans glided between trees whose foliage glittered like spun silver.

He paused to calm himself and remember why he had come. The open Gate flickered at his back, framing the muted, somber tones of earth. Ivy stood a few paces away, lips parted, her eyes taking in the countless marvels surrounding them.

"Welcome to Tir-na-Nog," Béfind said. She reached out to stroke Ivy's raven hair, sifting it through her fingers. "Welcome home."

As she spoke, Ivy's simple traveling dress melted into a drapery woven of minuscule precious stones and fibers so light that they rippled with the gentlest breeze. Ivy lifted her arms and spun about, laughing. The Fane across the meadow turned their faces, curious, and floated toward her, their slippered feet barely touching the ground.

Home. Donal trembled and clasped his hands together, struggling with his fear. It was irrational, he knew. Irrational and childish to fear what had no power to hold him.

But he was afraid, and not only for Ivy. He

took a deep breath and opened himself to this world, this paradise, defying his all-too-human emotions. He watched as Ivy wriggled her bare feet in a sparkling beck and giggled as scarlet fish nibbled at her toes. Her delight was unaffected. No one had forced it upon her. And still the Gate lay open.

The Fane lords and ladies drew near, their faces wreathed in smiles. They knew Béfind, and they recognized Ivy as one of their own. Their beauty was a joy to behold. They gathered close, raising musical voices in greeting, offering slender hands, showering this impressionable girl with praise she could not help but soak up as a flower absorbs the sunlight.

And then they came to Donal. He had not expected to be noticed, but the Fane gazed upon him with those same smiles and words of welcome, calling him by name: Donal. Donal, our brother, our kin. They drew him among them and surrounded him with warmth and soft touches, demanding nothing.

Gossamer threads of yearning wove about Donal's heart. Birds descended from the trees to perch on his shoulders, whispering of peace and plenty. Foxes and rabbits gamboled at his feet, and sleek-coated horses, whose backs had never known a saddle, nuzzled his hands. Not one would ever endure the lash of a whip or the shattering impact of a bullet.

None would ever share with Donal their pain at the viciousness of men, or bear the sorrows of captivity.

The murmuring of the Fane grew louder, interrupting Donal's dazed thoughts. The crowd parted, and a blinding figure appeared in their midst, her gown constantly changing color to match the hues of grass and flowers, leaves and sky.

"Titania," the Fane cried. "Titania." And Donal knew he was in the presence of the terrible creature he barely remembered from childhood, the queen who had forever cursed his father with the shackles of mortality.

She alighted on the earth, accepting the accolades of her subjects, and looked into Donal's face with a smile.

"So," she said, "you have returned at last."

Donal held his ground, refusing to be awed by her radiance or influenced by the instinctive mistrust that rose in his heart. "Queen Titania," he said, bowing.

"And you have come in good company," she said, gracefully indicating Ivy, who laughed as she accepted a plump, exotic fruit from the hands of a pale and handsome young lord. "It is indeed a day for celebration in the Blessed Land when two of our own are restored to us."

"I thank you for your welcome, my lady," Donal said, "but we have come only in agreement with the Lady Béfind, and our visit may not be a long one."

Titania's delicate brows drew together. "You would leave us, Donal son of Hern? You, whose blood gives hope for the preservation of your people?"

"My people." Donal glanced about at the perfect, pleasant faces on every side. "It was 'my people' who rejected Hern when he declared his love for a mortal woman . . . the woman who gave me the blood you find so valuable."

The Fane raised their voices in protest, but Titania held her temper. "You speak boldly, grandson," she said, "and not without truth. Yet we do not hold you responsible for the errors of your sire."

"Even if I have made the same errors?"

Titania brushed her fingertips across Donal's hair. "You were but an infant when you passed through our country, yet your life has not been unknown to us. You have not been happy in the world of men. Mortal love has not saved you, my child. It brings no peace, only torment."

Donal stepped back. "My life is not at issue. I came to protect an innocent child who knew nothing of her Fane blood until today. She must freely choose whether or not to abandon the life she has always known."

Once again he looked for Ivy, surrounded by a coterie of admiring Fane who appeared her own age but were likely centuries, even millennia older than she. It was all deception at its very core, but Ivy had already fallen under Tir-na-Nog's spell of endless bliss.

In time, she might come to recognize how brittle was the shell of Fane delight, how little happiness she would find among creatures that took every pleasure for granted. But she was very young, and if she were forced to make her decision before she learned the truth . . .

Donal turned and walked away from Titania and her court, beginning to contemplate the impossible. He knew without question that Ivy would discover only emptiness in this place. She would lose her untapped capacity for love, the spirit that made her uniquely herself . . . and she would hurt Cordelia terribly, perhaps beyond any hope of mending.

God knew *he* had done little enough for Cordelia. He had only complicated her life and brought confusion and pain, arrogantly upsetting the fragile balance she had created to deal with her past and her unwelcome passions. Whatever regret she might feel at his leaving would quickly pass if she had Ivy to love and care for.

It was simple, really. Many would benefit if Ivy returned to the mortal realm, but few would suffer if Donal did not. He had no real friends apart from those he had made at Edgecott. He had certainly done little enough to help the animals, whether in the Zoological Gardens, the Yorkshire dales or in Cordelia's menagerie. And now he had lost the only ability that gave any meaning to his presence on earth.

He had dreamed of traveling to other lands, seeking solitude in forest and plain and mountain. But if it was isolation he craved, he could find it as easily in Tir-na-Nog as any place on earth. The beauty he saw all around him was not limited to this one meadow and grove; it extended for uncharted miles in every direction, unbounded by human measurement, vast wildernesses where even a Fane might lose himself. If Titania expected him to contribute his seed to the High Fane bloodlines, it was a small enough price to pay for freedom.

He circled slowly back toward the watching queen, his steps heavy with sorrow. *It is best this way,* he told Cordelia's image in his mind. *You will still have purpose and work to bring fullness to your life, and Ivy will be beside you. Only give her time,* muirnín — *time and a little room to find herself. Give yourself leave to put the past behind you. Live fully, as you were meant to do.*

Forgive . . .

He stopped before Titania, his mouth gone dry. Béfind stood beside the queen, full lips curved in a mocking smile.

"Well, son of Hern," she said. "You bargained with me, and you have lost. Any fool of a mortal could see that Ivy has found her home."

"You've given her no time to decide anything," Donal said coldly, "but it doesn't matter." He turned to Titania. "I have a proposal, my lady. It was never my intention to remain in Tir-na-Nog, but I shall do so on one condition . . . that you allow Ivy to return to the mortal realm, there to remain unmolested to the end of her days."

"No!" Béfind burst out, but Titania silenced her with a flick of her fingers.

"An interesting proposition," the queen said, her voice as expressionless as her perfect face. "You offer your body for the siring of children?"

"I do, if I am permitted to go my own way when my services are not required."

"Ivy can bear children of her own," Béfind said. "You have no need of this —"

"Ivy is but one woman, who may never give birth to living offspring," Donal said. "One halfling male may provide . . . many opportunities."

"Yes," Titania said. "He speaks truth, Béfind. His seed could fill a hundred empty wombs with life."

A hundred empty wombs. Donal closed his eyes, sickened. There would be no love in such matings. Never again would he feel a flawed, passionate woman in his arms, or believe for one glorious instant that the curse of his loneliness had at last been lifted.

Cordelia.

"There is one other matter," he said. "No Fane must ever lift a hand against the woman called Cordelia Hardcastle or any member of her family. And I would request a week's leave to dispose of other business —"

"Other business?" Béfind repeated, laughing harshly. "Would that be punishment of the mortal Inglesham who made you all but his slave? I have already done you that service, halfling . . . and disposed of your precious mortal lover at the same time."

Donal snapped toward her. "What are you saying?"

"Why, your little hob informed me of the viscount's transgressions, so I gave Inglesham what he believed he wanted — the love and obedience of Cordelia Hardcastle, which I do not think he shall much enjoy once he has it." She cocked her head. "His work should be completed by now. . . ."

Donal spun on his heel and raced back for the Gate, scattering startled Fane left and right. He had no sooner reached the square of shimmering light than he nearly collided with a small, swiftly moving shape.

"Tod!" He caught the hob by his shoulders and lifted him high. "Where is Cordelia?"

"Here, Donal."

She stepped through the Gate and stood,

legs braced apart like some ancient Celtic warrior-princess, an iron poker in one hand. Her startled, awestruck face was the most beautiful thing Donal had ever seen.

"I understand you might require some assistance," she said.

CHAPTER
TWENTY-NINE

Donal gazed at Cordelia in astonishment while she absorbed the incredible scene before her, certain at last that everything he had told her was true.

There *was* an Otherworld beyond human knowledge or imagination, a place where even the earth seemed made of velvet and the air sparkled with motes of gold. There were such creatures as Fane, Fairies, Fair Folk. They stood before her now, gorgeous faces distorted in expressions of affront at her intrusion. Among them stood the woman she had known as Countess Pavlenkova, and another whose radiant gown set her apart from the rest; they stared at Cordelia as if they might strike her down with a word.

Tod escaped Donal's hold and darted back and forth, seeking the one they had come to find. "Ivy!" he cried.

"Tod?"

Ivy stepped out from a crowd of richly-dressed young men and women, her slender

603

body draped in a gown woven of gemstones and starlight. "Cordelia?"

"Mortal!" one of the young men hissed. Others took up the chorus, repeating the word as if it were the bitterest of curses. "Mortal!"

Donal turned to face them, planting himself between Cordelia and the speakers. "Are you all right?" he said over his shoulder. "Did Inglesham . . . did he —"

"Inglesham has been dealt with," she said, tightening her grip on the poker.

"I knew nothing of Béfind's plot against you. If I had —"

"I know, my friend. But now we have matters of greater import before us."

She caught the edge of his smile and knew that he was proud . . . proud of her, that she could stand here so calmly when most women would be swooning in their tracks. She had no intention of disappointing him.

Before he could speak again, the woman in the radiant gown came forward, floating several inches above the ground.

"Titania," Donal said. "Queen of Tir-na-Nog."

Cordelia swallowed her amazement and offered a shallow curtsey. "Your Majesty."

Titania glared at her from cat-green eyes, flinching from the sight of the poker in Cordelia's hand. "Mortal insolence," she hissed, "bringing Cold Iron into the Blessed Land."

She turned her icy gaze on Donal. "Who is this creature, grandson?"

Countess Pavlenkova — Béfind — came up beside her, almost snarling with rage. "This is the interfering female for whom Donal holds such great esteem."

"Indeed? Then it appears your plans for her were not successful."

"They were not, Your Majesty," Cordelia said, meeting Béfind's stare.

"And this hob," Titania said. "Is it not the one that belonged to him who was my son?"

"It is, my Queen," Béfind said.

Titania stroked her lower lip. "This almost becomes intriguing." She looked down at Cordelia. "And how is it that you have dared to enter the realm of the Fane, Mortal?"

"I have come to fetch Donal Fleming and the girl whom this lady stole away with lies and deceit. It is time for them to return home."

"But Ivy *is* home," Béfind said. "Or did you not know that your halfling made a bargain with me . . . that she should enter the Blessed Land and choose her own future?"

"It's true, Cordelia," Donal said, keeping his back to her. "Béfind had the means to force Ivy through the Gate, but she agreed to let Ivy make her own choice . . . if I agreed to accompany them."

"A trick," Tod said, hovering anxiously at Ivy's shoulder. "A trap set for my lord. Do not —"

"Silence," Titania said. "We have laid no trap for our kin. You may see for yourself." She beckoned to Ivy. "Come forward, child."

Ivy walked slowly toward them, Tod beside her. The veneer of playful flirtatiousness she had worn only moments before had gone, replaced by the hesitant bewilderment of a child. "Cordelia," she said, her eyes welling with tears. "Donal, I . . ."

Béfind stepped in front of her. "We have tolerated enough mortal interference," she said. "My Queen, banish these creatures and their cursed Iron, and let us see them no more."

Cordelia met Titania's gaze. "Did I not just hear that a bargain had been made . . . or can it be that the people of Tir-na-Nog do not hold to their agreements?"

Titania's nostrils flared. "We hold to them, Mortal." She turned to Ivy. "Speak, child. You have seen the glories of the Blessed Land. You have witnessed the horrors of the human world. Which do you choose?"

Ivy glanced back at the assembled Fane. They called to her in their lilting, beautiful voices, a cluster of soulless, flawless living jewels.

Cordelia stood by Donal's side. "Come home, Ivy," she begged. "I know that I have made mistakes. I have tried to mold you into something you can never be." Her voice broke. "You were right when you said that I saw you as my sister. I wished a second chance to save her by saving you. But my error does not lessen your value to all of us. You are needed, my dear. Needed and wanted."

"What if I can never be like you?"

"You will be yourself, loved for yourself alone."

"Aye," Tod said, defying Titania's command. "As I love you, my lady." He knelt before her and bowed his head. "I will go where you go, and serve you all my days."

Tears ran down Ivy's cheeks. "Tod, my dearest friend."

"Love," Béfind spat. "Shall I tell you of the curse that made this creature what he is today?" With scornful relish she spoke of the magic that had transformed a lord of the High Fane into a lowly hob, and how only one of Queen Titania's power might break it.

"Tod," Donal said, his voice thick with sorrow. "You never told me. . . ."

Tod bowed his head. "I had accepted my punishment," he said, "until Ivy. . . ." He met her gaze. "I do not deserve your regard, my lady, but I know now that love is the greatest mortal gift. You will not find it here. You will grow cold and hard as these fine lords and ladies. There will be no going back."

Béfind raised her hands to strike Tod down, but Donal caught her arm and held tight.

"Tod is right," he said. "Go home."

One of the Fane began to laugh, a silken sound of scorn and amusement. The others joined in, filling the air with cruel music. A lord dressed in shades of ruby and amethyst negligently lifted a finger, and Tod shot up into the air. A fine lady bent her wrist, and Tod flew to her like a child's plaything flung by careless hands, bounced from one Fane to the next.

"Stop it!" Ivy cried. She charged the nearest Fane lady, seizing handfuls of trailing silken sleeves. "Let him go!"

Tod tumbled to the ground, groaning softly. Ivy knelt and gathered his small body into her arms.

"Take me home, Cordelia," she said, her voice hoarse with weeping. "Take *us* home."

Cordelia closed her eyes in gratitude, fear and awe supplanted by untrammeled joy. She set down the poker and held out her hands, one to Ivy and one to Donal.

Donal did not take it. He released Béfind and backed away, stopping beside Queen Titania.

"I cannot go with you," he said in a whisper.

"What? But it is over. Donal —"

"You must return without me," he said, raising his voice. "It was never my intention to come to Tir-na-Nog. But now that I am here . . ." He stared up into the silver trees. "I realize that I belong among the Fane."

Cordelia stared at him without comprehension. "But you . . . you belong here no more than Ivy does. Every word Tod spoke to her was true."

"True for her," he said. "True for one who requires love to live. But I am not like Ivy."

"I don't understand." She moved toward him, sickened to the core of her soul. "I do not blame you for being angry at my refusal to believe your stories. I was a fool, Donal, I freely admit it. I was a fool about a great many things."

He shrugged. "You are human."

"And you are half human!"

"My humanity has been my cage. I have no desire to live at the mercy of primitive mortal emotions for the rest of my life."

Cordelia stilled her trembling. "And what sent you here to help Ivy, Donal? What drove you to save her in the first place? What of the animals you have served with your compassion and your healing gifts? Do they mean nothing?"

"They will do as well without me."

But I will not, Cordelia cried silently. She clenched her fists. "I ask nothing of you, Donal. I expect nothing, only that you grant yourself the same understanding you did Ivy. You need not stay in England . . . the whole world awaits you."

"I have a whole world here," he said. "In Tir-na-Nog I can serve some purpose and escape mortal suffering. What more could I ask?"

All at once Cordelia felt something she couldn't name, a certainty that welled up in her like a dry spring come to life. She knew without question that Donal was lying, and that he did it to protect her and Ivy and all those he loved.

"No," she said. "I don't believe you, my dear . . . you were never very adept at prevarication."

His head jerked up, and a flash of emotion crossed his face. "Leave this place," he said. "Leave now, Cordelia Hardcastle, and be glad you pay no terrible price for your freedom."

"But I do pay a price," she said. "*You* are the price. You, the man we love. The man *I* love."

He turned sharply away. "You speak to no purpose, for I cannot love."

"Even if I believed that, it changes nothing. I will not let you throw your life away." She signaled to Ivy. "Go through the Gate now, and wait for us."

Ivy obeyed, taking Tod with her. Drawing up her skirts, Cordelia raced back for the poker and snatched it up, holding it before her like a sword. "Your Majesty," she said to Titania, "you will kindly release Donal from whatever bond you have placed upon him."

"Cordelia," Donal whispered. "Go, I beg you."

"I shall not." She wielded the poker in a wide circle, sweeping it from side to side. Titania, Béfind and the other Fane fell back with shouts of rage and fear. Righteous anger bubbled up in Cordelia's heart, anger such as she had not allowed herself to feel in years, a wildness and ferocity that gave her the strength and speed of ten Othellos. She advanced on the Fane like a tigress defending her young, and they retreated in astonishment.

"Now, Donal!" she cried.

Still he didn't move, staring at her as if he had just witnessed something beyond his imagination. With a snarl of impatience Cordelia seized his arm, flung him about and ran for the Gate.

Donal's feet touched solid earth, and almost at once the seductive spell of Tir-na-Nog began to leave him. He blinked, aware of Cordelia's hold on his arm, and slowly returned to himself. He saw Ivy sitting on one of the fallen menhirs, Tod and Sir Reginald nestled against her, and a man with a horse a little farther away . . . a man Donal recognized with disbelief as Sir Geoffrey Amesbury.

For a moment all Donal felt was a profound relief and the overwhelming desire to take Cordelia in his arms and kiss her to within an inch of her life. But then he remembered, and exaltation crumbled into despair.

"I must go back," he said.

Cordelia lifted her hands to his shoulders and gave him a firm shake. "Nonsense. We are safe now, and —"

"Safe?" He shook his head, laughing at his own stupidity. "You shall never be safe again if I betray my bargain."

"To remain in Tir-na-Nog in Ivy's place?" she asked, her face unyielding.

"It was necessary," he said, pulling away. "Ivy would be destroyed —"

"And you will not?" Cordelia jabbed the end of the poker into the ground, grinding it deep into the soil. "I saw what would become of you, Donal, and I shall not permit it."

"You are one woman, Cordelia, no matter how brave. They have millennia of magic behind them."

"Believe me when I say that if any of them attempts to steal either you or Ivy, I shall kill her." She smiled. "I see by your expression that you do not believe me. Do you think me incapable of such violence, my dear, such mad and reckless behavior? But you did not know me when I was young."

"Cordelia . . ."

She might have said more, but the Fane had no intention of allowing such leisurely conversation. The Gate hummed, the square of light trembled between the menhirs, and Béfind plunged through, her face a mask of rage. She strode directly for Ivy.

Donal knew he had to stop the Fane before Cordelia risked her own life, but it was clear that Béfind would not listen to reason. She had no interest in Donal's bargain; she wanted what was hers, at any cost.

With a whispered prayer, Donal wheeled, snatched Cordelia's poker from the earth and opened his mind to the beasts. He sent a call far and wide, to every creature large and small that might serve to distract Béfind from her purpose.

He knew in an instant that the animals would not answer him. Paralyzed with fear, he spoke to Sir Reginald. The dog ignored him. He listened for the horses' thoughts, but all he heard was silence.

Cordelia was already halfway to Ivy's side when Donal caught up to her. They were both too late. Béfind was reaching for Ivy when Tod surged up between them, defiance in every line of his little body.

Béfind struck. A bolt of power shot from her hands, piercing Tod in the chest like a spear of light. Ivy screamed. Sir Geoffrey, who had remained utterly still since Béfind's appearance, ran toward the Fane like a man possessed.

"Béfind!" he cried.

She froze. Cordelia halted her headlong rush, and Donal watched in amazement as Fane lady and mortal man stared at each other with devastating recognition.

"Béfind," Sir Geoffrey repeated, his voice cracking on the word. "You do remember me, even though I have changed and you have not. You *do* remember."

"Geoffrey?" She ignored her victim and weeping daughter, bewilderment in her glacial blue eyes. "Why are you here?"

"To see you." He fumbled inside his coat and brought out a silver bracelet of intricate design. "I have waited all my life for your return, but you never came."

She thrust out her hand to ward him away. "You have no part in this, Geoffrey. Leave the girl to me."

"Not yet, Béfind." He displayed the bracelet on an open palm. "Do you not remember when you gave me this token of your affection? Do you not recall the promises you made to me on the day you left, the vow that you would grant me any gift within your power to give? Today you will fulfill that vow." He stepped forward, took her hand and clasped the bracelet around her wrist. "What I ask you must do."

"You forgot to whom you speak, Mortal," she said. "I am —"

"I know who you are. You are the woman I loved."

Suddenly she smiled. "And you would have that love again, my bold Geoffrey? You would come live with me in Tir-na-Nog?" She stroked his cheek. "You would have such happiness as no mortal can imagine, *leannán*. Only speak the word, and I shall grant it."

He trembled, his gaze sweeping past Ivy and Tod, coming at last to rest on Cordelia. "No," he said. "I ask that you go from this place and never trouble Ivy or my kin as long as the sun rises in Tir-na-Nog."

Her mouth twisting in fury, Béfind wrenched the bracelet from her arm and threw it at his chest. "Foolish Man," she spat. "You have lost your final chance. Now all of you shall —"

"I think not, Béfind."

Donal and Cordelia turned toward the new voice. A man had emerged from the Gate . . . a Fane tall and stately, his eyes glittering with amusement. Béfind seemed to shrink in on herself.

"Idath," she whispered.

"The game is over, Béfind," he said, "and you have lost."

Ivy stared at the Fane lord. "You," she stammered. "You are the man who gave me my pendant when I was little. The man I thought was my father."

Idath inclined his head. "I remember. But I am not your father, child."

"Who . . . who is he?"

Idath looked at Béfind. "Will you not tell her, *a mhuirnín*?"

The Fane woman grimaced in such a way

that even her beautiful face turned ugly. "You hated him," she said. "You hated that I bore his child, and that is why you kept Ivy from me. You —"

"Hated Sir Geoffrey?" Idath said. "Not at all. You'd become too arrogant, Béfind. It amused me to teach you a lesson."

Ivy shivered, her gaze darting to Sir Geoffrey. "*He* is my father?"

Sir Geoffrey looked just as stunned as she. Cordelia's expression was caught between joy and disbelief. "How can that be? Ivy is seventeen. I would have known if my father . . . if he had —"

"Forty years passed in your world since Béfind became this man's lover," Idath said.

"And time is different in Tir-na-Nog," Donal said, almost numb at the revelation. "In the months that Béfind was with child, years would have passed here."

"And more years before I learned my child was alive," Béfind said. She extended her hands to Ivy. "Come back with me, my daughter. Remember how these mortals lied. . . ."

Idath laughed. "No mortal can match a Fane at deception." He turned to Ivy. "Stay here, little halfling. The son of Hern was correct when he said that you are no more than a precious object to the one who bore you." He held out his hand to Béfind. "Your time here is finished. Come home."

Béfind seemed to crumple, diminishing into an ordinary woman before their eyes. Idath led her toward the Gate and turned, meeting Cordelia's gaze. "Yours is a power greater than any we in Tir-na-Nog possess," he said. "Use it wisely."

He and Béfind stepped into the Gate. It vanished behind them. Sir Geoffrey stared at the standing stones until the last faint vibrations had faded, turned to gaze at Ivy, and then fell to his knees, his head buried in his hands.

Death was very near. Tod felt its cold hand on his chest, pressing against him, making it difficult to breathe. But he clung to life for Ivy's sake, and for Donal's, knowing that there were things he must say before he left the world.

He listened to Sir Geoffrey speak of lost love and broken promises. He felt the Gate between two worlds close forever. And then Donal was beside him, holding Tod's small hand in his large fingers as Ivy stroked the hair from his eyes.

"How are you, my friend?" Donal asked with infinite tenderness.

"Tod is . . . very tired, my lord."

"Save him, Donal," Ivy begged. "He never harmed anyone. All he ever did was love us."

"I know." Donal met Cordelia's eyes, his

own wet with tears. "There is nothing I can do."

Cordelia touched his hand. "You said you cannot heal people," she said, "but you must try, my dear. You must."

He bent his head. "My gifts have left me," he said. "I can no longer call or hear the animals."

"That cannot be," Cordelia said. "Did the Fane —"

"The Fane did nothing," he said, withdrawing his hand from hers. "It is in my nature, Cordelia. I —" He broke off, no longer capable of speech.

Tod groaned, his guilt so terrible that he wished he were already dead. He tried to rise. "My lord," he said, choking. "I have betrayed you."

"Hush," Donal said. "Don't trouble yourself —"

"It was because of the curse," he said. "I knew that Ivy could not love me . . . like this. I hoped that Queen Titania would lift the curse, and that Béfind would allow Ivy to choose her own fate. I was wrong."

Donal folded Tod's hand in his fingers. "If only you had told me," he said. "I would have helped you. I've been a poor master and a far poorer friend. . . ."

"It is no matter," Tod whispered. "Forgive me." He trembled, feeling the weight sink deeper into his chest.

"Oh, no," Ivy said, sobbing. "He did it because of me, Donal. You can't let him die. Please. I'll become a proper lady, anything you ask. Only save him!"

"I have no power," Donal said hoarsely. "Nothing —"

"I refuse to believe it," Cordelia said. She leaned across Tod, cupping Donal's face between her hands. "Whatever has weakened your gift, it cannot be gone. I know this, because for the past eleven years I shunned a part of myself I thought I hated — the wild Cordelia who would not accept a cage — a part that seemed to bring only grief and shame. I believed that I must become what Lydia wished to be, that somehow in doing so I might atone for her death. I did not know how greatly I was deceived until you saw through my disguise, when you accused me of hatred for the creatures in my own menagerie. I had become a 'Lotos-Eater' of Tennyson's poem, seeking peace that was not peace at all, only self-deception."

Donal closed his eyes. "Yet the old Cordelia survived."

"Yes. I learned that she had a purpose. That she's part of myself, and I can no longer pretend she is not." She laid her hand over his. "*You* have a purpose, and that is why I cannot believe that your abilities have deserted you. Idath said that we mortals have a power greater than any in Tir-na-Nog possess. That power is love, Donal. Your love for Tod. His love for Ivy."

"And mine," Ivy said. "And mine for him."

Donal said nothing for many heartbeats. Tod knew he battled the fears he had nursed since childhood, fears Tod had fostered with grim deliberation. But it was too late to speak of that now; it was right that Tod should die and pay the price for his treachery.

But he did not die. Donal laid his hands on Tod's chest and flung back his head, silently drawing upon the very emotion he believed would rob him of his gifts. Tod felt the love pour into him like the blood of life, beating in his veins and rushing into heart and lungs and brain. It filled him to the brim and overflowed, stretching his flesh, expanding muscle and bone in waves of pain and ecstasy.

Donal lifted his hands, his eyes wide with astonishment. "Good God," he said. "The curse . . ."

His heart in his throat, Tod gazed down the length of his body, down and down to the long legs and slender, elegant feet. He felt the strong, half-familiar bones of his face, and then he looked at the fine, graceful hands attached to lean and muscular arms.

"You did it, Donal!" Ivy cried. "You healed him!" She leaned over Tod, grinning, joy and love shining in her beautiful eyes. Tod didn't have to see his own face to know what she saw, what he had become. He was himself again.

He sat up and met Donal's gaze. "Thank you," he said, his voice deep and sure. "Thank you, my friend."

Donal grasped his offered hand. "What should I call you?" he asked.

He met Ivy's gaze. "Aodhan is my name. But I will always be Tod to those I love."

Donal looked at Cordelia, as foolish and besotted as any young mortal with his first girl. "You were right, Cordelia," he said. "The gift isn't gone." He laughed as Sir Reginald leaped into his lap and licked his face.

Abruptly Cordelia rose, walking swiftly away before Donal could see the ridiculous, selfish sadness in her eyes. It was wrong to feel so, she knew it . . . wrong to think of herself when there was so much to be grateful for. Tod had transformed from a strange little man to a splendid young god; Ivy had her love, and Donal his beasts . . . what more could anyone rightfully ask?

I have no right, she thought. *There is still a great deal to be done. Inglesham must pay for his crimes, my father has just lost the love of his life, Ivy is coming home and we must think of an explanation for the sudden appearance of an entirely unknown and very handsome suitor in the neighborhood. . . .*

"Cordelia."

Donal came up from behind, wrapping his

arms about her, and she thought she would come undone.

"You're trembling," he said, his breath caressing her temple. "What is it, Cordelia? What's wrong?"

"Why, nothing." She half turned, smiling. "It is just that so much has happened, don't you agree?"

"Indeed."

"Theodora must be wondering what we are about, the poor dear, standing watch over that blackguard Inglesham. And Sir Geoffrey . . ." She glanced toward her father, who still sat with his head in his hands. "He sacrificed the dearest wish of his heart for our safety. Ivy is his daughter; that knowledge cannot fail to alter him. Perhaps there is a chance for a new beginning in our family. As soon as we are home, he and I must have a heart-to-heart talk. And then I must see the animals and apologize, even though they won't really understand —"

"Cordelia."

She caught her breath. His lips grazed her ear, her cheek. Tears started in her eyes.

"I know you must go," she said. "You never deceived me, even when we . . . it was always very clear. I shall be forever grateful for everything you have taught me . . . taught all of us. Of course Ivy will miss you, and Theodora, but perhaps when you have seen something of the world you will come back and —"

"Cordelia!"

"Yes, Donal?" she said meekly.

He turned her about to face him, clucked his tongue, and sat her down on the nearest stone.

"You didn't believe me when I told you the stories about the Fane," he said.

She shook her head, unable to meet his eyes.

"Then why did you believe when I said I had no desire to deal with primitive human emotions?"

"I . . . I didn't. . . ."

He folded his arms across his chest. "In Tir-na-Nog, you told me that you neither expected nor asked anything of me. Is that correct?"

"Yes."

"And then you said you loved me."

She hid her face behind her hands. "Yes."

"Which was the truth?"

She stiffened. "I was not lying."

"You love me, yet you want nothing of me."

"Nothing but your happiness."

"Very noble and selfless of you, *a chuisle*."

"I am not noble."

"Then there is something you would ask of me, after all."

She glared up at him. "No."

He sighed. "You have always been a stubborn wench." He glanced toward the little wood at the edge of the stone circle. Cordelia noticed a rustling of leaves, a movement in the grass beneath the trees . . . and suddenly they came, animals of every size and sort: waddling badgers and prickly hedgehogs, darting shrews and bashful voles, russet foxes and chestnut stoats, tufted squirrels and leaping hares, sleek fallow deer and white-rumped roe. They advanced upon Cordelia like a mismatched army and came to a halt, gazing at her from eyes black and brown, large and small.

Cordelia sat very still. "What do they want?" she whispered.

"An explanation."

"*I* cannot speak to them."

"I will translate for you." He cleared his throat. "They wish to know if Cordelia Hardcastle is capable of wanting anything for herself."

"What? I —"

"Does she plan to spend the rest of her life in selfless sacrifice and dull propriety, or will she allow a little of that wild creature loose again?"

Cordelia's cheeks flamed. "I cannot go back."

"Then you must go forward."

"Naturally."

"And you will do so alone."

"I am perfectly capable of . . ." She saw the twinkle in Donal's eye and stopped.

"Always capable, my Cordelia." He cocked his head. "My friends are still not satisfied."

"What more can I tell them?"

"This time they have something to tell you."

She squirmed on her stone seat. "I am listening."

He gestured to the ranks of animals. They began to chatter all at once . . . grunts and snuffles and groans and yips, a chorus of music only another beast could fully appreciate. Cordelia swallowed a reluctant smile.

"I did not quite understand," she said.

"With pleasure." He shuffled his feet and stared at the ground. "They wished to tell you that Donal Fleming has lost his heart."

Cordelia blinked rapidly. "And they want me to help him reclaim it?"

"Oh, there is no need for that. You already possess it."

She began to shake. "I . . . I don't —"

He dropped to one knee and met her eyes. "I love you, Cordelia Hardcastle. And I am perfectly willing to have my friends repeat it as many times as necessary to make you believe."

"That will *not* be necessary." She slid off the stone and knelt before him. "I will never again dare to disbelieve the Lord of the Beasts."

And she kissed him then and there, savage as a tigress claiming her mate, until he begged for mercy.

CHAPTER THIRTY

"So it was all a deception," Cordelia said. "Tod was so afraid of losing you to a mortal woman's love, as he had lost your father, that he convinced you that you would also forfeit your powers if such a love ever came to you."

"Yes, and I believed him." Donal stretched his legs out on the cool grass beneath the ash and pulled Cordelia closer, gazing at the river with lazy eyes. Only a week had passed since the final confrontation and healing among the standing stones, and yet everything had changed. Even his memories.

"Tod was my closest companion all through my later childhood," he said. "I had seen my father become more and more like an ordinary mortal after he was exiled from Tir-na-Nog — no longer able to make plants grow in an instant, or summon the animals from the forest."

"And that frightened you."

"I worshiped my father. But I had spent my early childhood alone, with only the animals

626

for company. I couldn't conceive of losing that gift. The older I grew, the more terrifying such a prospect became."

"Of course," Cordelia said, stroking his hand. "Anyone would feel the same."

"It was easy to believe what Tod told me. I often had nightmares about my brief time in Tir-na-Nog with my father, but I never stopped to think that perhaps my father's changing was the result of Titania's curse, and not because he had learned how to love."

"Yet you stopped hearing the animals when you realized you loved me — first with Othello during the animals' escape, and then at the standing stones."

He lifted her hand and kissed her palm. "There was another time as well," he said, and told her about his affair with the Black Widow, how he had believed himself in love and temporarily lost his ability to communicate with the animals.

"My poor darling," Cordelia said. "No wonder you could not admit to loving anyone."

"I severed myself from the animals through the simple conviction of my own mind. I was so certain of suffering the loss that I created it."

Cordelia smiled wryly. "We are very good at punishing ourselves, are we not?"

"It is a very human talent."

She turned to look into his face. "Why

didn't Tod tell you the truth when he was dying?"

"I think by then he had become 'human' enough that he was prepared to accept the penalty of death for his betrayal." He frowned, wrestling with the guilt that had plagued him since Tod's transformation. "It was my fault that he was driven to Béfind. I neglected him shamefully after I arrived at Edgecott, and he feared I would leave England, and him, forever."

"How often we fall prey to our fears," Cordelia said. "And how often our fears are mistaken."

"My fear would have permitted Tod to die," Donal said gravely, "but you gave me the strength to heal him."

"The strength was always within you, my love."

"Perhaps. But I don't think I saved Tod at all. I think it was the love in his own heart, his willingness to sacrifice his life and his deepest desires for all of us."

"As even my father, in the end, was willing to make such a sacrifice. As you have for me."

"In what way?

"By agreeing to remain at Edgecott, even though your heart would go wandering in the wilderness."

"It is no sacrifice."

She pressed her finger to his lips. "I know better. But I have decided to take your advice and become quite selfish in my happiness."

He sat up. "Indeed? Tell me."

She leaned her head against his shoulder. "Perhaps you have noticed how much Sir Geoffrey has changed."

"It would be difficult not to. I would say that he has become a new man."

"He threw off the bitter shackles his unrequited love for Béfind had placed upon him. I consider it truly a miracle."

"He still has much to answer for."

"That may be. But have you seen the effort he makes to win Theodora's good opinion? He is quite the gentleman. And he and Ivy are becoming fast friends."

"That is an odd pairing if ever I saw one."

"Yet they have something in common. Both have been deeply touched by the Fane."

"But Ivy will have Tod."

"Eventually . . . when she is old enough to know her own mind, and he has established himself as a respectable *human* suitor."

"My parents will see to that, as they're arranging for our special license." Donal grinned. "I think they're quite relieved that a respectable woman has accepted me."

"Alas, they have not yet met me. They may change their minds." She gazed into his eyes. "We shall have to arrange a meeting very soon, this coming week if possible. I fear we will not be available afterward."

"Not available?"

"I have booked a passage on a ship leaving England in three weeks' time, and we have a great many preparations to make."

"Leaving England?" He caught her by the shoulders. "Leaving for where?"

"I thought Africa might be our first stop. If we can restore Heloise and Abelard to their homes in the wild, then perhaps there is hope for Othello and the other menagerie inmates." She grinned. "You see, I have decided that I can serve and be selfish at the same time. With your gifts we can free the animals, Donal, you and I . . . and we will learn to be free again."

He stared at her. "But what of your work here . . . your responsibilities, the charities —"

"Theodora has expressed great interest in my projects. Between her and Sir Geoffrey, I believe that Edgecott and its dependents will be in excellent hands."

He pulled her against his chest. "You're sure, Cordelia?"

Beside the river, Desdemona stretched her neck and gave a piercing whinny while Boreas bobbed his head in an emphatic nod.

"I believe you have your answer," Cordelia said. "And here, my friend, is another."

ABOUT THE AUTHOR

Susan Krinard never expected to become a writer, but fell into it accidentally when a friend suggested she try writing a novel, which sold to a major publisher two years later. A longtime reader of science fiction and fantasy, Susan began reading romance — and realized that she wanted to incorporate fantasy into her romance novels. Since then, she considers herself incredibly fortunate in finding a career so perfectly suited to her.

Susan makes her home in New Mexico, the "Land of Enchantment," with her husband, Serge, her dogs, Brownie, Freya and Nahla, and her cats, Murphy and Jefferson. In addition to writing, Susan's interests include music (New Age and classical), old movies, reading, nature, animals, baking, and collecting jewelry and clothing with leaf and wolf designs.

Readers are invited to visit her Web site at www.susankrinard.com.